OBJECTS OF DESIRE

Also by Roberta Latow

A Rage To Live
Love Chooses
Her Hungry Heart
Cannonberry Chase
Cheyney Fox
Three Rivers
Tidal Wave
Soft Warm Rain
This Stream of Dreams
White Moon, Black Sea

OBJECTS
OF DESIRE

Roberta Latow

HEADLINE

First published in 1995
by HEADLINE BOOK PUBLISHING

10 9 8 7 6 5 4 3 2 1

A catalogue record for this book is available from the British Library

ISBN 0 7472 1135 3

Typeset by
Letterpart Limited, Reigate, Surrey

Printed and bound in Great Britain by
Mackays of Chatham PLC, Chatham, Kent

HEADLINE BOOK PUBLISHING
A division of Hodder Headline PLC
338 Euston Road
London NW1 3BH

For Claude Ury
who understands that every lady needs
a knight in shining armour.

With grateful thanks and love
Roberta

'Make certain your love for me will be long,
Not in haste, the days of our heat,
the nights of our lust.
We are not creatures of the moment,
but lovers, whose flame burns hot and bright.
A gift from Eros, more rare than rubies,
this erotic fever'   – *The Epic of Artimadon*

HUSBAND AND WIFE

Chapter 1

'I don't mind dying. I don't mind being dead.'

Mark Boxer said that to Martin Amis when he was in hospital and dying. He was not a man to blame anyone for anything.

Robert Rivers had read Amis's account of that meeting and now he was hearing those very same words from Elizabeth Lacey. She was not his friend the way Amis had been Boxer's friend. Robert was Elizabeth Lacey's surgeon, a man in the business of life and death. He was trained not to break down and cry. But he did wonder why it was that essential people of this world were the ones who tried to make it easier for those they were leaving behind; or, as in this case, those who had failed them.

Robert took Elizabeth Lacey's hand in his and stroked it. It was physical rather than verbal confirmation that she was indeed going to die. Far better, far kinder, than a doctor's double talk which evaded the issue.

Dr Robert Rivers and his patient, the several other doctors in his team and the nurses, had been through so much together. Elizabeth had come to them from London by air ambulance as good as dead, and they had performed near miracles to save her. After months of a slow and painful convalescence, Robert had stood at the entrance to the Harley Rogers Clinic with these same people now standing around her bed and had waved goodbye to her as she walked down the main stairs to her waiting limousine. Once on the pavement, she had turned to face them and give one last wave and a smile of thanks.

Minutes later, Robert had been walking through the busy lobby of the Harley Rogers Clinic to the lift that would take him to the operating theatre where he was due, when he heard running footsteps behind him, commotion, shouted orders. He had needed no one to tell him. The look of urgency on Nurse Coleman's face, the sound of it when she had called out his name had been enough. Together they had raced from the building. His staff had been working on Elizabeth right there on the pavement.

Robert took charge. It had always been a possibility that her heart might be too tired, too worn out, to carry on, but there had been no indication that that was the case during the many weeks they had monitored her in the hospital. That had been several days ago. She had rallied once again under his care. But not enough. Now it was just a matter of time, a very short time: days, hours.

Robert stood for several minutes outside Elizabeth Lacey's room talking with his colleagues: two doctors, two hospital interns, the floor's head nurse and Robert's Nurse Coleman, who was directly responsible for the nursing of his patients. From the private wing of the hospital they went down to Intensive Care to check their patients, and from there to the wards where the less affluent patients received the exceptional medical care the hospital was world famous for.

Several hours later Robert shook hands with the last of his patients and walked from his examining rooms to his office. Nurse Coleman removed the stethoscope from his neck, walked around him and reached up to help him off with his white coat. She held his waistcoat out for him and he slipped his arms through the arm holes and began buttoning it. She was at the ready, holding his jacket for him to slip into.

Nurse Coleman and Dr Rivers had been conducting this final ritual of his working day for more than ten years. She was not only very astute about the emotional state of his patients but just as sensitive to the state of her idol's feelings at any given moment, as was Mrs Winkler, Robert's secretary.

After a brief knock at the door Mary Winkler entered the office with a smile, carrying a cup and saucer and a plate containing one Ry-King, lightly buttered, a paper-thin slice of baked ham neatly covering the crisp bread. She placed them on his desk. Looking up at him, she told Robert, 'No emergencies. All the calls can wait until morning except one. The palace wants to know the date you plan to fly to Morocco for the King's check up? I've pencilled in the twenty-fourth to the thirtieth of next month. You could do with an extra few days away.'

'No appointments?'

'There are always appointments. But none that I can't juggle around.'

Robert ran his fingers through his hair, then pulled down on his waistcoat. It fitted perfectly over his slim muscular body. A broad-shouldered man of only average height, almost embarrassingly handsome, looking more a cinema version of what an eminent doctor should be than the real thing, he was pampered and admired by all who worked for him as well as his patients and peers.

A cautious man, a perfectionist, a man dedicated to medicine and science. A man of intelligence and skill, creative, innovative, he commanded respect, even adoration. Dr Robert Rivers of the Harley Rogers Clinic was a man loved and respected as well as feared. This fear was imposed not by Robert's wrath, he never showed that, but by a desire not to be banished from his working or private life. The very thought of a harsh word from Robert made those around him try that little bit harder, to avoid making mistakes.

'You are a wonder, Winkels.' He sometimes called her Winkels when they were alone and he was seriously distracted. 'That sounds good to me. Make the arrangements.'

Mrs Winkler picked it up immediately: a sense of indifference in his voice, maybe even a sadness he was trying to cover up. Resignation? He usually looked forward to his bi-annual visit to the King. He liked the man and the country and enjoyed the hospitality heaped upon him by the monarch and his court. She looked at Nurse Coleman. The nurse too had recognised that something was not quite right.

'The usual arrangements?'

'Yes, the usual arrangements.'

Two first-class seats together in one name, Dr Robert Rivers. He never took his wife. He always drove himself to New York's Kennedy Airport. A limousine from the palace waiting for him on the tarmac as he alighted the plane, and the reservations – those were all the arrangements Mrs Winkler ever made for Dr Rivers on these occasions. Now, after so many years, she still had no idea who occupied the other seat on his travels, if indeed anyone did. She could only surmise that he had a secret travelling companion because on his return there was some inexplicable sense of renewal about her employer. He seemed happier, more vital, than on a return to the clinic after a holiday *à deux* with his wife.

'Do you have any other instructions for me, Doctor?' asked Nurse Coleman.

'Nothing special. Just keep a close watch on Miss Lacey. And don't hesitate to call me if there is any change in her condition.'

The two women made their retreat. Robert sat down at his desk and, taking the cup of strong black coffee in his hand, swivelled his chair around to gaze out of the window overlooking the lake. It was a view he never tired of – a thick, luscious wood circling the large placid lake. The few buildings around were hidden among the trees. Robert was as fond of it now, shivering in the cold under an icy grey sky, as he was during any of the four seasons. The trees, bare and tall and proud in deep sleep, were nowhere near ready to come to life, as they always did with the return of spring. The pine trees, voluptuous boughs heavy with long needles, each one sheathed in ice from the rain several days before, looked like thousands of millions of long, slim crystal prisms in the late-afternoon light.

Robert sipped his coffee, remembering Elizabeth Lacey's whispered words: 'I don't mind dying. I don't mind being dead.' The look of peace, contentment, love in her eyes . . . It had affected him profoundly when she had uttered those words to him. What dignity, what character. The lack of malice, for one who had all but lost her life then fought back to live again, only to be struck down for the final count before she even had an opportunity to take advantage of her second chance at life. How well she must have lived her life to feel that way.

Robert rose from his chair and stood by the window. Only the realisation that he could not in truth express those same sentiments as Elizabeth Lacey made him realise how *un*well he was living his life. It was at that moment that Dr Robert Rivers changed it. Not thought about, or considered, nor contemplated, but actually acted upon a need. He picked up the telephone and called his wife.

Anoushka Rivers could not hear her telephone ringing, she wasn't home. She was at an exhibition of Jasper Johns paintings, a retrospective in the University's art gallery. Robert was very keen on Jasper Johns' work. She only quite liked it. They owned three. She had taken her time in viewing the paintings. She was trying.

That morning she had driven to West Grinstead to go shopping at Lord & Taylor's. It was nearly the same distance to West Grinstead as it was to New York. An easy hour's drive on the motorway, a short distance off that, park your car in the vast, near-empty, parking lot, a few steps from the car to the door, and there you were into the lush quiet of chic shopping. West Grinstead was easier.

Robert preferred taking her to Bendl's or Saks or Bergdorf's in New York; a little shopping and a great deal of art gallerying, a simple lunch somewhere elegant, drinks at The Carlisle to allow the evening traffic to die down, then on to the Saw Mill River

Parkway and the Auberge Gilles, for a dinner of roast duckling with white peaches and black cherries. Unless Robert was too tired to drive home, in which case it was dinner in the city and a night at The Pierre. Her husband spoiled her.

Anoushka liked the salespeople more at the West Grinstead Lord & Taylor's. They knew her by name. The buyer knew her taste, what she looked best in. Anoushka knew Robert would like today's purchase – a Ralph Lauren evening skirt of black crêpe-de-chine and a loose blouse of cream-coloured satin, sensuous for its cut and its full, long sleeves that buttoned tight on the wrists, and a narrow belt solid with black jet beads. Had he been with her (he liked to go shopping with her, and did most of the time), he would have been more extravagant than she had been with herself. He would have insisted she have the Lauren *and* the Armani evening suit.

Loaded down with dress boxes and smart carrier bags, she had lunch in the Bird Cage Room. Anoushka liked Lord & Taylor's restaurant: the several storeys' high round room with its New York chic window-dressing interior decoration, all atwitter with ladies chatter, pretty women preening their feathers. She ate hot corn chowder and a chicken salad sandwich, black coffee and dutch apple pie with vanilla ice cream. Her favourite Lord & Taylor's lunch.

Anoushka had been giving herself quite a nice day. All Anoushka's days were quite nice, that was her life. She was thinking about that and the Jasper Johns and seeing Robert as she turned up the sable collar on her brown tweed coat and walked down the stairs, braving the bitter cold wind whipping across the lake. They were going to a dinner dance at the country club. She would have rather had dinner alone with her husband. She never tired of being alone with Robert. She adored him and their life together. No one knew better than she what an attractive and special man she had married. How lucky she was that he loved her, was so devoted to their life together.

Anoushka never really enjoyed the country club functions. She had little in common with the women who belonged there. She was not a good golfer, preferred the ocean to a swimming pool, and had little interest in becoming a work-out obsessive, but for Robert's sake she made a half-hearted effort at belonging. And that was more than the club women did in befriending her. Thirteen years and they still continued to see her as an outsider. Robert River's mistake.

Robert, always the gentleman, the charmer, liked the use of his club, but managed for the most part to keep out of the socialising and club politics without offending. The dinner dance this evening was his once-a-year concession.

Anoushka missed the boys now that they were at school and only home for end of term holidays. She had fought hard to keep them at home but Robert and even the boys had been adamantly in favour of boarding school. Anoushka knew the boys loved her but she also knew that in the last few years they had drifted away from her to Robert. Anoushka tended to let things slide, in fact, she had chosen to ignore the changes going on around her until it was too late and they were gone to Groton.

Anoushka looked at her watch. How nice it would be if Robert could get away early. He worked so hard, she did worry about him. She had a sudden desire to see him. It was more than desire, she wanted Robert and now. Anoushka was very sure of herself, her marriage, her life, not a woman to fear loss. But suddenly she did. It was distressing, somehow inexplicable. It flashed by her, remaining only just long enough for her to find the sensation unpleasant, somewhat frightening, and she was much relieved once it had passed. Her immediate reaction was to miss her husband, and want him. Anoushka always wanted Robert. Not often, but on occasion, she did go to his office. Mostly, as now, when she wanted him so much that hearing his voice was not enough. On such occasions it was sexual yearning. She could never get enough of Robert sexually. That part of their life together was a very important factor in their marriage. She thought about it as she drove up to the front entrance of the hospital.

Anoushka switched off the motor and slid across the seat to check her face on the mirror on the back of the sun visor. It was a good face with strong features: a slim elegant nose, high, prominent cheekbones, dark blue eyes, and sensuous lips rouged a pale rose colour. Anoushka wore no cosmetics save for her lipstick. She tended to play down her near-perfect features set in a heart-shaped face that softened her, some claimed haughty, others exotic, looks. Most women who knew the Riverses were envious of Anoushka's looks, her having caught Robert for a husband, the seductive huskiness and hint of foreign accent in her voice, and delighted in her faults. And she did have faults, most of them glossed over by Robert.

She adjusted the sable beret she was wearing and ran her fingers through silky blonde, nearly platinum hair. Locking the car, she hurried up the stairs. Rocco, the hospital door attendant, saw her coming and opened one of the pair of large glass doors.

'Mrs Rivers, long time since we've seen you here.'

'Hello, Rocco, I won't be long.'

'Bad place to park, Mrs Rivers. Give me the keys, I'll move your car.'

'Couldn't you just watch it? I won't be long. Fifteen minutes?'

She was such a nice woman. Why not? He flouted the rules. 'No more. Now promise? I guess I can bend the rules for the doctor.'

Anoushka smiled and patted him on the shoulder as she hurried through the lobby. There were smiles from several of the women busy at the reception desk as she acknowledged them with a wave while swiftly passing them bound for the bank of lifts. Too hot. It was always too hot in the hospital. She opened her coat, ignoring the fact that there was a button missing.

She stepped from the seclusion of the lift into the fifth-floor corridor. It smelled of hospitals and was filled with white-starched uniforms, the occasional harried-looking intern, and concerned relations rushing about. Robert would insist on having his office and examining rooms right in the midst of his patients. She went to the nurses' station to greet the women briefly before heading for his office. She noticed the false smiles and the whispers. They never liked her visits. She represented a part of Robert's life they could never experience, except marginally for a few hours at the annual party for the nurses she and Robert gave every Christmas. They were all more than a little in love with Dr Robert Rivers and never thought her good enough for him. That was not a problem for Anoushka; other people's opinions just washed over her. She greeted one of Robert's colleagues, a doctor who was a close friend as well as one of his peers. They spoke briefly before she continued down the corridor towards Robert's rooms.

She passed a distraught-looking young woman, tears streaming down her face. Anoushka placed an arm round her and led her to the waiting room, offering what few words of comfort she could before she asked a nurse to try and help.

Anoushka had compassion and worried that she saw so little in the faces and actions of the pretty and perky young nurses. They exuded something more like aggression, authority, power over the sick through their nursing. It always disturbed her. She would yet again talk to Robert about it. More than once he had suggested to her that she had a romantic idea about nursing and suffered from a Florence Nightingale syndrome, believing that all

9

nurses chose their profession out of a deep sense of caring. True for many, but not all. Other factors, and the deeply disturbing aspects of working with the sick and dying, did sometimes eat away at compassion. As did the system.

Anoushka would listen but never really hear what he was saying. She always heard what she wanted to hear. It made life so much easier.

She entered Robert's office. Mrs Winkler nearly jumped out of her chair. 'Mrs Rivers. I didn't expect to see you.'

'That's because I'm a surprise. Hello, Mary.'

'It's always nice to see you, but you should have called.'

'What? For an appointment to see my husband?' And she smiled at Mary Winkler, meaning it as a joke.

It was not, however, taken as such. Mary Winkler was embarrassed and felt she had to defend herself. 'Oh, no, I didn't mean it that way. I said that because the doctor isn't here. You've just missed him. Shall I try to find him?'

'No. I just came on the off chance that he might be able to come home early for a change. I seem to see even less of him now than when the boys were at home.'

Mrs Winkler, normally extremely discreet about Robert's movements, felt strangely sorry for Anoushka. It prompted her to say, 'He did say, if need be, I could reach him at home. He's probably on the way there now. You've only missed him by a few minutes.

Anoushka felt a surge of delight which showed on her face. She smiled and thanked Mrs Winkler. The two women spoke for several minutes and Anoushka left for home.

The Rivers house was large and very beautiful. Nineteen rooms of crisp, white, New England, turn-of-the-century architecture, many chimneys and grey shutters, on a rise of green lawn carved out of a white birch wood only yards from the edge of the lake. Chimneys was one of those New England, picture postcard sort of houses. Anoushka never took it for granted, but always felt a surge of happiness when she drove down Longmeadow Road past her neighbours' houses. Those too were impressive, set back on large plots of land or down winding drives through the birch trees.

She drove up the drive and round to the back of the house, directly into the garage where she parked her Mercedes Estate next to Robert's Jag. She gathered up her shopping and walked across the lawn, now a white blanket of frost, and through the back door. The warmth felt good. It made her realise how raw and cold a day it was. She shivered and shrugged deeper into her coat. I could do with less grey and more sunshine, she thought, as she continued on through the house to the library where she knew Robert would be.

'Robert, I'm home,' she called out as she dropped her shopping on a chair in the hall.

'In the library,' he called back.

'I know,' she said, entering the room. 'I saw the lights from the road. How really nice that you're home early.'

Anoushka sat on the arm of Robert's chair, placed an arm over the back of it and, leaning towards him, gave him a kiss on the cheek. She briefly caressed the back of his neck and then looked away from him to the flames leaping in the fireplace. She removed her hat and shook out her shoulder-length hair. To be in the warmth and comfort of her own home was a great feeling.

'Oh, that looks just what I need! I've had a hard day shopping for clothes for this evening,' she told him as she caressed his hand and took from it the Lalique tumbler containing a vodka martini with a twist of lemon. She placed it to her lips and drank, at the same time placing his now empty hand on the top button of her coat.

Silently he undid the button and then the next and took notice of the one that was still missing, the threads that once held it in place. He nearly said something about it but didn't. He had, several times, and still it was missing. There seemed no point. Especially not now.

'You don't mind my pinching your drink?' she asked.

'Of course not, I'll make another,' he told her and rose from the chair to go to the drinks tray set on a Queen Anne table in front of the library window. Still with his back to her, he asked, 'Did you buy something really lovely, something special?'

Robert did so like beautiful things. She smiled because she knew how pleased he would be when he saw her shopping. 'Very. I was extravagant,' she told him as she balanced the glass on the back of the chair and finished unbuttoning her coat, slipping out of it, and removing her gloves.

'Good,' he told her. Still with his back to her he said, 'I knew you wouldn't mind. I've cancelled the country club this evening.'

'But my shopping! My new clothes!'

He was surprised to hear the disappointment in her voice but it had no bearing on his resolve. 'We can still get dressed up in our finery and have an evening together. Here, preferably. Dinner, a nice bottle of wine, some time just to talk.'

'Robert, what a charming idea. Much better, very much better than the club.' He felt a surge of relief to hear delight replacing disappointment in her voice. 'There isn't much in the refrigerator, I don't go to the supermarket until tomorrow. I know, there's some lobster bisque. We can have that to begin, and there's endive. I can make us a salad, and a cheese soufflé.'

'No!' It came as a shout. Robert hadn't meant it to, but the thought of Anoushka fussing in the kitchen: the whirr of the electric mixer's stainless steel whisks, the egg shells lying on the marble counter top, the flour leaving a light film over everything, the mess, all the same as usual, as if nothing had changed. Anoushka always made a horrendous mess when she cooked without the help of their cleaner-cum-cook-cum-housekeeper. Somehow tonight he could no longer turn a blind eye to it, something he was usually good at. He turned to face his wife. The look of surprise on her face prompted him to disguise his anger.

'No,' he repeated more calmly. 'That's too much work and mess. Something easy, or we'll go out for dinner somewhere nice. I don't want you distracted in the kitchen and me getting into a good book. An evening together is what I had in mind.'

Anoushka chose to ignore the sharpness in his voice though it had felt like a sharp slap. 'Then it's one of Mrs Cooper's casseroles from the freezer right into the oven, or we go out. Whichever you choose.'

'You put the casserole in the oven and I'll fetch us a good bottle of wine.' He took a sip of his drink. The chill and bite of the vodka in his mouth felt good. It was what he needed.

'The kitchen, the dining room, our upstairs sitting room? Where would you like to dine?' she asked.

'The dining room. We'll bathe and dress for dinner in the dining room, you in your new outfit.'

Robert walked back to the chair where he had been sitting and picked up the arts magazine he had been reading. Anoushka was still sitting on the arm. He sat down. They gazed at one another. He very nearly began to speak to her right then and there, but lost his moment when she deliberately slid from the arm of his chair on to his lap and in the process yanked her cashmere jumper up and over her head to drop it on the floor in front of the fire. She removed his glass from his hand and put that on the floor too, and then, taking his hand in hers, placed them on her naked breasts.

'This is not what I had in mind,' he told her, not unkindly, while cupping one of her breasts in the palm of his hand and caressing it gently with the other. The large and voluptuous weight overflowed his palm. He liked to feel the heft of her breasts in his hands. Robert had always liked her breasts, the dark and sultry-looking nimbus that circled the fat erect nipples. He had always found something powerfully decadent about Anoushka's breasts. He liked her much better naked than clothed. Her body suited his sexual fantasies, desires, his strong and restless libido.

Though he never yearned for her sexually, all she had to do was present herself in that light and he found her irresistible. She had always been like that for him right from the first time she had seduced him. The feel of her skin, her natural scent, made even voluptuous by the perfume she used: Paloma Picasso. He enjoyed her cunt, so soft and moist, and the deep coral colour of its fleshy and succulent outer and inner lips; the way it gripped him tight and teased him into powerful fucking. How clever and imaginative she was in her lust, the outright depravity she practised with her husband. In the dark, in the privacy of their sexual world, she was lewd, base even, and knew how to excite him. She fed his own sexual rauchiness with hers and he was always surprised how far they would go to experience sexual oblivion.

In their erotic life together, they gave in to the darker side of sex, wallowed in it. He never tired of her. Robert enjoyed satisfying their sexual hunger for each other. She had always had sexual power over him, and he had loved her for that. How well she hid her erotic soul from everyone but him. There was of course more to Anoushka than that, enough for him to have built a life with her. They had created two wonderful boys, been a family. Theirs had been a good life, but now he could see clearly as he fondled Anoushka's breasts, saw the lust come into her eyes and feel her squirm with pleasure as he lowered his mouth to bite into her nipples and suck deeply on them, that love, if it had ever really been there for him, was gone and had been for a long time. Lust had been carrying them for as long as he could remember. It came as a tremendous relief to him to see that so clearly and be able not only to admit it to himself but to act upon it.

He sat back in the chair, sighed and repeated himself. 'As I said, this is not what I had in mind.' He stroked her hair and caressed her cheek.

'Well, this is exactly what I have had in mind for the last few hours. So much so I even went to the Clinic to find you, meaning to induce you to come home and make love to me.'

'You were at the hospital?'

13

'I just missed you.'

Anoushka unzipped Robert's trousers. He tried to stop her but she laughed at him. It was a sensuous, wicked laugh. One that insinuated he was behaving foolishly. A knowing laugh that said, 'Don't be ridiculous, you'll not resist me.' She cupped one of her breasts in her hands and fed it into his mouth by first grazing his lips with her erect nipple until they parted and he hungrily licked and sucked with a wild abandon.

He was erect and in her hands, pulsating. It brought him to his senses. He eased her from him and gazed at her, touched the dot-sized beauty mark just above the right corner of her lips. 'You're not listening to me, Anoushka.'

'No,' she admitted happily and rose from the chair to stand facing him. She took her drink, drained her glass and handed Robert his. He too finished his drink. 'I'll be right back,' she told him.

Anoushka hurried from the library and Robert tried to compose himself. Not easy. He was still erect and full of lust which had no place in his resolve to implement the drastic change necessary to his life. In only a matter of minutes Anoushka was back. Seeing her enter the room, he yet again marvelled at how sensual a body his wife had. Still, after two children, she possessed the narrowest of waists. It was as if she were reading his mind. She went directly to him, delighted that his condition had remained the same as when she had left him. She bent over him, moved her breasts seductively, caressingly, back and forth, across his face. This woman, so sedate, cautious, somewhat remote in her public persona – who when clothed was a tinge slovenly and not very stylish unless prompted by her husband or an insistent saleslady – how whorish and exciting she could be in her sexual persona.

She was taunting him, denigrating his sexual prowess, and he didn't like it. He grabbed her by the wrist and she fell against him, whispering something obscene in his ear. When she stood up, he rose from the chair with her.

Anoushka began kissing him all over his face, and between kisses told him, 'I want to come in your mouth, feel you deep inside me, taste your come.' Pink with embarrassment now, she whispered again in his ear, 'Oral, anal, cuntal sex. Now wouldn't that be a lovely way to begin our evening?' He took her in his arms and kissed her deeply, and it was a kiss not devoid of genuine passion.

He saw happiness shining in her eyes, and felt a twinge of

sadness for her when she told him, 'How can you have any idea what a joy it is for a woman to be filled by the cock of a man she loves? To grip it inside her, vice-like . . . that for me is being alive and one with you.' This was the kind of talk she knew seduced him, set him free to explore the depths of his sexuality. He still liked her for that, but as one would like their favoured hooker, the mistress one kept but never married. Once more Robert felt relieved that he was already finished with her as wife or mother of his children.

'I adore you, Robert, and our life together. This is the best of us, right here and now, when we are in lust, and the world falls away. Every time we make love, I always feel you are fucking me for the last time. That's why I can never go too far, never want to stop, why I savour every drop of your come. Now take me to bed.' And she kissed him once more as passionately as he had kissed her.

'What if it is for the last time?' he boldly asked. Hoping it might stop her, make her think, listen.

No such thing. All he received was that wickedly sensual smile. 'You've said that before.'

'Have I?'

'Yes.' And she laughed and pulled him along through the library, the hall, and up the stairs. Once she turned round, looked at him and said, 'The sex is too good, and in that you are a very greedy man, Robert. I tie you to me with it, and since we love each other and are bound together there is no last time for us.'

'What about dinner?'

'It's in the oven. What about me?' They were just outside their bedroom door. She flung her arms around his neck and kissed him. Before they entered the room, she began to undress him.

'Once again, Anoushka, I'm telling you that I hadn't planned this. Sex is not what this evening is about.'

'It is now,' was her retort.

He had seen her like this before. Anoushka at her most seductive. The usually introspective, somewhat remote woman exposing her most intimate self to him in lewd and base expressions of her sexual hunger. Honest in her sexuality to the very core of her being, in that she was the rarest of women. Anoushka pushing all the sexual buttons that she knew he would not resist because of his own sexual lust. He went down on her, a taste of Anoushka to begin the last ride they would ever take together into the land of sexual oblivion. This was the first time Robert could admit to himself that lust, not love,

15

had been the foundation of his happiness with Anoushka, and it was no longer enough. They were finished, dead, over. But that didn't stop him. This, their last sexual encounter as husband and wife, was fierce and thrilling; the little death of many orgasms for her, his parting gift.

Chapter 2

Anoushka could hear the sound of a cello; the music of Villa Lobos drifting up from the drawing room. She cut the sales tag hanging from the cuff of her new satin blouse, straightened the skirt over her hips and adjusted the belt of black jet beads. It suddenly seemed very important that Robert thought she looked perfect – beautiful and perfect. He was angry with her. Though he had not said so, she sensed his anger, had experienced it in the sex they had just experienced together. There was always a little anger in Robert when he was out of control sexually. At those times he turned his anger to passion and uninhibited sex, sex with no boundaries. Base and lewd and so exciting. That was why she drove him to it, used her sexuality to seduce him into streams of orgasm they both enjoyed. There was nothing else like sexual bliss with Robert, that and to hear him tell her how much he loved her.

How she revelled in his protestations of love during their orgasms together. But not this time, not once had Robert used his sexual rage to call out his love and passion, and tell her, 'I love you, my wife,' or 'I love you, Anoushka.' Once spent, it was always the controlled, kind, generous Robert asking, 'Happy, babe?' or telling her, 'Something special. You deserve something special in your life. Go and treat yourself to something you want.'

Some little thing he was too much of a gentleman to make an issue of, that was it. The button missing on her coat? She had seen him take notice of that. Something she should have done and had let slide? She was more curious than concerned. She knew her Robert. Something must have happened at the hospital. But he never brought the hospital home and into their personal lives. Anoushka shrugged her shoulders and tried to put Robert's anger out of her mind.

She took a long steady look at herself in the mirror, and what she saw gave her confidence that Robert would be much pleased with her. Just out of a dress box elegance, everything in place and shining. He liked his women to look as if they had stepped directly from between sheets of crisp white tissue paper or walked off a fashion runway. Once again she vowed to herself to keep up her standards for the man she loved.

She could smell the casserole, lamb and lemon, rosemary and thyme, wafting through the house from the kitchen. She turned from the mirror, and as she passed their four-poster bed Anoushka found Robert's absence from it disturbing in the same way she had done when she had awakened and he had not been there. She left the room immediately and blocked all worries from her mind.

Anoushka was aware that her marriage was the sum of many little rituals. Dressing for dinner was one of them. It kept an edge on their togetherness, their making an effort for one another and leaving the day and the outside world behind them, to be viewed with a degree of emotional detachment as a voyeur might. It was one of the rituals they both enjoyed whether dining at home or out in some smart restaurant before going to a concert, the theatre or cinema. Had they not planned to go to the country club for dinner this evening, Mrs Cooper would, as she did most of the evenings they were at home, have been serving them a splendid meal. It was neither laziness nor not wanting to be home alone with her husband that prompted Anoushka, on entering the kitchen and seeing Robert dressed in his dinner jacket and black tie, to suggest, 'It's not too late for us to change our mind, Robert. I think I would like to go to dinner at the country club.'

He ignored her words. He was standing at an angle to the cooker, tending a saucepan. 'Your timing is perfect. The rice is done. I used the Basmati, butter and black pepper. Another fifteen minutes and the casserole might have dried out.'

'We can eat it tomorrow. Let's go to the club,' she insisted.

Robert placed a lid on the saucepan and turned from his cooking to gaze across the kitchen at her. There was something in his eyes that she had never seen before. It was unnerving. And his silence – she felt something hostile in his refusal to answer her. That strange sense of fear that had seized her earlier in the day returned. She shivered. Robert turned his back on her. There seemed something terribly exacting in the way he turned the knobs of the cooker off. From the warming oven he removed a handsome porcelain soup tureen containing the lobster bisque. He walked with it past Anoushka to the dining room.

She followed him, trying to tell herself nothing was wrong. It was just Robert changing his plans. The candles were already lit in the dining room and the table set for two. He at the head and

Anoushka on his right. After placing the tureen on the table, he went to Anoushka and took her by the hand.

'You're a very beautiful lady, and the clothes are marvellous. You would have made a dazzling impression at the country club.' But his voice was as cold as stone.

He held the chair back from the table and, zombie-like, Anoushka sat down. Robert sat down in his. 'There's something very wrong this evening,' she commented.

'Ah, you've noticed.' He poured a serious and grand old style claret, a La Mission-Haut-Brion into each of their glasses.

'What's going on, Robert? You're frightening me,' she told him.

'There's no point in being frightened or anxious about this. We are going to be civilised and deal with this rationally. As much as I would like to make this easy for us, there is no way to be kind and get the job done. It's *over*, Anoushka. I want out of this marriage as quickly and with the least harm to the children as is possible.'

'What *are* you talking about, Robert?'

'Divorce.'

She all but jumped out of her chair and in the process knocked over her glass of wine. It smashed and the wine soaked in a pool of red into the white linen cloth. She quickly stepped back from the table to stop the wine staining her skirt. Robert rose from his chair to cover the ugly red mark with his napkin and to take Anoushka by the arm and lead her away from the table, through the dining room into the drawing room. 'I think something stronger perhaps,' he suggested as, still gripping her arm, he walked her to the table where they kept a drinks tray.

'Is there another woman?'

Robert looked away from the drinks tray and met his wife's eyes. How blind Anoushka could be when she chose to! So many years living with him and not to have known that. He felt no sympathy for her. Incredibly, her question angered him. 'There has always been another woman,' he told her.

'What are you talking about, Robert?'

He splashed two large measures from the bottle of vodka he had earlier removed from the freezer into small crystal glasses. He knocked his drink back in one swallow and Anoushka followed suit, closing her eyes and trying to catch her breath, shocked yet still not believing what she was hearing.

Robert took her by the arm and once again walked her to one of a pair of French Directoire round chairs, sitting her down in it.

He grabbed the other by its elegant arm, carved in the shape of a swan, and drew it from its usual place to sit opposite his wife. He could see it in her face. She was blocking out the reality of the situation, just as she always did when something threatened the peace and happiness of her life. She was trying to minimise the damage. But this time he would not make the slightest concession, as he had done all their married life to date. Not for her, the children, nor their marriage. Even he was shocked to find that his marriage to Anoushka was quite finished. How indifferent he was to the years or even the pleasure he had had with her and family life.

'Anoushka, we can do this the easy way or the hard way, but it's going to happen.'

'I can't seem to take this in, Robert. If there is a problem, let's talk about it, work it out.'

'Anoushka, the problem is this marriage, and I don't want to work it out. It's over.'

'Why?'

'Don't do this to yourself.'

'Do what?'

'Ask me the whys and wherefores.'

'Oh, I'm just to remain silent and make it easy for you to destroy my life!'

'Talking about why I want a divorce will only hurt you more, and not make this any easier for me. It's over, we have to go forward with our lives.'

It was as if Anoushka had not heard his words. Once more she asked, 'Why are you doing this?'

'I want to live my life differently.'

'Then we'll both live our lives differently.'

'Stop! I don't want to live with you. This divorce is all about not wanting to live the remainder of my life with you. We're both still young enough to make other, more rewarding relationships for ourselves. Ones that will make us really happy.

'I *am* really happy.'

'Well, I'm not, Anoushka, and I don't want to live one more day of a life filled with regrets. Not even one more hour.'

'I can't believe this is happening to me. I'm going to wake up and this will have been a bad dream, a nightmare.'

'You are very much awake, Anoushka.'

'We're a family.'

'Yes, we are at least that. You can see the boys any time you want to see them.'

'I can't seem to take this in. You love another woman and always have? And you are giving me permission to see my own sons when I would like to? Have I done something wrong? OK, if I have then I'll make it right. If you're unhappy with some aspect of our life, we'll solve the problem, Robert. I love you and I know you love me.'

She rose from her chair and paced the floor. Angry now, she confronted him with, 'How dare you tell me you haven't been happy, that we haven't had a good life, a family and home that was everything you ever wanted?'

'It was everything *you* ever wanted, I always wanted more but made do.'

'That's cruel.'

'That's the truth, and one we should have faced years ago. Now let's be civil about this.'

'It's difficult to be civil, Robert, when I have been so deceived.'

'I take full blame for the dissolution of our family.'

'Oh, Robert, that's rich! You destroy my life in one swift blow and don't mind taking the responsibility for it. Who is she? Is she demanding that you divorce me and marry her?'

'No. She knows nothing about this. And she has never, not once, made a demand that I leave my family for her. Quite the opposite in fact. It was she, many times, who tried to break away from me to save our family.'

'Taking my husband anyway! How pathetic I must seem in your woman's eyes. How rotten of her, how rotten of you. How long have you not loved me?'

'You are determined to have this out, aren't you?'

'You bet I am.'

'I won't lie to you so some things are better left unsaid. Believe me, it's best for us merely to work out some arrangements.'

'Better for you, but not for me. I want the truth.'

The man standing in front of Anoushka was a Robert she had never seen before. All kindness, generosity, gone from his face; instead anger and bitterness and hatred. She shivered, felt sick and collapsed into the chair where she had been sitting.

'I never wanted this marriage. I *had* to marry you. Now does that make this any easier?'

'Because I was pregnant?' It was more a gasp than a statement.

'Yes. You trapped me into marriage. I did it for my unborn children.'

'You loved me!'

'Yes, for being the mother of my sons, and stayed with you

21

because we had become a family.'

'We had a good marriage, Robert. You can't deny that.'

'A very good marriage, but it's over.'

'Over?' she repeated, and once having said it understood for the first time that Robert did mean to leave her.

'I made the best of a situation. For years, Anoushka, for so many years. Now I want more than just making the best of a situation.'

'You've been planning this for a long time. Is that why you insisted the boys go away to school? You were setting me up to throw me out.'

'No. I hadn't planned this at all.'

'You can't just toss us away.'

'I am not tossing my boys away. We'll work out an amicable settlement.'

'I want you, Robert. And my life as it is.'

'Well, I don't. And that's final.'

They remained silent for several minutes. He poured them more vodka. After some time, Anoushka asked, 'You mean this, don't you?'

'Yes, I do.'

'You're angry with me?' she asked, more out of puzzlement than anything else. How unfair Robert was being. What had he to be angry about?

'I'm angry with both of us. Me for being so weak and not having done this long ago. And you for always closing your eyes to the reality of my unhappiness.'

'Oh, so now this is all my fault?'

'Yes. Actually, I believe it is.'

'This is why we're not at the country club tonight. It wasn't love or sexual passion that made you change our plans. Although one would hardly have guessed that by the performance you put on upstairs in the bedroom. Fuck me and leave me! How despicable. Not worthy of you, Robert, to end it with one last fuck.'

'Do you expect me to defend myself? If you do you will be sorely disappointed. Or would you prefer me to be crude and hurtful and tell you that this evening, like most of the sex during our married life, was predominantly your hunger, your lust? It turned me on, you were too good a fuck to resist, and why not? Sex made you happy, made us both happy. Maybe I even did it as much out of a sense of guilt because I never loved you, so I fucked you well, gave you as much pleasure as I could because I couldn't really give you what you wanted. Me and love. Because I was giving that elsewhere.'

'I can't bear it. All these years you've been playing a role in some cheap melodrama.'

'A role you cast me in. There's no point to this conversation. I have done everything for the boys. I always will. I hope you feel the same.'

'What exactly do you mean by that?'

'The boys are old enough to understand that we want to go our separate ways.'

'*You* want to go your separate way. Let's just get that straight.'

'All right, I want to go my separate way. I can sell this place and give you half of the proceeds. It will buy you a small place in a less affluent neighbourhood here in Lakeside. You can take what you want from the house.'

'Bust up our home?' It seemed unthinkable to Anoushka.

'I'd rather not do that. There are alternatives. I would like to keep the house intact for me and the boys. They love Chimneys. This is their home.'

'The home you're breaking up.'

Robert chose to ignore her remark and continued, 'Their home has always been a stable environment for them. I know we would both like to keep that for them.'

'But without me?'

'Yes, without you.'

'God, you're a bastard.'

'I will, of course, settle some money on you. Half of what I have. But we live so high, there isn't much to divide. I'll give you a portion of my income, keep you until you can find a new life for yourself.'

'And how do you suggest I do that?'

'Go look for it. Get out into the world and find out who you are and what you can do for yourself. You can't do it here, not in Lakeside.'

'Are you running me out of town now? Proposing I should leave Lakeside?'

'I'm proposing one of us should leave Lakeside. It would be practical, it would be constructive for all of us if *you* were to choose to leave. You cannot easily, if at all, make a life on your own here in this community, not after a divorce. Half the lifestyle you know and are used to is all you might manage at best. Too tough. It would be easier for you to begin again elsewhere.'

'No husband, no house, and now no town to live in. I suppose

23

what comes next is to take my children away from me?'

'I wouldn't have put it exactly that way, but yes, I do want custody of the boys.'

'Never!'

'Don't say never, Anoushka. The burden I'm taking off your hands gives you the freedom to go out and start again. You won't exactly be homeless. If you agree to leave Lakeside and let me help to support you financially, I'll make our house in the Caribbean over to you. You've always liked that house and living there. You can take the boys there on their holidays, live in some degree of elegance or travel. Begin again.'

'Oh, you're not going to take our island home away from me. At last a sacrifice on your part! What if I don't like these plans of yours?'

'They're hardly plans. I may have wanted out of this marriage for a long time but until now it was a vague thought which I never acted upon. I have never planned how we should part. I'm talking this out for the first time.'

'Well, I don't like your plans for me. What are the alternatives?'

'I can leave Lakeside and the clinic. You can remain here in this town and take custody of the boys, give them a diminished life, and have a thin time yourself. Anoushka, divorced women like you – well, let me put it this way. You can never regain in this community the same life we had as a family. I'm offering you a better deal than hanging on in Lakeside. If you're smart, you'll take it.'

'Oh, so now this has come down to the best *deal?* I can't believe this is happening to me! The boys – do you think they will choose to live with you rather than me?'

'I think they'll choose to stay with their father here in their family home where they are happy and secure and have their friends all round them, and know that their mother is at the end of a telephone when they need her, that they can see her whenever they wish, as you can see them whenever you want to. They will understand we gave our marriage the best shot and it somehow missed the target. Alexis and Mishka are mature boys who have seen more than half their friends come from marriages that didn't work. Our boys understand the realities of life far more than you think. They're kids with lots of savvy, like most children of the 90s, stable, well balanced and very bright. They will know that within this unfortunate break-up between you and me . . .'

24

Anoushka interrupted Robert, 'Oh, you do at least agree it's unfortunate?'

The look of utter disdain he shot at her made her shiver. He chose to ignore her remark and continued, 'They love us both, and trust us, and will see that we are doing the best we can for all of us.'

Anoushka covered her face with her hands. She felt the tears staining her cheeks and swallowed hard, drying her eyes with the back of her hands. 'You're stripping me of my life, my whole world.'

'No, just your lifestyle. I won't be able to keep you lavishly but I promise you will never be destitute.'

'Oh, and I'm supposed to thank you for that? Next you'll be telling me that I'll thank you for this one day.'

'No, I would never have uttered that cliché, but it's probably true.'

'What happens next?'

'We go and see the boys and then our lawyers who will make a meal out of this. Unless we are careful they will come out financially better than either of us.'

This time it was Anoushka who rose from her chair and went to the vodka bottle. She poured herself a large measure of the powerful clear liquid. After emptying her glass she went to stand next to the fireplace. For several minutes she remained silent with her back to Robert. Quite suddenly she whirled round to face him. Anger shimmered from her. 'What if I say no, no divorce? If you leave me, you leave with nothing.'

'Then I will leave you without a divorce, and with nothing if need be, and you will have destroyed our sons' lives and most probably your own chances of ever finding a man to love you better than I have done. You do that and I promise the boys will hate you for your selfish vindictiveness. And so will I.'

'Even more than you do now?'

'Hate is the wrong word. I'm indifferent to you now, Anoushka, and that's the result of years of love and hate. Love for being the mother of my children, for your lust and for keeping a family together for us. Hate for having trapped me into marriage, for your own pride and self-satisfaction in being my wife.'

'You bastard! You're blackmailing me into this divorce, using Mishka and Alexis. I never dreamed you could be so despicable.'

'Desperate.' The bitterness in Robert's voice penetrated to Anoushka's heart.

'I don't deserve this, Robert.'

'Who said life is fair?'

'Who is she?'

'Does it matter?'

'Of course it matters.'

He clenched his hand into a fist and slammed it hard on the table, dislodging a lamp, an ashtray, a silver-framed photograph of himself, Anoushka and the twins. Robert's anger, held in check until now, turned to rage. He pulled his wife out of her chair and held her by the arms in a painfully tight grip. He raised a hand to slap her hard across the face and she pulled back in fear. Robert trembled. He managed to retain a semblance of control over himself, enough not to strike his wife. Instead, he pushed her hard and she fell back into the chair.

He told her, 'You don't listen. No, that's not true, you do listen but you don't hear. You always hear what you want to hear, see what you want to see. You *will* pursue this questioning. I'm trying to spare you, but why do I bother? You enrage me. So much so, I want to beat you into the ground. That comes of years of concessions in our marriage, of being separated from the woman I really love and want to build a life with. That comes from my weakness, for not going out and grabbing the love and the life I wanted with the woman I love.

'One mistake, that's all it takes, one small mistake. That's all we have been all these years, and now that mistake is over and still you don't let me go. Still you question my life, my need to be free of this marriage. You have not the least understanding or feeling that this breakup is happening to *us*, not just you, that all questions are irrelevant, as are all the rehashings of our life together. Your unwillingness to face up to the misery of our situation drags me down to brutality. Spare you? In my own fashion I've been trying to do that. A mistake. Now I will spare you nothing. Rosamond Rogers is the other woman, and we have been lovers very nearly from the day you and I returned from our wedding trip. And she is the woman I will marry as soon as I am free.'

'It's not possible,' Anoushka gasped.

'Rosamond and I always knew that our love for each other, if ever discovered by you, would be a blow you might never recover from, so we turned ourselves into cheats. We, and especially Rosamond, suffered embarrassment at having to sneak around for stolen moments and hidden corners, strange hotel rooms, or empty offices after dark, so that we might be together. No

26

humiliation was too much for our lust and love for each other.'

'Oh, now you want me to feel sorry for the woman who stole my husband away, invaded my life as a friend and betrayed me? A double betrayal. You and Rosamond . . . The happy life and love I thought was mine, all a sham.'

'Rosamond and I have had to live with the knowledge of that all these years. Protecting your feelings has not been easy for us. This marriage is breaking up because when I die, I want to be able to say, as one of my patients said this morning: "I don't mind dying. I don't mind being dead." Only someone who has lived their life to the fullest, someone who has fulfilled themselves, can die with such dignity. The way I live now, I am not a man who could utter those words. I would go in bitterness and regret, and I don't intend to do that.'

Robert's words had been spoken with such passion that for several minutes afterwards they remained silent listening to their own thoughts, their own pain. Rosamond and Robert, out of their desperation to be together whenever possible, had eased Rosamond into Robert and Anoushka's family life. Rosamond became their best friend, the person whom the twins loved and saw as a member of their family, a friend with whom Anoushka was happy to share her husband and children. All that flashed through Robert's mind and made him more angry; so many hints over so many years that Anoushka had turned a blind eye to. The thought and the memory of all those years the three had shared together prompted Robert.

'Making Rosamond a friend, sharing your husband and children, our life with her – a magnanimous gesture to a lonely woman. That's been the role you have played with Rosamond all along, and not very subtly, I might add. Enduring that was very difficult. Consideration for your feelings, guilt for not loving my wife the way I should, love for Alexis and Mishka, a belief in the family, the home – so many excuses turned Rosamond and me into cheats, and me into an adulterer. We began to despise ourselves. The relief I feel now because that's over for me and Rosamond is immeasurable. And now that you know the truth, it must be for you.'

Anoushka regained her voice. 'We went everywhere together, she was a part of our lives. She added joy, became as close to us as any family member could be. Surely not? It can't be? How could you and Rosamond deceive me? The two people I loved the most aside from my sons. I gave her my home, my family, because she could find none for herself.'

'All those years you were treating her with pity for her aloneness and sharing our life with her, she was wanting what you were so possessive of, and feeling the pain of what she was missing. Yet she stayed on for my sake, for our family's sake, because she knew that she was my happiness and I would abandon you all if she left me. How cruel you've been to us both by not opening your eyes and seeing what was there between us. We gave you so many hints. Could you not understand that there had to be something wrong with our marriage when half of the time I insisted she be part of it? No, not you. You simply couldn't see what was right there before your eyes, how Rosamond gathered the crumbs that you threw her and lived and loved off them.

'How do you think she must have felt all these years, always waiting for that invitation to the house from you, for your suggestion that she travel on holiday with us, and then having to go to her room alone at night while you crawled over me lustily, insinuating how sexually compatible we were and showing it off publicly. Only my acknowledging that it was true, albeit as subtly as possible, would calm you down so not to make your behaviour more embarrassing for Rosamond. For all our friends as a matter of fact.'

'You pig, to speak to me like this now! You took her into my home and deceived me, both of you, right in front of me. And when she was not with us, what an actor! The good and generous husband and father and, I might add, the extraordinarily lustful lover. Love for Rosamond never stopped your hunger for sex with me, did it? What treachery, what disloyalty. Why didn't you just leave me if as you say you didn't love or want me?'

'Pity. Rosamond pitied you. She said she would never break up the family, she loved us as a family.'

'And kept silent, and made love to my husband behind my back. You were indeed discreet about that. How, when, where?'

'Drop it, Anoushka.'

'No, tell me, you deceitful bastard.'

'Every chance we could get.'

'My life has been a sham,' she said barely above a whisper. She was beaten, pummelled by Robert's revelations. She was feeling like a boxer whose opponent had him on the ropes and was clinging on not to go down for the count. It showed in her face, the manner in which she sat slumped in her chair, hands gripping the arms, knuckles white.

'Yes. But it had to end.'

'You were always going to leave me? You would have long ago but for the boys?'

'Yes. Rosamond and I agreed not to make a move until the Alexis and Mishka were of an age where they would not be damaged by divorce.'

'You would fuck her and love her and make serious life decisions with Rosamond, and then come home to me? I think I'm going to be sick.' Anoushka placed a hand over her mouth and retched, but nothing happened. They were both silent for a moment while she composed herself as best she could.

'You never knew. It never harmed you, Anoushka. I never denied you sex, affection, respect, and never embarrassed you.'

'Am I supposed to be thankful for that? Next you'll be telling me sex with her enhanced our sex life?'

'That's true. Sex, love with Rosamond, the excitement of an illicit affair, they all added to my life. I did come home and was able to cope with you and family life. She makes me feel free and alive, not trapped and suffocated by love and duty.'

The pain of what Anoushka was hearing was overwhelming but she could not help herself. She had to know more, every detail of Rosamond and Robert's heinous exploitation of her loving good nature. She was baffled as to how she had never received a hint of what was going on. Once more she imagined that what was happening to her was not true. It was madness, but she kept wanting Robert to prove to her that it was. 'Where? How? Does everyone know?'

'You won't be satisfied till you hear it all. Do you think if I have this in-depth confrontation with you, these revelations will somehow change things and what is happening will go away? You can shove it to the back of your mind, and we can pick up our old lives again? It's not going to happen.'

Anoushka knew what Robert wanted was for her to accept the inevitable, be a lady, and walk away giving him his freedom in a civilised fashion. Her interminable questions more than angered him now, she saw clearly that he was enraged because she would not let go as gracefully as he had lived out his unhappy years with her. Anoushka didn't give a damn about this anger, or the rage she saw in his face. Her gaze was as hard and mean as his now.

And it was that look in her eyes that prompted Robert to tell her now, somewhat sadistically, 'How? In secret, discreetly. When? Stolen moments, frantic sex when you vanished for short periods of time to see to the dinner, here in this very room, Rosamond bending over the back of the very chair you are sitting in, on that sofa, that floor. Hard and full of passion for each other, desperate to be alone and intimate, we would couple. I would move in and out of Rosamond until she came, then hurriedly withdraw, zip up and caress her cheek with my hand, and thank her for being there for me. When you would go to pick up the boys from their friends' houses, when you bathed or dressed, anytime you left us along together and I felt we were relatively safe from your walking in on us, we had each other.

'And at the hospital on those evenings when I was supposed to be there on clinic business, we were having sex, glorious, thrilling lust on the floor of my office. Weekends when I went away on seminars, trips abroad on consultations with colleagues or to visit some of my more celebrated or seriously ill patients, were stolen days of bliss for us. On the grass, in a wood, in out of the way places where we were not known.

'And when we were on holiday with you and the boys, I had it all, you and Rosamond. I revelled in the lust provided by two women who loved me. It became my way of life but the down side was that the arrangement turned Rosamond and me into fraudsters, fakes, hypocrites. For two people such as Rosamond and I who despise such venal behaviour to find ourselves dedicated to it was anathema, suicide to the soul. Self-inflicted poison, drop by drop. I hate you for that.'

'Don't lay this on me Robert! You could have stopped at any time.'

'You fool. Don't you think we tried, many times?'

'Not hard enough.'

'I despise you for this, Anoushka, putting us through this confrontation now.'

'Do you think I care any more about what you or Rosamond think about me? Rosamond! She's worse than you. I opened my home to her, shared my life, my husband and my children with her. And don't think there weren't times over the years when I would rather not have done. And all the time she was stealing you and my children away from me! Oh, I did notice how much a part of our lives she was, I wasn't altogether blind. But I never saw or imagined that she could steal you away from me, that she was crawling into my life to push me out. Despise? Don't you use that word about me. If anyone should despise, it is me. I despise Rosamond for what she has done and think you both disgusting. No, I take that back about her being the worse of you. She's bad in my eyes, about as bad as you can get, but you're worse, much worse. Controlling me with love and lust all those years, your

30

power and charisma dominating me and my life. I've spent my entire marriage doing everything possible to please you. I was so grateful for love and fidelity from such a handsome, clever, attractive man. A man who made other women's husbands look grossly unattractive. A man the entire world of medicine admired for his humanity and genius, his devotion to his work.

'What a joke on me! I always thought you were able to be all those things because first and foremost you had the security of home and hearth with me, your one and only true love, me and the boys. That we inspired you to greatness because we were your real and only true life. That your love for us made it possible to go out into the world a hero. You pig!'

'And there is your insufferable vanity speaking.' Robert raised his hand once more to her. Only this time he slapped Anoushka hard across the face. The act stunned them both. He closed his eyes and took a deep breath.

'I suppose you've wanted to do that for years,' she said with incredible sadness in her voice.

Robert opened his eyes and gazed into hers. The icy coldness with which he looked at her made Anoushka take a step back. She formed a fist and placed the knuckles of her hand in her mouth.

'Yes, many, many times.' With that he walked from the room and out of the house.

ANOUSHKA RIVERS

Chapter 3

The sun was out, white-bright in a blue sky on a bitter cold day. It made things appear to be less frozen than they were, gave an illusion that soon this hard winter would be over. Everything looked sharp, crystal clean. All a lie. Nothing was either crystal clean or clear as far as Anoushka could see. Darkness, emptiness had taken over her life.

She gave Robert everything he wanted: the house as it was with all its contents down to the last pot, pan and book; custody of their sons; a discreet and immediate exit from Lakeside for her in exchange for a promise of no lies to Alexis and Mishka. Instead she and Robert would see the boys together but she would be the one to explain the traumatic events changing all their lives.

The boys' best friends were the Holland children who lived next door, and Betsy Holland was the closest friend that Anoushka had. Close but not intimate, they were hardly women who confided their troubles to one another. There were reasons for this. Anoushka never had any troubles. She was a woman who'd never allowed anything to cloud her idyllic life with Robert. And Betsy? It was quite simple; she was more social, had other friends with less satisfactory lives who felt angst about things Anoushka never did. It was easier to share intimacies with them. And there was a second reason. As much as Betsy liked and got along with Anoushka, she like most of the Riverses' friends, had grown up with Robert and liked him more than his wife. There was always something a little remote, smug, not quite New England about Anoushka, she'd felt. Or was it a fiercely independent pride in who she was, what she had, that was offputting. It gave her, rightly or wrongly, a condescending attitude. Like others who knew Robert and Anoushka as a couple, Betsy could see what Anoushka never did: that Robert had not married the right woman. Betsy often felt sad for them, but mostly for Robert and the concessions he had made. She had always wished she could have liked Anoushka that little bit more.

Others were not so scrupulous. Far from pitying Anoushka after they learned of Robert's defection, some of her neighbours were keen to distance themselves from her. It was as if they saw divorce as a contagion – or perhaps Anoushka as his wife a threat to their own propped-up and patched-together marriages.

It was to Betsy and David that Robert went after walking out on his wife. David was his childhood friend and attorney but until Robert rang their doorbell that night, he had never dreamed that Robert and Anoushka would not stay married for always. Robert had indeed buried his unhappiness deep. It was Betsy who let herself into the Rivers house to comfort Anoushka the best she could. And it was Betsy and David who were now driving her into New York where they were to join Robert and the Riverses and Holland children for lunch in the Oak Room of The Plaza before Anoushka sailed out of their lives on the *QE2*.

This lunch was not easy for any of them, but designed for Alexis and Mishka's sake, to make light of the devastation of a family. It was dressed up as a treat for the boys, having their best friends with them and going to see their mother off on the first lap of her travels round the world. Anoushka thought of Robert flying the four boys down from Groton for the day. They were probably at The Plaza by now.

Traffic was building up, it had been since Riverdale but kept moving along. Panic set in as Anoushka was riding alongside the Hudson River. She seemed mesmerised by the water and a ship going upriver. Betsy turned in her seat to look at her.

'Won't be long now. Are you all right?'

David shot a look at his wife that said, 'What a stupid question.'

'Sorry, Anoushka, that was a silly.'

'If I can only get through this lunch and sail away without upsetting the boys, that's all I care about. *All right* hardly comes into it. But I know what you mean, Betsy. Bearing up is more like it. And, yes, I am doing that, I think.'

To herself she thought, Just about. She placed a hand to her temple and closed her eyes. She was trying to be rational about the boys' reaction to the news of the divorce. What had she expected? That they would beg them to stay together? That they would choose to live with her in lesser circumstances, in another town, another country? That they would abuse their father for devastating their lives? Yes, she had wanted and had expected them to do all those things. They hadn't.

The very next day after Robert's announcement that he was

leaving her, he had called the headmaster of Groton and received permission to take the boys out of school for the day. Robert had arranged for a suite of rooms at a four-star country inn near the school and to have a sumptuous lunch served to them in its sitting room overlooking a lake. He knew that would be a plus for the boys because Alexis and Mishka were always ravenous, most especially during school term with nothing to fall back on but school food, and packages from home. The privacy would be a plus for them all. Under the circumstances, no public dining room would do.

The boys had been full of news of themselves and school and hardly said anything about being allowed to play truant for a day. But they were too, as Robert had suggested, mature for their years and not unaware that something was amiss. It was not long after they had entered the suite before Alexis asked, 'What's wrong, Dad?'

Mishka added, 'If it's bad news, Dad, let's have it.'

'Nothing wrong, just different.' That was how Robert had answered the boys. Those words, and the cold tone of his voice, stung Anoushka now just as they had then in that pretty sitting room overlooking the lake.

Why, she wondered, didn't they look to *me* for answers, ask *me* what was wrong? They had kissed her, cuddled her, been obviously happy to see her. But no more than a kiss and a hug and then it was to Robert that they gave their attention. Had it always been this way? Should she have handled it differently? No? Yes?

For the hundredth time she ran through her mind how she had handled the task of breaking the news to the twins. No, she concluded. She may have been unhappy with their reaction, may not have heard what she wanted to hear from them, but what she had done had to have been right for the boys, or at least she had to believe it was.

'The lying bastard,' she mumbled.

Thankfully neither Betsy or David heard her, or at least they said nothing, and Betsy did not turn round to look at Anoushka. Again she agonised over what she had said to her sons. 'There is no easy way to break this to you, boys. Your father doesn't want to live with me any more. He wants a divorce from me but not from you. He has made it clear that a reconciliation is impossible. None of this is my doing. None of it is what I want.'

Anoushka had watched the colour drain from Alexis's face, Mishka's eyes fill with tears. Why hadn't she held her arms out to them, given them a chance to rush into them? Just standing by the window, unable to put her pain away, had been her fatal mistake. Anger and bitterness had grabbed her and would not let her go. They had consumed her and left no place for her sons to slip in and comfort her, sapped her of the energy she needed to comfort them. Instead she continued, 'Your dad wants you to stay with him in our house, for me to make a new life for myself elsewhere. He's running me out of town, blackmailing me with your happiness.'

'Anoushka!' Robert's shout made her jump with anxiety. She was way out of line. She had gone too far. The boys looked horrified, disbelieving, she could see that in their faces. Her hysteria frightened them. They looked not to her but to their father for an explanation of her behaviour. Robert went to his sons and sat between them. He placed an arm round each of them. Mishka placed his head against Robert's shoulder.

Why hadn't the boys run to her, tried to soothe her? Seeing her sons and her husband together made it somehow worse for Anoushka. She was unable to help herself. The sight of them all cosy with each other had only hardened her resolve to state the facts, tell her side of it. She wanted to show Robert up for what he was doing to them all. So she had continued.

And now, in the back seat of the car crossing town to The Plaza, her words were haunting her: 'I have agreed to your father's terms not because I want to but because I love you both with all my heart and don't want to uproot you from home and friends. Dad says our divorce has nothing to do with my relationship with you boys. We can see each other whenever, wherever we want. I'm keeping the Caribbean house, and you can have your holidays there with me. We can travel. I'll be at the end of a telephone whenever you want me.

'All that is true, but hardly the same as us all living together as one family. Your father would like to think it's simple for us all to dance to his new tune. Well, maybe it is for him, for you boys, but it certainly isn't for me.'

They had been shocked by their parents' intention to divorce. Concern for where their mother would go, what she would do, was in every question they had asked. Alexis had come out with, 'Is it sex, another woman? Is that why Dad has stopped loving you?'

That was the question that had hurt the most. And she had done no better with that than she had with any of her other answers. She told her sons, 'Your dad has lied to us all. He was only making believe he loved me, he says for our sakes, yours and mine. There has always been another woman he loved more than me, but I'll let him explain all that to you as he has so cruelly explained it to me. She's a traitor, like your father, and they have both cheated me for the last time.'

Anoushka knew her answers had been filled with bitterness and sniping at Robert, blaming him for everything, that she had kept babbling on about him irrationally, one minute attacking him, the next telling the boys they were staying with him because he was a good father who wanted the best for them all. The crossed signals she was sending out only drove Alexis and Mishka further away from her and her unhappiness and closer to the calm, quiet support their father was emanating. Anoushka had been appalled when she realised that the boys, prompted by their father, saw her plight as nothing more than glamour, a great adventure for her to go out into the world and construct a new life for herself. They would all have new lives with the old one as a foundation to build on. She wanted to kill Robert.

David interrupted her thoughts. 'Anoushka, I feel there is something that must be addressed and this is the last time I will be able to have a quiet word with you before we get to The Plaza.'

Though she barely heard the words, David's voice snapped her back to the present. 'You're using your attorney's voice, David.'

'I guess I am. As both friend and attorney I am advising you for the last time that you are being rash and very foolish. You are acting out of pain and pride in not going for a better settlement from Robert than you have chosen to take. Your own lawyer has advised you of that, and though I am Robert's attorney, I as a friend, and Robert as my client, advise you to take what he is now offering. You will be much better off.'

'Throw Anoushka another bone? Is that what he has instructed? Everything I take from him, David, makes me feel like a dog hungry for the leftovers of a life I once had with him. To learn that I have been living off the scraps and bones of his generosity all these years when I thought it was love is humiliating enough, don't you think? I only want what *I* want. And I wish I had money of my own, something of myself to fall back on so I could walk away from him taking nothing. I'm not the dog he thinks I am, and I don't want his generosity. I have had my fill of that. The house in Barbados, twenty-five thousand dollars, first-class travel for a year, and one thing, any thing, from the house that I want. And I am only taking those things so I can get on my feet. He got away cheap.'

'That's what he's worried about.'

'Tough, he'll have to live with that.'

'You're not being rational or practical, Anoushka, just stubborn. You can't make anything like the life you are used to with nothing but twenty-five thousand dollars and all your travel expenses for a year. What about when the year is up? How will you live? Even in Barbados?'

'I don't know how I'm going to live through this lunch, never mind anything after that. So stop asking me, and telling me what a fool I am. Don't you think I know that? If you're a friend then watch over my boys for me. I can't think of anything else you can do except change the subject.'

They were waiting in the lobby of The Plaza: Robert, Alexis, Mishka, and the Holland boys, Rudi and Joe. The moment Anoushka came through the door she saw them all standing together, eyes on the entrance. Mishka had an armful of long-stemmed white roses and Alexis carried a massive box of chocolates, wrapped beautifully in silver paper with a gold bow. They rushed forward to kiss their mother. They did indeed think her departure a great and happy adventure for her, she could tell by the smile on their faces, the enthusiasm with which they greeted her and were looking forward to seeing her aboard the *QE2* and having a tour of the ship. Robert had covered himself well.

Robert. The moment she saw him standing there in The Plaza her heart skipped a beat. How handsome and sexy he was. She wanted him. She was still attracted to him. It was purely physical. The chemistry for her with Robert was still there as strong as ever. As the boys hugged her and presented her with the sumptuous gifts, she smiled and kissed them and thanked them and put on a good show for them, but her heart was with Robert. She wanted him, yearned to be lost in erotic bliss with him. She wanted to come, for him to transport her into the erotic world she was so happy with him in. But it was gone, that would never happen again. An exciting sexual life with the man she loved, that too was over for her. For the first time since that dreadful night less than a week ago she realised the extent of her sexual loss. That was something else she would have to learn to live with. Yet another thing to traumatise her.

They gazed across the room at each other, his face as hard and cold and angry with her as it had been since that night when he blew her world apart and left her with the dregs of a life. He used his anger like a shield, deflecting all Anoushka's grief and hurt at his actions as if he was afraid to confront them face on. He was not a man devoid of compassion, but as a doctor had long ago learned how to bury it deep.

Rudi and Joe left Robert's side to greet Anoushka. They gave her a kiss and presented her with gifts until her arms were full; they too were caught up in their friends' mother's departure. From her side they rushed away to greet their own mother and father. To anyone in the lobby of The Plaza, here was a happy family party. A birthday? An anniversary? Some mysterious and exciting rare occasion that was cause for a party? One would hardly have guessed a divorce. It was left only for Robert to join them.

He walked across the lobby and greeted Anoushka. 'You look very chic. I always did like you in that hat.' He took her lightly by the elbow, wanting to usher her through the lobby to the Oak Room. She pulled away as discreetly as she could without making a scene. He managed a whisper to her.

'For the boys' sake, please, no scene. Christ knows we have had our scenes!'

Anoushka's reply was to walk quickly from his side, to join Mishka and Joe and ask them, 'How about helping me with all these terrific presents? What a lucky lady I am.'

'Postcards, Mum, lots of postcards.'

'And for me too please, Mrs Rivers,' had been Mishka's and Joe's reply to that.

All through lunch Robert was at his most charming. He had planned her farewell magnificently, leaving not a thing undone so that it should seem the most happy of celebrations. Bitterly she thought, well, it is for him, but kept that thought to herself and suppressed the misery she was feeling every minute of that lunch, every second of her last day with her family and friends.

They had a large table by the window. The bowl of flowers in the centre were white tulips, her favourite. They were served oysters Rockefeller, turtle soup, rock Cornish game hen, wild rice, baby peas, candied carrot and sweet potato, a green salad with Roquefort dressing, chocolate mousse. All the boys' favourites made up the menu for the Rivers party.

The twins had been seated on either side of their mother and the Holland boys on either side of them. Robert had seated himself where he and Anoushka need not confront each other across the table. The boys' youth and innocence, love, their enthusiasm for her new adventure and endless talk about where they would go, what they would do if they were the ones sailing into the unknown, charmed and melted Anoushka's heart. It

41

eased her pain and she lost herself for a few hours in their dreams.

Afterwards it was to be coffee and petit fours in the Palm Court of the hotel where tables had been arranged for them. There was yet another farewell surprise too. Alexis and Mishka had vanished from the party for a few minutes only to reappear with guitar and flute.

The boys had been studying music since they were five years old and Alexis's mastery of the classical guitar was something very special. The flute, played by Mishka, exquisite at the worst of times, was today ethereal, tender, so very sweet. Alexis took the chair placed in the centre of the court under a palm tree and Mishka stood ready to play next to him. They gave Anoushka a farewell concert, announcing first, 'We have arranged this piece as a gift for our mother.' The piece was composed by Joaquin Rodrigo, which the twins had adapted so that they could play it together. Several times, as one played solo, the sound of the other's instrument seemed to linger and ride for a few seconds on the notes of the other. In duet, they were equally impressive.

The surprise was almost Anoushka's undoing. She had been saved from breaking down by a combination of feelings: rage, anger, love, pride and despair. Self-pity for her plight. Betsy, sitting next to her, reached out to take her hand, squeeze it, and whisper, 'It was all their idea. You're being terrific. When they are older, and understand, the boys will always remember you for this with admiration.'

Those words helped Anoushka to keep herself together. Never was she as proud of her boys as during their concert! They had heart and soul and genius with their music. How had she failed to realise that until now? By the time they had played the last note the Palm Court was ringed with people. Alexis and Mishka took their applause with ease and a smile and blew a kiss to their mother before joining her. They needed no words to tell them how much she had enjoyed her surprise. It was hugs and kisses from her, and more from Betsy, and shakes of the hand from Robert and David, a pat on the back from Rudi and Joe. 'You get it from my mother . . .' Anoushka began. The boys broke in and finished her sentence with her '. . . she was a master on the balalaika as a child, famed in St Petersburg for her skill with the instrument.' Everyone began to laugh, even Anoushka herself.

'You always say that, Mom. Every time we finish playing something you like,' said Mishka.

'Do I?'

'Every time,' repeated Alexis and Robert in unison.

Robert should have kept quiet. It broke the spell, cast her back to the reality of her situation. But once more she was saved, this time by strangers who made it easier for Anoushka by breaking into the Riverses' party to praise the boys.

Later, walking up the gangway of the luxury liner with her family and friends there was a moment when Anoushka did falter and think she could no longer go on with the charade. To die right there and have it all end, this sham of a life she had led, how she wished it could be over right then and there! But death is not all that merciful, not so easily achieved when you want it. Something made her reach way down into herself and, against her will, struggle on through the afternoon.

There came a moment when Betsy and the boys decided they would accept the captain's invitation to have a look round the bridge of the ship and Anoushka was left alone in her cabin with Robert and David. Her immediate reaction was to head for the door. She had nothing to say to him. David looked uncomfortable. Robert asked in that same cold and indifferent voice he now reserved for her, 'Anoushka, do you have everything you want?'

She swung round to face him. 'What a very stupid, insensitive question. What do you think? You're a smart man, supposedly a man of genius. Answer that one yourself.'

'I meant, have you chosen what you want to take from the house? I'll have it shipped wherever you like, whenever you like.'

'Oh, that. Tie up the last detail, end it clean and neat, and then nothing left except civility between us for the rest of our lives. For the sake of the children.'

Anoushka caught the look of irritation with her on Robert's face as he shot a glance across the stateroom to David. 'Don't worry, Robert, I made a deal, I'll abide by it for the sake of my sons. Tie up the loose ends? They're tied up, you hard, mean bastard! I've already taken a memento of my life with you.'

'Don't call me mean, Anoushka, you could have had more than one thing from the house. Hard, yes, I'll confess to that – something I've had to be with you to get on with my life. Learn a lesson from that.'

It was David who, sensing the ugliness behind what was happening and how it could escalate, stopped it with, 'That's enough. It's all been said. There's no point in your beating up on each other any more. It's not worthy of either one of you. Now, just for the record, what have you taken, Anoushka?'

She seemed to pull herself up. Walking tall, she crossed the stateroom to look in a mirror. She adjusted her hat, ran the pads of her fingers over her face as if she were wiping away the stress, all her anxieties, then turned to face them. Adjusting the magnificently luscious lynx collar of her camelhair coat she looked David directly in the eyes and told him, a degree of hauteur in her voice, 'The Greek and Roman coin collection.' Then she looked past David to Robert and for the first time since their estrangement challenged *him* with a look of pure vindictiveness.

'You've never shown any interest in the collection. You've rarely taken the time to look at the coins and know nothing about them except that I am a passionate collector who had traded up my grandfather's collection since I was a child. You took the one thing you knew I could not bear losing. It never entered my mind you could be so vengeful.'

'Now you know how it feels.'

Anoushka walked from the stateroom with Robert's and David's voices ringing in her ears.

'You wanted your freedom, Robert, it seems the price is the coins. Having signed a paper declaring Anoushka could have anything she wanted from the house, you'd better abide by that document and take this like a man.'

'She knows nothing about them. She has no idea what she has there.' He was protesting but there was resignation in Robert's voice. And pain.

Anoushka had known very well that was the only loss that would pain Robert because for all his love of beauty and rare things, he was not a materialistic man. He could sustain the loss of anything else without too much distress. Things were things to Robert. Life was something other than things, and she had always admired him for that. But the coins had always been something else for him, representing the special passion and excitement that all collectors live for. He would suffer this loss, agonise over what she would do with them. The coin collection was a lifetime's love and work. She had hit him a blow she knew he would never recover from, and not only because she took it, or didn't care about it, but because she knew absolutely nothing about the coins. Robert despised ignorance. The collection had been his very private thing. He had always been as reserved and secretive about it as he had been about not loving her. Oh, yes. She had got him where it hurt and that raised her spirits considerably.

The farewells were dreadful, and not only for Anoushka. At that moment, on deck, just before they were about to take leave of the ship and go down the gangway with their father, mother and sons kissed and hugged each other and made promises to write and for Anoushka to call once a week from wherever she was in the world. Tears welled up in the boys' eyes and were fought back. There were smiles on trembling lips. It was Alexis who said it for them all: 'We're OK, Mom, it's all just too new and a matter of getting used to.'

'A new door opens and all that,' chimed in Mishka, and placed an arm round his brother's shoulder.

'In a way you have to like the excitement of the drama Dad has created,' said Alexis.

'Well, maybe not *like* but play the role each of us has been cast in it,' answered Anoushka.

That seemed to strike a chord in each of them and simultaneously they all laughed and tears vanished. Anoushka laughed too but asked herself, 'Is this black humour?' And then she was alone.

How had it happened? How could she have lost everything? Her boys? Her husband? Her lifestyle? Her home? How did she get to be last in line and so utterly alone? Good questions. Unanswerable. Maybe she was too bruised by events to find answers. Curious, but too crippled to seek any answers. And what, after all, did it matter now?

Feebly Anoushka waved from the rail on A deck to the boys and Robert down below on the dock. They looked so happy, so full of life and enthusiasm. And why not? They were going home. Robert had everything he wanted. She tried to paste a happy smile on her face for the boys' sake and thought, How cruel youth can be. How insensitive, selfish, self-centred. She kept reliving the last three days. How was it possible she was in this hell? Only a few days. It seemed a lifetime.

The boys were waving now with both arms, great arcs in front of themselves, throwing kisses as the ship was slipping its moorings and lumbering away from the dock. How she loved them. They were the only people on the dock except for the longshoreman pushing the covered gangways, working the massive hemp cables that helped launch the ship.

Her husband and sons were there because of Robert's connections. Always Robert's connections. Those little privileges that men of skill and renown are rewarded with, were part and parcel of Robert's life. She asked herself with some bitterness whether famous doctors' ex-wives still got favours, whether the cachet of achievement by their ex-husbands still rubbed off on them. Tears appeared at the corners of her eyes and now she too waved with both arms and pretended enthusiasm as she bid farewell to life as she knew it.

A bitter cold wind was whipping off the river. Her family were dancing, hopping from one foot to the other to keep warm as the mighty Cunard liner backed into the Hudson River. The blast of her horn, a dramatic, romantic sound, echoed against the buildings on either side. Anoushka leaned out over the rail and watched Robert and her children recede: become smaller and smaller, mere dots, pin points of people against the massive landscape of the terminal and Manhattan rising majestically behind them. A gust of wind whipped under her sable-crowned, wide-brimmed felt hat and blew it from her head. She grabbed for it but in vain. Anoushka watched it tumble and turn on the currents of air before it drifted down between the side of the ship and the terminal. A longshoreman watching the English liner make its grand exit chased after it. The elegant Adolfo head gear eluded him and drifted down further to the water.

The boys broke away from Robert and ran towards the end of the dock, trying to catch it. They missed and the river made its claim on Fifth Avenue, taking possession of the hat. It bobbed along on the waves created by the churning of the massive ships propellers and then, quite suddenly, drowned, disappeared, never to be seen again. The last indignity. She had even lost her hat.

Chapter 4

'Clearly, this is not about a hat, though it was a very pretty one.'

Anoushka turned from the rail to look at the man, tears streaming down her face. She'd not been aware of him standing next to her. His words only added to her distress.

The man opened his coat and drew a clean white handkerchief from his trouser pocket. He pressed it in her hand. Anoushka covered her eyes with it and struggled to compose herself, but it was impossible. She was sinking under the weight of too much misery. She clung to the rail of the ship for support as her knees buckled. Wiping her eyes with his handkerchief and a trembling hand, she asked barely above a whisper, 'Help me.'

The tall broad-shouldered man looked round him for a ship's officer, a fellow passenger, anyone, to come to her aid. But they were virtually alone in the bow of the ship, the other passengers having sought shelter from the wind and cold in the enclosed section of the deck.

She saw him looking round and grabbed on to his arm. 'No, please, discreetly. I don't want to make a scene.'

He placed an arm round her and that did give her the physical support, the comfort she so desperately needed. The warmth and strength of his body seemed to energise her. She pulled herself up and tried to walk. Her steps were unsure, wobbly. 'I'm so ashamed,' she told him through her sobs and gasps for breath. 'Embarrassing, this is so embarrassing.'

'Let's just get you out of here, and to some private place where you can cry and beat your chest, if that's what you want.'

Anoushka wrenched her arm away and glared at him. 'You think I'm enjoying this?'

He supported her once more, his hand on her elbow, and kept her walking. 'It doesn't matter what I think,' he told her. With that he pulled open the doors to the glassed-in area and indicated to her that she should step over the threshold. Under his breath he mumbled, 'Shit, how I hate women in distress.'

She struggled to release herself from him and told him, 'Then just go away.'

'What's your stateroom number? I'll see you there. That's the best thing to do if you don't want a scene. You look a mess, clearly not in control of yourself, and if I don't help you someone else will have to.'

She told him the number of her stateroom. Then, all control lost, burst into tears again and leaned against the stranger.

Anoushka woke up in panic. She had a tremendous headache. The room was dark. Completely disorientated, it took her several seconds and the movement of the ship to remind her she was on the *QE2* crossing the Atlantic Ocean. Groping in the dark, she finally found the bedside lamp and switched it on.

The room had three portholes and was panelled with a warm honey-coloured wood. She was lying on an overly large bed. Her coat was draped over the arm of a wing chair. She swung her legs off the bed. The headache seemed to be concentrated in the back of her eyes. She covered them with her fingers and pressed gently then dropped her chin on to her chest. She sat there like that, head lowered, for some time and with the most peculiar feeling.

Emptiness, a profound sense of meaninglessness, had taken possession of her. Somewhere in the depths of sleep and despair her emotions had somehow petrified. Had they magically vanished, or were they merely deep frozen, to be resurrected at some future date? Who was to know? And what did it matter? Whatever had happened to them they were gone, and there sat the same Anoushka Usopova Rivers looking like herself but not at all the same person she had known herself to be. She had awakened as a woman with a past that no longer meant anything to her. Worse, she was aware that Robert, Alexis and Mishka were still in her life, to be dealt with more than loved. Emotional burn-out. Anoushka was aware of that but could do nothing about it. The fact of the matter was she no longer cared.

She rose from the bed. She was barefoot. She looked round the room and spotted her shoes placed neatly together on the floor next to the wing chair. The man. She flushed pink with embarrassment and touched the side of her cheek. She half expected it to be sore where he had slapped her hard. He had been escorting her to her cabin, but rather than calming, her hysteria seemed to have intensified. Her sobs had been uncontrollable, and she had been hyperventilating so badly that her body had been shaking violently.

Once he had her in his stateroom he had actually to pull her up and brace her with one hand, then slap her hard across the face, saying, 'Sorry 'bout this.'

It had worked. He shocked her sober and she had covered her face with her hands and cried softly as he led her to his bedroom and sat her down on the bed. He left her to return with some tablets and a tumbler of whiskey, and ordered, 'Drink this down.' She had. He then pulled her up from the bed and removed her coat, then sat her down again and swung her legs up on to the bed. That was the last thing she remembered, except that the man had muttered as she was passing out, 'Damn it, how I hate hysterical women.'

He had loosened her clothes. She went to the mirror to adjust them and was shocked by how pale she was, how messy. Her mascara had smudged in dark circles round her eyes and rivulets of tears had streaked her cheeks. In the bathroom she washed her face and tried to make herself more presentable, at least as presentable as red and swollen eyes would allow. She had to get through the corridors of the ship to her own stateroom without attracting any attention. All she wanted was a hot bath and to go to sleep again.

There were signs of the man everywhere. Damp towels lying over the edge of the bath or dropped carelessly on the floor, shaving brush and razor, after-shave, scented soap, a leather sponge bag. Toothpaste with the cap off and squeezed from the top lay on the washstand. A dirty shirt in the laundry basket, a black sock draped over the basket's edge. He had obviously bathed and changed while she had been asleep.

Anoushka rubbed her forehead, trying to remember what her good Samaritan had looked like. She couldn't. Somehow not being able to put a face to him motivated her to hurry from the bathroom and slip into her shoes and coat. She looked for a handbag for several minutes until she realised she had left it in her stateroom when she had gone on deck with her family and friends.

Opening the stateroom door to leave, Anoushka was surprised to find that it was not the corridor she stepped into but a large beautifully appointed sitting room in creams and beiges among more polished wood panelling. A large vase of dark and fully blown long-stemmed red roses sat on a circular marble table in the centre of the room and a Persian carpet, dramatic for its subtlety of colour and pattern, was unexpected in a stateroom on what was after all a commercial ocean liner. All the lamps were turned on and cast a warm, soft glow around the room. There were stacks of books piled on a desk, a sheaf of white paper, a typewriter and laptop computer, a mug with dozens of sharp pointed lead pencils sticking up in it.

Old habits don't die easily, not even when you are emotionally dead. An avid reader herself, any book was of interest to Anoushka. She looked at the title and was surprised to see that it was a Japanese edition, the one directly underneath the French edition of the same book, the next a Russian title, all of which she could read. All three book titles translated differently but the author was clearly the same – Hadon Calder. A name she knew well, in common with the rest of the world. Had her Good Samaritan been Hadon Calder? The very possibility sent Anoushka fleeing from the room.

To have imposed on someone she had admired for years and not even known who he was, if indeed that had been him, only proved to her what a state she had been, was still in.

It was two in the morning and the corridors were empty, a relief for Anoushka because she got lost and had to accept a cabin steward's help in finding her way. The moment she stepped into the room, attractively appointed and with a small private balcony, the day and its events loomed up in front of her.

Anoushka spent the next three days in her stateroom taking only breaths of air on the balcony where she stared empty-minded across the cold Atlantic waves. The events that had taken place on her arrival were completely blanked from her mind. She picked at the food served to her in her room. She neither read nor watched TV. All concentration gone, she did little but sleep and take long baths and drifted in time and space.

It wasn't so much boredom as claustrophobia that finally, on the afternoon of the fourth day, drove Anoushka from the confines of her room. She needed the wind on her face, and space, and to walk. And walk she did, endlessly, like a lioness escaped from her cage.

A new face in first class, she was not the only one feeling the claustrophobia of a luxury ship's crossing. Many a passenger was to lower a book or paper, thrilled to see a new face, a mystery woman. She ignored their smiles, the occasional friendly greeting.

Anoushka did not feel the adventuress she was supposed to be, more a wanderer with no place to go. In limbo. That was it. She was in a place of oblivion, and once she realised that, she came out of the living coma she had suspended herself in since the *QE2* had pulled away from the dock, leaving her life behind her. Where do wanderers go? More to the point, how do they work out where they want to go? Where was she going? Southampton to dock, London, and an open ticket to the world. Daunting. But something to contemplate.

She asked the deck steward for a chair out in the fresh air and the sun, somewhere sheltered from the wind. And there she sat, tucked under a blanket, and thought not about the future but the several days she had locked herself away on the *QE2*, in mourning for the death of a marriage, her life as she had known it, her happiness. Lost days and nights of which she could remember nothing. Time, *her* lifetime, lost forever, wiped out of her share of existence. Suddenly she made the decision: Never again. No more lost days. She wanted to live every minute of every day, no matter what it was to bring.

She felt the warmth of the sun's rays on her face. It made her skin tingle and she felt herself coming alive. A minute at a time, a day at a time, to live every aspect of life, and want nothing from it. How else would she be able to discover herself again, new, fresh, without carrying the heavy baggage of the past on her back? She sighed and felt as if a great weight had been lifted off her. The lid of her coffin? She couldn't quite smile. Resurrection was one thing, happiness a great deal to ask for. To live again seemed quite enough. Another deep sigh, and she mumbled aloud, 'Come on, Mr Sun, do your stuff, heal me.'

She enjoyed a cat nap, short and sweet and very comforting. And when Anoushka opened her eyes she felt if not a new then certainly a different woman, possibly one with a new sense of adventure. She could almost understand the enthusiasm her sons had felt for her voyage into the unknown.

The sun was very low in the sky when Anoushka abandoned the deck for her stateroom. The moment she opened the door she knew that it was not a happy choice. The walls seemed to close in on her. One more night. You can live with that, she told herself. She had found some strength to fight off her demons and that realisation lifted her spirits enormously. She went to the wardrobe and chose the dress she would wear for dinner. A stone coloured crêpe-de-chine full-length evening dress, strapless and pencil straight with a slit up the back, worn with a three-quarter-length silk chiffon coat of the same colour and banded in the same crêpe-de-chine. Robert had bought it for her in Paris. She had only worn it once, and until now had considered it too young and glamorous for her.

She walked across the room holding it up against her and looked in the mirror over the chest of drawers. Anoushka was shocked at what she saw. She looked drawn, drugged with despair, like someone who had suffered a tremendous shock. It was all in the eyes: shock, pain, suffering. She touched her cheek with her hand; at least the sun had given her some colour. Anoushka ran her fingers through her hair. Still a pretty woman, but how had she allowed herself to become so – well, matronly, there was no other word for it. She had of course been right about the dress, it needed a vivacious woman. The woman Robert had wanted her to be or he would never have bought such a dress.

Clearly a visit to the beauty salon was in order. A tall order for Anoushka who detested the hairdresser's and all those beauty treatments other women were so fond of. They had never been a part of her life. Clean hair, a little mascara, lipstick, and that was it. Her good looks and Robert's love had always been enough. Now that was gone. She fled from her stateroom to the first-class beauty salon.

She was the last to leave, but when she did she looked more glamorous than she had done for many years. That look of a well-to-do suburban matron and mother had been buffed away considerably. She received a few tips from the salon's beautician, Denise: a touch of mocha-coloured shadow and more than a hint of dark brown mascara, a lip pencil outlining the sensuous lips coloured with the same soft shade of lipstick she favoured, a blusher of soft tawny beige, all added so much, masked to some extent the traumas she had suffered. Her shoulder-length hair looked more silvery-blonde. Layers had been cut into it by the endlessly chattering and morale-boosting, hair stylist, Charmaine. It had more lift and body and a soft wave to it. Gone was the ten-year-old straight and sensible bob.

Walking back to her stateroom Anoushka noticed that the few people she saw were dressed for dinner – black tie or evening gowns – and all heading for the dining room. She was late, very late, and still in her wide white flannel culottes and white silk Armani shirt. She passed one of the cocktail lounges and went in for a glass of champagne. It was deserted except for the staff and one couple on the far side of the room. She felt no compulsion to rush, merely asked the waiter to call the dining room and say that she would be late for dinner.

That was Anoushka's first realisation that she could do anything she wanted to do. There was no husband, there were no children, home or commitments to consider. Just herself. A fact of her new life, too strange even to dwell on. The waiter brought some cheese straws and refilled her glass.

'You mustn't forget your books, Mrs Rivers,' said the young man, placing two dictionaries, a pad of paper, a notebook and a Mont Blanc fountain pen on the small table.

She was about to protest that the books were not hers, but having been taken by surprise was too slow. The waiter was gone through the glass doors from the lounge into the corridor before she could say anything. No matter. She would merely leave them there for someone else to come and claim.

It didn't take long before curiosity got the better of her. Clearly someone was doing a translation from Japanese into English, and badly. Without much thought she took the pen in her hand and corrected nearly two paragraphs. Lost in the work and relaxed for the first time in weeks she was not aware of the man who drew a chair up to her table and sat down. He startled her with, 'I hate other people using my fountain pen.'

'Oh. I'm so sorry. I got carried away. It's so badly translated. I thought I could help.'

'You know more than *sayonara*, so you think you're a translator?'

'I said I was sorry.' And Anoushka replaced the top on the pen and shoved the papers and books across the table. She rose from the banquette, very embarrassed and wanting to leave.

He stopped her with, 'Oh, sit down. You seem to be continually barging into my privacy. How badly?'

'How badly what? And I don't barge into people's privacy, not the people I know, and certainly not a man I have never seen before in my life.' With those words Anoushka once again tried to take her leave.

Hadon Calder was astonished. She was not play acting, she did not remember him as the man who had come to her aid. He was fascinated that she could block him, possibly the entire incident, out of her mind. She looked a great deal better to him than she had when he had handed her his handkerchief and she had asked for his help.

He decided, for the moment, not to pursue the fact that they had indeed met but instead rose quickly from his chair and blocked her way. 'I'm being rude. Inexcusably so. But I am rude, and paranoid about my privacy, difficult at the best of times, selfish and self-centred. A pig, actually. I can, however, also be devastatingly charming when I want something and very pleasant and amusing if I'm not put upon.' He took her hand in his, and, as

53

if to prove a point, lowered his head and placed the perfect continental kiss upon it. 'The translation, is it very bad?'

'I don't think I want to get into this.'

'Please, how bad?'

'As you so rightly pointed out, knowing the words doesn't make you a translator. I really must go, I'm very late for dinner.'

'Dine with me.'

'Impossible.

'Why?'

'I'm not good company, I need to be alone.'

'Maybe that's just what you don't need.'

'How would you know what I need?'

'I only said maybe.'

'I don't know you, I don't dine with strangers, and frankly I don't much want to make the effort of getting to know you.' Anoushka could hardly believe she had said that. She quickly added, 'Or anyone else.'

'That's perfect. I don't particularly want you to *know* me. Quite the contrary. And have no fear, I certainly don't want to *discover* you. Just pick your brain, and talk about translations. Something to amuse ourselves while we dine well. Shall we say back here in an hour, dressed for the last dinner aboard ship before we dock in Southampton?'

Anoushka hesitated.

'Oh, shit, who needs this?' He gathered up the books, placed the fountain pen in his pocket, and said, 'I can't stand indecisive women. It's a really irritating trait. If you prefer a boring evening dining alone, then don't come.'

Anoushka surprised Hadon when she stepped around him and left the room without a word. He had misjudged her reaction, had expected her to crumble and accept his invitation. He had after all seen what a vulnerable woman she was.

Few people knew what Hadon Calder looked like. There were no author photograph on his books, and his TV and newspaper interviews were rare. His acerbic tongue, quick wit and passion for privacy were all there in his writing, and that he felt was enough. Anything left over was for him. His genre was the big novel, a cross between the geo-political thriller and existentialist thinking. Some wag on *The Times* had labelled him 'Camus for the masses'. He was that rare thing in the literary world: a formidable writer that the public read, and still he remained a private man, wealthy from the work he loved, who could roam the world with a certain degree of anonymity.

He was one of those people who believed that work was more fun than fun. That his writing was as much a business as an act of creation. His books were widely translated. No. 1 bestsellers in ten languages. Hadon Calder made it a policy to have translations from the foreign language editions sent to him. He had recently had to hire new translators for two editions after the death of a man whose work had pleased him for more than ten years.

This neurotic woman who had now crossed his path twice was right – the new translator was just not good enough. He was missing the power and beauty, the subtle, smooth, expansiveness of Hadon's prose. This new translator had lost the heart and essence of Hadon's writing. He had somehow been heavy-handed, used leaden words that killed the pace. The Calder images no longer gleamed with magic and poetry. He watered down the evil and uplifting goodness, the mix that Hadon Calder's novels played with so brilliantly, and where was the wit?

Hadon's first impression that something was very wrong was the first time he saw the proofs of the book. They were more than one-third the size of the English, French and Italian editions. The man would be fired, the translation junked, but that was not enough for Hadon. In London he and his publishers would interview a number of new candidates for the job but this time Hadon would be there to listen and approve or disapprove. Line by line, they would get it right because Hadon would have done his homework, analysed what was wrong with the present translation, be able to indicate where the losses were in the translation.

It was not an easy job at the best of times but it was twice as bad now when Hadon was angry over every omission, the stupidity, the waste of time and money with every sentence that went wrong. It made for a lesser book, a bad book in his eyes. For a perfectionist who insisted everything be right, having the wrong translator was a seriously bad business.

Hadon was late. He had taken his time bathing and changing into evening clothes. A royal blue silk handkerchief frothed from the breast pocket, his only deviation from the formal dinner jacket so elegantly cut, so perfect with its wide black satin lapels, the white linen shirt and soft black silk bow tie.

The bar was deserted, except for the bartender and two waiters who snapped to attention. Hadon went directly to the bar and asked for a double martini, no olive and a twist of lemon. He seated himself a table near a porthole, drawn to that particular place because of a white full moon that cut a path of silver across the water. He ordered a second martini and asked the waiter to fetch a menu from the dining room for him. She was approaching the table while he was still talking to the waiter. He added to his other instructions, 'You'd better make that two menus,' and rose from his chair to greet Anoushka.

'I didn't think you'd come.'

'Well, that makes two of us. Neither did I.'

And for the first time they smiled at each other. He kissed her hand and they sat down. 'What made you change your mind?'

'The idea of dining alone, of getting bored with myself.' This time the smile was teasing. 'No, none of those reasons.'

'Then dare I ask why?'

'No. I think not.'

He ordered a martini for her and after the waiter departed, he said, 'That's quite an evening dress. You're a lady full of surprises.'

'No. My husband was full of surprises. He bought me this gown.'

'Oh, there's a husband?'

'I thought we weren't going to pry into each other's lives, not discover each other? You weren't interested, remember?'

'And neither are you?'

'No.'

He drained his glass while Anoushka sipped from hers. 'I'm famished,' she declared, and picked up the menu.

Hadon was surprised to find he liked her. She was interesting, complex, vulnerable and strong-willed. How else could she have blocked him, her Good Samaritan, so completely from her mind? He couldn't decide how bright or clever she might be, but he knew enough about character to know that she had been cheating on herself for a good many years. He could wager that that family she had left behind on the dock in New York had buried the real woman in her years ago. Wife, mother, matron of suburbia, she was more than that. Did she know it? He liked her looks, whereas he hadn't considered them when he had seen her at the ship's rail, although, he had earlier this evening. Now he found her down-right attractive.

'Caviare and quails' eggs,' he ordered, looking across the table at Anoushka for approval. 'To get on with.'

'And vodka, not chilled but very cold, don't you think?' she asked.

He raised an eyebrow approvingly. 'Yes, you're quite right, caviare and vodka, perfect mates. And followed by, for your first course?' He waited for her to choose. Watching the indecision on her face made him suggest, 'Shall I order for us?'

Anoushka lowered the menu. He was amused by the look that came into her eyes when she answered. 'No. I had a husband who used to do that, take me over, and all the time I thought it was a charming gesture. Not any more. I'll manage, thank you.'

A flash of hatred, was that what he had seen in her eyes? And she had used the past tense. He was even more intrigued by his dinner guest.

'I'll have the foie gras en croûte, consommé, baby lobster, lamb cutlet, potatoes rosti, Caesar salad. And for pudding, Baked Alaska.'

'May I at least make a suggestion? The lemon sorbet, served between the lobster and the lamb, to clear the palate, as it were?'

She smiled at him and answered, 'Suggestions are acceptable.' And turning to the waiter, added, 'The lemon sorbet, please.'

'I don't have a problem about women taking *me* over, on the rare occasion that is. I consider this a rare occasion.' He closed the menu and handed it back to the waiter, telling him, 'The same for me. And could you have them call us when our table is ready?'

'I don't know what to say to that,' Anoushka commented.

'You're not expected to say anything.'

'That's good to know. Do I seem awkward to you?'

'An odd question? No. Not particularly.'

Anoushka looked pleased. She smiled and said, 'Oh, good, that's a start.'

'Would you like to elaborate on that.'

She hesitated, not sure whether she did or didn't. Was he irritated by her silence? She thought he might be and told him, 'I sense that hesitation annoys you. You should be more tolerant, especially with strangers. Not everyone can be quick, or may want to be. My timing is not the same as yours.'

That's quite sharp of her, thought Hadon. She gets better and better. He raised his glass and toasted her. '*Touché.*'

'I haven't dined alone with a man other than my husband since my marriage thirteen years ago. The experience is new, I hardly know how to behave.'

'You're doing just fine.'

Anoushka relaxed enough to consider this man for the first time. He was, she thought, in his early sixties, very fit and quite handsome. Big and very rugged, John Wayne, Texas, kind of big. She imagined he lived on a ranch. His masculinity was appealing. The ache returned, the loss of Robert, the security of having a

57

man to care for her, a man of her own, a man to escape with into a world of sex and fulfilment, erotic oblivion. She looked across the table at this attractive stranger and the ache diminished. There were other men in the world, if not for love at least for sex. How had she not thought of that once in all her years with Robert? Blind love had indeed a great deal to answer for.

On the way to the dining room, she stumbled and Hadon caught her with an arm round her waist. Pulling her up against him was instinctive. He liked how she felt in his arms, the sensuous body discernible under the crêpe-de-chine. Sensuality and vulnerability, for him a real turn on in a one night stand. A crude thought, Fuck her and leave her. A few seconds, that was all it took for him to deduce what a very sexual woman this lady was, and how much years of marriage, children, husband, and the security of family life had taken her over. Here was a woman of carnal desires who was hiding behind respectability. She gave out enough signals, albeit without intending to.

He was amused by his discovery, and also excited. He had a taste for carnal ladies, women who left love and all its trappings out of the bed. Hadon Calder was a genius at the three-day romance, but even better at the twenty-four-hour, sex 'em and leave 'em.

Chapter 5

Hadon felt Anoushka draw back as they entered the dining room. Her explanation was, 'All these people, chatting and laughing together. I've been dining alone in my room too long.'

'Are you all right?'

She hesitated then answered, 'Yes. It merely took me by surprise.'

'Just another restaurant, only it floats. People out to have a good time. It's all quite ordinary.' With that he took her firmly by the arm and they followed the maître d' to the table reserved for them and resplendent with flowers. Their places were set with a bowl each of the best Beluga caviare sunk in a larger silver bowl of crushed ice, individual small carafes of vodka and small-stemmed shot-sized glasses. They were hardly seated before one waiter arrived to fill their glasses, another with a mound of hot buttered toast.

Anoushka raised the glass to her lips and said, with a hint of a smile, '*Nastrovia*.' Then she drained the glass in one swallow, the right way, the Russian way. Hadon was impressed.

'*Nastrovia*,' he toasted, and drank it down in the same fashion.

'My name is Anoushka Usopova Rivers.'

'And I'm Hadon Calder.'

'Oh.'

Hadon placed several triangles of the buttered toast on his side plate and took up the polished amber pallet, one of the traditional ways to scoop some caviare on to toast. If possible one never used silver. He had written that in one of his books. Remembering made him smile.

'The writer?'

'I've never heard there were two Hadon Calders, though of course there might be,' he said, not unkindly.

'How presumptuous of me, correcting your work. You were quite right to be angry.'

He reached across the table and refilled Anoushka's glass. 'A woman who likes to go at her own pace, you told me. I'll leave it to you then to pour your own vodka after this one gentlemanly act. Don't be embarrassed, your presumption is what got us here dining together.'

'I do have an excuse,' she told him.

'You don't need one.' He was genuinely trying to put her at her ease.

His assurance did not stop Anoushka. 'It was such an insensitive translation. I know your work, am in fact an admirer, you've given me many hours of great pleasure. I didn't realise it was your work I was reading. I should have, but I'm not quite myself. What I did know was that line for line the work was losing something in translation.'

'The toast will be cold and the caviare is delicious.'

Anoushka spread some caviare on a corner of hot buttered toast and squeezed drops of lemon on the succulent black beads from a wedge wrapped in muslin. She ate with gusto.

'Where did you learn your Japanese? How is it you chose to learn Japanese? It isn't exactly like taking up French or Italian.'

Anoushka looked across the table at Hadon. 'Oh, how wrong you are. It's exactly like taking up French or Italian.' There was cynicism in her voice. 'I had done those: beginner's and advanced courses, plus art appreciation, literature courses, poetry. I was running out of the courses the local university offered for the bored and ambitious housewife who wanted to better herself and impress. As it happens, I impressed no one. There was only Russian, Chinese, and Japanese left and I was already fluent in Russian. It is after all my native tongue. I favoured Japanese first because I like the modern Japanese writers, Mishima and many others. No doubt Chinese would have come next, only my circumstances changed quite suddenly and there was no longer spare time to fill. Now it's all just spare time. Have you brought that sheet of paper I was so audacious as to work on?'

Hadon drew from his breast pocket the sheet of paper now folded in four. He handed it across the table to Anoushka without comment on what she had just revealed. She placed it on the table next to her plate and filled her glass. This time she took a sip of the vodka, smiled quite charmingly at Hadon and then emptied her glass in one swallow. He had been preparing another triangle of toast heaped with caviare. Carefully he handed it across the table to Anoushka. She ate the delicacy before she picked up the paper and read several sentences written in English by Hadon, then she read the same sentences from the Japanese translated back into English. She saw the rage rising in Hadon's face.

'Butchery,' he exclaimed.

Anoushka became very bold. She held up a hand to silence him and then proceeded with the translation she had made from English into Japanese, and then read how her translation from the Japanese read back into English. She watched with some pleasure the calm that replaced his rage. Anoushka folded the paper again and handed it back to him. 'I hope this vindicates my intrusive behaviour.'

'And more,' he told her as the waiters returned to the table to clear and produce their first course: foie gras en croûte.

Over dinner they spoke of nothing but the two paragraphs Anoushka had worked on, the nuances, how the juxtaposition of words can make poetry of even the most banal thoughts, can create art from intelligence, imagination, and passion. Anoushka was quoting from the Japanese writer Shusako Endo which prompted her to quote another passage, from 'A Midsummer Night's Dream'. She stopped mid-sentence and all the enthusiasm seemed to drain from her face.

Hadon said nothing, merely observed the change in Anoushka. Her head lowered she said, only just above a whisper, 'I used to talk like this sometimes to my husband. Only now do I realise he never heard me, only pretended to.'

Hadon remained silent. What after all could he say to that? Marital unhappiness . . . how boring, how unnecessary, and why would a woman live with that? The waiters returned. The main course arrived. Hadon cut into the lamb cutlet, done to perfection, pink, sweet and succulent. He was enjoying his food and felt some disappointment that his dinner companion had suddenly gone off hers.

'You really should try these baby cutlets.'

Anoushka took a deep breath, a sigh, and then raised her head and gazed across the table at him. ' "Conversational French, and my wife speaks conversational Japanese." I always thought those many many times Robert said that, to his friends and colleagues, it was his pride, and love for me that prompted him. Not only was I blind but deaf. Only now do I hear the scorn in his voice.

'All those lessons for all those languages, a married lifetime of lessons, of filling in time – and for what? For my husband so he might be proud of me in front of his friends, so that they could smirk and make wry comments about my penchant for learning and my linguistic abilities that I never used. "Conversational Japanese, for someone who has never been to Japan and has no

61

particular desire to go. Now we are obliged to so Anoushka can practise," he once said at a dinner party, then kissed me sweetly on the lips and patted my cheek, took my hand in his and kissed it.'

Anoushka's eyes were brimming with held-back tears. Hadon watched her bite on the corner of her lip and take her fork and knife in hand, making an attempt on the food in front of her. She looked utterly miserable, but more glamorously so than she had at the rail of the ship. That was what prompted him to say, 'I don't really want to hear about your husband or about your conversational Japanese. You're more than that, much more. I'm offering you a job as literary translator for my work.'

'I don't want a job. I don't need a job. I want my marriage back, my husband, my family. I don't want to change my life. I was happy with the old one, but that's gone, wiped away. I am married to a most important and extraordinary man. He was my life, my whole world. He created it for me and then destroyed it. He dumped me for another woman. Threw me on the rubbish heap like some object he once desired and no longer had a use for.'

The pain and humiliation, her catastrophic losses, threatened to swamp her once again. Hadon thought for a moment that she was going to lose control of her emotions as she had when she had said goodbye to her family. The very idea annoyed him. About to say something to that effect, he was stopped by the manner in which Anoushka raised her chin just that little bit higher.

'I shouldn't have accepted this invitation. I'm sorry, but I think I must get some air.' She placed her napkin on the table and rose very slowly from her chair.

Hadon followed suit. 'No, please. Stay. Finish your dinner. Don't be stupid. I hate women when they play the martyr while they suffer.'

Anoushka sat down again. She wanted to play no more roles. The two waiters who had come to draw their chairs retreated and Hadon sat down. He picked up his napkin and draped it across his lap, then his knife and fork and continued his meal. 'The rosti potatoes are delicious,' he told her.

'My suffering has nothing to do with you, and martyrdom has always disturbed me.'

'Then why do you constantly inflict it on me. Is it some kind of a female ploy of yours.? If so it's very unbecoming. You have other far more interesting female traits to practise on a man. Drop whatever is eating away at you and get on with your meal.

Enjoy your life, the shackles are off.'

When had Anoushka heard such straight talk from a man? Hadon Calder's manner had certainly never been Robert's. He pacified, charmed, showed affection and passion. But only now, listening to Hadon Calder, did she realise how Robert had pandered to her weaknesses, accepted them, or pretended to. He had never coped with her faults, and almost never bothered to point them out. What a fool she had been to think that his silence was caused by love for her.

She found it impossible to eat, merely toyed with the food on her plate. She did, however, manage the Mouton-Rothschild claret quite easily. Hadon watched her in silence for some minutes then asked, 'How would you say in Japanese, "One doesn't wait for tomorrow, every minute is another day?" ' And he smiled. It was a generous smile, not one that warmed the heart but one that declared, 'I'm your friend.'

Anoushka translated for him.

'And, "Live in the heart of every one of those minutes." Go on, I want to hear how it sounds in Japanese,' he told her, a distinct twinkle for her in his eyes now.

Again she answered him, only this time it was Anoushka who smiled. There was a spark of life in her smile that he had not seen before and he knew, though he had not expected it, that she would reveal more of herself to him before this night was over. Not a man to hesitate, he asked, 'You would really like to get out of here, wouldn't you?'

'Only when you've finished your meal.'

'Let's go. We'll have that flamboyant dessert you ordered elsewhere.' And he placed his napkin on the table. This time they both rose from their chairs at the same time. After Hadon asked the waiter to have the Baked Alaska and coffee sent up to his suite, they left the dining room together.

The cabin steward was in the corridor. He rushed forward to open the door to Hadon's suite. Hadon watched Anoushka and was convinced that she still had no idea that they had met before. An attraction had sprung up between them. As it usually is with these things, it was difficult to pinpoint just when it happened between them, but it was most definitely there.

To block him out of her mind was one thing, but could she block out the rooms where she had, in some hysteria, passed out in his arms? He hoped so. How nice it would be for them to leave their first meeting far behind them, if only for this one night.

Anoushka walked across the room to the desk and placed a

hand on one of the books. It wasn't going to happen. He could see recognition on her face. There was no embarrassment in her voice, just a sudden hint of too much pink on her cheeks. That surprised Hadon.

'I had forgotten about these rooms. The good Samaritan who put me in his bed. I'm very good at blocking things I can't cope with out of my mind. Why didn't you say something?'

'There seemed no point.'

A simple enough statement but one that changed everything between them. They fell silent and something new was born between them. Something erotic sparked, began to smoulder for them. It was instantly physical and exciting. Faces liking faces, a body wanting a body. The new and the fresh, flesh coming alive, wanting to make contact. A shiver of pleasure for Anoushka brought passion into her eyes. Not missed by Hadon. He walked across the room and, raising her hands to his lips, kissed them, first one, then the other. Then, very gently, he kissed her on her lips. He led her away from the desk close to the marble table in the centre of the room. The scent of red roses enveloped them. Very slowly, as if he were savouring every second of the act, Hadon removed the transparent silk jacket from Anoushka's shoulders. His hand grazed the side of her neck and she yielded by dropping her head to one side and caressing his hand with her cheek. Like a pussy cat begging for affection, wanting to be caressed.

He liked the feel of her skin. It was warm and soft, so smooth, yet taught over firm voluptuous flesh. His hands roamed sweetly over her chest and shoulders, down her arms. He played with her fingers, so long and slender, and liked the smoothness of the long oval-shaped fingernails. An almost imperceptible sigh of pleasure from her delighted him, prompting him to turn her hand over in his and raise it to his lips and kiss it.

'How sweet and erotic the scent of red roses,' she told him as she raised his head from her hand by placing a finger under his chin. Then she put her lips very carefully upon his and licked his lips, nibbling at them.

While her kisses were taking him over, he caressed her breasts through the sensuous silk covering them. When Hadon slipped his hands under the strapless bodice, Anoushka's sigh was one of a woman experiencing exquisite pleasure. To feel again the caress of a man's hands on her naked breasts, was to trigger pent-up sexual need. The very thought of intercourse, orgasm, that moment of 'the little death', strong and powerful, a coming that triggers a moment of perfect bliss, and the beat of a rampant penis taking possession of her, blocked out everything in life that was less than sexual. She closed her eyes and enjoyed his caresses and the sexual excitement she'd seen in Hadon's eyes. She gave into him, raised her arms and draped them round his neck, and everything in Anoushka Usopova Rivers gave herself over to all things sensual in Hadon Calder.

She was more, much more than Hadon had anticipated. How well she hid the fire, the passion, her sexual hunger. It took him over, incited his own. He found the fastenings on her dress, fumbled with them and gave up. Unable to wait, he tugged at the strapless bodice. When it lay crumpled round her waist, he buried his face between her ample breasts and drew in the natural sweet perfume of her flesh, an aphrodisiac for Hadon. He licked and sucked her into his mouth. She tasted divine. He pressed the sides of her breasts against his face. The sensation of being smothered by her voluptuous flesh incited him to bite into her: love bites, leaving passionate tracks to her nipples. The large and dark nimbus round the already erect, long and succulently fat nipples was sexy in the extreme. He held one breast in both his hands. It overflowed his fingers, this firm fleshy wonder of erotic delight, and he lowered his mouth to it and sucked deeply, using his teeth to taunt and tease.

Anoushka writhed with pleasure. Her breasts had always been unbearably sensitive. She murmured just above a whisper, 'That's wonderful. Don't stop. Please, don't stop.'

She caressed the nape of his neck, ran her fingers through his hair and grasped it tight, pulling at it as her excitement intensified. From there her hands found their way under his jacket and to caress his flesh. She tore off tie, jacket, shirt, and Hadon crushed their naked bodies together in an embrace. He held her tight, two bodies entwined, until he could bring his passion under some control. When he released her it was just enough to step back and admire her breasts. Once more he caressed them. His fingers tweaked and teased the raunchy dark nimbus, pinched hard at the nipples. He liked watching her. She was trying so hard to control herself but her face, and the way she squirmed, gave her away. She was coming and wanted more and stronger orgasms. He wanted total out of control sex for them, erotic oblivion.

Anoushka's hands had been busy, wrapped around his semi-erect penis. He knew now that she thrived on sex. She was a lady who knew not only how to handle it but had a passion for it. The manner in which she toyed with the knob of his penis – teased at the eye with the tip of her fingernail, the rhythm she used in her fondling of him, pressure and release, to stimulate and excite, sliding, grasping; hands, fingers used with as delicate a touch as a feather's, up and down the shaft, the shiver of delight that went through her when she cupped his scrotum, they were messages relating her lust for phallus and the joy she derived from her own sexual cravings.

There was a knock at the stateroom door. It was as if Anoushka had not heard it, or if she did, didn't care because she continued to caress Hadon. He smiled at her, kissed the tip of her nose, and with much less haste now raised the bodice of her gown to cover her breasts. He adjusted their clothes so that they looked presentable and reluctantly removed his hands. He led Anoushka to a chair and took one opposite her. Finding it impossible to answer the door in his erect condition, which showed no signs of abating, he called from the chair for whoever it was to enter.

The cabin steward and a waiter entered the room, the waiter carrying a silver platter covered with a large domed cover, plates, coffee pot, and demi-tasse cups. Once they had set the table where the red roses were displayed in all their glory, and had placed chairs there for Anoushka and Hadon, the two men stood at attention. One whisked the domed lid away. Baked Alaska appeared, a confection of ice cream covered in meringue and baked to a golden colour.

'Something extra from the chef, his own special addition to the traditional baked Alaska.' With that the waiter poured over the domed pudding a thin *cassis* sauce and struck a match. Blue flames leapt into the air and the scent of blackcurrants filled the room.

After the right comments from Anoushka and a wry smile from Hadon, the flames finally spluttered out. The waiter asked, 'Shall I serve, sir?' and held a chair out for Anoushka.

The cabin steward was more astute. He suggested, 'Or would you care to serve, sir?'

'I think we can manage, thank you.'

The two men retreated and once the door was closed, Anoushka turned to Hadon. 'That was quite a performance, and the Baked Alaska looks marvellous, but why did you answer the door?' Disappointment echoed in her voice.

'Because you wanted Baked Alaska.'

'But I wanted sex more.'

'You can have both. Baked Alaska does not preclude sex,' he

told her as he rose from the chair and went across the room to her. Taking her by the hands, he pulled her from the chair and up tight against him. He held her there for a few seconds and then swung her off her feet and into his arms.

Hadon carried her to the bedroom door where he stopped. Anoushka reached down and turned the door knob and he kicked the door open and walked with her to the bed. There he stood her on her feet. He had hastily put on his shirt and jacket when they had been interrupted by the arrival of the Baked Alaska. Now he wasted no time removing them while gazing intently down at her. He needed no words. His eyes instructed her to disrobe.

Naked, Hadon appeared much younger than his years. A fit body, sensual, exciting, and not the least frightening despite the exceptionally well-endowed and very erect penis, and the large scrotum hanging low against his muscular thighs. Anoushka's heart raced with desire for the power and beauty of such a phallus. Merely to imagine how it would feel to have such a sexual organ as his ease itself into her, take possession of her, to be riven again and again by Hadon, was thrilling beyond measure. Seeing this staff pulsating with life and sexual vigour was to incite even stronger yearnings in Anoushka. Such imaginings and the sight of him standing before her were just enough to whet her appetite, to titillate her for all things carnal with this man.

How good it felt, such overpowering sexual desire, what excitement this giving oneself over to free-wheeling sex with a stranger. How had she not realised she had missed that during all those years with Robert? She reached out and took Hadon's hands in hers and placed them on her breasts, directing them how to caress. His touch was to electrify her further. She placed them under her breasts and held them there so that they could feel the weight of them in his hands. She pressed his hands hard against her own flesh, wanting to feel even more the sensation that his hands could instill in her. His fingers bit hard into her flesh and she felt luscious, scary erotic pain, lust. She drew his hands away from her breasts, now moving them over her back, down over her bottom. He had no further need for her to direct him now. He took over.

He was a voluptuary, that was clear from the way he enjoyed the fleshy but tight orbs of her bottom, caressing between their cheeks. Clearly he liked the curves, the weight and shape, so sensuous and perfect, something further to excite his own lust for sex with this woman. She widened her stance and with searching fingers he explored the hidden recesses, so private and mysterious, the essence and heart of female sexuality, except for moments like this when a woman wanted to share that part of herself with a man. He wanted more and found more, a tight place and past that a moist and lusciously soft slit: fleshy, satiny, long, slim cunt lips, a bud ripe for the taking. She shivered with delight.

But Anoushka wanted to be in control of this glorious fondling. Quite gently she removed his hands and placed them over her hips, indicating that she wanted more caressing, for him to know all of her body. Hadon obliged Anoushka with many kisses, and always the roaming hands. It was easy to give her what she wanted, liking as he did the feel of her, all of her: the slight swell of the belly, the very blonde almost white silky triangle of pubic hair. He spread his fingers through it, and combed it, and grasped the fleshy mound beneath. Once more she took control and directed his hand to the cleft of that voluptuous Mound of Venus, so seductively captivating to men.

He slipped searching fingers between the warm lips, even more moist now from the light, almost imperceptible orgasms she had been enjoying. This time she did not remove his fingers. Size, reaction to touch, a clitoris used to agitation . . . this was a noble female sexual organ that gave untold pleasure.

She was unexpectedly free sexually. A lady and a libertine, or a lady wanting to be one. Everything about her sang a song of sex, lust, hunger for sexual oblivion with no holds barred. This once wife and mother had true sexual audacity.

It was confirmed when she very slowly, wanting him to savour every bit of what she was doing, turned round with her back to him and bent over. She spread open the cheeks of her bottom to give him an exquisite view of female genitalia. He was mesmerised by the voluptuous act, enraged with lust, throbbing for Anoushka's cunt.

She was beautiful, unbelievably raunchy and provocative, like a lovely, exotic female of the wood, an animal in heat lusting for cock and sperm. She was offering herself, teasing and taunting him with open cunt. But she wasn't an animal. This was a luscious lady, naked and desperate for sex and to come alive in lust. A lady with a voluptuous body, long and shapely legs encased in cream silk stockings that culminated high on her thighs and were held tightly in place by a wide band of white lace. A lady standing in high-heeled tarty shoes who was used to playing the role of part wife, part whore. One of those rare and special kind of women who knows how to keep a man with her cunt.

Hadon was impressed and felt himself slipping under her sexual spell. He placed his hands on her waist; she moved back against him until their bodies touched. She reached back and wrapped her arms round him and leaned that little bit more into him, rubbing herself up and down against him.

He caressed her back and then her bottom, and beneath that, and without ceremony, pulled apart as far as was possible her cunt lips and inserted the knob of his penis against her. He slid it up and down and round the opening and felt the shiver of excitement rend her body as he pushed hard to insert the head of his penis inside her. He teased it by gentle withdrawal and forceful thrusts, always sliding that little bit more of himself inside her. She was tightly wrapped round the tip of his cock and it felt sublime for both of them. Moist as she was, it was not enough: cream or butter, saliva, oil of jasmine or gardenia to make her ready for the more easy passage of such an ample penis was what was needed. He liked her courage for wanting all of him, no matter how. He kissed her on the nape of the neck.

'Great sex takes time. You're not a woman to be rushed,' he whispered in her ear, a husky lust in his voice.

He felt her push against him as he thrust into her. He liked her hunger for more of him. All the while he was moving the knob of his penis in and out of Anoushka. Her sighs of pleasure inflamed him. 'Deeper, I want more of you, all of you inside me. Please, now, I'm so ready!'

Reaching round her, he filled his hands with her breasts, now so sensitive to touch that she pulled back into him as if she had been scorched. He withdrew abruptly, turned her round and took her in his arms. His lips devoured a nipple and all its dark and sultry nimbus now puckered with passion, while he swept her up into his arms. There were tears of uncontrolled passion, frustration, pent-up sexual hunger in her eyes.

'Everything. I'll give you everything sexual you hunger for. We'll take our time, get lost in the sexual depravity we crave. For us, tonight, there'll be enough come to get drunk on, sexual bliss beyond measure.' He smiled at her and demanded, 'Now tell me you're happy, that I know what *we* want?'

She placed her arms round his neck and rested her head on his shoulder but remained silent. He smiled, understanding her inability to tell him how she felt. 'That'll do as a yes and "I'm happy",' he answered for her.

Anoushka lay down on the bed. She held her hands out to Hadon and he took them in his and lay down next to her. He pulled her high against the pillows, adjusted them behind her head and shoulders and placed a quick kiss on her cheek. He took a nipple in his mouth. She squirmed. He had her raw, so sensitive to his every touch. Now he placed himself on his knees between her legs. He raised one and removed her shoe, kissed her ankle and dropped the shoe on the carpet. He ran his hand up and down her other silken-clad leg, and again dropped a shoe on to the carpet. Bending her legs at the knee, he placed her feet flat on the bed and pushed her legs wide apart. Naked except for stockings, she was even more sexy than merely naked; more whorish, more exciting.

Her most private self, totally exposed, cunt ready and waiting for him, Anoushka was filled with a sense of joy, as she always was when she could be that way for a man. It had always been like that for her from the very first time she had experienced sexual intercourse. She handed Hadon a pillow and he placed it beneath her bottom, then another. It was as if she could not show enough of herself to him, and wanted to be in a position to receive the deepest penetration during fucking.

He placed his face between her legs and it was she who held back the outer labia of her cunt, she who showed herself pink and open and yearning for his lips. She felt his tongue, his teeth, nibbling at this most sensitive, tender place. Such exquisite caresses. Fingers tormented her with pleasure, put her on the edge. Desire released in a series of brief, gentle orgasms. Her come covered his fingers.

He liked playing this sex game with her. For Hadon foreplay was delicious, but only as a first course to whet the appetite for more. He was on the verge of turning from such gentle lovemaking to the two playmates, lust and debauchery, who would take him over. Anoushka, a willing stranger, and one he would never have sex with again, was an extra bonus. Her openness doubled his excitement, added a frisson to uncomplicated sex. The only kind of sex Hadon ever practised.

Withdrawing his lips was to release her, and sitting back on his haunches he viewed his willing prey before slipping on to his side next to her. Hadon took Anoushka in his arms and kissed her. A kiss of adoration? One of respect for lust unbound, the sexual freedom she possessed? She thought so, sufficiently to trust him to take her down the erotic path she yearned to travel with him. There would be no harm. Pure bliss would be there for her, a different kind of rainbow, the ultimate pot of gold.

Before Anoushka slid down off the pillows and on top of him, slithered snake-like down his body, leaving a trail of sensuous kisses, culminating in one on the knob of his penis, and sucked him into her mouth, they already knew this was to be a sexual odyssey to remember but never to repeat. It was too perfect: the intensity of their desire for each other and where they wanted to go with it, the time and the place. A moment in each of their histories. Anoushka intended to make the most of it.

'I'll always remember you for this night,' she told him. And he stroked the top of her head as she took his rampant phallus further into her mouth.

Only a woman as experienced, as appreciative of oral sex as Anoushka, could take a man of such exquisitely large proportions whole, suck him so passionately deep into her throat. The sensational sucking rhythm as she fondled his scrotum lovingly in her cupped hands gave Hadon sexual pleasure so intense he lost himself in her. He gripped her head between his hands, pulled at her hair during those moments when he had to fight hard not to come, once, twice, several more times before he eased himself still throbbing with desire for orgasm from her. He was her object of desire as much as she was his.

Once more he pulled her up and arranged her against the pillows. 'Don't move. Wait here, just like this,' he ordered, and slipped off the bed and left the room. Anoushka's heart was still racing, her mind was filled with nothing but thoughts of tasting his come, of having this virile sexy man's sperm filling every orifice of her body. She closed her eyes and tried to calm the sexual fires raging within. But her imagination had taken flight and would not settle: the sweet and salty taste of come, a strong and copious orgasm flowing over her lips, her cunt wet with the mingling of both their orgasms, those moments when they would ride out on the wings of eternity into oblivion as they came together.

Hadon returned to the side of the bed. She looked incredibly raunchy: sexual hunger raging in her eyes, her arm across her breast, her hand in her mouth. She was biting into the loose skin on the top of her hand, the soft flesh between her thumb and forefinger. She was holding her breath. He watched her body go taut. Anoushka came, and came again, and closed her eyes. Release, glorious release. Her body relaxed and went limp. It was all there in her face, that exquisite look of sexual ecstasy. He waited, choosing to remain silent so as not to divert her pleasure, nor his, for being there to watch it. Her eyelashes fluttered and, quite lazily, she opened her eyes, removed her hand from her

71

mouth. A deep sigh, and a languid smile for him crossed her lips.

Hadon had two plates heaped with thick slices of melting Baked Alaska on them. He spoke to her. 'That looked as if it was *very* nice.'

'Very nice indeed,' she told him with no embarrassment for having come without him, or for him having seen her in the most intimate of moments.

'They'll get even better,' he promised.

'Oh, I know that. More intense. And they'll last longer, because you'll be there.'

He leaned forward to kiss her, liking her very much for being so honest. He wondered as he handed her one of the plates and sat down next to her how long it had been since she had been as sexually honest with herself as she was with him? He spoonfed her from his own mound of melting ice cream and meringue.

'This is wickedly good,' she told him with a smile.

'I always hate the pretension and performance of a great pudding, especially Cherries Jubilee and Baked Alaska, but my taste buds don't,' he admitted.

'That's me too. I hate the pretension of all the best things in life,' she told him.

Something as casual as two people sitting on a bed eating ice cream did nothing to dampen the ardour these two naked people had for each other. Hadon sitting cross-legged was still maintaining a massive, erect penis and Anoushka, reclining against the pillows, erect nipples surrounded by a dark nimbus of sexual excitement. Sexual tension was building, still building for them as they fed the confection from their plates to each other.

Hadon handed his empty plate to Anoushka and walked back into the dining room only to return bearing the silver platter with the remainder of the Baked Alaska. He picked up a pillow that had fallen on the floor and placed it on the bed between them and the platter on it. He broke off pieces of the meringue and ate it, feeding chunks of it to Anoushka. She ate them from his hand and licked and sucked his fingers into her mouth, seductively, one at a time. Playing with him, she would occasionally give his throbbing penis a long, wet and sensuous lick, trailing rivulets of vanilla ice cream over it. Her warm tongue, the cold ice cream . . . an irresistible tease and taunt. He retaliated by rubbing the back of the silver spoon between her cunt lips. Sexual game playing? She was good at that, seductive as hell with it. So could he be, but he had had enough. He no longer wanted to play with her but to fuck her.

The mound of melting ice cream was all that remained on the platter. Anoushka scooped some on to her fingers and placed it on her dark nimbuses' and nipples. The cold made her squirm and she laughed. Hadon watched it trickle over her bosom and lowered his head, enabling him to lick the trickling cream with his tongue, then suck it clean away. He fed her more ice cream, dribbled more of it over her breasts, and found her very erotic lying naked against the pillows, the ice cream on her lips, the warmth of her body melting it into pools of cream running over her breasts and down her torso. He had held back enough. He removed the tray from between them and placed it at the foot of the bed.

'We can do better for each other than ice cream, no matter how good it tastes,' he told her, and she knew he was right.

Anoushka closed her eyes. She was trying to get possession of herself, but it was too late. She knew what he was promising and lust had her under a sexual spell. He had held back long enough. With a spoon, he attacked the now collapsed mound of ice cream still left on the platter. He would penetrate a cunt through swirls of vanilla, chocolate and strawberry. The very idea both amused and excited.

'Madness, this is madness.' But it was not a protest from Anoushka more an observation.

'That's right, Anoushka, delicious madness to pave the way for us,' he told her as he raised her legs and placed them high on his shoulders. The tray clattered to the floor but they were barely aware of that. He grasped her by the hips.

The cream made it easier for Hadon. One thrust and the knob of his penis was tightly lodged inside her. It felt marvellous, much too good for her to keep silent. 'Hadon, how wonderful! More, now.' Her heart was racing. She drew in a deep breath and held it.

Hadon moved his hands from her hips to slip them under her arms and over her shoulders. He would pull her on to his cock as he thrust into her. Anoushka felt him move in deeper, slowly take possession of her until she could feel him tight up against her cervix, his scrotum slapping against her as he fucked her slowly, sensitising her to the slightest exchange, every nuance of a great fuck.

He did nothing to stop her cries of pleasure. They excited him and he didn't care who, if anyone, in the adjacent cabin heard them. Hadon and Anoushka took their time. This was to be no violation, this was to be sex and coming, carnal desire fulfilled at its very best. They were cunt and cock in flagrant togetherness, working in total harmony. So many positions to excite, for another sexual sensation so that they might go that little bit further into an erotic landscape from which neither one of them ever wanted to return. They revived themselves periodically with catnaps and a bottle of Bollinger, the taste and scent of sex at its very best. And so went the night and the beginning of a new day.

Chapter 6

'You don't have to say anything about last night. In fact it's better if you don't.' There was nothing nervy in Anoushka's voice, it was more matter of fact.

'Not even if it was to say thank you for a great brief encounter? You will at least allow me that?'

Hadon reached across the table where they were having hot croissants and coffee and took Anoushka's hand in his. They gazed into each other's eyes.

'No more than that, please.'

There was something in the way she said it that made Hadon agree. 'All right, but just answer me this – you're not sorry about last night?'

Anoushka was quick to tell him, 'Certainly not. Overwhelmed that I should have had such great sex with a stranger, grateful to have come so alive again when I thought my life was over. Not sorry. But it will never happen for us again. I'm sure you understand.'

Hadon kissed the hand he held and remained silent. He liked the romance of their situation: two people who gave themselves entirely and forever in one encounter, then passed on to other lives and other worlds. She was of course right, and once more he was surprised by this woman, how sensitive and romantic and very honourable she was, how incapable of tarnishing one night of perfection. For a greedy woman that said something, and he had no doubts that she was a greedy woman, or had certainly been one until her fall.

They were sitting on the private terrace off his suite of rooms, Anoushka dressed in her gown of the evening with his coat over it. There was little wind, and the ocean looked calm as the liner cut through it. The sun was high in the sky but there was warmth in it. A waiter slid the glass doors to the sitting room open and announced breakfast was served, and they left the terrace to sit at the table with the red roses on it.

There they were presented with omelettes stuffed with a ragoût of shrimps and mushrooms in Normandy sauce. They were accompanied by diced potatoes sautéd in black butter, purée of creamed spinach, and a mound of crisp bacon. Hot brioches and hot black coffee followed.

After serving, the waiter reminded Hadon that disembarkation at Cherbourg was at eleven o'clock and Southampton at approximately four o'clock that afternoon, and then left the sitting room leaving them to dine *à deux*.

The information seemed to Anoushka an intrusion of the real world she would rather forget.

'My luggage goes ashore at Cherbourg, but I disembark at Southampton. By the time I get home tomorrow evening my luggage will have been unpacked and my things put in their proper places. I live in Nice.' That was the only thing Hadon had volunteered about himself, and that was too much for Anoushka. Anonymity, Hadon as a man of mystery, was easier for her to deal with.

'I'd almost forgotten that great ocean liners have schedules. They dock and people get off and resume their lives,' she told him.

'That's what ocean voyages are for, to cut yourself off from everyday existence. You can meet yourself for the first time on ocean crossing. Have adventures that can change your life, your thinking. Or some people can.'

Anoushka listened to Hadon and had to agree with him. In his presence she felt somehow a very different woman from Anoushka Rivers, wife of the eminent Dr Robert Rivers of Harley Rogers Clinic, and it felt good. This man, the night before during their sexual escapades, and the way he was with her now, gave a boost to her damaged self-esteem. She was living every minute with him and enjoying it, feeling so very much alive that there was no time for thought, the past, the future, concern over what impression she was making; nothing mattered except being herself. She felt high on herself, as if she had had too much vodka, or, she imagined, had smoked too much dope. She was excited, but about what? A new life? No, just being alive.

It was a strange sensation this feeling so good, having her head in the clouds. She hardly knew who she was, where she was going, what she was going to do – and it didn't seem to matter. Strange sensation or not, that was how she felt and didn't question it.

She looked up as Hadon rose from his chair to cross the room and place a disc on the CD player. Music from the court of Louis XIV, fragile and sweet, the sound of harpsichord and the flute. It didn't so much fill the room with sound as soften the atmosphere, whisper exquisite chords, ethereal sounds, that triggered the imagination.

Hadon broke off a piece of brioche and buttered it. She watched him. Anoushka liked the way he ate, with gusto and appreciation of food; he had the same lust for it as he had for sex. He broke into her thoughts. 'Is it Cherbourg or Southampton for you?'

His question took her by surprise. That was the first time he had asked her about her life. Who she was, where she was going. All he knew about her until now she had volunteered. 'South-ampton,' she answered him reluctantly.

'And then what?'

Again she was surprised that he should ask her to explain herself. She had thought they had come to an understanding: no questions asked. A brief interlude, never to be forgotten or perpetuated. His questions were like invisible threads drawing her back to the reality of her situation: rejection, pain, deceit. Of having to face creating a new and different life for herself, maybe even a new persona. She was sorry he had asked, and didn't answer.

He was unabashed by her silence. 'I'll give you a card, my London agent's. I'll see him for dinner this evening and tell him I have met someone I would like to take on the translation of some of my manuscripts. He'll have instructions from me that if you should want to work, we'll give you a chance. It's what I would like, and it doesn't matter when if you do decide to do it. It doesn't even matter if you decide never to do something with your languages, not to me anyway. Everyone is replaceable, you'll find that out soon enough. Unless you have already. For example, last night.'

A mean and leading statement, the twinkle in his eye, the insinuation that it might have been he who had replaced Robert in sex with her. If he was trying to provoke her, he hadn't succeeded.

'I think you've spoilt me,' she said.

'Oh?'

'You've dined me so well and wined me and taken me to an erotic wonderland, a trip to be remembered, one to last a lifetime.'

How clever she was in changing the subject of working on his

77

books, with flattery, reminding him they were to be nothing more than a one night stand. She was smiling at him. He couldn't help but laugh and tell her, 'You're such a coquette, a seductress *par excellence*. You show me only flashes of it, but I do see it. One day I might write about a woman like you. Make you the heroine that I think you probably are. But I would describe you as a young woman before you married the wrong man.'

He held up his hand to stop her before she made a protest. 'No, don't defend yourself or him. I don't want to hear your story. I'm only telling you what I see, what I know from the few facts I have learned about you. A writer's imagination will do the rest. Something I write one day might well be inspired by you. I'll make a deduction. That is, if you will allow me?'

Fascinated, she said, 'No, don't tell me. Write it on a piece of paper, put it in an envelope and seal it. I'll place it in my handbag. A year from now I'll open the envelope and we'll see if you were right.'

Amused at the idea, he told her, 'If you prefer.'

'Yes, I think I do.'

She rose from her chair and went to the desk, returning with pencil and paper and an envelope.

He wrote several lines and then folded the paper and placed it in the envelope, sealed it and slid it across the table towards her. She caught it before it fell to the floor and looked at the envelope. He had addressed it to Anoushka Usopova. She stared down at it for a very long time, trying to remember the last time anyone had written to her using her maiden name. Puzzled, she gazed across the table at him.

'That is who you are. Had you forgotten? If I were to think of you – but I am a heartless man at the best of times, so I probably won't – but *if* I did, I would like to think of you leaving this ship more whole than when you arrived. A little less Mrs Rivers and a great deal more Anoushka Usopova. Broken hearts take time to heal and rebirth is painful so I will not think about you in that light. I prefer to think of you as I have known you sexually, and as an adventuress who is out there creating a new and exciting life for herself. Those sparks of seductive femininity you possess – use them well, Anoushka. Seduce lots of handsome young men who can satisfy your voracious appetite for all things erotic. Play with them, have the best of times. You're free. If you need someone to answer to then let it be yourself. You're no longer the appendage of a husband.'

Anoushka was not displeased at his advice, more amused. She

threw back her head and laughed. A throaty, sexy laugh he'd had no idea she was capable of. 'Talk of seducers, talk about charming! You're a dangerous man, Hadon. How is it that you make me feel safe, while all the time I know when I'm with you I might come to harm?'

'That shows how desperate you are, my dear. I'm a bastard.'

There seemed no answer to that. Anoushka knew he was telling her the truth. She had sensed it during their hours of sexual madness, for at some point that was what it had turned into. Had she not been the willing partner she had been, would anything have stopped him from taking her as and how he wanted to? She doubted it. But ever since she had met him at the ship's rail when the liner had been pulling away from the New York dock, he had been many things to her and a bastard had not been one of them.

'Not to me, Hadon,' she told him.

A look of understanding passed between them and then there was nothing more to be said. They finished their breakfast, lost themselves in the beautiful music and drifted further and further apart. Finally Anoushka rose from her chair and went round the table, to place her face among the long-stemmed red roses and breathe deeply of their scent, a perfume she wanted never to forget. Then she walked to his side and placed a hand on his shoulder.

'I think this is goodbye.' That was all he said. He slipped a card with his agent's address on it into her bag and walked her to the stateroom door. There they stood facing each other. She half expected him to ask, 'One more time?' and take her then and there. She would have liked that.

But he didn't. Instead he said, 'Ships that pass in the night,' and opened the door for her. He stepped into the corridor and called the cabin steward. 'Mrs Rivers would like to return to her cabin. Would you please escort her there?' There was one last smile for her. She returned it with one of her own then turned away from him and never looked back.

Anoushka was by no means living in dreamland; she knew that as soon as she had returned to her cabin. Bathed and changed into something more appropriate for disembarkation in Southampton, she found reality if not easier to deal with then at least something she could face. The voyage across the Atlantic and her encounters with Hadon had given her strength to reach down into the core of herself and there had found her remaining self-esteem.

Opening suitcases and folding clothes absorbed her for a while until memories began to intrude: so many years of packing and unpacking cases for the family; holidays, long weekends away with Robert, summer camps for the boys, a second honeymoon in Europe. Anoushka felt herself slipping into a cold and distant place, a void she feared. She sensed that black clouds were about to envelop her and so was depression. She had had enough of that so rang for the maid, someone else could pack, spare her the ordeal she had always loathed and been made to do for herself and her family.

Anoushka handed the woman a twenty-dollar bill and said, 'Please pack for me. That's for the packing and for seeing that my luggage is put ashore.' Then she took out a fifty-dollar bill and handed that too to the woman. 'And this is for taking care of me during this voyage.' And she gathered up her things and fled from the cabin, hoping that she was leaving behind that black cloud.

And she did feel better standing at the rail in the bow of the ship. The sun had grown even brighter and the wind had not risen. The salt air felt clean and fresh, healing her. Anoushka had control of herself again and wondered if she had tipped the maid enough. There were others to see to but she felt quite lost in dealing with travel etiquette. There had always been Robert to deal with such things. She had however remembered what he had told her once, when she had travelled alone to visit a dying uncle in St Petersburg: 'A lady alone will be considered a bother but not if you are a seriously good tipper. If you want service just pay over the top for it and your travels will be much easier.'

Anoushka felt good about being here among people, and watched the other passengers with interest. She even greeted a few, smiling pleasantly at others. She was sorry that she had wasted so many days in some deep dark coma of her own making. Being so utterly alone in that cabin during the crossing had been a lesson that she knew would last her a life-time. She would never again allow her despair to get on top of her as it had. It was killing. Here was rebirth.

She felt the buzz of excitement that is created on board when the voyage is over and the ship is about to dock. Suddenly the real world is about to intrude: luggage to oversee, travel connections and time tables to meet, shipmates parting with promises of continuing friendships, never to meet again. It was happening all round Anoushka, was something she could see but did not feel in any way a part of. She remained isolated from it, preferring to remain in limbo on the ocean waves.

'Look, the first sight of land. It's Lizard Point,' she heard someone shout excitedly. People rushed camera in hand to the ship's rail but for Anoushka the most southerly point of the British Isles, south-west Cornwall, rising up out of the Atlantic Ocean, was something she was not quite ready for. A brief look at the magnificent coastal scenery and she turned her back on it and walked away.

'So what?' she said aloud just above a whisper, and walked into one of the nearly deserted salons and ordered an espresso. Some time later France appeared on the horizon. At Cherbourg she watched the grand lady of the oceans and seas dock, and thought about Hadon Calder's luggage being manhandled from ship to shore then driven to Nice. Her imaginings stopped when she realised she had no real image of him or his luggage, what his life was like outside their brief encounter. One of the most exciting and intimate nights of her life, and when they had been together their souls had never touched. At the time she'd thought they had.

Anoushka ordered another espresso. She was feeling better about her aloneness, and did in fact quite like sitting by herself in the nearly deserted salon. Was it any different from a chicken salad sandwich eaten alone at Lord & Taylor's? And that was the first time that she had realised how lonely she had been in her marriage. For the first time she began to face the truth, even to accept that she had been less than honest about her perfect marriage. Could it possibly be that Robert had not given her all that she wanted? Had there been a great deal of 'Let's pretend' on her part as well as his? That question demanded a truthful answer. Yes, she thought. What followed was revelation, a genuine surprise.

The bell rang. Her last meal aboard this ship of fools. Yes, that was how she would always think of herself and her fellow passengers. Fools of one sort or another, trying to escape from something, most probably themselves. 'Hello,' Anoushka said. It was as if she were meeting herself for the first time. Hadon *was* wise. An ocean voyage can be one of self-discovery.

Lunch was a perfect cheese soufflé and a green salad with a raspberry vinaigrette dressing. Anoushka ate two desserts: chocolate mousse with a crème fraîche, and a bowl of fresh strawberries. She enjoyed her lunch and being the odd one out in the room of laughing and chattering diners. It suddenly occurred to her that she had, all her life, been the odd one out except when she had been with Robert and the children. How sad for her to think that that belonging she had so cherished, had so taken for granted, had been an illusion. She had not been wholly a part of anything.

The docking of the *QE2* in Southampton was an awesome sight, like the beaching of a great whale. Anoushka was riveted. Soon she would be walking down that gangway. In spite of herself she felt some excitement to think that, as Alexis and Mishka had said, adventures were to be her life.

A driver was waiting, wearing the black emblem of a Rolls-Royce driver in his cap, though he was driving a Bentley. He was holding a card with her name on it. All was just as Robert had said it would be. He whisked her through the English countryside to London and Brown's Hotel on Dover Street, Mayfair.

A family hotel: smart, chic, low key, just Robert's style. It served the best English breakfast, a delightful English tea. All Americans loved Browns'. It went with the rain and grey skies, the damp English cold that eats into the bones. It was central to everything Americans like Robert enjoyed about London: it was walking distance from everything for the super window shopper, and aimed at the cultivated traveller rather than the tourist. Mayfair was a happy hunting ground for the discreet, well-heeled buyer with taste. Bond Street and Mount Street, Savile Row, Bruton Street and Piccadilly – old English gentility holding its own in the new England.

Brown's in Mayfair was where the Rivers family had always stayed in happier times. Robert had made the reservation for her. A mistake she saw now, and she was at the desk being greeted by name by the concierge and the manager while being asked for her passport and to register.

Everything was familiar, too familiar. She could only relate to the place by being there with the boys and Robert. She actually looked around for them, to see that the boys were not getting into mischief, and for Robert to hand over the passports and register for them. Her husband had always taken care of such things. She had never gone through the process of getting into a hotel without a man to do what was expected. But there was no Robert there, nor were her sons in London with her. Anoushka was, for a moment, taken aback by her memory lapse. She turned to the manager and with a trembling hand signed the register in the place he indicated.

It felt decidedly odd being there alone. Walking towards the elevator, accompanied by the manager and a porter, she was involuntarily keeping her eyes on the entrance to the hotel. She was half expecting her husband and sons to come rushing through the door into the lobby.

Hers was a pleasant enough bedroom, even having fresh flowers. As soon as the hotel staff had left the room, Anoushka rushed over to them to read the card. From Robert? Alexis and Mishka? She pulled the small white rectangle from the envelope, even thinking she might read 'Hadon', on it, but then remembered. They had parted, and he knew nothing more than that she was going to London.

Was there no end to her disappointment and humiliation? It had been signed by the manager, 'Compliments of Brown's Hotel'. Another slap in the face to bring her back to the reality of her situation. Gazing round, she realised that she and Robert had stayed in this very room the last time they had flown to London for a long weekend. Her imagination conjured him up. He was sitting on the side of the bed next to the telephone, making calls even before he had taken off his coat – his usual habit on arrival at the hotel.

Savile Row for appointments with his tailor, Lobb's to say he was in London and wanted two more pairs of shoes. Robert with his pencil and small notecards housed in their slim leather folder planning out his advance on Mayfair: visits to Christie's and Sotheby's, Spink's on King Street, the Cork Street art galleries. The Tate would not be missed. Another phone call to see what was on at the Royal Academy.

Anoushka placed her hands over her face, not in despair, she was through with despair, but merely to block the images from her memory. No more hauntings from the past, thank you.

Too tired to venture out to one of the many restaurants that she and Robert had known and enjoyed, she took her dinner in the dining room. Miraculously, that night she slept very well. Over breakfast in her room the following morning, she made a decision not to stay one more night in this hotel. She was through with Robert's organising her life, in or out of marriage. After more than a dozen calls to other hotels, she still could not find one to accommodate her. Then, remembering how it was always impossible to get a hotel room in London when you wanted one, she dialled their London Mr Fixit.

Wherever they travelled, Robert had a network of Mr Fixits. The London man was a Harley Street doctor, a colleague of Robert's, a heart consultant, Sir Bramwell Stokes. Bramwell did not fail her. That afternoon, as promised, she called her sons from her hotel but now it was The Connaught. The boys were full of themselves and sounded happy, no different than if she had called them from her own drawing room in Lakeside. They wanted to know all about her crossing. She tried to make it sound thrilling but there had been no hundred-foot wall of waves, no crashing storm, the ship did not founder and they'd had no need to be rescued. She realised she would have to do better than this to keep Alexis and Mishka interested in her travels.

Reluctantly, she made another transatlantic call to Robert. Unusually, he was available for her. When they had been living together, it was rarely convenient for him to speak to her immediately. She felt real hatred for the man the moment she heard his voice. She was through with him, but her change of hotel must be made known, in case of an emergency.

'Then you arrived safely at Brown's? A good crossing, I hope?'

The ice in his voice! Indifference glossed over with politeness and an undercurrent of annoyance. Those same things she had heard so many times for so many people, but never had she dreamed that they would one day be for her. Did he wish her dead? Well, she wasn't and didn't intend to be for a long time yet.

'No, I'm not at Brown's. Too many memories there. I called Bramwell and he managed to get me a room here at The Connaught. I thought you should know where I am.'

A long pause, and then he spoke. 'Anoushka, you don't have to call me every time you change hotel.'

'Just how do you expect me to stay in touch? Emergencies? If you should need me?'

'Anoushka, we don't live from emergency to emergency. A postcard when you have changed countries, sent to your attorney, should do. If I or the boys ever need you, we'll find you through David.'

Silence was the only thing Anoushka could manage, all that her anger would allow. Finally it was Robert who broke it. 'Look, Anoushka, I don't want to be harsh with you, but a clean break, that's what we need. Not just because that's what I want but because, under the circumstances, it's best for you as well. The boys will be fine. I'll be fine. We'll all come through this. All it takes is time. A chance for separate lives to develop.'

'Ah, the doctor speaking, and with his best bedside manner!'

'Yes, if you like, a doctor's advice. You would do well to heed it.'

Another ghastly silence. Again it was Robert who broke it. 'How's the weather in London?'

'I didn't call to give a weather report, Robert, just to tell you where you can find me.'

'Anoushka, moving to The Connaught was not what I arranged for you. That's all right, but I want to remind you that you are not very good at formulating plans. You'd better learn to be. The happy-go-lucky existence you have had with me doing the planning in our lives is over. You're on your own and with little money. London is costly, even with me picking up your travelling expenses and hotel bills. I'm not going to quibble about your staying at The Connaught but you do have to think about the cost of your food, your day to day living in London, or any other capital city for that matter.'

She interrupted him. 'How I live and what I do are none of your business. Remember, you're through with me.'

'Anoushka, you'll need more money or you'll have to get a job, and that won't be easy. You have no qualifications. I'll come right out with it. I'm prepared to buy my coins back from you.'

'So that's what this is about?' Anoushka had forgotten about the coins. 'And would that make my life so much easier, you being in possession of your coin collection?'

'Yes, if you *sold* them to me.'

'I wouldn't even consider selling you *my* coin collection, Robert.'

'Then promise me you will save them, put them in trust for Alexis and Mishka?'

'It really bothers you that they are mine, doesn't it?'

'Yes. Be careful with them, Anoushka, they're your most precious asset.'

'No, you bastard! I'm my most precious asset. You miss your coins, do you, Robert? You're broken-hearted over losing them, are you? It hurts losing something you love, doesn't it? Good. Now you know how I feel.

'Begin again, Robert. That's what you told me to do to ease the pain of *my* losses, so that's my advice to you if you want a coin collection. And don't ask what I'm going to do with those coins. I will, however, give you a hint. You will never see them again, except possibly in several other people's collections.'

Then Anoushka hung up the telephone and broke the connection between herself and her husband forever.

London had always been a city that she'd thought she could happily live in. It was a civilised city with just the right amount of pomp and circumstance. It had chic, elegance, culture, and the sense of many villages working together to make one great city.

The old as revered as the new. It had always been a place where she had felt comfortable, almost at home in. Not so any more. That feeling would come back again, she kept telling herself.

She dined at The Ivy, at Claridge's, The Connaught, The Hard Rock Café when she wanted a hamburger and was lonely for her sons. Mr Chow's and the Tandoori on Curzon Street when she wanted a taste of other places. At The White Tower she recognised Bernard Levin, the journalist, and eavesdropped on the conversation around his table. That evening she felt less lonely. She began looking at people and seeing them properly, especially the men. It felt good to be attracted once more to the opposite sex, to think about the company of a man, the joys of sex.

Every day she was up and out, walking the streets of Mayfair and Knightsbridge and Chelsea. She took long walks in St James's Park and Hyde Park, and sat in the Farm Street Gardens every morning. She began to shop, buying an entire new outfit at Brown's on South Molton Street, another at Ralph Lauren on Bond Street.

A new attitude seemed to come with the new clothes. Now when dining alone there was a flirtatiousness about her that made heads turn. It was far more enjoyable than the many evenings when other diners had looked through her as if she didn't exist. That had hurt. It had been soul-destroying, that feeling of being invisible while you were still alive, flesh and blood, a human being with feelings.

Those days and nights hardly bothered Anoushka now, neither did visiting the familiar places she used to go with Robert and the children. The only exceptions were Fortnum's provisions counter, and Harrod's food hall, the patisseries and specialist food shops in Soho, where she now had no need to buy bread and cakes for Alexis and Mishka, olives and shaved thin slices of Parma ham for Robert, who liked to have a snack with a Campari and soda in their hotel room rather than tea. Buying four champagne truffles, or one croissant for herself, when she used to buy at least a dozen for her family, saddened her.

The weather never lifted during all her weeks in London. The clouds would break, the rain would stop, and then just when she thought the sun would appear the clouds would close in and the rain come down again. Grey, grey, was London this winter. One day rushing down Cork Street in the rain, Anoushka saw a reflection of herself in the store front windows and wondered what she was doing walking around in such grim weather.

She had been several weeks in the city and it felt as if she had been there a lifetime. She decided to pack her bags and leave for Paris where she hoped for better weather, and if she didn't find it there she would go to Rome or head for Athens. Anoushka *could* formulate a plan. How surprised Robert would have been.

Chapter 7

Anoushka never filled in her cheque stubs. In fact, until her stay in London, she had very rarely written a cheque. She was a woman accustomed to using plastic for whatever she wanted, and the bills went directly to Robert's office. How she spent money, a demand for receipts, a budget, the usual financial talk between most husbands and wives, had been non-existent between Robert and Anoushka. Not an extravagant woman, money had never been a problem between them. She was ignorant about money and what day-to-day living could cost, having never paid an electricity bill, insurance, anything to do with an automobile. Even the price of a London taxi surprised her now, and she realised grimly that all the years she had thought Robert was protecting her by taking care of their finances, he had been making her unfit to manage alone.

On her return from her morning walk, the concierge handed Anoushka some post with her key. Her heart leapt. News from the boys? They had been bad about replying to the long and loving letters she sent to them, and she was beginning to think her weekly calls to them were not such a good idea. Without them, Mishka and Alexis might make more of an effort with the fountain pen. But there was no letter from the boys. Instead the envelope contained her new credit cards, ones in her name, Anoushka Usopova Rivers, instead of Mrs Robert Rivers. They had been forwarded from David Holland's office. With them came a note from David assuring her the boys were well and saying that he hoped she was saving receipts and keeping cheque stubs.

Anoushka understood that she had to think about money; that in fact she did not have very much. She suddenly became aware she'd been living her life as one long holiday. How much money had she spent? She could only judge by going to the cupboard and looking at her wardrobe, by counting her blank cheque stubs, thinking about where she had gone, what she had done in her day-to-day existence in London. She sat in a chair in one of the public rooms at The Connaught reliving her days and nights, trying to fill in the blank cheque stubs from memory.

Anoushka went to her room and sat at the dressing table still thinking about money. It had always been an abstract thing in Anoushka's life. She had never really learned about it from her mother, and there had never been a father to teach her about it. He had died when she was five years old. There had been hard times and easy times before she met Robert, but even in the bad old days she had survived with dignity. There had always been someone there to provide for her, and if there hadn't been she soon found someone. Money had always been a by-product of something more interesting in her life.

Anoushka opened the velvet bag containing her divorce settlement. She spilled the Greek and Roman coins, each in their own small velvet envelope, on to the table. Opening one, she slid out a coin and looked at it, then placed it on the table in front of her. Eleven coins that until she had taken them had meant little to her. Now they seemed very beautiful, and had about them something more than beauty. Thousands of years old, they held in them history, the passion of many lives. She smiled at herself for being fanciful. She was not usually a fanciful woman. She slipped each coin back into its case, and the velvet bag where they were kept into her handbag. Then she dressed to go out into the rain again. She did not to go Spink's, the coin dealer's, which was where Robert would expect her to go. Instead she went to the British Museum to look at their Greek and Roman coins.

Anoushka could see that hers were as beautiful as some she saw in the museum. It was true what Robert had said, she had absolutely no idea what she had taken from him in her vindictive rage. Clearly she needed advice.

The following day she called the British Museum and asked for an appointment to see the curator of Greek and Roman coins. Two days later he met her at the museum. Studiedly calm expressions on the faces of the curator and his colleagues who had been called in to view Anoushka's coins could not dispel the excitement, even tension, she sensed mounting in the room. Finally, after knowing glances from one authority to another, the questions started. 'How, Mrs Rivers, have you managed to assemble such an impressive collection?'

Anoushka liked 'impressive'; it validated her instinct that these coins were indeed as important as some she had seen in the glass cases in the galleries.

'When did you collect these, Mrs Rivers?' asked another expert.

Before she could answer the chief curator interrupted. 'This is an extraordinary collection, Mrs Rivers. We would be pleased to know anything you can tell us about them. Where, for example, they came from?'

Anoushka had no idea and so could give them no answer. She had been indifferent to Robert's hobby, his obsessive passion. He had always been secretive about his coins. It had irritated her enough for her to have taken little interest in them, to have for the most part blocked them and his passion for collecting out of her mind. Somewhat embarrassed at her ignorance in this matter, she turned their questions back on them. 'Before I tell you what I know about my collection . . .'

'Then they are yours?' interrupted one of the men standing round the curator's desk.

'Oh, yes, they're mine. May I continue? As I was about to say, I would appreciate it if you could tell me what, if anything, you know about these coins?

The curator picked one up and held it in the palm of his hand.

'The last time I saw this, it was in a collection up for auction at the Hotel Baur au Lac in Zurich. The collection had belonged to Bruce McNall, a Los Angeles millionaire, what you Americans would call whizz kid coin collector. An aggressive dealer in ancient coins and artefacts. Athena Funds, his company, was selling off forty-five thousand coins including some of the most famous in existence, such as the Ides of March – a gold Aureus minted by Brutus to commemorate the assassination of Julius Caesar. This coin in my hand came from that collection and was sold that day to a Los Angeles collector, Morton Holmby.'

The curator put the coin down on the velvet cloth on his desk and chose another. 'And this one was for many years in a French collection owned by Monsieur François Audren, while this,' here he chose another coin, 'belonged to Prince Ahmad, a member of one of the royal families in the Gulf, who prides himself on having one of the finest collections of Greek and Rome coins in the world.

'These,' he told her, and drew aside three on the cloth, 'I saw displayed in a conference room in Zurich in 1974 when a dealer buying for an Arab king outbid buying agents for Aristotle Onassis and the future French President, Valéry Giscard d'Estaing.'

All eyes were on Anoushka. Clearly she was stunned by what

she was hearing. 'Shall I go on, madam?'

'You put my collection in illustrious company. How can you be sure these are the same coins?'

The curator handed the magnifying glass to her. 'They are of phenomenal quality, and have been well recorded. I recognise their marks – all ancient coins have their marks. They are, so to speak, the coin's finger prints.' He held the glass over one for Anoushka to look at. 'A silver decadrachm. Might I ask – I think I must ask – how you came by these?'

'Not in any criminal way, if that's what's concerning you, gentlemen.' They all looked embarrassed now.

Overwhelmed by what she had learned, Anoushka asked, 'May I have a glass of water?'

'I think we can do better than that for you, Mrs Rivers. May I suggest we would all benefit from a cup of tea?'

It was evident to everyone in the room that Anoushka Rivers was as puzzled as they were that she should have such a collection in her possession. Over tea and biscuits they chatted about her stay in London, what she had seen at the theatre, what exhibitions she had attended. About anything but the coins. Finally Anoushka felt composed enough to address the curator.

'I'm not a very worldly woman. I needed to discover whether my collection was a significant one or not, and hesitated to go to a dealer. Now that I know it is, I feel I must put your mind at rest and tell you how the coins have come into my possession.'

Looks of satisfaction crossed the men's faces. Decorum held back sighs of relief. Museums do not like to be faced with the darker side of antiquity collecting such as smuggling or theft.

'They are part of a divorce settlement. How my husband came by them I can only guess. I imagine that they are gifts from grateful patients. My husband is a doctor, a heart surgeon, Robert Rivers of the Harley Rogers Clinic in Lakeside, Connecticut.'

Anoushka could see general recognition of the name. She continued, 'Each of the men whom you have mentioned as being the last owner of a coin has had his life saved by my husband. Wealthy and generous patients must have known my husband to be a passionate numismatist, and I assume that is the means by which he came by these coins. Ancient coin collecting was something they must have had in common.'

'It seems unimaginable that your husband should give this collection up.'

'I guess he wanted his freedom more than his coins. And I have no doubt he thought my ignorance about and disinterest in the coins would in due course lead me to exchange them for a better financial settlement than I already have. It would never occur to him that I would investigate my asset and deal with anyone other than him about it.

'You see, I have always deferred to my husband and his wishes. I'm not clever about such things as money, assets, business, nor do I have or understand the passion for collecting. But I do understand my husband. The fact of the matter is that he did not offer me the coins in settlement – I took them, or tricked him if you will. I took the one thing I knew he prized. An act of sweet revenge for his destroying my life. But at the time I had no idea just how sweet. Their value, their rarity, even their beauty, none of that came into it. So you can understand that what I have learned here today poses a tremendous problem for me.'

How very American of me, and stupid, she, thought to herself. To spill out such a personal story to these strangers – reserved Englishmen, who shun the emotional coming to the surface of life in any way or form. Robert would have been appalled to know that she had spilled her guts to scholars at the British Museum. Could that have been why she'd done it? She viewed the men's embarrassment but hardly cared about it. However, she, like everyone else in the room seemed relieved when the curator broke the embarrassed silence that had followed her revelations.

'May I ask what you intend to do with them? I ask only because the museum has a vested interest in all such beautiful and historical objects.'

'I have no idea. Yesterday I thought I would sell them. Now I will have to think further. My decision will depend partly on my financial situation.'

'May I suggest, should you make a decision to sell, that you offer them back to the collections whence they came? Each of those collections is large and important, and bound to end up in a museum one day. Alternatively you might consider offering them to us in some capacity.'

It was dark outside and rain was beating against the windows of the taxi. Anoushka had walked some distance through Bloomsbury in the downpour before she had found a cab. Wet nearly through to her skin, she only realised how uncomfortable she was when the powerful heater in the back of the taxi steamed up the windows, and the musty scent of drying wool filled the passenger compartment.

Riding through the rain-drenched streets, back to The Connaught, she thought about Robert and how he had deceived her on so many fronts. Not once had he told her about the generosity of his patients, nor had he ever indicated to her that the coins were of such great value. Why hadn't he told her that they had a multi-million-dollar nest egg? Why had he never confided in her? How was that possible for a couple who had been so close, so intimate as she had believed them to be? His last words to her about the coins had been that he would buy them from her. Buy them? And how much would he have offered? This man she had believed to be the finest, most honourable man in the world.

Anoushka knew that as a family they were well off, enough to have everything they wanted, within reason though certainly what they had was not on the scale of wealth enjoyed by some of the names she had heard in connection with *her* coins this afternoon. Had she agreed to sell to Robert, he would have tossed her a pittance, deceived her, cheated on her yet again. She burned with hatred for him and his deceit.

The doorman at The Connaught held the huge umbrella over her head as she paid the taxi driver. Still lost in her thoughts, she let the doorman take her by the elbow and usher her from the rain into the hotel. Anoushka went directly to the bar and ordered a vodka martini, then after giving her wet things to the waiter she chose one of the bar's comfortable chairs at a small table.

There she sat drinking martinis and wondering why she felt so unhappy about the coins when she should have been thrilled to know how valuable they were. Her future financial security, something she had not even thought about, was set for life by the mere fact that she owned them. She was wealthy in her own right now, and thought about that though it held little meaning for her. All she could think about was that she had lost the great love of her life, that her husband had robbed her of her family, that she had been thrown out in the world utterly alone.

The next morning Anoushka packed her bags and left for Paris. The sun was out there, and Anoushka felt uplifted seeing the brightness and gaiety that French life had to offer. Paris was a city she had always loved, but her life there was no different from life in London and after five weeks she had had enough. She wanted to go home to Lakeside.

The moment she heard David's voice Anoushka knew she had made a mistake in calling him. He would not tell her what she wanted to hear.

'Anoushka, nice to hear you. How are you getting on?'

Just hearing his voice seemed to settle her. That was strange because in all the years she had known Betsy and David, he had had little time for her. It was Robert who was his friend, her husband whom he had got on with. But since the break-up, she had found David her only truly compassionate friend, the only person interested in her welfare in spite of representing Robert in the divorce. Though he had found Dan Konicosh, a young man in another firm to represent her in her divorce from Robert, David had agreed to handle any of her other affairs.

'Not very well, David. I want to come home to Lakeside.'

He remained silent on the other end of the line. Finally, he spoke. 'I'm not so sure the time is right for you to come home, Anoushka.'

'I miss my home, my family. It's so hard, this endless holiday I'm on that's no holiday at all, more like a penance I am being made to pay. Glamorous, velvet-lined if you like, but a penance nevertheless.'

'That's tragic. Anoushka, and you can't become a tragic figure, you owe it to yourself and to the boys to be better than that. You're still a young woman, and beautiful. You have a brain. Do something for yourself.'

David had never spoken to her like this in all the years he had known her. How was it that he felt he could now? Was she so different as someone other than Robert's wife? But his words gave her no real direction, merely a hint of one. She needed more. 'Why don't you think it's the right time for me to come home?' she asked.

'Think about it, Anoushka. What have you got to come home to? To become another statistic in that vast number of women trying to recapture the life they had with their husbands. Not many of them make it. Divorced women, especially ones whose husbands have walked away, are the new underclass. When you come home I would like to see you as one of the few who survive the destruction of one life, and watch you build a new one for yourself and your boys. And if you can't, then at least give it a try. There are hundreds of thousands of women just like you having to begin again and few of them have what you have as a jumping off point. What have you done, if anything, about making new friends, finding a vocation for yourself, having a real adventure?'

'Nothing.'

'That was part of your problem here at Lakeside, Anoushka.

95

Robert was your only friend, your only life. Otherwise you liked your own company more than anyone else's.'

'That's not wholly true, David. Robert, my boys, my lifestyle as Mrs Rivers, that was everything I ever wanted. And I enjoyed my solitude, as something precious, all for me, Robert understood that even if his friends didn't.'

'There you have it, they're Robert's friends not yours. My case rests. Robert's gone forever, Anoushka, and you have to get a life together for yourself before you come home. Get out of The Crillon and into a flat, go to a café and make a friend, get a job – it doesn't matter what, but something to occupy your mind. Solitude is all right, a luxury, wonderful – if you can afford it. For the moment you can't. You're still trying to live on memories of your great love, and that's not living. If you come back here now you'll never find as good a life as you had with Robert, and what you should be looking for is a better one. Be brave, think not what is expected of you, or what others do in your situation, but of what you want to do this second time around.'

'You make me sound pathetic.'

'Well, it's a pathetic situation you are in, but only you can turn it around.'

'You give good advice, David. Hard to take but too sensible to ignore. You make me see what a long road I have to travel.'

'Just take the first step, Anoushka, that's always the hardest. Get into your stride, and I'm sure you'll surprise us all when you walk back to Lakeside.'

'Isn't it strange? I never liked you as much as I do right now, David.'

'Not so strange, Anoushka. You never opened yourself up to me before. Friendship has to do with just that. Well, maybe not just that. I have to go, I have someone waiting on the other line. Stay in touch.'

Who is to know how and when a profound change happens, one that comes from within and is to last a lifetime? That sort of change is real and fundamental. Anoushka was trying to avoid at all costs changing her life. But it did happen to her, while sitting in the sun outside the Café Flore, drinking Pernod and eating salted cashews while reading the *International Herald Tribune*.

She put the paper down on the table and sat back, feeling suddenly different, more relaxed in herself. All the tables were filled and the passing parade of Parisians seemed somehow to look even more attractive and full of life than usual. Paris was flourishing in the springtime. The Parisians' passion for street life, as well as home and all things pertaining to the enhancement of the senses, was infectious.

A smile appeared first at the corners of her lips and then spread across her face. She laughed aloud, at first softly then louder and even louder. She seemed unable to stop and it was laughter so full of joy and sweetness, that people around her could not help but smile. Anoushka felt as if she were cleansing herself. A smile still on her face, she raised her hand to call the waiter.

'Will you allow me to offer you a drink?' asked the man sitting at the table next to hers.

The woman with him bent forward to add, 'Oh, do let him. He's charmed by your laughter, and he's quite a nice man.'

'It had something child-like and innocent, it made me feel, for one moment, as if I were five years old.'

'How odd. That was the way I felt while I was laughing.'

'And how do you feel now?' he asked.

'Wonderful, ready to eat up the world.'

'Bravo,' he said.

'Well, how about starting with having a drink with us?' suggested the woman.

Anoushka's heart was pounding with excitement. She was moving. Accepting a drink from a stranger was a little thing but she was doing something *she* wanted to do, not what she thought she should do. Was this the first step that might distinguish her from her old self, the one that might help her to become a new individual? Was this her first step to going home?

'A Pernod then,' she heard herself say.

'I am Hervé Lacoste and this is my friend, a compatriot of yours, the lovely Page Cooper.' He gave Anoushka a seductive smile that charmed.

He was handsome, but it was not his looks that attracted so much as his obvious sexuality. He wore it like a woman wears a jewel, with pride and coquetry, an adornment to attract the opposite sex. Anoushka sensed he was a rogue with women, he had about him that whiff of danger that some women like. Before Robert, marriage and Lakeside, she had known men like Hervé Lacoste, and had found them exciting; dangerous but electrifying. She had almost forgotten that such men existed. It had been men like Hervé who cultivated the sensuous in her that had so enchanted Robert. Paradoxically, the libidinous nature honed by such men as he had given her the security and happiness she had always sought. For a time at least.

Hervé's approach to Anoushka was smooth, clever, intelligent,

97

provocative. Five sentences and he had hooked her on to his line. He began to reel her in. 'A tourist?'

'You would prefer that I was a cellist? An opera singer? No, I'm afraid not, just another American tourist.'

'Somehow I think not,' he told her, rubbing his chin. He was a man in his fifties with blond hair gone white, and cut short with some chic. Dimpled cheeks when he smiled, and a sensuous mouth, mischievous lines at the corner of his eyes, but otherwise a taut youthful skin over fine masculine bone structure. He wore steel-rimmed glasses and took them off now to wipe the lenses. He did not take his gaze off Anoushka. 'And how would you know what my preferences are?'

Page entered the conversation, 'You're quite right, Anoushka – I may call you Anoushka? You can call me Page. He has a penchant for beautiful, talented, accomplished and clever women. He is an authority on glamorous career women.'

'Are you a career woman, Page?' asked Anoushka.

'She has been,' Hervé answered for her. Was he telling her they had been lovers, past tense?

He placed an arm around Page and kissed her, first on one cheek and then on the other, and once more. He turned back to Anoushka. 'In Paris we always kiss three times. In the provinces only once.'

'Are you here alone, Anoushka?' asked Page.

'Yes.'

'I would have guessed a husband lurked somewhere round the corner,' Hervé told her.

'The husband no longer lurks.'

'How lucky for us. Then we can ask you to join us this evening.'

Anoushka gave no answer. As attracted as she was to Hervé, she held back from accepting his invitation. He smiled but did not push the matter. Instead he asked her, 'An American with a romantic Russian name who speaks French with a French accent? Not your average American tourist, I think. Born in?'

'St Petersburg.'

'Ah, I thought Russian-born.'

'Now how would you know that? I am completely Americanised,' she told him, laughing and quite enjoying his interest in her.

'The hair, the elegant features, high cheekbones, the way you laughed. You may look like Mrs America but there was the Russian soul in that laugh. My guess would be background white Russia, lifetime red Russia.'

'You are uncannily right.' Anoushka talked past Hervé and spoke directly to his companion. 'Page, is he always so astute?'

'Always. He's part Rasputin, part Svengali, but mostly Don Juan.'

'A dangerous man,' teased Anoushka.

'But irresistible to women,' he added.

'Oh!' Anoushka declared, feigning surprise, but in truth she was already aware of that, and thinking, No, not irresistible but fatal.

'A fact. I'm not bragging, Anoushka,' he told her, a wicked twinkle in his eyes.

This was café society, and not just at the Flore, the Deux Magots, or Brasserie Lipp, but at any French sidewalk bar. People at their leisure with the knack of conducting amusing conversation, intelligent banter, urbane philosophy, while always using their eyes to check on who is coming, who is going. It was a disease, this people watching. Even Anoushka caught it. She liked to watch writers scribbling on a pad, painters working out their next canvas over a pastis, the beautiful people cruising the beautiful people, the elite communing with the successful.

Once Hervé broke his conversation with Anoushka and Page to say hello to someone passing by their tables. The second time he merely nodded his head and waved. This time he stood up to greet Roman Polanski and Jeanne Moreau who stopped at his table.

He kissed Jeanne Moreau and shook Roman's hand. Page and Moreau exchanged smiles while Polanski kept his gaze on Page. They talked briefly and then after an apology from Hervé there was an introduction for Anoushka. She was too impressed, too dazzled by it all, and barely said hello. Hervé excused himself and walked away with the actress and director to a table some distance away.

Page and Anoushka looked across the empty chair separating them and it was Anoushka who spoke first. 'I hope I didn't look too impressed. Was I awkward?'

Page began to laugh. 'You were fine.'

'I was just so surprised.'

'If you are with Hervé, it's always like that. He is one of the world's great photographers. He has photographed the most glamorous women and men of our time, and his war work is memorable. Everyone wants a portrait by Hervé. He likes you, was probably photographing you in his mind while you were laughing. You did change, looked so extraordinarily pretty, so ethereal – not at all the lady who had been sitting there for an hour looking lonely and lost.'

Anoushka was astonished. For so many years people had looked through her and seen nothing in her to speak of. Not knowing what to say to Page, she asked, 'Are you in the theatre, a celebrity of some sort too?'

She began to laugh. 'No, but I do know many people who are. I'm a designer.'

'In Paris?'

'Yes, and London and New York. I have offices and shops in those cities but I travel everywhere on my commissions. I am the florist for people with discerning taste – I create floral spectaculars for all sorts of events. Fashion shows for the haute couture collections, palaces for formal occasions . . . all sorts of fascinating jobs. Sometimes just a single orchid or daisy will do for the right occasion.'

'How wonderful.'

'Yes, it has been wonderful, years of hard workaholic living with short pauses for hard core playing. It made up for a lot of things I lost out on in my life. Or at least I thought it did. What about you, Anoushka? What do you do?'

'You mean what have I done? I have done wife and mother. One might say I'd done it to death.'

There was something in the way Anoushka spoke that made the two women burst into laughter. 'I've done flowers and you've done marriage.'

'More like marriage has done me.'

'I don't know what to say to that,' said Page.

'There's not much one can say. Past tense is past tense. After the initial shock of having been dumped by my husband and, as my attorney said, becoming one of the new underclass in society, I have finally come to see the only way to survive is to let the past lie firmly where it is, and do something with the now, not as compensation but in the spirit of adventure.'

'Well, that's something I wish I had learned long ago. I think we should celebrate. A rebirth? Yes, maybe what Hervé and I saw in your laughter was a newborn woman. How exciting.' Page lifted her arm to catch the attention of the waiter. 'House champagne and three glasses.'

'What a good idea,' said Anoushka, feeling somehow close to this beautiful stranger who seemed to understand her. Had she too, at some time in her life, faced emotional trauma? Could Page possibly have felt the pain of loss on a grand scale such as

100

Anoushka was feeling? It was the first time she could remember feeling such interest in a female acquaintance – one she sensed could very easily become a real friend. After the months of travel, the years of feeling interest in no one but Robert and their family, Anoushka found the prospect strangely appealing.

'I too am looking for a new life,' said Page. 'I and my demons have struggled through the old one and I've had a good time, a great time. But I'm burned out. I'm going on an adventure, a great safari, seeking what has so far eluded me. Wrong paths, bad choices . . . who hasn't taken those?' Page shrugged her shoulders and then asked Anoushka, 'What about you?'

'I don't know where I'm going, or even how to take the first step. I've forgotten who I am, what I want, where I want to go with my life.'

Like fellow conspirators the two women fell silent on seeing Hervé returning. Page leaned across the empty chair. Lowering her voice, she told Anoushka, 'I can tell he wants to bed you. Don't mind me. I have had him for years, on and off. Strictly sexual lust. An arrangement, so to speak. I'm sure he would like us both. Don't look so shocked, Anoushka. You have to begin casual sex somewhere, and it might as well be with him.'

But Anoushka was shocked. Shocked that she was excited by the idea of sex with Page and Hervé. Page was as Hervé had described her: lovely and seductive. Ever since Anoushka had made their acquaintance she was aware that there was not a man who passed by their tables who did not look at Page with lustful interest. She had sensual charisma, that certain mysterious something that men find irresistible. She spelled out in body language, 'I want to be taken, so take me if you can.' Anoushka had the feeling that keeping Page Cooper was not as easy as getting her.

Anoushka was not naive. She saw the flirtatious looks, the brief but definite come on Page gave every passing man who showed interest. The envy in women's eyes for the inexplicable quality she possessed that was more than beauty. Intelligence and sexual charisma are seductive to men.

Hervé took his seat between the two women. He looked at Page with lustful eyes, grazed her face with his hand, her lips with a finger. She kissed his fingers. He caressed her shoulder, kissed her hand and whispered something in her ear. Anoushka yearned to be in her place. They drank their wine, and Hervé caressed Anoushka's thigh. His smile promised more. She sensed the years slipping away from her and felt young, almost child-like. Again it happened. That smile came to her lips, laughter rose from her soul. She tossed her head back ever so slightly and enjoyed the laughter of youth. She felt alive, frivolous, drinking champagne with Hervé and Page at the Café Flore. Where had the Lakeside matron gone? she wondered, and then told herself, Good riddance to all that. Her laughter had the ring of freedom to it.

Anoushka wanted Hervé, in the same way she had wanted and had Hadon. She wanted, too, to be someone in her own right again, as she had been before she had given herself up to Robert and marriage, always trying to please and belong. Like some Svengali or mystic, Hervé understood that through her laughter one woman was metamorphosising into another. He bent forward and whispered, 'I'm going to take you home and make love to you, get inside that laughter. Sex in the afternoon, in Paris, with a stranger.' And he finished his wine.

'What a good idea,' Anoushka told him. Raunchiness put her on edge, took her over. She wanted sex, an erotic encounter, intense and exciting with Hervé.

He answered her need by raising one eyebrow, cocking his head to one side and saying with great Gallic charm, 'Ah, delicious.' Then, turning to Page he told her, 'We're going home, the three of us.'

'The two of you,' she said with a smile. There were protests about not wanting to break up Page and Hervé's afternoon together from Anoushka, cajoling from Hervé. Nothing would change Page's mind.

PAGE COOPER

Chapter 8

Hervé and Anoushka watched Page weave her way round the tables and away from the Café Flore, in the same way others watched her, with admiration. Page knew how to move, she had the body and stature to walk through a crowd as gracefully as an animal would pick its way, in long, cautious strides and seductive steps. The rich auburn hair and sensuous green eyes, fair skin and pointed chin set in a perfect oval face – she was Vivien Leigh as Scarlet O'Hara, Garbo as Queen Christina.

'She's a heroine, isn't she?' remarked Anoushka, thinking of those women.

'With all the beauty and all the flaws, and a dark secret she keeps well hidden like most heroines.' Hervé took his gaze from Page to fix it on Anoushka. 'Men fall in love with Page for her beauty, her sensuality, because they are unable to resist her seduction of them. We have all fallen into erotic love with Page, and she has walked away when we ask for more. She never gives herself over to men, not even when she is in the throes of erotic bliss. A place she likes to dwell in. She's a fascinating woman.'

'I would like to know her better.'

'In what sense?'

'Do you always think sexually?'

Hervé laughed, 'Yes, always. I cannot pass by a woman without thinking of her sexually. I like sex in all forms – body to body, reading pornography, looking at porn – it's a basic instinct.' He smiled at Anoushka and asked, 'Have you not had sex with a libertine before? Or is it the female libertine that excites your interest? No, I think not. You're not a lesbian. Then *how* would you like to know my Page?'

'As a friend.'

'She has no women friends.'

'Neither have I.'

'I find that very sad. Then you too must have a secret buried very deep, one you want no one to know about. I have always

105

found that people who don't want friends and can barely tolerate acquaintances are usually maintaining distance so as not to be discovered.'

'You may be wrong.'

'I'm sorry Page wouldn't join us. Are you?' Again the sexual connotations, the sensual look in his eye.

'In truth?' Anoushka teased.

'In truth,' he answered her, taking her hand in his, raising it to his mouth and licking the centre of her palm delicately with pointed tongue.

Anoushka closed her eyes, savouring the kiss, the feel of his lips against her skin. How hungry she was for him to make love to her. All thoughts of Page vanished. Orgasm and that moment of sexual ecstasy that could be so true and pure, only that was on her mind now.

'No. I want you all to myself. For you to take me and no other woman this afternoon. A libertine you call yourself?'

He rose from his chair and, still holding her hand, pulled Anoushka from hers. They stood looking at each other for several seconds. A flower lady passed by them and held out a small bunch of violets. Hervé let go of Anoushka's hand long enough to select several bunches for her. He was leading her through the maze of tables and people, and when they stepped on to the pavement in front of the café, turned to her and said, 'Nothing will be the same for you after today.'

He needn't have said anything. Anoushka knew that already.

Page had two things to do that afternoon. One was to place an ad in the *International Herald Tribune* and the other was to say goodbye to François. Page had been saying goodbye to François for five years now, and though he didn't believe it, this time was to be the final farewell.

He had picked Page up at a party at the Eden Roc in Cap d'Antibes. He had actually tried to snatch her away from a friend of his, but Page would never give up Jean-Paul, nor any other man she fancied, to live exclusively with François. French high society was appalled that he should be besotted by a mere florist, someone in trade. A man of his breeding, taste and intelligence! He was a cultivated man of great inherited wealth, and patron of the arts, with a beautiful wife, children, mistresses, and a reputation as a lover of beautiful, intelligent women. Neither François nor Page cared to make their on again, off again sexual trysts particularly public; privacy suited them both. She floated in and out of his life as and when she chose. There was gossip, but discreet gossip, about their sexual preferences but the French care little about sexual scandal, it has no real meaning for them. A man's preference is a man's private affair. Whereas across the Channel in England, sexual indiscretion discovered means scandal and disgrace.

Page had had many lovers from all walks of life. A biker or millionaire, plumber or solicitor, judge or doctor – they were all fitting objects of her desire. She was a self-made woman who had crawled her way out of poverty by dint of her good looks and ambition. The Page Cooper of today could not have grown wealthy and worldly, sophisticated and a success story, without the business tips she gathered from the men she had become involved with. She used her men the way most men use women: for sexual pleasure, to pave an easier passage through life, to wear them on her arm as a badge of success. Page's life: a rewarding business success story, lovers she could not love, a crippled personal life because she could not have the one man she wanted.

Loveless promiscuity had been her personal life, ten years of it, a long run, before she realised that it was no longer enough for her. An endless stream of attractive men and great sex had given her snatches of pleasure but did nothing to quiet the emptiness and despair that haunted her soul. She had never buried the past, the past had buried her. At last she had to admit a need to create a new and better life for herself was upon her. And she had every intention of doing just that, even if it did mean she had to drop the torch she had carried for Oscar. Give up the dream that one day the one and only love of her life would return.

François had a magnificent eighteenth-century house and gardens near the British Embassy, almost next-door to the Rothschilds, and a house in the Place de Vosges. He called it his play house. The Place de Vosges house was where Page was headed. People whispered about François's play house, how he kept it as his very private hideaway. Powerful and wealthy people have a way of ensuring their own privacy. François was a master of the art. People said about him that after he survived his heart operation, he changed. His near death experience gave him an even greater appreciation of life than he already had. He was even more kind and generous to his friends and family, but now lived in a world of his own as well. One where he denied himself nothing, lived for the thrill of the moment as if there were no tomorrow. All of which was true.

The butler let Page in, and she was shown to the first-floor drawing room. There she found François, Jean-Paul, and another admirer of hers, a man, twenty years younger than his host and host's friend.

'The founding members of the Broken Heart Club,' François quipped.

'Take pity on us, Page, we hate to lose you,' said Jean-Paul.

'So you've banded together?'

'Only to give you a farewell party,' said the young man, Timothy, who went directly to her to place an arm round her and kiss her sexily on the lips.

The four had had a party before, several times. Page was aware that this one had been arranged by François because he of the three was the only one who believed that if she did walk away from them it would be forever. A parting party he had suggested to her. All three men knew how much she enjoyed being held in the arms of one man who caressed her, while another sucked on her breasts and a third took possession of her with his penis. Nothing was more exciting for Page sexually than to have men such as these who adored her, loved and respected her, make love to her, take her sexually one after the other, changing places so smoothly that she hardly knew where one man began and another left off. A night of one long fuck, such as few women ever have.

Each of them in their own right was a virile lover with endless stamina for sex and orgasm. Page could expect sexual oblivion, and long and exquisite orgasms to match theirs, but it would be she who would have to beg them to stop, she who would be worn out by an afternoon and night of coming. They would feed her, care for her to keep her from fainting with exhaustion from her own many orgasms. There would come a time during their orgy when she would at last lose herself in sex, become no more than an object of sexual desire, when all thought was gone and animal instinct drove her libido.

These men understood her, loved her for her passion for all things sexual, her appetite for men's seed and desire to taste it, to be filled by it, till it flowed from every orifice of her body. The excitement of having three men at a time, their thrusting penises, the several orgasms each would issue, was thrilling for her as it was for them. Four people who worked in sex as one. Her obvious pleasure ruined them for sex with other women who loved it less, who played games of: 'Oh, no. Oh, yes. Well, maybe I do like sex.'

Page held her men enthralled because no matter how much she

gave sexually with men, as a friend, as a lover, as a whore in bed, she held something back. There was always something more to be had from her that she kept, they believed saved, for some mystery man in her life. It was what each of them wanted from her though they knew it would never be theirs. It was impossible to hate Page. Had it not been these two Frenchmen and the young American would have, for being unable to capture her heart. Instead they loved her and feared the loss of her, every time she walked away from them.

Because Page had made it quite clear that she wanted nothing but what she had sexually with François, Timothy and Jean-Paul, they had each been generous with gifts to her, but cautious in their generosity for fear she might feel compromised and drop them. The three men were aware that there was no future for them with Page, either together as libertines or individually as lovers, in anything like a permanent relationship. They suffered her promiscuity, more so because each of them sensed, to their sadness, that one day there would be a single man who would capture Page's heart. Or already had.

They began their afternoon party with champagne and ended it with breakfast in the yellow dining room overlooking the Place de Vosges. Page was dressed in a cream-coloured diaphanous dressing gown of the finest silk, spun as sheer as a spider's web and trimmed in heavy cream-coloured lace – a gift from François that she kept with several other gowns in his house. It showed off her body seductively. The full breasts so high and firm, the narrow waist and flat tummy, the rounded bottom and just the right amount of flesh on the hips, the long shapely legs and comely thighs. Her skin, so taut and smooth as satin, was the colour of thick Devonshire cream. She was woman made perfect from her graceful hands to her long slender feet. A luscious woman physically, with the personality of a femme fatal. Not the least and possibly the most beautiful and seductive thing about Page was her face, how she used it to give people pleasure: a smile to enchant, a twinkle in the eye to bring light to people's lives, lips that were sensual but sweet, so very kissable. A face of sugar and fire. Men and women alike were intrigued by the way Page moved: with grace and sensuality. It was in her walk, the manner in which she sat, crossed her legs, used her arms and hands. Even her shoulders. François had often told her she spoke with her shoulders.

The four were silent over breakfast. As they consumed strawberries and crème fraîche, eggs scrambled in black butter and garnished with truffles, brioche, and paper-thin slices of ham, puff pastries spread with peach preserve, the occasional word or smile seemed sufficient. Everything they had had to say or express to each other had been accomplished during their many hours lost in sexual abandon. These were people bound together in lust. What need for mere words?

Page rose from her chair and walked to stand behind the still seated François. She placed a hand on his shoulder. He took it in his and brought it round to kiss it, then placed it delicately back where it had been. She bent her head and kissed the top of his. Next she moved over to stand behind Jean-Paul. She grazed his cheek with the back of her hand and then turned his head round to kiss him sweetly on the lips. Timothy scraped back his chair and turned to look at her. She sat down on his lap and raised his hand, opened it and kissed the palm. Then she rose and told her swains, 'I'll be back,' and walked from the room.

François reached for another brioche. Timothy rose from his chair with the coffee pot and walked round the table refilling empty cups.

'And my mistress Mai Choo thinks she is the great courtesan of the 90s,' was François' only comment on Page's exit.

Timothy placed the silver coffee pot back on the table and went to the window. 'She's more than that,' he said, still with his back to the other two men.

'Of course she's more than that,' said Jean-Paul, 'and that's what makes her great. She is a most unusual woman, a courtesan without a patron. Page manipulates men magnificently for her own means. All of us in this room and how many other men can testify to that?' There was admiration, not criticism, in his voice.

Timothy returned to sit at the table. 'I love her. I want to marry her but she won't have me.'

François laughed.

'Are you laughing at me, François?'

'No, I'm laughing at the situation. You see, Timothy, we too have been where you are now. We love her just as much as you do.'

He ran his fingers through his hair. 'I'm not going to get upset about this notion of hers to turn her back on us and strike out for a new life. How many times before has she said she was leaving us?'

The men fell silent again. Jean-Paul concentrated on his food or at least seemed to be. Now it was François who rose from the table to stand by the window looking down into the Place de Vosges. After several minutes he rang for the butler and asked

110

for a chilled bottle of champagne, vintage Louis Roederer Cristal Brut, and a jug of white peach juice. Returning to his seat once more after serving himself with more scrambled egg from a silver chafing dish on the console set against the wall, he looked across the table to his friends and remarked, 'One of the many things about Page is that she always leaves us hungry for more.'

The three men had to laugh at themselves; they were not easily besotted by women. Their laughter seemed to change the subject and somehow bring them back from their erotic reverie into the present. They spoke of politics. Timothy, a political journalist based in Paris but writing exclusively for an American news magazine, always had political tidbits to offer for the interest of his two older friends.

The three had become good friends, bound together in their lust for womanising, and especially because of their partying with Page. They were neither bisexual nor homosexual, yet through their partying with her had learned the excitement of each other's bodies, gained added pleasure from knowing intimately each other's sexuality.

The Place de Vosges, a series of handsome, much sought after Paris town houses where once the kings of France's courtiers and favourites lived, was quiet. Every street was muffled, registering as an intrusion on this special sunny rectangle in the midst of Paris. The quiet in the house, as in the square, made every sound seem significant.

François was the first to hear the tap of her heels on the stairs, then passing the dining room, the front door opening and closing. 'She hasn't said goodbye. Page said she would be back,' said Timothy.

'But she never said when.' That was François.

Several minutes of silence and then Timothy broke it. 'I must go.'

'And so must I,' added Jean-Paul.

François told his guests, 'You won't find her, you know. She will have arranged to have a cab waiting close by.'

'I didn't expect to,' said Timothy, and went to his host. François rose from his chair as Timothy extended his hand and offered an invitation. 'Come to lunch with me? Tomorrow at the Grand Véfours, a thank you for your hospitality, for the best times of my life.'

François had been correct, Page had called for a taxi from his bedroom phone and as she rode away in it from the Place de Vosges into the morning traffic, looked at the cars and the people, the beauty of the buildings and the glamour of the shops, the chestnut trees just bursting into bloom, the twisted and tortured plane trees turning green with newborn leaves, and understood how finite all this was for her.

She felt happy, a new kind of joy surging from the depths of her soul. Not since the days when she and Oscar had been in love had she felt anything like this. She rolled down the windows and took deep draughts of air to fill her lungs. Slowly breathing out, she felt herself letting go.

A sense of gratitude for everything she had accomplished, for everything she had been in her life, was there – the good and the bad. Like some invisible shawl, who and what she was wrapped itself around her, embraced her, and she knew that whatever paths she had taken to get where she was with herself, right or wrong, she had done the best that she could and had no regrets. Of the many men who had come and gone in her life, François, Jean-Paul and Timothy, even Hervé, were the men who understood her best, accepted and loved her for what she was, and what she would never be. Never had she felt as deep an affection for them as she did riding away from them and the erotic world they had created for her. Perverse? Maybe so. But that was how she felt.

The sexual party, orgy if you will, such as she had experienced with them the evening before, was still very exciting to her, as fresh and new as it had been the very first time. Sex without guilt, without strings attached or having to pretend. Sex with no past to consider or future to be concerned about. Adoring men and a constant flow of sexual oblivion experienced almost to death could still thrill. But there was more for Page: sex as good as she had had last night but with one man whom *she* could love – that was still missing from her life. She had tasted it once and that had spoiled her forever. What was this extraordinary life she had carved out for herself if she could not love again?

From her handbag, Page took her mobile telephone and punched in Hervé's telephone. His assistant Sylvie answered.

'Sylvie, this is Page Cooper, I must speak to Hervé.'

'He's setting up for a shoot, you know how he is. No calls when he's working.'

'Tell him he *must* take my call.'

Seconds later Hervé was on the telephone. 'This had better be good, Page.'

'I need a favour, Hervé.'

The tone of annoyance vanished immediately. 'Of course.'

112

Page smiled to herself. That was Hervé. No questions asked. A real friend, a great lover. 'You've always wanted to photograph me?'

'Yes.'

'Now. Now, Hervé, please. I'm leaving Paris this afternoon. I will need three prints, and I want to look wonderful. I need them. They're farewell gifts, thank you notes, mementoes of me . . . call them what you will. I want to give them to three special friends.'

'I'm photographing a princess who for security reasons shall remain nameless. A *Vogue* cover shoot. It's supposed to happen in an hour's time but she'll be late, her plane has only just taken off from London. So get over here now, Page, and I mean *now*, and we'll have a great time doing it.'

'Hervé, we're just heading for the Pont Neuf. I want the real thing, the grand Hervé portrait – hairdressers, make-up men, dressers, the lot.'

He laughed. 'So I am at last going to catch you, make you mine forever. Your timing is perfect. The hairdressers are here, and the make-up man, and a rackful of clothes. The dressers are waiting round drinking coffee and doing nothing. After all these years of my begging to snap you, and your distaste for being photographed, what's suddenly changed your mind?'

'The end of an era, the beginning of a new one.' And Page cut off their conversation by the flick of a switch.

Page was feeling depressed, not about herself but about the women who had answered her ad, so many lost women roaming the world looking for a life. It was heartbreaking. When she had placed the ad in the *International Herald Tribune* in the hope of finding two women not unlike herself who wanted to change their lives and share an adventure of discovery and new horizons, she never dreamed how few of them were truly looking for a second chance. Most only wanted to slip back into the world they had known and had been ostracised from for one reason or another. It seemed that all they wanted was to recapture their former lifestyles and the husbands who had abandoned them or died, or lovers who had become bored and dropped them.

She had been one of those women for the last ten years, fooling herself that she was building a lifestyle that had nothing to do with the past. A lie. All she had done was manage to survive on rather a successful and sometimes rewarding scale, when in truth what she wanted was to have Oscar back and the lifestyle that went with him. She could understand those women, have pity for them, for she had at last come through the pass and into a greener valley.

But if she were disappointed by the women she met who had answered her ad, they were equally disappointed by Page. They had hoped that the woman who had placed the ad was going to be a lady who knew where she was going. One who was planning every step of her future, setting out on a new life which they could latch on to. No such thing. Page was offering nothing except to join hands with women of like mind who were prepared to jump off the deep end into a loose and free existence. No plan except to go where the wind blew them, travel the globe together to get a new perspective, and just live. They each of them would create new lives for themselves and as sisters under the skin might learn one from the other as they learned for themselves, a better way to live and find peace and contentment.

Eleven women she had interviewed, and she had no desire to have lunch with one of them never mind travel the world for a year. Women in their fifties or forties; one had been over sixty but looking more like thirty-two years old. They had Elizabeth Arden faces, Daniel Galvin hair, and work-out bodies. They had been impeccably well turned out; designer labels to keep them warm instead of men. One woman, a fifty-five-year-old earth mother who had gone through four husbands and was looking for a fifth, and dressed in expensive ethnic, had at least been amusing about what she expected travelling with a couple of women. Beverly Campbell-Royce had her itinerary all worked out: India, Kathmandu, Goa, Eastern Europe. She was in search of yet another new guru, and dope. Dope she told Page was essential to her new voyage of discovery. Dope and young men – rock hard flesh. 'I'm not ashamed to say, I'm into orgasm.' Page had wanted to say: 'Who isn't, you silly cow?' But merely told her when the woman offered a macrobiotic lunch, 'Thanks, but no thanks.'

One woman, no great beauty, very bright but spinster-like, rejected Page when told: 'I don't care where I go, what I see, who I meet, what I do with my time. I intend to take it as it comes and so will my companions, otherwise there is no point in going on an adventure.'

A Swedish blonde was the one who asked the most interesting question: 'Why don't you go alone?' And Page had answered her honestly. 'Because I don't know how. I need friends, companions, who don't know how to get a new life together either. Together we can struggle through to get where each of us wants

114

to go. Hopefully we'll support each other, learn from each other.'

It was a bright and sunny day and Page took a long walk through Mayfair, thinking about all those women she had met. She had known it wouldn't be easy but was still prepared to carry on with the exercise. She had travelled alone for long enough.

She still had that sense of happiness she had discovered in Paris. It seemed to be a part of her life now. She stopped at the tea shop Richoux in South Audley Street and ordered tea and cucumber sandwiches, then sat back and people-watched. Women and more women, not unlike those she had been meeting, not unlike herself. All her adult life Page had known women like these. She had worked for them, dashed in with flowers to brighten their already bright lives, and dashed out again. But she had never had the companionship of women, and somehow now, at this stage in her life, she understood that she had missed out on something. Yes, she would try and find women who needed to have women friends in their second time around in the life game.

She remained a long time in the chic tea room, watching the women come and go and wondering about their lives. Several men took a table near to her and she saw the marked difference it made. The women, including herself, perked up; men did put the edge into being alive. They did make a difference in women's lives.

Page went with her bill to the cashier and stood next to a man buying a cake. He smiled at her. She knew men's smiles such as his, and smiled back. 'For your little girl?' she asked.

'No. For me. I have a sweet tooth and no little girl.'

He wasn't a particularly handsome man, but he had sexy eyes and a good body, was well dressed in that attractive Savile Row tailoring. Experience had taught Page to recognise a good lover. He was one, and for a moment she was tempted. She left the shop before he did, but he followed her.

'This is awfully forward, but will you come home and share my cake with me?

'How sad for me,' she said, 'but I've just had tea and sandwiches and I don't have a sweet tooth.' And giving him one of her most charming smiles, she added before she walked away, 'Maybe another day our paths will cross.' She always left an admirer with hope.

Page sat for half an hour in Grosvenor Square. She thought about that man, the image he had of her, and pondered on something she had never thought of before she received the print of Hervé's photograph that had arrived that morning. She looked in the mirror every day and thought she knew very well what she looked like, just how attractive she was. Then the photograph arrived and she realised that what she saw was not the same as what other people saw. Hervé had caught an image of her that she did not know. With all the men who had fallen in love with her, those who had chased after her, even the occasional one night stand, still she had no idea how very beautiful and desirable she looked. She really had a different vision of herself from the one that she projected. Did most women? She thought probably they did.

She was just in time for her next appointment. Maybe this woman would be better. This one she was meeting in the bar of The Connaught. It had been the other woman's suggestion. Page was just walking up the steps to the entrance when Anoushka came through the door.

'Page!' she called out.

She had to think for a moment, having totally forgotten Anoushka once she had given her to Hervé. Nevertheless she was pleased to see her again.

'What are you doing here, Page?' asked Anoushka.

'I've come to meet someone in the bar. And you?'

'I'm staying here. It's really so nice to see you again, Page. Can we meet?'

'Well, if you have nothing better to do, then come along and have a drink.'

'I don't want to intrude.'

'You won't be. I don't even know the woman.'

'Oh.'

'I should explain. I'm interviewing her. I placed an ad in the *International Herald Tribune*: "Woman seeks others who are interested in adventure. A year's travel in search of new horizons. Only apply if you have left the old ones behind." '

'I wish I'd seen it.'

'Would you have applied?' Page asked, a smile on her lips, knowing very well that Anoushka would not have.

'Well, I am looking for a new life.'

Page liked Anoushka. She had liked her right from the first when they had met at the Café Flore. She liked her still when she had encouraged her to go with Hervé. She could just possibly be the right travelling companion, thought Page. She had after all been game enough to accept a sexual tryst with Hervé. 'Well

116

then, come on, let's talk about it. Champagne cocktails are terrific here at The Connaught.'

Together they walked through the entrance to the bar. The woman Page was to meet hadn't arrived as yet so they took a table in a quiet corner of the room. Page ordered the drinks. 'What are you doing in London, Anoushka?'

'Life can be so strange. We create richly patterned routines for ourselves only to find life has no pattern. I suppose that's how I happen to be in London again. That and Hervé. It was actually meeting you and him that set me thinking I should do something with myself.'

'Oh?' Page was puzzled.

Anoushka took a sip of her drink and then told Page, 'It was a strange thing what you did, giving me Hervé, emboldening me to go off with him. And even stranger that I should have done it. I'm not very good at promiscuity, too long a faithful wife. A generous gift to a stranger. I don't ever remember any woman being so generous with me.'

'Don't read too much into that, Anoushka, it amused me to do it.'

'You were right when you told me I would have a great time with him. I enjoyed myself thoroughly. He was a wonderful lover. Do you mind if I tell you something about it?'

Page sensed that Anoushka had to talk about it to someone. 'No,' she answered, being more kind than curious though she did try to show interest for Anoushka's sake.

'Hervé was happy enough with me, or at least expressed happiness and declared me sexually an exciting woman. But at five o'clock in the morning in a bistro, over bowls of onion soup and chunks of hot bread and butter, he could barely hide how bored he was with me, my mind, me as a person rather than a sexual playmate. I couldn't believe we had nothing to talk about, but we didn't. I was a boring housewife to whom he gave a great fuck. I could see that was what he was thinking. It was there in his face, in the conversation he was trying to have with me. It was very humiliating because I knew he was right. I have had two men since my husband dumped me, Hadon Calder and Hervé Lacoste.'

'Anoushka, I *am* impressed! They're after all men of fame and fortune, and very discriminating in their choice of women.'

'Don't be. Both men were appalled that I was satisfied with achieving less than my potential, though Hervé had the good grace not to talk about it whereas Hadon didn't.'

'It sounds to me like you're being hard on yourself, Anoushka.'

'Don't be kind, Page. You can't tell me that you didn't see that very same thing at the Flore. It's true. I was perfectly content with what I had. What need did I have to stretch myself when I had a husband and family to pamper me and tease me, I thought lovingly, for my inadequacies? You can't tell me it's not true that men like Hadon, Hervé and Robert don't admire women with some substance to them.'

'Well, I don't know the other two men, but that's true of Hervé. You have substance, Anoushka. If we hadn't seen that in you, heard that in your laughter, we wouldn't have bothered speaking to you.'

'But not like you, Page.'

'Maybe not, but I worked awfully hard at being a woman of substance, and maybe that was because I didn't have the husband I wanted or the children to cater to and hide behind. But never mind all that. So you came back to London.'

'Yes, to see a publisher and get a job.'

'And did you get it?'

'Yes, only yesterday. I'm going to translate one of Hadon Calder's novels.'

'Into what language?'

'Japanese.'

'How wonderful, and how extraordinary that you are fluent in Japanese.'

'Well, nearly fluent.'

'So you'll stay here in London?'

'Oh, no. I have six months to do the translation. I can go anywhere I like to do it. *And* he's paying me.'

'I should hope so.'

'Quite a lot of money. More money than I have ever earned before.'

'Have you ever earned any money before. Anoushka?'

'No, actually, not with my brain.' And Anoushka smiled. She was obviously delighted with herself.

Page raised her glass. 'I'm happy for you. Anoushka. Here's to new beginnings.' She brushed back her hair with her fingers so that it fell away from her face. She did it with grace, a sensual gesture that came naturally, one that charmed men and was a Page Cooper habit.

'Oh, your earrings! They're coins. How beautiful.'

'Yes. My favourites. They're special to me.' Page took one off and showed it to Anoushka. 'Are you interested in coins?'

118

'I never was before, but yes, I am now.'

The coins were mounted in a double band of gold and hinged in a manner that allowed them to be swivelled so that they could be worn with either side of the coin facing.

'Oh, I love them, Page. How clever. I have some coins. Would you mind if I copied the idea some time? Where did you buy them?'

'I didn't. I have a friend who has a fine collection of Greek and Roman coins. He gave them to me for my birthday one year. These are Roman. Do you collect coins?'

'Well, not exactly.' Page could hardly miss the look of embarrassment on Anoushka's face. 'I took them as part of a divorce settlement, and frankly I'm confused as to what to do with them. In fact, I'm going to Zurich tomorrow to see some dealers there. I'll try and sell one.'

'But you mustn't sell to a dealer! Sell direct to a collector. You'll do very much better financially. My friend, for example, might buy one. Probably all of them. I could give you his telephone number and you could call and ask him if he's interested. You can say you're a friend of mine and that I suggested you call. I can't believe he wouldn't give you a better price than a dealer. He's a true collector, discriminating and honourable, more an academic than a businessman about his coins. There are many rogues in antique coin collecting, but you would be safe with him.'

'It would be such a relief if I could sell one. I have such mixed feelings about the coins, even about disposing of one, but I've been foolish, and I need the money. They're very valuable and one sold would give me the financial security that I'm looking for to live and travel and work. I have to establish myself with this first book before I can expect to be self-supporting.'

'François is your man.'

'No! François Audren?'

'Yes, exactly. You know him?'

'No. Only of him. I can't go to him.'

'Whyever not?'

Anoushka was in the middle of her story about her coin collection, what she knew about the coins and how she thought Robert had come by them, when a waiter appeared at their table to announce that a Miss Sally Brown had called to say that she was going to be there a little late and would Miss Cooper please wait?

'Well, that's a few strikes against Miss Brown. She's already

119

fifty minutes late. She won't work out.'

The two women went back to their conversation about the coins. Page was intrigued by it but sorry to see how confused and unnerved the telling of it had made Anoushka. Page could see that she genuinely did not know what to do about the coins. 'A word of advice. Presumptuous of me, but I would like to give it.'

'Please,' answered Anoushka.

'The first thing is to stop being emotional about the coins. The second is to do something constructive with them, so call François. Tell him you're a friend of mine, offer him one of the coins, and not the one that he gave your husband. Don't even mention that coin or your husband. Don't give François your married name, you can always do that at a later date if you choose. This way you leave all your options open for the coins and how you want to deal with them in the future.'

'How clever of you, Page. I wouldn't have been able to work that out on my own.'

'Have the coins been valued?'

'No. They have been given a provenance by the British Museum, but they haven't been valued. They don't talk money at the British Museum if they can help it.'

'Then first thing tomorrow morning you go to Spink's and tell them you want a valuation of your coins for insurance purposes.'

'They know me at Spink's, and they know Robert, and I don't want to go where we're known and questions might be raised. I don't want Robert to know what I'm doing with *my* coins.'

'Then get the British Museum to tell you the name of the best dealer for valuation in Switzerland. Fly there with the coins, get your valuation, then fly to Paris and sell the most expensive one to François. Do you have a Swiss bank account?'

'No.'

'You *are* a babe in the woods. Fly back to Zurich, open a deposit account and get a safe deposit box, the Credit Suisse is good, then deposit the coins in the box for safekeeping, except for the pair you want to make into earrings. And the proceeds from the sale to François, deposit them in your savings account which you can draw from as you need to. And don't tell your husband what you've done. You don't have to tell him everything, you know, Anoushka.'

She seemed both amazed and encouraged that things could be done like this. She admitted, 'I'm not very good at things like this, Page.'

'Well, you'd better be. If you'd been able to manage your

affairs for yourself, you might not have been placed in the position you're in now. A guess, of course.'

'What does that mean, Page?'

'Oh, I don't know, Anoushka. And what does it matter what it means? That was the past and this is now.' She took a pencil and small pad of paper from her purse and wrote down François's telephone number and his name. 'There.' The finality in her voice gave Anoushka the message. That's done, now let's move on. Page ordered two more champagne cocktails.

'This Sally Brown . . . points against her keep mounting. Where is she?'

PIERS HAMILTON
STEVEN
GEORGE HAZLIT

Chapter 9

Everything that Page had said about finances and the coins kept turning over in Anoushka's mind. Life had suddenly become exciting: contracts to be signed at the publishers, a more stable financial future. She was doing something interesting with herself, for herself, by herself.

After Anoushka's problems had been ironed out, the conversation had turned to the women who had answered Page's ad.

'They sound to be what my attorney calls "the new underclass". That's what he called me.'

'Am I a new underclass?'

'Hardly. You're different. You've done something with your life and now you're doing something else with it. The new underclass are women like me who have been abandoned by their husbands, and dumped out into the world after they have had their families broken apart and their lifestyle ended. Women who want only to get back what they've had stolen from them, and can't. That's the new underclass and there are millions of us, so David says, and few who ever succeed on their own.'

'I find that abhorrent.'

'It is.'

'I somehow don't see you as one of those women, Anoushka.'

'I'm not so sure. I loved my life, my home with Robert and my children. I can't envisage anything better. What might save me is that I hate the idea of being labelled an underclass almost more than being one.' Here Anoushka hesitated.

'*And?*' asked Page, who found Anoushka increasingly more interesting.

She drained her glass in one swallow and then, gazing intently into Page's eyes, said, '*And,* my life is as valid as Robert's. Who and what I was before I met him and turned myself inside out to make him happy, to be the love of his life, his wife, the perfect mother of his children, and to reap the rewards His Eminence provided for me, must still be there. My happiness was built on a foundation of deceit. He spoiled me and destroyed me, underminded my self-esteem so cleverly I never knew it, thought it was love. He stole my life from me and I intend to have my revenge. They say it's sweet. I want to taste it.

Anoushka fell silent. Flushed with embarrassment she finally said, 'I've given away too much. I don't know what's the matter with me. When I was married I never spoke of my personal life to anyone. But then I was so self-satisfied and felt so superior to other women who complained about their lives. I had nothing to complain about. I had it all. Now I seem to be spilling out my intimate life to anyone who will listen. You should have heard me at the British Museum!' Anoushka found herself so ridiculous she shook her head from side to side and a smile crossed her face. She began to laugh at herself. 'The British Museum no less – how ridiculous. But a classy place, if you have to do it.'

That brought a smile to Page's lips as well. 'Will you stay here in London, Anoushka?'

'No. I won't find the sort of life I want here.'

'Then come with me on my adventure. I think you'd make a good travelling companion. We like each other, are two civilised human beings. Joining forces might not be a bad idea for either one of us. Maybe it could turn out to be a great idea. Anyway it's not a marriage, just travelling. You have your work which you say can be done anywhere, we won't be on the road all the time. A sail boat or a motor yacht for a home, maybe a house on a Greek island where it's peaceful and quiet when you want to work.'

'See Lake Victoria, learn to sail, return to Alexandria, maybe even St Petersburg?' added Anoushka.

'A house in Bali on the beach, or a beach house in the West Indies.'

'Oh, I've got one of those, we could certainly stay there. It's wonderful. I couldn't bear to think about returning there alone, but with a friend or friends as the case may be, that puts a different picture on things.'

'Then you'll come?'

'Do you think I can afford it?'

'You'll have the money, Anoushka. You have assets, remember, assets that can be converted into money, and it will cost money to take a year off and travel the way I want to make this journey. Let me put it this way. Frankly, I don't think you can afford not to afford it. Where else have you got to go?'

The two women remained quiet for some time, contemplating

their future, what they might be committing themselves to. It was Anoushka who called for yet more champagne cocktails. This time potato crisps came with them.

Piers Hazlit walked into the bar and looked round the tables for the woman he was to meet. A dozen or more people were drinking in the bar but not one of them resembled the tweedy, plain-faced lady libber he thought he was looking for. He glanced at his watch. She was late. No matter, time was irrelevant to Piers. He went to the bar and shook hands with the bartender. 'Hello, George.'

'Haven't seen you for a long time, Mr Hazlit. Been somewhere interesting, I expect?'

'Yes, very. How've you been, George?'

That was Mr Hazlit, polite but aloof, interesting without bragging about it, a real gentleman. George was sure to read about his latest adventure in the papers. Mr Hazlit was often in *The Times*, they favoured him with profiles every time he returned from some remarkable expedition. He was one of the last in the tradition of the great English traveller, explorer, writer – when he wasn't exercising one of his many other passions. A Cambridge scholar who could recede into his books and be as happy and content there as he was on the move: a mountain to climb, an ocean to sail. The world knew him to be a superior travel writer and lover of nature. His friends a cricket enthusiast, a lover of young, beautiful and frivolous women. The gentleman aristocrat playboy, one of the best of the increasingly dying breed who still lived for the big adventure.

'A malt whisky, no ice,' he told the bartender.

'Certainly, sir.'

Piers looked around the room again. No, for certain she wasn't there. 'George, when a Ms Cooper comes in, would you send her to my table?'

'She's here. Over there. She's the lady with the red hair.'

Piers walked across the room, mesmerised by the two attractive women having drinks together. He recovered himself when he was standing in front of them enough to ask, 'Ms Cooper?'

The puzzled look on the face of the tall, slender young man with the aristocratic good looks was obvious. Page answered him. 'Yes, I'm Miss Cooper,' she answered, emphasising 'Miss'.

'Oh, I stand corrected.'

'Sorry, an idiosyncrasy of mine. I hate that American tag the liberated woman has forced on the world in the name of something I have never understood.'

Anoushka watched Page and the young man who were sparking off each other. She listened with some interest to Page ask, 'And you? Who are you?'

'Oh.' The question seemed to snap the young man back from a mini-flirtation with Page. 'I'm Sally Brown.'

Page and Anoushka looked at each other, 'Well, you're a surprise,' said Page.

'And you're not exactly what I expected. May I sit down?' He drew up a chair before Page could answer and made himself comfortable. The waiter arrived at the table and placed his drink on it.

'Do I call you Sally or Miss Brown?' asked Page.

'Sally! Oh, how stupid of me. I meant, I'm here for Sally Brown.'

'Well, that's quite different then,' said Page, and the three of them began to laugh.

'I'm Piers Hamilton Hazlit.'

'Well, you already know I'm Page Cooper, and this is Anoushka Rivers.'

'Hello. Can I offer you fresh drinks?'

'No, these will do,' answered Page, and the conversation suddenly stopped. Piers kept staring at her.

'Is something wrong.'

'Wrong?'

'Yes, wrong. You keep looking at me as if I were a ghost.'

'Oh, no, not an apparition. A surprise. You're not at all what I expected.'

He broke into a smile that completely changed his quiet, almost serious, good looks. The sexiness in his face excited and charmed: his relaxed manner, with his sureness of self, sent a message to the two women: dangerously attractive man, too easy to fall in love with, caution. At all costs, caution.

'Well, what did you expect? Why did you expect anything?'

'The ad in the *International Herald Tribune*. That's what I'm here about. I mean, that's what Sally's here about.'

Page and Anoushka looked at each other, then Page asked him, 'And you expected what from that ad?'

'Well, certainly not a vivacious, beautiful woman.' He turned to Anoushka and really looked at her for the first time. 'Sorry, have to correct that. Two attractive ladies. I suddenly feel very stupid, and find it rather awkward being here at all.' And he smiled at them once more. He seemed to enjoy laughing at himself.

128

He was the sort of man who smiled with his eyes. Anoushka found herself immensely attracted to him. It was more than physical, but it was that of course too. His manner was cool, with an outward reserve about him that hid a fiery soul, a passionate nature. It was all there in his face, the way he carried himself, and in the eyes – they told everything. The joys of waking up in the arms of a man such as Piers Hazlit, the warmth, intimacy and security, that's what she missed the most.

Looking at Piers she yearned once more for the security that comes from intimacy and commitment. She tried to shrug off the desire she had to fill the hole in her life that came from not going to sleep every night and waking every morning next to a warm body. One that is as much a part of you and your life as your very own skin. She quickly started to block out the pain of loss, only to realise that somehow Piers Hazlit had read her thoughts and her heart. She could see it in his eyes.

She lowered her own and it broke the spell of whatever had been going on for them for a few seconds. She felt uncomfortable with her longing to get close to this man, enough to tell Page, 'I think I'll go make a phone call to Paris.'

Well, thought Page, 'Maybe Anoushka *is* a mover and a shaker after all.' She smiled and said, 'I think the British Museum first for a name, remember? Then Switzerland for an appointment, then Paris.'

Anoushka thought, A caring friend, smiled and said, 'Yes, I remember.'

Piers rose from his chair as Anoushka prepared to leave the table. Their eyes met again almost accidentally but she pretended to herself that they hadn't. She took only a step or two before she felt compelled to turn round and look at him again. To Page she said, 'I won't be long.' But to Piers she said nothing, only gave him a dazzling smile.

He watched her as she walked from the room. It registered with him at once that she was a sexy lady, one he would like to know in the biblical sense. But wrong time, wrong place. He returned to his seat and looked across the small table at Page. 'I can almost wish that I was Sally Brown, except that I enjoy being myself too much,' once more giving her a smile so sexy this time she understood that he had been turned on by Anoushka.

Page watched her disappear through the door. 'I find that very interesting, Mr Hazlit.'

Piers realised that Page Cooper was a woman men didn't put things over on. He liked her. She was not his kind of woman,

Sally Brown was his kind of woman. But he liked Page, enough to give her another flirtatious smile and tell her, 'Sorry to repeat myself, but you are a surprise.'

'We've been through that, Mr Hazlit. Why don't you tell me what you're doing here?'

'Actually, I'm the one who saw your ad. I'm the one who was intrigued by it and brought it to Sally's attention. She doesn't read the *International Herald Tribune*.

'Oh.'

'Please let me explain. I saw it as an opportunity for her and suggested that an adventure, striking out into the unknown, was an opportunity she would be a fool to miss.'

'I take it she is your special friend?' Page was fishing, trying to catch what was going on here.

'We have been close friends.'

'A close friend who wants her to take a long voyage to far away places? And you've come to check me out.'

'No, nothing like that. Well, maybe it's a little like that. You see, I would never want her to be unhappy.'

'You're assuming that I'll accept her as a travelling companion, and even before I meet her.'

'I care about her and so will you, and I can assure you she is amusing and charming company.'

'I hate women who are late.'

'Well, that is a fault, I agree. She is habitually late. You will have to make excuses for that.'

'I don't *have* to make excuses for anything.'

'I'm not doing this very well.'

'No, you're not.'

'This time she's late on my account. Something personal between us.'

'I don't get this. I don't think I want to get this. Are you here to vet me?'

'Yes, actually. Sally needs a new horizon, the sun has set on her old one, only she doesn't want to believe it. She needs a new perspective, if she wants to be happy.'

'And you know what will make her happy?'

'Yes, I do, as a matter of fact.'

'Are you so sure?'

'Yes.'

'Then what are you doing here, instead of her?'

'I felt it was my responsibility to check you out.'

'Because you talked her into the idea?'

'That might be part of it. I wanted to make sure you were the sort of person she might like. And she will like you. You're beautiful and glamorous, and Sally likes the pretty people of this world.'

'Oh, I'm beginning to see. You thought . . .' And Page was amused at what she thought he thought.

'Yes, I expected middle age or more, jolly hockey sticks and rough tweeds.'

'You forgot a little moustache and tightly permed hair, thick cotton stockings and sensible shoes.' At that point Page crossed her sheer-stockinged, long, shapely legs shod in high-heeled black snakeskin shoes. She liked teasing him. They both began to laugh.

'I think we understand each other,' he said as he stood up. Page extended her hand in friendship. He took it in his and lowered his head to place a gallant kiss upon it. 'Sally will be with you in just a few minutes.'

Page was by now intrigued to meet her. A few minutes ran into fifteen and the return of Anoushka. 'How did you do?' she asked.

'You are clever, Page.'

'Well, unfortunately I have had to be.'

'Everything went surprisingly well. To be honest, I think I'm a little overwhelmed by it all.'

'I thought for a moment there that Piers Hamilton Hazlit might have done a little overwhelming himself,' Page teased.

Piers stepped from the hotel into Carlos Place and discreetly slipped the doorman a five-pound note for watching Sally's black BMW cabriolet. He took several long strides towards Sally who was not as he had left her, sitting in the car, but standing by it talking to a friend he vaguely recognised. Sally had so many friends: shopping girlfriends, and lunching girlfriends, health club girlfriends, old girlfriends and new girlfriends – too many friends for his liking.

Looking at her, he felt a moment's sadness, something poignant, for all the things they had not been to each other. He could still look at Sally and like her, want her, in the same selfish way he had always wanted her and had kept her. Sally was a perfect little package of feminine delight. That was the problem: she was nothing more and nothing less. He made no excuses to himself or to anyone else for liking her Barbie-doll looks, nor for tolerating her frivolous life-style. The superficial values that governed her life, her lack of ambition, her exquisite passivity, her adoration of

131

him, had all suited his needs. She had taken little thinking about.

Piers Hamilton Steven George Hazlit was a man mindful of his background and his obligations who was smart enough to manage his affairs through delegation to estate managers and agents so that he was free to play as he wished. His relationship with Sally had always stopped short of love; it was more easygoing fun, convenient sex. She was, if nothing else, a fun girl, an uncomplicated personality. That was good for a man who wanted an affair that takes little, if any, effort at all.

Piers had liked the way Sally was there, always waiting for his return. But he had always been aware that they were two people adding nothing to each other's lives. Because they shared nothing together but great sex, it had always been in his mind to end their relationship. Doing so had become an imperative because she had made the fatal mistake of pressing him for marriage and children.

There was a little guile in Sally. She had undermined her case for a wedding band and a white dress when she was honest enough to admit to Piers that she saw marriage and children as a hedge against old age and loneliness, and that she did not expect that they would change either Piers's or her lifestyle which she was perfectly content with. She had played the wrong hand, gambled and lost.

As he looked at her, he realised he would miss her. Her tininess. Everything about Sally was petite: hands, feet, the perfect little breasts, the slim beautifully formed figure. She had often teased him. 'How clever I am to have been born the right size and shape for Piers Hamilton Steven George Hazlit to play with.' And she was clever enough to know she was a toy. How many times had she told him she didn't mind being his play thing, she liked being a full-sized Barbie doll? That was the problem: he could never understand that that was all she wanted to be.

He had told her from the beginning that he wanted more, but underneath her up-market doll's looks there was a fiesty, amusing and sexy lady who hung on to him tenaciously. What Piers could give her was what Sally wanted, and because he gave it to her, she loved him. She'd waited him out, year after year, and now the years were up as far as he was concerned. She had become boring, the life they lived together too stale and predictable.

Her long dark blonde hair highlighted with streaks of ash and frosted white reflected different shades of gold in the afternoon sunlight. The perfect small pointed face with its turned-up nose and beestung sexy lips, rouged in pale coral lipstick, the huge brown eyes and long thick lashes . . . She was like the whipped cream on a Viennese hot chocolate. Delicious. He heard her laughter and watched her stand back from her friend, one hand on her hip as she twirled round, as if modelling her Jean Muir wide trousers and long, perfectly cut, soft jacket of the palest pink cashmere, so soft and feminine, so delectable.

The woman, a brunette not nearly as pretty as Sally, but well turned out, said, 'I love it.'

They saw Piers approaching and the women kissed the air on either side of the other's face, the girlfriend farewell. They greeted Piers, and the other woman left. He thought rather hurriedly.

'Do you know what Evelyn said when I told her you've dumped me?'

'I wish you wouldn't put it that way.'

'How would you like me to put it?'

'We're leaving each other on amicable terms because there is no future for us.'

'Maybe not for you, Piers, but there was for me. Don't look so worried. I lied. I've been kinder to you than you deserve. Amicable was the very word I used.'

'You know that it's right for us to go our own ways, you just don't want to admit it.'

Sally had a conspiratorial look about her. It prompted him to ask, 'Evelyn looked at me as if I were the enemy, I can't help but wonder what else you've told her and the army of girlfriends you run with?'

'That you're sending me on a trip round the world as a consolation prize, to ease your conscience, because you think I need a change of scene as well as a change of life – so I can't make lunch next Thursday.'

'Change of scene, change of lifestyle, Sally, and well you know it. You make it sound like a penance. You don't have to go, you know, you can spend the rest of your life lunching with the girls at San Lorenzo.'

'Don't worry, Piers, if I don't like Page Copper, whoever she might be, and her travel plans, I *will* be lunching at San Lorenzo next Thursday.' And she started to walk past him.

He stopped her with a hand on her arm, 'You'll like Page Copper, she's not at all what I expected.'

'Well, let's hope she's not what I expect her to be like.'

Piers placed his arm round her. Looking down at her, he said, 'I'll wait here in the car for you, Sally. Friends? We were never

133

each other's great love, you know that as well as I do. We just suited each other for a long time. It's not me you'll miss, it's the lifestyle you got used to. Friends?' he queried again.

Sally knew he was being honest and genuine; she wanted him to be less honest, less genuine, and less right. He was one of the great catches in the bachelor stakes on the English aristocratic circuit and she had lost him, he had wriggled off the hook. She felt her failure and the loss too deeply to talk of friendship now. She did hope that Page Cooper was all right, though, because the truth was that it wouldn't be easy facing those girlie lunches, having to get a job, going on the open market for a new man in her life. Travel, all expenses paid, did sound like a penance but was her best option until everyone got used to her break up with Piers, and especially Sally herself.

'Maybe,' she told him, and hurried away.

Piers watched her walk into the hotel. She would be all right. He had no doubt they would some day be friends again. What she could not understand, what he had always understood, was that they had been friends who fucked well together, had good times, nothing more than a happy-go-lucky couple who ran with a fun crowd when it suited Piers, and where Sally ran alone when it suited Piers.

Sally had come a long way in the years since he had picked her up at the Dior counter in Harrod's. He smiled to himself, remembering how enchanted he had been by her Lancashire accent. It somehow didn't fit the pretty, petite, soft and sexy look of her. Even now he found her northern accent, though fainter after living in the south and running with upper-class-accented girlfriends for so many years, sexy and appealing. She had stood out from the other sales ladies plying their wares under the bright lights for not being heavily made up and looking just a little vulnerable. Piers had always had a fondness for vulnerable women.

He took a cigar from the case in the inside breast pocket of his jacket, a silver cutter from another pocket. Cutting the tip of the long, slim, hand-rolled Havana cigar, the same brand his father had always smoked, he dropped it in the ashtray. He turned the cigar slowly as he placed the flame of a match to it and puffed. It burned evenly just as the flame reached his fingertips and died. He lit a cigar in exactly the same way his father had. Piers did many things precisely as his father had, he was very much his father's son.

He turned to look over his shoulder through the rear window of the car. If Sally was not coming through that hotel door that was a good sign. She had taken a look at the women and had liked them enough to sit down and talk to them. He would give her fifteen minutes. If she was not out by then, he would leave a message with the doorman that he had gone to White's, his club, and would see her later at home.

He turned back in his seat and relaxed. Home. It brought a smile to his lips. Not the four-bedroomed Hays Mews house, once large stables that had belonged to the family's eighteenth-century Charles Street town house, where he lived when he was in town, but the house he really considered home, Chalfont, a crumbling mansion with a fifteen-thousand-acre estate less than two hours from London. His smile was in memory of the first time he had brought Sally home for Sunday lunch with the family. Well, the family and sixteen others.

Chalfont Under Edge was not quite the picture postcard image of the perfect Cotswold village but close enough. Its residents took a snobbish pride in being part of Wiltshire and not the tourist-ridden Cotswolds. Piers had pulled his black two-seater Jaguar up before the village pub, The Horse and Hounds, for a drink before going on to the house. It had been packed with people. Heads had turned and the pub had fallen silent when Sally entered but then the chatter and buzz resumed the moment Piers entered behind her. There were pats on the back, hand-shakes, greetings for him. He had ushered her through the pub to the bar and ordered them drinks. Piers introduced Sally to the publican Jim Withers, the barmaid Sheryl, and several other men standing at the bar.

'The crowd from the house has been and gone, Piers.'

'Were there many, Jim?'

'Quite a few.'

He had turned to Sally and said, 'Chalfont has a good table.'

'I don't know what that means, Piers.'

'It means people like dining at my mother's table because she serves good food and wine in abundance. The flowers, table settings, silver, even the guests, are never boring or mean.'

She had smiled at him. It had been an enigmatic smile and when he held the car door open for her he had asked, 'Why did you smile when I told you Mother had a good table?'

Quite charmingly she had risen on to her toes and kissed him on the cheek, answering, 'You're a real toff, so very upper-class sometimes, and I love it. I suppose I'll love it even more when I can stop thinking it's a joke you're playing on me.'

135

He puffed on his cigar and opened a window. He could still be amused by remembering those early days with Sally. His mind drifted back again. They had only known each other a few weeks that first time he had brought her to Chalfont.

He drove through the massive ornamental iron gates swung back on stone plinths topped by weatherworn lions with broken tails, the odd leg or ear missing too. The five-hundred-year-old trees and parkland with its lake, the crumbling stone bridge over a stream that fed it, a gentle rolling landscape that Capability Brown had had something to do with, a private English parkland that had seen better times and many more gardeners, was still a place of majestic beauty. The Jacobean stone house, mellowed by the centuries, with its towers and turrets, its lead domes and roof and its many chimneys, was not huge by stately home standards but reeked of history and upper-class privilege. To most first-time visitors it brought gasps of astonishment, admiration, wonder.

But not to the Lancashire lass, Sally Brown. She was a girl who took everything in her stride. She showed none of the awe that many other girls had when he brought them home for Sunday lunch. Her only comment had been, 'This house suits you. What fun to be born in a house like this.'

His mother and father had been alive then. His mother, Lady Elspeth, not a great beauty by any standards in her youth, had never improved as some women did with old age. She had, however, been a woman of infinite charm, and famous for her independent spirit and eccentricities. It had been from his mother that he had inherited both his fun-loving nature and his desire for solitude, as and when he wanted it.

Lady Elspeth's comment, the only one she had ever made to him about Sally, was: 'She is a nice young thing, Piers. When you're through playing with her, see you don't throw her away like a broken toy.'

His father was a handsome man whom Piers admired and resembled not only in looks but in spirit: they shared the same wanderlust, always a challenge to be taken up, an exploration to organise, an expedition to join, some romantic adventure to embark on. That had been his father's life, and he taken his family with him sometimes, his son certainly from a very young age. Before he became a cabinet minister, he had been an unofficial emissary who travelled abroad to sort out problems for Queen and country. He had been charming to Sally, and when he and Piers had taken an after-lunch walk to the folly on the edge of the lake, had told his son, 'You are like me in so many ways, my

136

boy. In my day there were showgirls, actresses, pretty things like your Miss Brown. They're usually more clever than you think.'

And Sally had been clever, very. She had understood his character and had inched her way into his life by seeing to it that he didn't have to think about her. Sally was just there. Not at all obtrusive but there, a presence in his life that he hardly had to think about. His friends, the women as well as the men, travelling companions and literary associates, all became her friends.

Harrod's had soon been left behind. She had been nineteen when he had picked her up at the perfume counter and six weeks later he allowed her to move into his London mews house. He liked keeping her. Every day she learned a little bit better how to fit into Mayfair society and his world, and bettered herself effortlessly. He liked her, respected her for that, that she was changing her life, up-grading herself without losing the essential character he was so attracted to. And she did it without making a great issue of it, that was important to their relationship. How clever she had been to know that. He had been amused by the frivolous life she had chosen for herself: the gossiping, the lunching with girlfriends. Her life became one of shopping, beauty salons, hairdressers and dressing up, most of all just being pretty and amusing and there for him when he wanted her.

He had always known what she was and was not to him, and it had been to his credit that he had never allowed her to become a house slave. She never had to clean and cook for him nor play valet in exchange for his keeping her in style. The sexual favours? That had always been a tricky one, though less tricky when after a few months they realised that was what kept them together. All the rest was trimmings.

They lived separate lives and had a life together, and that suited him. Sally came and went as freely as he did. There had been many times during their life together when he had extended invitations and she had accepted to go with him on some of his expeditions or adventures. When he had climbed the Eiger, she had watched him through a telescope from a hotel in the valley and waited for him to return. She partnered him in a motor race of vintage cars through five countries. And if she didn't go with him she was always waiting where he'd told her to be. But there were other times when he was away without her for months on end: his expedition up the Amazon, or the year he entered the Whitbread Round the World Race, to come in second. The years of Sally just being there slipped by.

Often when he was away he would forget that she existed, and yet at other times, such as when he made a camel trek across the Sahara, he had dreamed about her. For days afterwards he had thought about her, how he spoiled her, and how much she enjoyed it. He thought of her lunching with the girls and the shopping and waiting for him to return, how she had ambitions for nothing more. What a boring life she led, and how happy she was with the life she had made for herself, and he was pleased for her. But out in the desert that night she suddenly became a cause for concern when he saw that they had nothing in common, not even love.

It had been during that same night, under a sky black and silky-looking, not unlike silk velvet, and studded with millions of bright stars, that memory brought his mother back and he remembered how she had been with Sally. She had liked the same things in Sally that he had: her lack of guile, simplicity, self-awareness. Lady Elspeth befriended Sally. It was she who sent her to Winkfield to learn flower arranging, she who by example taught Sally the manners expected in upper-class circles, but never by instruction. His mother had chosen to sit on the lawn and drink with Sally and Piers's sister Caroline during her last days when pain had been her constant companion.

That night all sorts of memories came flooding back to him. How proud he had been to have Sally Brown standing with the family at his mother's open grave. And then later, after his father's death when he had inherited the title and Chalfont which he had always adored and had now become the centre of his world, Sally had taken up residence with him as she had done in London, remaining in the background of his life.

Now, sitting in the car awaiting her return, he remembered that extraordinary night in the desert where he had felt closer to God than ever before. The past had flooded in and the future had somehow presented itself as a blank. When new beginnings became something essential, like a new dawn.

There was an inch or so of ash on the end of his cigar. Very carefully he deposited it in the ashtray, and sighed. He felt such relief that Sally was still inside the hotel with those women. The rest was up to her. He felt a sudden surge of elation at being free from Sally; at their, each of them, being able to get on separately with new people, and intimate relationships governed by love.

Piers gave the doorman a message for Sally and walked away from The Connaught to Berkeley Square and then up Bruton Street heading for his club. He kept looking at the attractive women passing by, and each time he registered some interest in one, it brought a smile to his lips.

Women. There had been so many lovely women in his life, even during the years he had lived with Sally. But never when he was in England. In England she had been there, ever present and satisfying. The other women were in other places: all sorts of women, objects of his desire, mini affairs and one night stands and call girls. He had never been averse to paying for sexual favours: an elegant and expensive prostitute who guaranteed great sex – why not? His was a voracious appetite for women. Not a man who thought about love or romance, yet he was a romantic.

He had a penchant for the exotic and the erotic in women, but women such as that jarred the emotions, signalled involvement, something that took time and energy and reached into the core of his being. Something to flirt with but to be cautious with, on guard against, because that was the sort of woman he could give himself up to, reveal himself to. He had always shied away from relationships that might develop into commitment of the heart and soul, ones where he might not be in control, hold the power and the passion. Not yet. He was not ready, too promiscuous, too hungry for new and exciting sex – and he had Sally Brown waiting at home.

Walking down St James's a woman dropped a parcel and he bent down and picked it up for her. Their eyes made contact. She had the same colour hair as Page Cooper. She thanked him and rushed away. Page Cooper was that sort of erotic woman, sensuous and as liberated sexually as he was. A man can sense that in a woman. The other woman, Anoushka Rivers, he had for a few seconds tuned into. There was a woman he would like to discover, peel away the layers she was hiding behind. He sensed she was a woman with a sexual secret and he would have liked to discover it.

Piers had always seen women as no less interested in all things sexual than he was himself. Most only pretended differently, and enjoyed it in various degrees as their right as much as his. Sally and sex . . . There had always been something about Sally and sex for him. He had but to look at her and lust came into it. He liked fucking Sally. Her enthusiasm for sex was there and though she could lose herself in it, after a few years he understood that it was for Sally as superficial as the rest of her life. Good, great for him, was what seemed to matter to her. After that discovery, he wondered just how much sex really mattered to Sally, but not enough to speak to her about it.

What had made life so easy with her had been that she didn't love Piers for himself but for the good times they had together, because he had added so much to her life. That was what made her wanting to marry him and have his children so impossible, so unworthy of her. It was also what made him realise he was yet to have a love relationship with commitment that was worth building on.

SALLY BROWN

Chapter 10

Anoushka and Page watched Sally Brown cross the room and make direct for their table. Having met her lover, she was not at all what they expected. Though neither woman said anything, the look that passed between them sent out that message.

'Disappointing?' mumbled Page under her breath. But before Anoushka could whisper her impression, Sally spoke to them with a smile that was friendly, sweet even.

'Hello, I'm Sally Brown, here about the ad in the *International Herald Tribune*.'

There seemed little to do but ask her to join them, though Page thought it a waste of time. This girl on face value did not seem to be someone she wanted to spend any time with.

'I'm Page Cooper. You're very late but do sit down. Are you habitually late?'

'Yes, I would say so,' she answered, not looking at all contrite for having kept Page waiting.

'They say that's indicative of something.'

'More or less indicative than being always punctual?'

Touché, thought Page. Anoushka put out her hand and Sally Brown took it and smiled at her. 'I'm Anoushka Rivers.'

'Champagne cocktails, that will do me just fine,' Sally told Page, and turned to call a waiter.

Page stopped her with a hand on her arm and said, 'No, please let me.'

Sally seemed comfortable with them, almost as if the three were friends. Here was a pleasant manner, winning even. Page realised she was an uncomplicated person. With Sally Brown, what you saw was what you got. Page's first impression of her changed.

'Placing that ad in the *Tribune* was a brave and generous thing to do, Page. I can call you Page, can't I?' Before she could answer, Sally continued. 'And very like an adventuress. I've been thinking about it ever since Piers brought it to my attention. Why would a woman do that?'

'You wouldn't have?' asked Page.

'No, never in a million years. Not from choice.'

'But you're assuming I had a choice.'

'Oh, you didn't?'

'I didn't think so. It occurred to me that there were other women out there like myself who feel, as I do, that they have to strike out for a new life, different and exciting, to add to the lives I've already created for Page Cooper thus far. I had objectives. I'd accomplished them all, save one, and was rewarded with many successes. The realisation of success has to be ultimate happiness, the pot of gold at the end of the rainbow. I'm a treasure hunter out on the hunt. A rocky road to travel, hence the ad. Like minds on a great adventure was something I thought was called for.'

'To live anew and find the missing pieces, or those lost to us through our own or others' carelessness – now that is a big adventure. One might even call it a challenge,' said Anoushka.

'How are you answering this ad, Sally, with hope or despair?'

'Reluctantly, is the honest answer. I like where I've been, what I've done, my lifestyle. I don't want any more than that, but change has been foisted upon me.'

'It seems that I'm the only one of the three of us who has voluntarily walked away from one lifestyle to seek another. I must have been very unhappy.'

'You sound as if you didn't know it, Page.'

'I didn't. I was having a wonderful life. I had everything and every man I ever wanted.' There was a naughty glint in her eye. Neither Anoushka nor Sally missed it and for a moment they envied her, though neither woman had ever wanted a man other than the one they had been committed to. Until Page added, 'Save for one thing, and that loss I buried so deep I thought it was forgotten.'

'Life's just a bugger,' said Sally.

The conversation halted. The women remained quiet sipping their drinks. Finally it was Page who said, 'I can't remember how many of these cocktails I've had but I do know I daren't have another, and I'm famished.'

'Join me for dinner, both of you. I'm meeting some girlfriends for Chinese. It'll be my treat.'

'You have dinner with girlfriends? You have girlfriends?' asked a surprised Anoushka.

144

'Dinners and lunches and tea and drinks. Have I got girlfriends! They're my life, my fun. Don't you have girl-friends?' Sally looked genuinely astonished when both women said simultaneously, 'No.'

Page added, 'I've always preferred men friends.'

'And I had my husband and my marriage, I didn't need friends.'

'Boy, have our lives been different!' said Sally.

'I've never travelled with women before. I'm suddenly a little apprehensive but maybe because we're so different we'll get along,' said Page.

'I've travelled with a woman, many times, but that hardly counts. My husband and I allowed her to join us, friend of the family and all that. Some friend! She's sleeping in my bed now.' Tears welled up in Anoushka's eyes. 'I'm not sure I'm going to get over this. What kind of a travelling companion will I make with such a mess of a life as I have?'

'Everybody's got something, Anoushka,' Sally told her.

She lowered her eyes and tried to bring herself under control. Sally rose from her chair to go to Anoushka and sit down next to her. She placed an arm round her shoulders. 'You're not alone. We'll be there for you when you're having one of those deep-darkies – that's what I call the blues.' And she looked past Anoushka to Page and smiled at her.

Without realising it the three women had made an alliance. Page raised her glass and so did Anoushka and Sally. 'New horizons,' was her toast.

'I suppose it would cause a scandal if we smashed the glasses on the floor?' said Sally.

'It seems as if this is a momentous occasion and we should do something dramatic, but getting thrown out of The Connaught . . . no, I don't think that's it,' said Page, suddenly quite excited about taking off with these women.

'We could go shopping.'

'The shops are closed at this hour, Sally.'

'We could hire a hit man to shoot my husband,' said Anoushka, not a trace of a smile on her face.

'Not a good idea. Just keep imagining he's dead. It's a safer bet,' was Sally's advice.

'I wish there was a bordello for women. That's what men would do. Celebrate with a great night of booze and sex in some grand whore house.' There was a look of surprise on Anoushka and Sally's face. Or was it shock? Could it be that Page's travelling companions were no more liberated sexually than they were from the men who had finished with them and thrown them into the arena of women without men.

'You mean, pay for sex?' asked Sally.

'You have heard of gigolos?'

'Yes, of course, but not for me, Page. Not even for one night of fun in a male whore house, if there is such a thing. I'm the one who likes to be rewarded in the game of sex. Have you ever paid a man for a fuck, Page?'

'Sally, really! That's a very personal question,' said Anoushka.

'Oh, we're not supposed to ask personal questions? If that's one of the ground rules, we have a problem. I'm always asking personal questions. Friends do that, you know. Ask *and* confide in each other.'

'Ask away, Sally. I think we should accept that we can ask each other anything, confide anything, but not to have to answer. Ground rules? I haven't thought about that nor do I want to. Let's just make them up as we need them, if we ever do need them.'

'That sounds good to me,' said Sally. And both women looked at Anoushka.

'I guess I can live with that. I may have over-reacted, Sally. I'm not used to people being so direct with me. I just assumed that everything in my new life would continue as it always has, all politeness and subtlety. Intimacy locked away in some cupboard to be taken out on the right occasion.'

'Good,' said Sally, and Page nodded her approval. And the three women smiled and felt very pleased with themselves. There was a feeling that they would get on.

'There are a few things I would like to make clear – not ground rules, simply how I feel about our travelling together, and the marked difference between us. I may have placed the ad in the paper, have been the motivating force that has brought us together, but my responsibility for the three of us and our travels ends right here. There will be no leader of the pack. If there was it wouldn't work for us. We should be open with one another, discuss things, and make unanimous decisions. That makes things easy.'

'Sounds right to me. What about you, Sally?' asked Anoushka.

'Fine, seems OK.'

'There's one thing that is markedly different about us.'

'I'm certain as we get to know each other we'll find many,' said Anoushka.

'I'm sure you're right,' said Page. 'But the one that is important for us to remember right from the start, so we understand each other's view point, is one that I have observed already. We three are going on this odyssey and only one of us is making this voyage without anguish, and that's me.

'From the little said here this afternoon, and what I deduced from having met you in Paris, Anoushka, the chief reason for your and Sally's anguish is your difficulty in facing the end of a relationship, and your lives as you have known them for many years. I have more to say but if this is too personal for either one of you, I'll stop now.'

'What you say is true in my case, anyway,' said Anoushka.

'Why don't you say what you have to say, Page?' suggested Sally.

'I've been where you girls are now. It's going to take time and a great deal of work to rid yourselves of your anguish. It did me. I no longer desperately want everything to continue as it is, and so I no longer have to believe that things will always stay the same. That's make believe. Things don't stay the same. You may believe that your lives should have stayed the same with the men you loved, but believing it has little or nothing to do with reality. Girls, you built your lives on make-believe, with its misinformation, idea and assumptions. Oh, my god, those lethal assumptions! Do I know about them. Those are rickety foundations on which to build. Do we take notice of the truth which keeps interrupting our dream of forever? Oh, no. No matter how much the truth keeps breaking in we keep up our pretence that nothing will ever change. We keep on going with hopeless bravado to hold on to what we have, never wanting change or to disrupt our perfect worlds.'

'Why do you think we do that, Page?' asked Anoushka.

'Because you, just as I once did, always think of changes as signalling loss and suffering. And when they happen, these changes, as in this case, you two out on your own after a long time of belonging to someone, you try and anaesthetise yourself as far as it is possible. Take my word for it, that doesn't work.'

'Then what does?' asked Sally.

'You have to grow up and stop assuming that permanence provides security. You have to accept that impermanance is the reality of life. Men seem to understand that better than women. Impermanance is about the only thing you can hold on to. That's what I believe and that's the way I live. I've stopped clinging to things and people. Everything I have done in the past is like a dream to me. I keep leaving things behind. Now, this moment, is real to me, but in a few minutes it will be a memory.

'I have compassion for what you girls are having to deal with, but thought it best to speak out now so that you can understand where I'm coming from since it's a very different place to where you are.'

At that moment Anoushka could not help but think of how dazzled she had been on first meeting Page Cooper. How, having expressed it to Hervé, he had agreed that she was indeed a very special lady with whom men fell in love though they could not possess. She was once again dazzled by Page, her looks, her seductive charm, and now the very core of this new friend's being. Page had been right to say something because it made clear to Anoushka something that had been a mystery: why she had given Hervé to Anoushka, and more importantly why Anoushka had had the courage to go off with a stranger for an afternoon of lovemaking. Page now understood Anoushka, had zeroed in on her because she had once been where Anoushka was still stuck. She had been saying to Anoushka, 'Live now, this moment.'

Sally Brown kept looking at Page. She had found her incredibly beautiful and sophisticated, but as she had been speaking, Sally understood what Piers had meant when he said that she would like Page Cooper. Here was a woman who spoke from the heart, lived from the heart. She was more like Piers than anyone Sally had ever met. How Page must have suffered, what tremendous loss and pain she must have felt in her life to have fought back to live in a world of impermanence and like it. Sally admired her for what she was but more so for her honesty. She knew that she would never live on the same plane that Page did but it didn't matter. They would be friends, respect each other for their differences. That, after all, had been what Page had been saying. Sally found a new enthusiasm for this odyssey she was about to embark on. Somehow she sensed this was the best afternoon of her life.

Heads turned when Anoushka, Sally and Page entered the Chinese restaurant. Theirs were such contrasting beauties: Page's sophisticated, seductive look with its hard edge of excitement; Anoushka, fair-skinned and with blonde, blonde hair, her sensuous body dressed down to appear a touch matronly; Sally with all the shine and sparkle of youth in chic clothing.

They of course had no idea how others viewed them. They

148

joined Sally's friends and enjoyed themselves. Having seen what a success their dinner was, and how much her friends liked Anoushka and Page, she took courage and told them, 'It's over for Piers and me. He dumped me.'

Until that moment there had been a great deal of laughter and chatter. Page and Anoushka had found these young women to be amusing, pretty and fun. But Sally Brown was in a league of her own as somehow original and special. The other young women, with their upper-class accents, had received a better education and had good jobs. At Sotheby's for one, as an interior decorator for another, and Lady Caldera was a charity organiser who, one imagined by her conversation, did her job between social engagements and beauty therapies of one sort or another. These girls, whose boyfriends or one husband had been in one way or another a friend of Piers, respected and had a deep affection for the girl who had never lost her Lancashire accent. If Anoushka and Page were friends of Sally's that had been enough for the girls to accept them on their night out. They gossiped about their mutual friends, Binky and Bonky, Winkie and Wonkie, Pussy and Feeny, as if Page and Anoushka had known them all their lives. At one point Page asked, 'Don't any of your friends have real names?'

They had been good-natured and charming, laughing at themselves and the little world they lived in, and admitting, 'Not many that we use.'

Page had thought she'd be bored at such frivolity but she hadn't been, not in the least. They were intelligent and amusing and lived in different worlds, just as interesting and valid as hers.

These English beauties with impeccable backgrounds, born to privilege, made the older women as welcome in their circle as they had Sally. They were full of chatter about a shopping expedition the following day. On the hunt for hats for Ascot, they invited Page and Anoushka to join them and then go on for lunch at San Lorenzo.

Page heard herself say, 'Why not?' That seemed to make them all jollier than ever.

Anoushka said, 'I would like a hat with a crown of egret feathers.' And everyone laughed.

It had seemed to Sally that this was the right time to make her announcement. The chatter stopped instantly. The smiles vanished from everyone's faces. Chopsticks were poised in mid air and tears welled up in Sally's eyes. She fought them back.

'Piers would say that that was not an accurate way for me to state the case. He would prefer that I said it was amicable. Well, it is amicable but only because I have no choice.'

This was where the famous English reserve came into play. Her three young friends remained silent. Not a word of shock or surprise, none of sympathy. Had they known what Sally had not, that it had always been on the cards? Yes, probably. Page and Anoushka had thought that after their first look at Sally Brown, and having met Piers Hazlit for only a few minutes.

Anoushka felt Sally's pain and reached across the table to take her hand in hers. This woman had only known her for a few hours whereas her friends had known her for years. Yet until Anoushka had made that gesture of friendship they could not reach out to her. Sally had embarrassed them. Anoushka had to remind herself how the English despise embarrassment, how they tend to ignore it. It was to them somehow bad manners to create a situation that might cause it. For the first time Anoushka understood that and, surprisingly, thought the English were right.

Until a few minutes ago Sally was a friend to these girls. Now she's an embarrassment, in the same way I would have been to everyone I knew had I stayed in Lakeside, she thought. Between the pancake rolls, the chicken in ginger and spring onions, the duck and plum sauce, the beef in black bean sauce and the fried sea weed, Sally had become one of the new female under-class.

Fiona put down the bowl of rice she had been holding. Her deep sigh attracted the attention of all the women round the table. 'Well, Sally, it won't be the first time you've had to go to the Royal enclosure without Piers. We've the same party we have every year going to Ascot. You'll just have to put on a brave smile and wear a bigger, more elegant hat than usual.'

The other two girls brightened up. That obviously seemed to be the right attitude to adopt to this uncomfortable news their friend had just announced. They actually returned to their food with enthusiasm until Sally's next announcement.

'I won't be going to Ascot.'

'But we're all going shopping for hats tomorrow. Of course you'll go, *and* have a good time. You'll be with us, and there will be plenty of dishy men there. Many admirers of yours,' said Helen.

Again silence fell round the table, good friends not knowing what to say to make it better for Sally. Finally Fiona spoke up again. 'Where are you going to go? What are you going to do? Oh, this is dreadful simply dreadful of Piers. I've known him since I was a child. He's kind and generous and would never just

150

throw you out. He'll provide for you. Oh, Sally, he is doing that, isn't he?'

'We haven't discussed it.'

Lady Caldera said, 'In my grandfather's day they bought their women hat shops.'

There were gasps of astonishment from the other two girl-friends. 'Cally, you're so insensitive!' said Fiona.

'And stupid. And what exactly do you mean by "their women?" Sally was never some kept mistress of a married man, like one of your grandfather's women. She and Piers have been sharing a life for years,' said Helen. 'This is like a divorce.'

'Not when you haven't been married,' said Fiona. 'Sorry, Sally. We're saying all the wrong things.'

'Are there any right things to say? Actually there isn't much to say. Let's just accept the bad news,' she said.

'I wasn't referring to my grandfather, Helen, merely what happened in his time,' said Lady Caldera defensively.

'Oh, *please*, Cally, everyone in London says if it hadn't been for your grandfather and his voracious appetite for beautiful and clever women, and his fortune, there would be no Bond Street. It's always been a standing joke that the chic shop was created in bed.'

That brought smiles to everyone's face. It seemed to break the gloomy atmosphere that had settled over the table. When Cally admitted, with a puzzled look on her face, 'I have heard that, and always wondered what it meant,' they all broke into nervous laughter, but laughter nevertheless.

'What does this really mean in practical terms?' asked Helen. 'I mean, where will you live, what will you do now that you no longer have Piers to look after? Oh, this has to be ghastly for you, Sally. You did look after him so well.'

'It is beastly. Piers and I have been together a very long time. I never thought about it ending. I've a life with him, I don't know what it's going to be like without him.'

'The same,' said Fiona.

'Never. You're either trying to be kind or you're fooling yourself if you think that. I know it, and so does Piers. And you, my friends, have to understand it too. That's why I won't be buying a hat for Ascot this year and nor will I be going.'

'You can't just hide yourself away, Sally.'

'I don't intend to. I'm going on a great adventure, leaving old horizons behind and looking for new ones. And Page and Anoushka are too. We're joining forces.'

151

'I don't understand. You're leaving London?'

'Yes.'

'For good.'

'I've no idea. But I would doubt that.'

'Leaving for where?'

'Don't know that either.'

'There are an awful lot of don't knows, Sally.' That was an apprehensive Helen.

'Yes, isn't it exciting?' And having said that, Sally realised that it was. Very exciting.

'Oh, Page, Sally's being so vague. Do tell us what you three are up to, where you're going?' asked Cally.

Page could sense the atmosphere round the table changing, a less distressed look on Sally's face than had appeared when she had broken the news to her girlfriends. 'It's all quite simple, Cally. The adventure has gone out of our lives. We seem to be missing something essential so we're going in search of it.'

'Men.'

'Fiona!' This time it was Sally, Cally and Helen who were aghast at the gaffe.

Page began to laugh. There was a certain charm and innocence about these young English beauties. Like rare hot house flowers they flourished in their enclosed little world. Naive about both good and the bad, everything outside that charmed circle they lived and thrived in. Page envied them and hoped that they would remain cushioned from the rough and tumble of a hard cold world, with all its excitement and despair. They were in their way fragile flowers. 'Fiona, do we look like women who can't get a man when we want one?'

'Hardly. Actually when you walked through the restaurant to join us, I saw you as an impressively attractive trio. So did every man in the room by the way heads turned. But, Page, you're not looking for men, are you?' asked Fiona, a note of incredulity in her voice.

'No, Fiona. I can't speak for the others but I can for me. Men, yes. Sex, yes. But I want more. A new skyline to stand against, maybe many new skylines to stand against. New things to see and learn from and to extend myself with, and maybe even love, a deep, abiding, mutual love. I discount nothing, no longer seek anything in particular. It may come, it may not, but the bottom line for me has to be ultimate happiness. I've had everything else.'

Anoushka listened to Page and wondered why she could

152

articulate what Anoushka wanted, what Anoushka had so mistakenly believed she had. Had her ego blinded her to the reality of her situation? Did it take a stranger to speak for her? Obviously it had, and did. Years of loving Robert, wanting to please him at any price, had blinkered her. If she had known what she had been doing there was something whorish about that. Another ugly realisation about herself. She couldn't bear thinking about it and so did what she was used to doing, blocking any unpleasant challenge out of her mind.

Sally reacted by accepting that Piers was taking care of her, maybe not with a hat shop but he had found Page and Anoushka and was interested in her happiness, even though, or was it because, it was to be without him? The male mind could be so perverse.

Helen asked, 'Do tell us more, where are you going? When will this adventure begin?'

Anoushka, Sally and Page looked at each other and shrugged their shoulders, then began to laugh. 'I guess we haven't decided,' said Page. 'We haven't even talked about that.'

'Well, it's begun for me. I'm here having dinner with women. I've never had dinner with a group of women out on a night on their own. I'm going to Switzerland tomorrow, and then on to Paris to strike a deal in Greek and Roman coins of antiquity and become an independently wealthy woman. Off on a great adventure and I don't know where, how or when,' Anoushka said with a look of excitement which until then had not been evident to the women round the table.

'And it's begun for me. I've never had a girlie dinner. And I've never wanted to share my adventures with other women. And I've never solicited for companions through an international newspaper,' said a smiling Page. She looked at Sally, hoping that the adventure had begun for her too.

'My adventure has certainly begun. I'm not having lunch with Evelyn on Thursday. And I'm not going to buy a hat for Ascot tomorrow. And I won't be in the Royal enclosure with you girls and without Piers this year. And I'm running away from a world I love and know one day I will come back to when I have it all, *and* ultimate happiness, not just a tentative piece of it.'

All three girls were clearly intrigued. 'How will you decide where you're going?' asked Cally.

'A pin in a map? Not a bad idea. We might like to visit or even take up residence there for a while. well, why not? We're all going to do our own thing, whatever that is, wherever we go. I

153

have a job, one I never dreamed possible. Nor I'm sure did anyone else. I'm going to translate the works of Hadon Calder into Japanese.'

Helen and Fiona were clearly impressed with Anoushka's announcement. 'Have you met him?' asked Fiona.

'Yes,' she answered. And realised that all the women at the table were interested in her in the way she always hoped Robert's friends might have been, for herself, for what she was doing with her life, not merely as an appendage of her husband's.

'Maybe we can do a little better than a pin in a map. For example, let's say we ask ourselves whether we want to stay in London. A question and answer thing like that,' suggested Sally.

'Good idea,' said Cally.

Sally's friends were taking a real interest in this voyage of hers and in her new companions. It was somehow flattering for the would-be travellers, to confirm that they were on their way.

'London?' questioned Fiona.

'No.' A loud reply in unison from the women.

'Paris?' that was Cally again. The no was unanimous again.

'Rome?' suggested Helen.

This time it was a shaking of heads. No, Rome held no interest for them.

'It seems to me that you don't want to stay in big cities,' said Cally, who seemed to be seriously fascinated by the women's adventure.

'Do we?' asked Sally.

The three women looked at each other. 'Not for the moment anyway,' said Page. And the other two agreed, saying that they did not discount a city of their choice when the time was right for them.

'Well, at least you have established something. In fact the one who should be sitting here is Piers. This is just his kind of thing, an expedition to God knows where, for who knows how long?' said Cally.

A rolling of eyes and a loud whisper from Helen. 'Cally, you clod!'

Sally, who was sitting next to her, placed a hand on her shoulder. 'It's OK, Cally, I'm not going to burst into tears every time Piers' name is mentioned. In fact it was Piers who found the ad and brought it to my intention. He's even met Anoushka and Page.'

'More like vetted us,' remarked Page.

'Well, that's a relief. That means he intends to pay for it, and you'd damned well better let him, Sally,' said Fiona.

'Money?' said Anoushka. 'I suppose we should talk about that.'

'You aren't very organised if you haven't even worked out the money side of things. You're extremely casual about this expedition of yours,' said Helen.

'Yes, I guess we are,' said Page.

'And hopefully we'll stay that way. I've had one life where my husband organised me to death,' added Anoushka.

A look of surprise at such frank talk shone on all the English girls' faces.

'Oh, damn, there I go revealing too much at the wrong time. It's getting to be a habit with me,' said Anoushka, so charmingly everyone came out with some little word to put her back at her ease. The best of which was Cally's.

'Would that we English could be more open, it would certainly make us easier to live with.'

'But less English,' said Fiona.

Almost in unison the English girls at the table said, 'Oh, no, wouldn't like that, not one bit.' They liked their Englishness and all it stood for.

'Not to worry. Such openness is not in the genes,' said Cally. That brought smiles from round the table.

'About the money? Let's get back to that. All expenses split three ways?'

'Perfect, Sally. Agreed.' The three of them were resolved.

'The amount? How much will we each put in the pot?' asked Sally.

'Fifty thousand dollars and see how we go?' suggested Page.

'That's a great deal of money. I've never had fifty thousand dollars of my own to spend on myself, and actually I don't know whether or not I can afford it,' said Anoushka.

'Only you know whether or not you can afford to spend it. Remember, you do have a job, well paid you said, as well as your coin money. But I'm not one to tell another person how to spend their money. I can manage that. Are you all right for that sum, Sally?'

'No, but Piers is. I'm in.'

'Then so am I,' said Anoushka.

'Fifty each isn't going to keep you in five-star hotels for long,' said Cally.

'It will for the odd night,' said Anoushka.

'I don't want a five-star hotel life for us. We don't want to be spoilt, pampered tourists this time round. We're going out there to live in the real world. We'll rent wonderful houses with staff when we can and live life as it unrolls, make our expeditions from there into the hinterlands that interest us. We have to start somewhere, where would we like to go? The table is open for suggestions,' said Page.

What was left of the Chinese food had gone cold. The six women watched as waiters whisked away plates and serving dishes. They brought fresh pots of tea, and deep fried banana dumplings.

'I've always wanted to sail the Atlantic, test myself against the elements,' said Anoushka. That surprised everyone at the table who had somehow not seen her in that light.

'I can contribute something there. Piers's schooner, *Black Orchid*, has a crew of six and sleeps twelve comfortably. He's sending it to the Caribbean and won't be on it. He'll be on an expedition of some sort up the Amazon.'

'I always say I want to sail the Atlantic alone. But when it comes to the crunch, I doubt that I would have the courage. With a crew of six it would be scary, but, hell, yes! I'd go. The idea is thrilling. Very out of character for me, but then *I'm* out of character. What about you, Sally? Could you bear it?'

'*Black Orchid* is a fantastic vessel. I've never crossed the Atlantic in it though we did sail many times to the Greek islands, and the coast of Turkey. Sure, why not? I'm game. What about you, Page?'

'I want to go as crew – that is if we can get them to teach me to sail before the crossing. Now that I would find thrilling.'

'We'll all go as crew. What do you think, Anoushka?' asked Sally.

'If Piers gives us the *Black Orchid*, how can I say no?'

Rousing applause from the women at the table, and, 'Bravo, bravo!' from Cally.

'I have something to contribute. I own a marvellous house in the West Indies, on Barbados. We can live there and spend the winter island hopping,' offered Anoushka.

More talk about where to go and when to leave, and then finally the three intrepid travellers took leave of Sally's girlfriends who insisted they would pick up the tab as a treat, a bon voyage. The three English girls were then invited to visit with Anoushka, Sally and Page sometime, somewhere, during their odyssey.

The life went out of the party once Anoushka, Sally and Page were gone. 'Piers is a pig for destroying Sally's life. And he has

156

done, that's for certain. Let's hope she can find another Piers. Sally will never make it without a man to love, a man to keep her,' said Fiona, and the other two girls agreed.

'Pray that none of us is ever thrown out by the men we love. We'd be no less sad and desperate than those women are. And make no mistake, they *are* sad and desperate, no matter the front they're putting on. Very brave too, for trying to create new and better lives for themselves when their broken hearts aren't even in it. Three strangers to one another, binding themselves together with nothing in common but bereavement, loss of faith, profound loneliness. Maybe together they can get over those things,' said Cally, tears brimming in her eyes caused by the deep dread that one day she might be in their unenviable position.

Chapter 11

It was a strange choice, India and the Taj Mahal, for three women whose men had not loved them as Shah Jahan, the Mogul Emperor, had loved his wife, Mumtaz-i-Mahal. On the contrary they were women who had lost the great loves of their lives, and had been replaced by other greater passions above and beyond them. Not Page nor Anoushka nor Sally's chosen man had pined for the loss of them enough to build a monument in their memory.

But the Taj was their choice, a mausoleum constructed from pure white Makrana marble on which over twenty thousand workmen were employed over a period of twenty-two years. The building of white marble, delicately carved and inlaid with precious stones, so perfect in its symmetrical design, so reflective of Persian influence set in its formal gardens, Mogul architecture at its best.

Of all the architectural wonders of the world they could have chosen from, surely to pick the Taj Mahal was not only for its beauty but for the love story that went with it.

In London, Page had said, 'I have always wanted to see the Taj Mahal, but I want to see it without the mass of love-lorn tourists. I'll make a phone call to an admirer who always promised me I would see the Taj as no woman had ever seen it. Well, if he can do that for one, he can do it for three.'

Now they would know if Page's friend was as good as his word. The long flight from London to India was over, their first adventure together was about to begin.

'I believe that car is for us,' said Page and the three women approached it, leaving the other passengers to cross the tarmac and head for customs.

It was dusk and the sky above Agra was streaked with the hot pink of a setting sun against a bruised blue, waiting to turn into a night of black velvet shot with stars. From the shadow of the car's interior Jahangir leaned forward and at the same time the window

159

slid silently down and the women had their first glimpse of their host. 'What a pretty sight you are, ladies,' were his first words to them. A wave of his hand and the chauffeur opened the door and Jahangir slid to the centre of the cream leather seat. With the palms of his hands he patted it to either side of him, a welcoming gesture for the women to sit next to him. The third was offered one of the jump seats facing him.

Jahangir was younger than Anoushka had thought he would be. She guessed him to be in his mid-thirties or early-forties. He spoke with the perfect upper class, well-educated, English accent, honed by Eton and Cambridge in his youth, and frequent trips to London and a huge residence in Holland Park where he lived now. His was a sensuous, husky voice with just a trace of a Hindi accent. He was darkly handsome and wore his hair long; his eyes were sexy and seductive, mesmerising, and his mouth the same. One of the top Indian polo players, he was loved for that as much as for his palaces and his wealth. 'A decadent dilettante, but kind and generous and living on a grand scale, with chic and in luxury,' was Page's introduction of him to Sally and Anoushka as the Rolls slid silently away from the plane. He laughed uproariously.

'A rather indiscreet introduction, but quite accurate, my Eurydice,' he told her. And then he took Page in his arms and kissed her with obvious pleasure. No one in the back seat of that car could help but understand that he had taken sensual delight in Page before, that he was counting on having it again. There was about the kiss, the manner in which it was given and received, a subtle hunger kept in check. It excited the women, made him seem incredibly attractive sexually. Both Sally and Anoushka were aware of how much they wanted that male attention for themselves, wanted to feel sensual desire rise in them as they saw it happening to Page and Jahangir.

He had a mischievous twinkle in his eye and enormous charisma and charm.

'Why do you call Page your Eurydice?' asked Sally who was sitting opposite him.

'Ah, well, that's because once, for a time, she allowed me to play Orpheus to her Eurydice as in the Greek legend – a very happy time for me but too short-lived. Eurydice, as you know, was a wood nymph, and that was where I first met and made love to Page: in a wood on a Tuscan hill.'

She leaned into Jahangir and kissed him sweetly on the lips. She removed her white linen jacket, and her cream silk satin blouse with its wide bow-shaped neckline slipped to one side to

160

show a tantalising naked shoulder. He caressed it. They were both smiling, obviously delighted to remember what they had once been to each other.

'In legend Eurydice, a dryad, was the wife of Orpheus. Alas, not like Page and me.'

'I don't know the legend,' said Sally, completely enchanted by the idea of Jahangir and Page in love.

He gave Page a knowing look, caressed her hair and told Anoushka, while never taking his eyes from Page, 'Orpheus was in love with Eurydice when she died of a snake bite. He didn't want to live without her so he descended to the underworld to recover her, but then lost her forever. You see, he had been stupid, violated the conditions of her release. He turned to look at her before emerging from the underworld.'

Anoushka was fascinated; by telling the Greek Legend, and linking it with Page and himself, Jahangir had revealed himself as yet another lover Page had walked away from, yet another man who could not win her heart. Hervé had told Anoushka that that was part of Page's seductive charm, the way she enslaved men. When Anoushka had met François Audren, who bought a coin from her, he had spoken of Page in a way that made her understand that he too had loved and lost her. Anoushka had not missed the magnificent black and white photograph in a Fabergé frame he kept on his desk. Three men and how many more? And why couldn't she give her heart to them? Who was the man who stopped her, isolated her from true love? It had to be a man, Anoushka was certain of that.

As they rode through the crowded, noisy streets, drenched with oppressive humidity, full of a strange new world of poverty and colour, it was that thought which occupied Anoushka's mind. Would her friend ever feel close enough to Anoushka to reveal her story, bring it to light, brand it as the past and let it go? She very nearly laughed out loud. The pot calling the kettle black.

Jahangir did not live in Agra. He kept what he called his Taj Mahal pied à terre there for the times when he wanted to visit the mausoleum or put up guests: fifteen huge, sumptuous rooms in the sixteenth-century fort, the other monumental building in Agra. This city in Uttar Pradesh on the River Jumna had once been the capital of the Mogul Empire and had been ruled by more than one of Jahangir's ancestors. For that reason he was privileged to live in those rooms. It was there that they were driving to from the airport, and where they would begin their amazing forty-eight hours in India.

Jahangir's friends were not nearly as handsome as their host but made up for their lack of looks by charm and warmth, passionate natures, and their knowledge of how to attract women. To be with Jahangir was to fall under the spell of the sensual excitement he cast. A master at the game of seduction, few could resist him. The three adventuresses did not.

Anoushka, Page and Sally were dressed in sumptuous but understated white evening gowns at Page's suggestion. She had been so clever. In London she had told them: 'I know Jahangir. He will want us to be glamorous, chic, sensuous and exciting, to live up to the Taj Mahal and the evening he will prepare meticulously for us. Not only for him and the Taj but for ourselves we should be visions of shimmering femininity floating through the gardens in the moonlight.'

To that end they had chosen well. Anoushka was wearing a long white dress, a sheath of crêpe-de-chine with slip straps, and over her shoulders a short cape of the most sheer silk chiffon that finished just above her waist. It was bordered in clear crystal bugle beads. She wore no undergarments and the dress, cut on the bias, followed her form and moved as she moved. With her silvery-coloured blonde hair and soft make up she was perfection, and worthy of the night being prepared for her.

Sally was adorned in the dress that they had all loved and wanted to buy when the three had gone shopping together. She was the only one small enough to fit into it. A cream-coloured paper taffeta evening dress, its skirt was full and trailed longer at the back showing several inches of ankle in the front. The silk was very nearly as light as air and the entire dress could be crunched up and fitted in the hand. It was a masterpiece of design, cut and dress making. The strapless bodice clung to Sally's breasts, fitted to the waist as nearly as if it had been a second skin, and round her neck she wore a garland of fresh jasmine blossoms.

Page's dress was white, one-shouldered, of crêpe-de-chine, long and slit up the front. It was the most sophisticated of the dresses. Only a woman with confidence and stature could carry it off. It displayed one naked arm and shoulder, leaving the other shoulder partially covered. The dress skimmed her breasts in the front and was cut to expose most of her back to the waist. The single sleeve was wide and fluttered teasingly when she moved her arm.

The men were dressed in white linen suits: Armani, Ralph Lauren, a Savile Row tailor for Jahangir. They had travelled in an entourage of three cars. When they arrived at the Taj Mahal it

162

was after ten in the evening and all was shrouded in darkness. They were ushered through the gardens to their feast by servants carrying lanterns and dressed in the livery Jahangir's family had always used: white turban and jacket with plum and red intertwined sashes, trousers of midnight blue.

It was mysterious, an adventure. They had no idea what to expect, what they might see, what experience was about to take them over. But the sense of expectation was dizzyingly exciting. They were there in the centre of the gardens, in the exact spot where Jahangir wanted them to be when the white, nearly full moon inched its way across the sky towards the Taj Mahal. The building loomed majestically in the dark, its towers and domes silhouetted against the blackness of the night.

They drank champagne and settled themselves round one of the garden pools in comfortable chairs that had been brought in for the occasion, and nibbled by candlelight on Indian delicacies: bite-sized filo parcels filled with spiced shrimp and curried crab, duck, the flesh from tiny succulent birds.

Moonlight brushed an edge of the Taj Mahal from ground to sky, and the building suddenly sprang to life. As the moonlight inched itself slowly across the façade of the building, Jahangir had their lights extinguished. The party stood in the darkened garden and watched in awe as the Taj Mahal rose from the shadows of the night. Sounds of the sitar, running water, crickets, the muffled noise of a sleeping city somewhere off in the distance. The sweet scent of flowers. No one spoke, all too mesmerised by the regal beauty of the Taj.

The façade remained bathed in moonlight for quite some time. It was as if the moon had found something remarkable to embrace and, having done so, could not move on. There was an order for the lanterns to be lit once again and the party walked through the gardens to another place that had been prepared for them by their host. Their white figures looked in the darkness like so many ghosts floating through time and space to pay homage to love.

At the very foot of the building, now lit from above by the moon and lanterns from below, they sat and listened to the haunting sound of the sitar and watched the dancing girl perform for them in the moonlight with the pristine white marble entrance to the Taj Mahal as a back drop.

The sensuality of the night, the place, enveloped them all. The heavy scent of flowers and the aroma of Indian spices from the food being prepared in braziers, the oppressive heat and humidity, and

163

the taste of dust, the exotic power and beauty tantalised the senses and wrapped itself around the party, drawing them into a world of erotic pleasure. Jahangir took Page by the hand and led her to his friend, the Maharaja, who placed an arm round Page and, tilting her chin up to the light of the moon, kissed her lightly on the lips. When Jahangir approached Anoushka her heart raced. He kissed her on the cheek and led her to Alexander Maar, the English poet. Finally he plucked Sally for himself as easily as he might have picked a rose from the bush she was standing beside.

The moon moved on and the Taj Mahal began once again to face away into the night. The drama of the occasion was almost unbearable. But there was more to come. As the building slipped back into the night, a soft warm light glowed from within the Taj Mahal.

The party mounted the stairs and entered the Taj where a small army of Jahangir's household were just lighting the last of thousands of candles before silently slipping out of the building.

A table had been set in one of the halls, and there they dined while listening to the haunting sound of the sitar echoing through the marble rooms. The dancer performed and a poet recited sixteenth-century Mogul love poems. The guests came to life, conversation flourished, laughter rang through the halls, and all were lost to the idea of romantic love.

At last Jahangir rose from the table and announced that it was time to go. They left the mausoleum following him through the gardens. Dawn was breaking and at just the right moment he stopped and insisted that they turn round for a last look at Shah Jahan's gift to the world. The smile on his face gave away his intended surprise. They were seeing yet one last image of the Taj in all its splendour.

The sun was just rising in the sky turning the dawn light a bright pink. The Taj was bathed an exquisite shade of rose, from that to a golden yellow, and then finally a crystalline white.

All evening Anoushka's partner Alexander had been charming but reserved with her. He was tall and slim, lanky-looking and boyish in appearance. He was many years younger than Anoushka. There was a sensitivity about him, a vulnerable quality that she liked but which seemed not at all sexy to her. For sex she would have chosen Jahangir not Alexander Maar – until he stepped up behind her and, placing his hands on her shoulders, pulled her gently back against him.

They were standing together in her room, the light dim, since

164

the windows were shuttered against the oppressive heat. It was a large and beautiful room, deep within the massive fort, cool and heavy with the scent of jasmine. A room that was sumptuous and sensual. The soft white walls were hung with dozens of mirrors all in wide decorative frames inlaid in mother of pearl and ivory. The chairs were sixteenth-century ivory pieces carved by great artisans and covered in white and silver silk brocade. The chest of drawers was inlaid with ivory flowers and rose cut diamonds, banded in silver and inlaid with mother of pearl. Cut crystal chandeliers, large and dramatic, hung from the carved and painted ceiling. Everywhere were vases of white flowers: orchids, and lilies, and long-stemmed roses. And in the centre of the room stood a fourposter bed of carved ivory draped with the sheerest of white silk.

He kissed the nape of her neck and removed the short diaphanous cape from her shoulders, kissing her first on one shoulder and then the other. A shiver of excitement went right to the core of Anoushka's erotic being. He licked a small place on her shoulder with the tip of his tongue and she closed her eyes and sighed. A signal for him to speak, 'If for only this night you will give yourself to me completely, let me possess you as Shah Jahan possessed his wife, I promise you will not be sorry. We can pretend we're great lovers for all eternity and act out our love accordingly.'

His hand lingered on her shoulder and she covered it with hers and told him, 'Yes.' Her heart was racing at the very prospect of being loved like that. She repeated, 'Yes.'

After such a night at the Taj Mahal, Anoushka yearned for sexual oblivion. They hardly knew each other but what Alexander proposed could not be missed.

With great finesse he unzipped her dress and slipped the slender shoestring straps off her shoulders. The gown fell to the floor, 'Oh, yes,' he told her, admiration in his husky voice. He kissed her back and licked a trail of kisses down her spine to the crack between the cheeks of her bottom. He slipped one arm round her and caressed her breasts. With the other he reached beneath her and found the warm slit waiting for his caresses. He fondled her breasts and the soft pink flesh of her cunt lips and probed deeper with searching fingers, hoping to give them both the sexual pleasure they were so eager for.

Anoushka could sense his hunger for her and leaned back that little bit more into him. He bit into her shoulder and sucked her flesh into his mouth. She turned round and Alexander saw her naked breasts and her provocative nipples, the stunningly sensuous body he had imagined, revealed to him in all its glory. The triangular patch of blonde pubic hair commanded his attention. He lowered his lips to it and sucked the mound beneath into his mouth. And then, taking her in his arms, he kissed her passionately. He nibbled at her lips and whispered words of love between kisses while he removed his jacket.

Anoushka sensed an urgency in him as strong as her own. She helped him, tearing at his shirt. He unbuckled his belt and she helped him off with his trousers. In the dim light they saw reflections of themselves in the many mirrors round the room. So sensual, the many reflections of their nakedness and together-ness, the aura of sex. It added a certain air of depravity that excited their passion to come together.

'I love you. You're the passion of my life. I want to die in sexual bliss with you, many times, again and again, and always to rise again to give you love and more lust and to draw from you orgasm after orgasm. I want you spent with come.'

Heady sentiments although they knew it was pretence, but it was what was called for and sounded wonderful and Anoushka played her rôle, imagining herself to be loved as no other woman had ever been loved.

'I love you, my life, my heart,' she told him, and opened her cunt lips with her own fingers and spread them as far apart as she could so that he might see what she offered was real and for him. He raised her up off the floor by her waist and thrust her upon his rock hard, pulsating phallus. She watched his massively erect penis inch its way into her cunt.

Tense with excitement, Anoushka whimpered at being taken like that by this young poet. A man rampant, taking possession of an open and willing, more than ready cunt – she thought it one of the most beautiful sights in the world. She wrapped her legs round his waist and held on that way in a tight grip, bending backward so that he might penetrate deeper, so that she might feel the full force of his lust for her. His hands on her hips he moved her on and off his penis while hungrily sucking on her breasts. He walked round the room with her like that and they looked at themselves in the various mirrors. It incited lust and pride, a love of themselves as erotic souls living out their fantasy.

She was surprised how very sexual a man he was, how ardent he could be, the sexual control he had over himself – she hadn't been ready for that in him. At first he was subtle in taking possession of her, almost delicate in the way he used his lips, his

166

mouth, his penis. His penetrations were slow, exquisite, deep. His withdrawals tantalisingly sexy. He created a symphony of fucking, the rhythm increasing with the passion until the beat was a crescendo of lust for cunt and love. His violent passion had built slowly but now it took them over and excited Anoushka to come. She felt his body tense while she was coming. He kissed her and bit into her lips and mouth and told her between kisses, 'Next time hold your breath for as long as you can just before you come. The pleasure will treble. Your orgasm will be so intense you'll want to die in it.'

He took her to the bed and there leaned her over it. Clasping her by the waist, he took her from behind. She crawled on to the bed on her knees and raised her bottom. She felt his genitals slap against her cunt lips as he fucked her and more pleasure, more excitement took them over. He was at that point of animal lust when love vanishes and violent love-hate fucking reigns supreme. His fucking now was reminiscent of Robert's. She could drive him to that very same state. Anoushka squeezed hard with the muscles of her cunt and gripped Alexander. She created a rhythm of pressure and release that was as seductive as it was pleasurable for a man. It drove both of them closer to a state of sexual ecstasy. Anoushka took an even more sexually aggressive role now, and all their acts of love and lust began all over again for them.

Alexander withdrew from her. Gathering her in his arms he told her, 'You're fantastic. How poor I would have been had I not had this intimate few hours with you. I'm so grateful to have loved you, if only for this short time. If I were to die now in your arms, I would have lived a full and rewarding life, Anoushka.'

She wanted to weep for joy. To be loved like that. In all the years with Robert he had never made her feel as this young man did. There were more kisses and words of praise for her. His hunger for her was like an aphrodisiac. She came, and came again, and then lost track of her many orgasms. She had never been a woman ashamed of her lust or her ability to come as often as she did when she was in flagrante delecto. Quite the contrary, she was proud of her erotic soul, her ability to give herself up to lust and a man so completely.

She slipped on top of Alexander and he had her that way, raising and lowering her on his penis. Completely lost in lust, she never heard the door open or close. She was leaning over him, her breasts swaying over his face, his mouth catching them first one then the other to suck on, when she felt another pair of hands caress her bottom, another pair of lips kissing her back, another penis placed between the cheeks of her bottom. She came in a tidal wave of come, so intense she called out in a scream of pure pleasure.

'Hold your breath for as long as you can, make your body rigid and then when you're on the edge let go, collapse into sexual ecstasy. You'll have the ride of a lifetime.'

She did as she was told and during that time felt the coolness of a silky smooth cream between the cheeks of her bottom and in that tight secret place, then caresses and probings. But as intensely exciting as these new sensations and those created by Alexander were, she held on to her breath, held back her moment of orgasm for as long as she could. Then Alexander called out, 'Now! Come with me, now.' And they did. All three died in the arms of the god Eros, their god for the night. It was sex lost in the madness of ecstasy, pure sexual bliss.

Anoushka lost track of her orgasms and just before she submitted to exhaustion and a deep sleep that was more like slipping into a coma, felt the flow of warm luscious sperm and a strange peace and contentment.

When she awakened she was lying clasped in Alexander's arms. She kissed him awake. His first words were, 'I have never had a more exciting woman. I will always love you for giving yourself to me so completely.' He kissed her with passion and a love that was genuine. She watched his penis come alive again and, lying on their sides facing each other, he draped her leg over his hip and entered her. He throbbed with lust for her and told her, 'To die inside a woman, Anoushka. What more can a man ask for?'

They never mentioned the other man who had vanished as silently as he had arrived.

It was there in that beautiful room with her young lover that Anoushka came to terms with her real self, not the woman she had created for Robert, her sexuality, her struggle between the spirit and the flesh. After several days in Agra, she rediscovered the joys of her sexuality with several other men and enjoyed, as she once had before Robert, the desire they felt for her.

The next few months travelling with Page and Sally: in the Himalayas, Tibet, Ceylon, were a learning process for Anoushka which allowed her to realise how she had been deprived of attention, love and sexual passion without artifice or ulterior motive, and above all without deceit. She found a lost part of herself and her confidence in who and what she was kept building. Anoushka found she could respect herself again and there was no longer any doubt in her mind that she would find a love, rich and sensuous, loyal and true. But this time it would not govern her life, merely add to it.

The three women joined the schooner *Black Orchid* in Sicily. Piers Hazlit had allowed them to make the Atlantic crossing and was there to introduce them to the crew and instruct the captain. He had been swept up by the adventurous spirit of the three women. He, like them, found it thrilling that they should learn to sail for no other reason than wanting to crew *Black Orchid* across the Atlantic. How could he not give them his three-masted yacht as their training vessel?

Piers and Anoushka spent a night and a day together. They talked to each other, bared their souls, and found themselves slipping into love. An accident? Fate? Who knew? But Anoushka did not feel ready for anything as important as love with Piers. Oh, yes, she knew immediately that he was a man she could build the rest of her life with, share the good and the bad and the beautiful with. Here was a man she wanted her sons to know and love. A man she wanted to be part of her life for as long as she lived. But there were Sally's feelings to be considered. Loving Piers presented a dilemma for Anoushka, so she did what she always did, blanked it out of her mind, and placed Piers and her ultimate happiness on the back burner of her life.

Once the arrangements for their training had been worked out between the captain of *Black Orchid* and the women, Piers left for an expedition of Ethiopia. Anoushka, Page and Sally, enchanted by Italy, toured Sicily and Calabria. From there they journeyed to Greece to make Page's house in Hydra their base. The plan was for Anoushka to work on her translation for Hadon Calder, and for them to island hop as and when they liked.

For months, the flowers, the gifts and the love letters from Piers to Anoushka kept coming. No man, save for the poet Alexander Maar, had ever written verses for her or sent her love letters. They reached her wherever she was, and slowly Piers won her over until she was helpless to resist.

Chapter 12

Anoushka was sitting in the sun on the terrace of Page's house high above Hydra's port and looking down over the tiled roofs and terraces, the lime-washed island houses and narrow cobbled streets where donkeys were still the only mode of transport. She shielded her eyes against the sun and gazed across the Agean sea of dark rich blue, its waves silver-capped by the sun playing on the water.

She was thinking about the Taj Mahal and how she had seen it for the first time, by the light of a full moon. How they had picnicked in the garden by candlelight, an Indian feast, with Page and Sally, Jahangir and Alexander, the sitar player, a dancing girl, and white-turbanned servants. The scene was still vivid in her mind.

Church bells were ringing from the many little white-washed churches dotted round the rocky landscape of Hydra. They echoed over the island, some from far off, others from close by, and Anoushka closed her eyes and thought of that night in Agra. Despite being on a Greek island she decided one more time to relive that afternoon, the night, and the sunrise as it rose over the sugary white edifice dedicated to love. The same love she had once believed Robert had for her. What an ego!

Anoushka rose from her chair, poured herself another cup of coffee and walked with it to the end of the terrace where she sat down on the wall. Dressed in nothing but a near-transparent sarong made from a sari of royal blue silk, bordered with small hand-made cream-coloured silk flowers, that had been a gift from Jahangir, she placed her cup and saucer on the wall. Taking some of the fabric in her hands, she held it in front of her and looked at the view through it. She played with it, made sweeping movements of her arm. The flimsy silk danced on the soft hot breeze coming off the sea. It was reminiscent of the way the Indian dancing girl had moved seductively with her cream-coloured transparent silk scarf.

Seductive was surely the operative word for that entire magical night: indeed for the whole bewitching time with Jahangir in Agra.

That night had added much to Anoushka feeling quite different from the Anoushka who had sailed out of New York on board the *QE2*. Sometimes, when she spoke to her sons, the old Anoushka slipped back but more often than not the new one was listening to her sons, getting to know them. Every day something new was happening to her and as her confidence built, and she was able to deal with life on her own, she was more grateful for the company of Sally and Page. Together they had somehow managed to brave the past and leave it behind and each in their own way was working on their present as if there was no tomorrow.

One thing, however, never did change for Anoushka. Every night when she went to bed she missed the company of a man next to her. The warmth of a body, someone to share sexual passions with, someone to love and be loved by. Many hours passed, as they did now as she sat on the terrace wall in the sunshine, when her voracious libido wept for a mate. At those times, as now, she relived her time of sex and love with Alexander Maar on the night of their visit to the Taj Mahal.

She heard the sound of the ferry boat's horn, three blasts just before it rounded the corner and came into sight. It broke the excitement of erotic memory, mental masturbation, that had taken possession of her. Anoushka opened her eyes for only a second and then closed them again and sighed, a deep sigh of satisfaction. She had come several times while drawing that night of sex with Alexander from the recesses of her mind. She always did when she relived it. She bit into the flesh covering the knuckle of her hand and felt once more a strong orgasm. Her release complete, she called out, a little cry of pleasure, and opened her eyes.

Piers walked towards her. 'There's no running away this time, Anoushka.' Then taking her hands in his, he raised her from the wall where she was still sitting and took her in his arms. He held her close.

'How long have you been standing there watching me?' she asked.

'Long enough. Do you often come by yourself?'

She flushed pink with embarrassment and he smiled and kissed her on the lips, then the tip of her nose.

'What are you doing here, Piers? Why have you come?' she asked, trying to conceal her sense of joy at seeing him again.

172

'I love you, Anoushka, I came to tell you that. I'm here because I'm lonely without you, and needed to see you. Don't protest, I know you love me. I knew it that second time we met, and so did you.'

'Oh please, Piers, don't say any more. We promised each other time.'

'I'll give you time, the rest of my life. Is anyone in the house?'

'No. Sally and Page are spending a few days on the mainland. I stayed behind to work. But what if they had been? I told you, I will never hurt Sally.'

'Neither will I. Say you love me?'

'I can't.'

'You will.'

He took her by the hands and then stepped back a pace to look at her. 'You're so changed. I hardly recognise you as the woman I met at The Connaught.' He raised her arm high above her head and had her do a turn and when she was face to face with him again, he pulled on the sarong. It parted and like a massive, exotic butterfly crumpled to the terrace floor. Then he grasped her in his arms and kissed her passionately.

She knew she loved him. Sally and Page had known it even before she did. It had been Sally who had said, 'If he has to love anyone more than me, I would rather it be you than any other woman, then I can keep you both as friends.' She was being courted by Jahangir at the time, but had given no indication as to whether she was serious about him. Under the circumstances, it was magnanimous of her to have said that. Too magnanimous for Anoushka to accept it as truthful. Her own experience of Rosamond stealing Robert from her was still vivid in her memory and she simply could not bear to inflict that pain on Sally, on any woman for that matter. Yet she found herself falling helplessly in love with Piers. And now he was here in Hydra.

Without a word, she took his hand and kissed it and led him to her room. And there she kissed him on his lips, again and again, as she undressed him. This was their first carnal encounter. In whispers they spoke of love and lay down together on her bed.

'Anoushka, I love you.'

'I know.'

'I want you to be a part of my life. I can't imagine making a life with any other woman. We'll see the world together, create great adventures for ourselves. And we'll live in the most wonderful house: Chalfont.'

'Piers, I like having the same man in bed next to me every

night. I thrill anew every time I give myself to the man I'm committed to. But you had better know, I wasn't very good at being the perfect housewife. I'm sloppy in the kitchen, and I'm too lax with my children. I would have brought them up in an even more haphazard fashion than I have had it not been for my husband.'

Piers began to laugh but she stopped him, saying, 'It's not funny, you have to know the bad side of me, and there is one. I let things slide by, just happen. And I was smug, oh, so smug about having a handsome, famous, and successful husband. I liked his fame, his fortune, and loved him for his sexual soul and intelligence, the cool, orderly life style he demanded for himself and rarely got by being married to me. I had all that and loved it and lost it. And I'm still in shock, still smarting from my failure to keep a relationship together. I have a great many ghosts to lay because I tried to be the woman he wanted.

'Piers, never again will I pretend to be other than I am, no matter how much I may want to make you happy. I've done that, been there. Nor will I sit home and wait for you as if my world revolved round you. I've done that too.'

'Have I asked you for that? How can you think I would cheat you like that? I'm not Robert, Anoushka. Nor are you Sally. A marriage of convenience is not what I'm looking for. If it was I would have married her. Love, romance, passion, the chemistry that has happened between us, that's what I've been looking for in various ways all my life. It happened to us both and we are damned well not going to lose it.'

Anoushka kissed him. There were tears of joy in her eyes. She loved him for so many reasons, not least of all the genuine sweetness that combined with the virility of the man.

'Be patient with me. I have wounds that are still not healed. I want my life to be as valid as yours, and to be a whole person, respected for myself. I want to share my life with you just as much as I want you to share yours with me. Does that make sense?'

'A great deal of sense. What more can a man want from the woman he loves? Marry me. Say you will.'

'I need time.'

'For what?'

'To be sure. Not of you, but of myself. There are things to be done, people to confront, situations to be addressed, ghosts to be laid.'

'Do you love me?'

She smiled at him and confessed, 'Since that very first time we

174

met. For just a few seconds the world stopped still for me. We linked and the pain of the past fell away. We were together and it was finite. Then Sally arrived and I knew that I had to put you out of my mind. I did, but you never left my heart. Weeks later when we met again on board the *Black Orchid*, I told myself: Hold back, hold back. But love was there and overwhelmed me. We talked away those twenty-four hours we had together and fixed ourselves in each other's lives. In that short time we got to know each other better than Robert and I ever did, and I was married to him for thirteen years. Of course I love you, with all my heart.'

All the while she spoke Piers and Anoushka had been caressing each other. Now he lowered his lips to her breasts and kissed them. She kissed the knob of his penis, then continued fondling his erect phallus, his scrotum and the balls within the sac. There was no urgency in their lovemaking, it was as if they had been making sweet love to each other all of their lives.

He ran his fingers through her hair, and she said, 'There's Sally to think about. She's my friend. I can't betray her.'

'It was Sally who told me you were here.'

'She knows how we feel about each other?'

'She knows I'm in love with you.'

Anoushka's voice trembled. She fought back tears of shame and asked him, 'How could you do that? Tell her?'

'I didn't. She told me over lunch a few weeks ago. Sally is a remarkable girl, much wiser and more self-sufficient than you might think.'

'Was she upset?'

'No. She's in love with Jahangir and that's made her more sympathetic to what was missing from the life we had together. She's not stupid. Far from it. She always understood what was missing from our relationship, but was happy in it so didn't care. As she said over lunch, "What you've never had, you never miss, so I got on with being happy with what I did have with you".'

Anoushka felt relief at what she heard. But still something held her heart in check. The past? Other people's pasts and how they had affected her life? Could she believe that with her loving and being loved by Piers, Sally would feel none of the pain Anoushka still felt every time she thought of Rosamond and Robert? Deceit cuts deep. The circumstances were different, yes, but the pain of loss . . . that had to be the same for Sally as it was for Anoushka. That sense of worthlessness, the failure of being thrown over by a man, it had to be the same for Sally, for most women who had been tossed out of a man's life, been replaced by another woman.

175

She looked deep into Pier's eyes and saw his love for her there. It was unmistakable. When had she seen love like that? Maybe a hint of it once, and it had touched her heart then as Piers's love did now, but that had been so many years ago when she had been a mere child. Anoushka was overwhelmed by such love. She took Piers's hands, one at a time, and raised them to her lips. She kissed them, once, twice. A sigh came from the depths of her soul and she told him, 'There's so much you don't know about me.'

'Tell me?'

'Not now, not yet. Give me time, Piers.'

'And if I don't?'

'You will if you love me.'

He adjusted the pillows on the bed so that she was comfortable and then slid on top of her. He kissed her face, and then raising her arm kissed it from the fingertips to her shoulder. He continued his kisses over her breasts. Sucking Anoushka's nipples made her squirm with pleasure. With one powerful and deep thrust, for the first time Piers entered the woman he knew he would love as no other in his life ever again. She came immediately, a long and luscious, powerful orgasm. She screamed passionately. 'God, yes. Yes, help me!'

Anoushka felt herself slipping away, dying, in ecstasy. She tried several times to hold her breath, stem the feeling flowing out of her. Impossible. It was fucking as exquisite as she had ever had, thrusts filled with passion and love while they devoured each other's flesh with hungry mouths. Piers came and was no less vocal than Anoushka had been. There was something primeval in their howls to heaven. The sap of their souls flowing together was more sweet, more enriching than life itself. Together they were something special and very private, a force all their own that they had never experienced with any other person.

In the next few hours they lost themselves in each other. They covered each other with their come, tasted it in their mouths. Anoushka wanted to suck every drop of his seed into her womb. To hold it there forever. This was fucking governed by love, passion, yes, but respect and adoration too. When they lost themselves so completely in the erotic world they created for themselves, they became nothing more than pure sexual bliss.

Anoushka had never felt so complete in herself, so full of love and passion. She had it all. Pure happiness, sacred love, contentment.

All day they shared themselves with each other until they bathed and dressed and, hand in hand, walked down the steep

176

cobbled street and twisting stone stairs flanked by the high white-washed walls of other island houses. They went to the port for some supper. Over grilled *barbounia* fresh from the sea only hours before and a bottle of retsina, the resinated white wine Anoushka had at last acquired a taste for, there seemed little to say. Instead they watched the drama of the port coming alive in the early hours of the evening. Pure Greek theatre. The fishing boats bobbed up and down. People passed them by, smiled, greeted them, Anoushka being by now known on the island, as were Page and Sally. The scent of lamb and rosemary on charcoal, perfume to the hungry.

'You're very quiet,' said Piers.

'So are you,' she answered.

'I understand, Anoushka.'

'You do, don't you? Thank the lord for that. This is the most important time of my life, Piers.'

'You're the most important woman who has ever entered mine. I want to live with you, and love you, and die in your arms. But we'll not have any more lovemaking again, not until you're ready to make a commitment to me. Don't keep me dangling, Anoushka. Not if you love me as I love you.'

They remained silent while they both absorbed the importance of what Piers was saying and then Anoushka spoke.

'I want to make the Atlantic crossing with the girls on board the *Black Orchid*. Be there for me in the Caribbean when the boat docks. It's a long time to ask you to wait, so please don't. Get on with your life, and I'll get on with mine. If we still, each of us, feel the same about each other as we do now, then ask me to marry you again. I promise you'll have your answer then and there. Until then, think about us, Piers, take your time, look for someone else, make certain that you and I together forever is what you really want. I'll do the same. There can be no second mistake for me. Will you do that for me. No, for us?'

He hesitated. It was a great deal to ask of him they both knew it. 'Please, promise me?' she added, a tremor of emotion in her voice.

He smiled at her, reluctantly and said, 'You don't make it easy. I promise.'

She took his hand in hers and squeezed it.

He looked up at the sky. It was still bright but a moon was rising. 'I have to go before dark.'

'How did you get here?'

'A helicopter. It landed in Kamini.' Anoushka tried to rise from her chair. He stopped her.

177

'Piers, please.'

'No, don't come with me. No goodbyes. I'm too happy for farewells. Do what you have to to love me.' He rose from his chair and leaned over to kiss her lightly on the lips. Leaving some banknotes on the table, he walked away, never looking back.

Long after Piers had disappeared from her view, Anoushka thought about him and the life that they could build together. She had no doubt that the boys would like him, he was after all a real adventurer, not forced by circumstances to become one as she was.

Life was easy for Piers. He had no dilemmas, no past to overcome. When had he been a failure? He had never had his world torn away from him. He carried no baggage from the past to weigh him down as she did. She had no intention of carrying the burden of her failures and mistakes on her back like so much luggage into a new life with him. That would be too unfair on both of them. Anoushka loved him and knew that he was the right man for her, there was no doubt in her mind about that. But she could not bring herself to throw caution to the wind and run off with him. Not yet anyway.

She walked from the port through the darkened streets and up the many stairs to Page's large multi-level house, white against the blackness of night. It was in darkness and Anoushka fumbled her way through the gate in the wall and up more stairs on to the terrace. It was a marvellous night, still very warm, and the sky was peppered with stars. There was magic in the air, as there had been magic in her coming together with Piers. She felt as if she were going to burst with happiness.

Anoushka had not seen the ghost that haunted the house. Page believed that she had, many years ago, and Sally claimed that it was a man and that he had awakened her from a deep sleep, caressing her cheek. Though she could not remember what he looked like she did remember that as the dawn light slid into her room, he slipped away through the open window overlooking the sea. The locals all knew a ghost lived in Page's house, and that he was a good ghost, an old and wealthy sea captain who had owned many sponge boats at the turn of the century. He had built the house for the woman he loved, a young Egyptian beauty whom he wanted to marry. She led him on, promising she would give him her answer when the house was completed, and then kept asking for more rooms to be added, more terraces, more land, until even she had been satisfied by the house, then as now the grandest on the island, built in the most perfect setting. When the house was completed she refused him.

Heartbroken, he retired and lived in the house and waited for her to change her mind. She never did, and even after he was dead he refused to leave his house, or to stop loving her, and roamed through the rooms looking for her, waiting.

Anoushka thought about the sea captain and his love and was pleased that he was still there if in spirit only, though she wished his spirit would find rest eventually. That a great love would come his way and live with him there. He had waited so long.

There was something otherworldly about the place. More than once the women had spoken about the magic of the house, the spirit that lived in it. When Page had bought it some ten years before it had been empty, derelict, and it was to her credit that she had painstakingly restored it and kept it very nearly as the captain had built it so as not to spoil what he had given his heart to. That was it, the house had real heart. How Anoushka wished that Page and Sally were there with her to share this night and the magic of Hydra and Page's house perched high above the port.

But Sally and Page were not there. They were in Athens for a few days. Page to see an architect and go to the bank, and Sally shopping. Both planned to do the museums and go on an excursion to Delphi. It was hot and sticky and a dreadful smog hung over the city, the exhaust fumes of Athens traffic trapped in a cloud of unhealthy air. Page couldn't wait to leave this place she had once loved so much. This was certainly not the Athens of her youth with bright blue skies, a sun you could see clearly shining over the city. Athens at that time was a crossroads not for package tourists but for real travellers: poets and writers, painters and sculptors, philosophers and dreamers, romantics from every walk of life, in search of the Greek experience.

At the very same time of year, to the very day in fact, for very nearly seven years now Page would stop for one afternoon and one night in Athens before she took the ferry boat to Hydra. This was not that time of year but when Sally and Anoushka had both said they wanted to visit Greece, she had thought, Why not? They were a part of her life now, so she told them about her house in Hydra. They had been her first and only guests in the house, this most personal and private place. It had been a major step for her to open the doors of the Hydra house to them, and one she did not regret.

And now here she sat in her favourite café, at her favourite table, and watched the world go by over a cappuccino and a sticky

179

pastry. Nearly every time she sat here she would meet someone she knew passing through the city, just as she was. Invariably she saw faces she recognised: Greeks and expatriates who made Athens their home.

She bathed now as she always did in the warmth and generosity of the Greek people. Did any other love living in the street as the Greeks did? She doubted it. It had become just another cosmopolitan city when once it had been much more than that, the most charming, least sophisticated, largest village in the world. It was via Athena to Hydra every year that Page returned to fulfil a pact with destiny.

She saw Sally weaving her way through the lunchtime crowds. She was late as usual, but that no longer mattered to Page. She and Anoushka had got used to Sally's inability to take time seriously and she in turn had learned to accept the flaw of punctuality her two friends suffered from.

Sally, looking tanned and pretty as a glossy poster, was loaded down with shiny, brightly coloured shopping bags. Athens was a city not of a thousand and one nights but a thousand and one boutiques. You would have thought the Greeks had invented the word, the very idea.

Page laughed aloud when she saw an animated Sally in a white linen mini skirt and a thin silk blouse that left an inch of midriff showing, swing wide with a black and pink Yves St Laurent shopping bag and hit on the shoulder a middle-aged hairy and grossly unattractive man who was obviously failing to keep his pinching fingers to himself. Sally pressed on through the crowd towards Zonar's and her meeting with Page.

The man stopped in his tracks and loudly bellowed obscenities in Greek at her, while at the same time looking stunned. He had his rights. Some people laughed, others cursed him for his rudeness as they passed him by. And Sally left a trail of admirers turning their heads, stopping to watch her walk with head held high away from the scene. Not the most subtle of the Greek men. But she had mastered the art of dealing with their attentions within a few days of being in Greece. She was adroit in her own special way.

But who was she jabbering away to? Who did she have with her? Page couldn't quite see the face of the person Sally was with, obscured as it was by the crowd of people on the pavement. As Sally reached the corner she had to wait for a traffic light to change. The jaywalkers marched against the red light, the crowd thinned out and at last the mystery was revealed. It was Cally.

However had she found Cally? Well, that was Athens, and that was Sally. There were very few places where Page and Anoushka and Sally had been in the last few months where one or another of Sally's friends hadn't popped up from nowhere. She attracted friends and good times. She liked the sweet life and the sweet life liked Sally. It was to her credit that she knew what she wanted, what made her happy, and wanted nothing more. Indeed would settle for nothing less.

Page marvelled at how lucky she had been with her two companions. She had learned much from travelling with these two women so different from herself. They had become friends without even trying. They had been compatible when none of them had really thought they would be. Without any effort at all they became something important, very important, in each other's lives. Each had respect and admiration for the other's qualities and a courteous disregard for their faults.

Page had had no idea what her life was going to be when she had walked away from her work and the lifestyle she had been leading for so many years, and placed that ad in the *International Herald Tribune*. Change her whole life? Could it be done? Would she really do it? Others who knew her well doubted that she would. Page never thought about such things, merely got on with doing them. In fact it was far easier than people had told her it would be. Her timing had been right. Could that be it? Was everything in life a matter of timing?

Why did it suddenly seem so easy to do all the things you wanted to do? Have all the things you wanted to have? And with very little effort. Page watched Sally and her friend Cally scan the sea of faces outside the café looking for her. She raised an arm and waved.

'Hi. Look who I bumped into,' was Sally's greeting.

It was an amusing lunch, not much different than any other they had had with Sally's friends. But there was an appointment to go to for Page, and a Greek ship owner's yacht to board for a cruise round the islands for Cally. So there were hurried farewells and, 'See you in London. Or come and stay with us in St Tropez,' from Cally.

Sally divided the shopping bags between them and the two women went together to keep Page's appointment at the bank where she transferred a large sum of money into Greece. Some from the women's mutual account, some from Page's own. Sally watched and listened, and when they left the bank, she said, 'Then you've decided to build your greenhouse in Hydra and raise rare, exotic orchids?'

'Yes.'

'I think the sea captain would like that.'

Page looked at her. 'Funny you should say that. I think so too.'

'Jahangir wants to come to Hydra and stay with us in the house.'

The look on Page's face was one of sheer terror. The two women stopped on the pavement. Sally shifted all her shopping bags to one hand and with the other reached out and touched Page. 'It's all right, Page. I've told him he can't.'

'I'm sorry, Sally.'

'No need to be. I don't want him to come, he doesn't belong there. We're not insensitive, Anoushka and I. We know that Hydra is more than a house to you. Something very special and private in your life that until we came along you shared with no one. We feel very privileged that you allow us to stay there with you.'

The two women resumed their walk back to their hotel. Sally continued, 'I don't really want Jahangir there. I've become strangely possessive about your house, wanting to protect it and keep it safe for you and the captain. I know Anoushka feels the same way, just like Marika and Sotiri. You're lucky to have them watch over it when you're not there. It's the house, and the way you relate to it. It casts a powerful spell.'

'I'm so glad that I opened it to you and Anoushka. So pleased that you love it and the Greek islands the way I do. That you girls weren't disappointed in them.'

'I don't think I will ever forget Hydra as the ferry rounded the point of the island and I saw it for the first time. Magic, sheer magic! The crescent of houses, bright white under a burning sun, meandering lazily up and up, higher and higher, from the harbour to the top of the island. It took my breath away then and it does every time I see it. No wonder the captain loved it and built his house there. No wonder he won't leave it. Nor will you, I think.'

'No, I don't suppose I ever will.'

'Now that I know your house, Page, and I've met the captain – well, sort of met the captain – I somehow feel wherever I go, wherever I end up, I will have lived in paradise for a short time and on the edge of something miraculous. When we make one of our island jaunts and return to Hydra and that ferry boat blasts its horn and rounds the point and sails into port, I look up the side of the hill and feel the magic, the specialness of your house. The long elegant stone staircase rising from the terrace to the loggia, the tiled roofs as it rises tier above tier up the side of the hill.

'I'm a funny old thing you know. I loved Chalfont, Piers's country seat. I always knew I never belonged there. Too common, the Lancashire lass living with the toff and all that. I was never really part of it, it could never be mine. But none of it mattered to me. I loved being whatever I was there, waiting for Piers to come home to Chalfont and me. The house in Hays Mews – well, I loved living there too, felt it to be my home at least as much as Chalfont was. I've been privileged to live in those places, and now in Hydra, in your house. I don't mind that sense of belonging in someone else's place, someone else's house.'

'Do you still mind terribly losing Piers? I shouldn't have asked that. You don't have to answer. How indiscreet of me.'

'I might not have wanted to answer a few months ago. But now, why not? The answer is, not as much since Jahangir has come into my life.'

'He certainly is smitten, Sally, *and* persistent. Wow, is he persistent.'

The two women laughed and Sally said, 'And it's working. Every day I find myself falling in love with him that little bit more.'

'Then you do love him?'

'Oh, yes. I suppose that too is why Piers's falling for Anoushka is only causing me the slightest touch of pain.'

'She would be unhappy if she knew you were feeling any pain, no matter how slight, because of her.'

'Well, she'll have to resolve that one for herself. No one likes losing their life, she must certainly appreciate that. And let's face it, that's what Piers was to me, my life.'

The two women were walking up the stairs to the Hotel Grande Brittagna. Page was touched deeply by Sally's understanding that there was more going on for her in the Hydra house than anywhere in the world. The spirit of the place had rubbed off on Sally and Anoushka.

At the concierge's desk the two women handed over the shopping bags to be sent to their rooms and Page suggested, 'Let's go to the bar.'

'Why not?'

When had Sally not been agreeable? Her answer prompted Page to place an arm round her and the two women laughed and walked into the bar.

Seated, a chilled bottle of champagne opened and bubbling in crystal flutes, they raised their glasses and drank, a silent toast to the gods. They were happy.

183

'About Jahangir . . .'

'Oh, he's all right. He just misses me. Can't understand why I won't throw away the life I'm living at present and move into the Holland Park house with him.'

'He's asked me that same question enough times. Sally, I must confess, I'm surprised you don't either.'

'No more than I am,' she said.

'Then you want to?'

'Oh, yes.'

'Then why don't you?'

'Because I don't want to become a habit that Jahangir has acquired, the way I was for Piers. There, I've said it, admitted it to myself.'

She drained her glass and held it out to Page for a refill. Page saw the pain in Sally's eyes and didn't know what to say so she remained silent.

Sally drank more champagne and said, 'My life, the one I like and will have again with Jahangir, is the same lifestyle I had with Piers: being there for my man, waiting round for him to come home from playing elsewhere with his toys while I play with mine – shopping and girlie lunches, charity extravaganzas, gossiping on the phone, because that's me, what I want, what makes me happy. With only one difference: I intend for Jahangir to know very well before I move in with him how empty his life will be without me by his side.'

Was this Sally with the Barbie doll, empty-headed looks, and the passive, compliant nature, the answer to so many men's dreams? The Sally Page had so wrongly judged that first time they met in The Connaught.

'Don't look so surprised, Page. Just because I made myself a doormat for a man doesn't mean I didn't know how dirty I got. I had just never figured Piers would throw his mat out.'

'Oh, Sally,' said Page, pity in her voice.

'No, Page. Don't pity me. I'll give Piers this – living with him all those years gave me the security of a home, of having a man. If not wholly my own, at least a man who cared deeply about *me*, Sally Brown. Those years gave me time to build confidence in myself, learn who and what I am. He gave me time to better myself, and boy was I ambitious to do that! Because of him I learned to know my worth, enough so that if Jahangir wants me, loves me as he claims to, he'll have to bloody well make up his mind that Jahangir and I together, we're for keeps, and work at it as hard as I will. When he proves that, I'm moving in like a shot.

Once a doormat does not mean always a doormat.'

'Sally, you never cease to amaze.'

'Amaze? Well, maybe, but it's not easy. You see, I've fallen in love with the guy.'

'As much as you had with Piers?'

'Differently, very differently. With a greater passion in every way, even sexually. Piers always said he was leaving me because we didn't love each other, never had, that we suited each other first and loved each other for it. If I hadn't met Jahangir then I might always have believed he had said that just to get rid of me. This may sound perverse, but no matter if what Piers claims is true or not, I will always refuse to accept it. I won't cheapen those years we had together and my loving him, our loving each other, even if in the end he wouldn't make a commitment to me.'

'So you're waiting for Jahangir to . . .'

'Slip the ring on the finger.'

'He will, you know,' said Page.

'I know.'

And the two women laughed. They were irresistible to three attractive men at a table a few yards away. A fresh bottle of champagne was sent over to them and a message asking if the men might join them.

These were unusually attractive women quite used to the attention of men trying to make their acquaintance. When it suited, they could accept graciously.

'Why not? The man of your dreams might be right over there, Page.'

'The man of my dreams? Oh, I found him a long time ago. Like you, Sally, I await with anticipation the dream becoming reality.' Then she turned to the waiter and said, 'Tell the gentlemen it was kind of them to send the wine and we would indeed be delighted to share a glass of it with them.'

Chapter 13

The telephone rang once a day in the house in Hydra, and it was always Jahangir calling. Otherwise, the telephone remained silent. The women used it to call out but in deference to Page's wishes the telephone number had been given to no one else. They received all other calls at Sotiri and Marika's house down in the port, next to the post office. At first, Anoushka and Sally had thought it a strange arrangement to send a little boy running the steep climb from the port to Page's house screaming *Kiria* Cooper, *telephono*, or *Kiria* Sally, or *Kiria* Anna – he never could manage Anoushka. But after a few days they could see Page's point. What place did the outside world have in Paradise?

Anoushka was working well, she was two thirds of the way through the translation of Hadon's manuscript and feeling good about it. Sally was mixing with the in-crowd of foreigners living on the island, who Page had little to do with, so she was having fun. Page was reading and taking long walks or going out with Sotiri on a small kaiki for a day's fishing or exploring the far side of the island, when she wasn't doing work on the house. It was as if the women were in a time warp of lazy days of sunrises and sunsets. It was an idealic way to live. Simple, so very uncomplicated, from the purchase of a rough loaf of bread, to the taverna night life. There was no regimentation to their life on Hydra save for one thing: they were trying to get fit for crewing the *Black Orchid* across the Atlantic. It was the first step before their four-month training period. Sally was in charge of their regime since she was the only one who went to girlie keep-fit classes or did any running, as she had with Piers when he was training for one of his expeditions.

At six o'clock in the morning, no matter what, the three women ran from the house down to the port, from the port to the top of the island then down again, round the coast as far as the road went, and back. On their return to the port from their run they collapsed into chairs at their favourite cafe where they breakfasted on hot black coffee, fried eggs, sunny side up, bread and honey.

They were Hydra's morning attraction for the Greek men, admired by the foreigners, and thought quite mad by the local women. They returned home to twenty minutes of stretch exercises. Were they obsessive? Yes. But fascinating, and attractive, and living in one of the most beautiful houses of the island, and Page had always been generous to the church and those who had worked on the house, and so was respected by all the Hydriots. In a few weeks the *Black Orchid* would sail into Hydra's port to pick them up and they would be ready.

It was not as if the past was banned from these women's lives, they brought that with them, it was a part of them, what had made them what they were, influenced everything that they did. It was more that each of them had, without consulting the others, chosen not to talk about but to leave behind as much as possible the painful aspects of what had drawn them together. On the surface it appeared that both Page and Sally had or were making progress at coming to terms with that past, but Anoushka, possibly because of her sons with whom she regularly kept in touch, still felt deeply the humiliation and failure of her life. Only she carried that into their present.

They only had to look at her face when she returned after making her weekly call to the boys, or receiving a letter from her attorney with the merest mention of Robert, to know that.

Therefore when Anoushka, looking more disturbed than usual after a conversation with her sons, walked out on to the terrace where the three were having lunch under a two-hundred-year-old fig tree that was showing its new tender green leaves, Sally and Page were alerted to trouble.

'The boys want to say hello,' she announced, and handed the portable phone to Sally.

Page kept her eyes fixed on Anoushka. She seemed barely to be following the snatches of laughter and conversation of the dialogue. Finally Page spoke to the boys, answering the dozens of questions being fired at her across the Atlantic. It seemed they wanted assurances that they were going to have a great time with their mother during the summer holiday break without their friends, and TV, and the Lakeside country club. At last they seemed satisfied and hung up.

Page said, 'I think going out on the boat every day with Sotiri did it. I must say, Anoushka, I really do find your boys very clever for their age, very sure of what they want. I can't wait to meet them.'

188

But she hardly heard, she was somewhere far away in her thoughts. Page was certain that she did not imagine Anoushka's distress but looked to Sally for confirmation, and got it when she shrugged her shoulders.

'The boys sound fine, Anoushka, full of beans but very spoiled. All those present we sent them for their birthday – they really shouldn't have opened them yet. Now they'll have nothing from us on the day, and that's half the fun of birthday presents, getting them on the day.'

'What's wrong, Anoushka? Something is wrong, isn't it? Are you all right?' asked Sally.

She ignored the questions but answered instead with, 'You've both been wonderful about the boys. Striking up a friendship with them on the phone, signing my postcards to them. They always ask after you, want to know all about you. And you've been so generous to them. The croquet set from you, Page, all that polo gear from Sally.'

'Oh, that wasn't just me. That was Jahangir. We had great fun putting it together.'

Anoushka rose from the table and walked to the terrace wall and stood with her back to her friends, just staring out to sea. After some time she turned to the two women and said, 'This will be the first birthday my boys will have without me. Mishka is all excited about the party his father is giving them. I'm missing out on two things. It's Parents' Weekend at their school and their father will be there with Rosamond. The boys love Rosamond, have known her almost all of their lives. It's she who has arranged their birthday party as a culmination of the weekend.'

'Who's Rosamond?' asked Sally.

'Rosamond was our best friend. She's also, it turns out, the other woman, now sleeping in my bed. The family friend who managed to steal my family from me.'

'Oh,' said Page.

'I hate being so easily replaced. Parents' Day and the birthday – it hurts.'

'Do you want to be there?' asked Sally.

Anoushka, riddled with anxiety, lost her temper and snapped at her, 'What a stupid question, Sally. I'm their mother, I love them, of course I miss them and want to be there.'

Sally kept her calm and seemed not at all offended by Anoushka's outburst. 'It's not so stupid a question. If I wanted to be with my sons, I'd bloody well be there.'

Then she stood up and walked from the table. Anoushka

189

hurried across the terrace and grabbed her by the arm. 'Oh, Sally! Please, I didn't mean to call you stupid. I just feel such pain at not being with them, not being the one to plan their birthday party, not being a parent on Parents' Day, I just lashed out without thinking.'

'Don't worry. I didn't take any notice of it. But do tell me, why aren't you with them? Why don't you go?'

'Robert and David, that's my attorney, feel I shouldn't be jumping in and out of their lives during this time of adjustment for them. We'll have the summer holidays. I'm just being selfish, self-pitying.'

'Oh, really, Anoushka, don't be so wet! Fuck Robert and what he wants! And why are you letting your lawyer control your life? You want to go be with your boys on their birthday, so bloody well be with them. I would, and so I'm sure would Page.'

'Without question,' she answered.

'You do have visiting rights,' asked Sally.

'Yes, confirmed in writing.'

'Then why don't we all go? That's a great idea! We'll go along to give you support. Why should you have to do this alone? I'd love to meet them and see how they look in their polo gear,' said a very enthusiastic Sally.

Anoushka placed a hand on her forehead. It was a dizzying idea, one she had not even contemplated. How could she not have? Was she still so beaten down by Robert and his demands, his needs? 'You make it sound so simple. Just turn up. Robert will be furious.'

'Oh, really, Anoushka. Fuck Robert! You're not here on this earth to keep him happy, or had you forgotten that?'

'I'd have to face Rosamond.'

'So what?'

'Sally and I will be with you. Would you be happier if we all three went to Parents' Day and the birthday party?' asked Page.

'Would you do that for me?'

'Wouldn't you do it for us?' asked Sally.

'Of course, without hesitation.'

'So?' asked Page.

'I know I couldn't face it alone. It'd be such a surprise for the boys. They think we're such glamorous and adventurous ladies.'

'Well, we are. How many mothers and their girlfriends are planning to sail the Atlantic in a three-masted schooner?' asked a laughing Page.

'Oh, dare I?'

190

'Look, Sally and I don't know it all but from what I've heard and seen, Robert has walked over you long enough. You've regained your strength. Now don't you think it's about time you started to fight back?'

'I don't want to upset the children. They come first.'

'That's husband blackmail. What comes first is you and your children. You wait right here, I'm going for the calendar,' said Page, quite enthusiastic now that they had Anoushka motivated.

The enthusiasm slipped from Anoushka's face when she read the calendar. 'Well,' she told her friends, 'that was a great idea but impossible. Sally, you won't be here. You're written down here as going to meet Jahangir that weekend. And Page, you've made arrangements to be here alone for the next three weeks, from that Sunday, the last day of the Parents' Weekend and the evening of Mishka and Alexis birthday party.'

'And now it's you who has to pencil in the dates you want to be with the boys.'

Anoushka took the pencil and wrote, 'Connecticut, Anoushka'. Then she turned to her friend and said, 'That doesn't really solve the problem of facing this alone.'

Page took the pencil and added her name next to Anoushka's. Sally took the pencil from Page and did the same. The three women smiled at each other and Anoushka told them, 'I will never forget what you've both given up to help me through this.'

It was Page who rose from her chair this time and went to a far corner of the terrace to look out to sea. This year and one more to go, she told herself, and sighed. Returning to the calendar and her friends, she studied it well. She would not let Anoushka down but she would too have to be in the Hydra house as she had vowed to be and when she had vowed to be. It would take some planning.

'If we leave tomorrow for Paris, and Concorde from there to the States, with some fancy juggling we can arrive at the school on the Saturday morning, stay over for the Parents' Weekend and go to the boys' party. That's on the Sunday night, you said, Anoushka?'

'Yes, but there's a hitch. It's in Lakeside at our house. We'll have to arrange for transportation. Robert will probably fly down and take the boys back with him.'

'Then we'll do the same. A small plane from Kennedy Airport in New York to the school, a pickup and drop down the next day in Lakeside, then early the next morning I will have to leave to make Concorde back to Europe. The rest of you can stay on if

191

you like but if I am to keep my yearly vigil, which I fully intend to do, then I must be on the first Concorde flight out of the States. There. In theory we can do it.' She slammed the pencil down on the table and looked very pleased with herself.

'It's all too tight, it's asking too much of you,' protested Anoushka.

'Don't be so negative,' said Sally. 'Page has worked out her plans, and I'm giving nothing up. We'll take Jahangir with us. He'll understand and he'll be great, you'll see.'

Anoushka lost control of her emotions completely. She sat down, and cried, and was comforted by her friends.

The first call that went out was to Jahangir. Sally started the conversation with, 'Hello, darling. about this weekend – I have a problem. No, we three, Anoushka, Page and I, have a problem and we want to ask you if you will change the plans you've made?' And then she went to great lengths to explain the situation.

Page listened, in no doubt that Jahangir would acquiesce. The telephone was passed on to Anoushka. A stream of practical questions were issued from Jahangir. He then spoke to Page. When finally she placed the telephone on the table, she turned to her friends and said, 'We're in good hands, he'll have it all organised, well the mechanics of the travelling anyway. All we have to do is get ourselves to Paris.

Afterwards Sally looked extremely pleased with herself.

'Sally Brown, you look like the cat that swallowed the canary. Very, very smug. Do you have something you want to tell us?'

'He's wonderful! And so clever. When I said I needed him to change the plans he had made for our weekend together, he said, "They included a glorious setting for a dramatic proposal of marriage, one you could not refuse. However, the light has now dawned. I can see that if I am ever to get a yes from you, I will have to ask for your hand in marriage from Page and Anoushka, and more than likely consider them your dowry. Actually, I have for some considerable time been thinking that that's the way it's going to be. Marry you, marry them. Now, with this phone call, I am sure I've got that right".'

'Oh, Sally!'

'No, don't worry, Anoushka. I told him how clever he was to have worked it out. It's me and my two best friends he'll be getting.'

'What did Jaha have to say about that?' asked Page.

' "Well, thank goodness they're beautiful, and have charm and intelligence. And tell them I expect a yes without any further

192

hesitation. Do you hear me, Sally?" '

'And what did you answer?' Both Anoushka and Page were almost holding their breath with anticipation and in hope that she had given the right one.

'I said, "I think that's a great idea. Bring on the ring".'

'Sally, you've said you'll marry him!' said Anoushka.

'Yes, I guess I did. You'll both come along for the ride, won't you?'

There were whoops and hollers of joy and congratulation from Page and Anoushka, a few screams of excitement from Sally, and lots of kisses between the three women.

'What made you decide to give in finally? I know with Jaha you will live happily ever after, and it really will be till death do you part, otherwise he would never have pursued you as he has. Oh, I'm so happy for you! He'll give you back the lifestyle you love so much, and more of it than I think you have ever dreamed of.'

A laughing Sally said, 'And this time round, I know it's love for keeps for both of us. The deciding factor was Jahangir. His love and understanding were right there in something he said.'

'What? If you can tell us.'

' "As long as you have Page and Anoushka for best friends, I know you'll be happy with me." '

'When I asked him what he meant, his answer was so simple. I can't understand why I hadn't seen it myself. He said, "You'll never be lonely".

'I asked him what he meant by that and he answered me with, "I can be everything to you, your lover, your husband, the best man friend in your life, fulfil all your dreams, but I'm a man and you'll always love me as a man. That loneliness a woman has in her all the time, no matter how much she loves her husband and her children, the only real partner in that kind of loneliness can be another woman, her best girlfriend. You and Page and Anoushka, you absorb that loneliness you carry by being close to each other".'

Sally paused. It was an emotional moment for the three of them. Then she continued, 'And then he said, "Sally dear, this time try not to be late, and tell the girls I thank them. At least they've galvanised you to accept me and put me out of my misery".'

Until Jahangir had pointed out what best friends they were, none of them had realised what a cradle of support and inspiration they had become for each other. I have friends, was the thought that kept tripping over in Anoushka's mind as she punched in Robert's telephone number.

She checked her watch. The timing was perfect. She could see him now, in his office with his first cup of morning tea, Fortnum & Mason Royal Blend. He would be going over the night reports on his patients, studying them meticulously for the least hint of change or a problem before going on his rounds. He never operated before nine in the morning unless there was an emergency. How well she knew the pattern of his life. Out with the old wife, in with the new maybe, but she knew her Robert. When it came to his work it would not be out with the old pattern, in with a new one.

The ringing tone and a click. Anoushka's heart stood still. This was not going to be easy. Then the familiar sound of Mrs Winkler's voice, 'Hello, Dr Robert Rivers' secretary speaking.'

For a moment Anoushka hesitated, but only for a moment. 'May I speak to the doctor, Mrs Winkler?' There was hesitation on the other end of the line. 'Yes, Mrs Winkler, it's Anoushka Rivers.'

Mrs Winkler was all courtesy as she always was. 'So nice to hear from you. I hope you're well?'

'Yes, very well, thank you.'

'I don't know that the doctor's available . . .'

How many times had Anoushka heard that and accepted it as truth when it hadn't been? she wondered. 'I do know that the doctor is available. He's reading the night charts.'

'Then you must know too that he doesn't like to take calls during that time.'

'Frankly, Mrs Winkler, I don't give a damn! Tell him I am on the line and insist on speaking with him. It's very important. As important as his reading the charts.'

Several seconds passed and Anoushka rolled her eyes at Page and Sally who she insisted should remain with her. Then suddenly she heard his voice. 'Hello, Anoushka, I hope you're well?'

This was only the second time she had spoken to him since their separation and subsequent divorce. It did knock her a bit off balance, but she quickly regained her poise. 'I'm very well thank you, Robert.'

'What is it you want.'

'I don't *want* anything. This is a courtesy call.'

'Oh.'

Why had she never noticed when she had been married to him that he had nothing but contempt in his voice for her? She heard it now, so crystal clear, and hated him a little bit more for it.

'Robert, I spoke with the boys earlier and as a result have decided to fly over for Parents' Weekend and to be with them on their birthday.'

'I don't think that's a good idea, Anoushka.'

Now the voice had on its best bedside manner. The one he always used to talk her round to his way of thinking in some matter. Not this time, buster, she told herself, but what she said was, 'I don't care what you think, Robert. *I* think my boys have the right to have both their parents with them on Parents' Weekend and their birthday, separated as we are or not.'

'Divorced, Anoushka, divorced!' It was true, the divorce came through when she had been travelling in Sicily, but she tended to forget that. She ignored the correction.

'You've left this a bit late. How typical of you. Arrangements have been made.' There was more than annoyance in Robert's voice. Was it fury?

'Arrangements can be rearranged. Look, Robert, I don't want to get heavy about this but I do have it in writing, remember, visiting rights, any time I want to see my boys or the boys want to see me. I don't think this is an unreasonable visit and I'm sure you don't really.'

'No, of course it isn't. But I doubt that you will find any place to stay within fifty miles of the school. The inns and hotels will have been booked by the parents months ago. And then the party. . . it might be painful for you. It's in the house. They wanted a barbecue and all their friends from Lakeside and the school. I'm flying a dozen of the boys back just for the night.'

'It sounds wonderful for them. Tell them to bring sleeping bags. We'll need two of the guest rooms.'

'What are you talking about?'

'I'm coming with some friends, the women who will be playing host to the boys when they're with me on holiday.'

'That would be awkward.'

'Why, Robert? We have two sons we both love very much, and we don't want to create a tug of love situation or do anything to mar their happiness, do we? For their sake we'll be civil to one another, nothing more than that, and therefore you will open the house to me and my friends so we can be part of the birthday celebrations you've planned for them. I would expect to do the same for you on their next birthday.'

'And Rosamond?'

Anoushka chose to ignore the question. 'I won't like being there any more than you will like having me in the house, but yes, for our sons' happiness, I dare say we will be able to manage.'

'I don't like this, Anoushka, not at all. I concede your right to be at the Parents' Weekend, even to be with them some time on their birthday, but to crash in on a party Rosamond has been planning for months . . .' Here he hesitated for a few seconds then continued, 'That's so unfair of you.'

'Unfair! To stand up to Rosamond and remind her that they have a mother, and no matter how much she crawls into their lives I will still be there? Yes, I suppose it *is* unfair of me not to lie down and die for Rosamond so she can take over even my sons as she has taken over my husband and my life.'

'You see, there will be scenes. Is that fair to the boys?'

'No, you're wrong there, Robert, there will be no scenes. I wouldn't ruin the boys' weekend for the world.'

'Why do you and your friends insist on staying in the house? It's my house and I don't want you and some strangers in it.'

'My friends are not strangers and don't insist on staying in the house. I do. I want the boys to understand that you and I, Robert, no matter what our differences, will be together in bringing them up. That they live with you and Rosamond but I am welcome there as their mother and in Lakeside, and am not just some reject, some lowly untouchable who has been made to wander the world. I want them to see I have a life and friends, and am not the lonely woman you shipped off into exile, as I so stupidly agreed to.'

'Anoushka, you don't have friends. I have never known you to have a real friend in your entire life.'

She tried to keep her anger within bounds, but that last remark cut deep because it was so true. She had never had or wanted anyone but him from the very first time they met. 'Robert, you're a real prick, and I have had enough of this conversation. I've told you what I want. You see that I get it.'

'And if I don't?'

'Oh, I suggest you do, because if ever you hope to see those precious antique coins of *mine* again, either in your hands or in trust for the boys, you'd better come to terms with me.'

'That's blackmail.'

'Yes, it is, but at least I don't use my sons to get what I want.'

There was a long pause. No matter how many antique coins Robert might receive as gifts in the future, he knew that to lose even one irreplaceable coin was tantamount to disaster. He stressed, 'No scenes. Do I have your word on that?'

'You have my word. Robert. I didn't have to call and tell you

196

that I'm coming, but I'm glad that I did. Believe me, I will treat you better than you have done me. Don't tell the boys. I want it to be a surprise. I'll call the headmaster myself.'

Anoushka disconnected before Robert had a chance to say another word, placed the instrument on the table and her hands over her eyes. She felt quite exhausted.

'I think that's called playing hard ball. You were terrific,' said Sally.

Anoushka removed her hands. There was no sign of distress on her face, all anxiety was gone from her eyes.

'How do you feel?' asked Page.

'Just great. I'm going home.'

Later that evening the women walked down from their house and through the pretty narrow streets to a small taverna in a large walled garden. The proprietor placed a table and rickety wooden chairs in a quiet corner, against a wall hung with a trumpet vine.

They ordered lamb chops cooked over a fire of charcoal and sprigs of rosemary, a salad of tomatoes and feta cheese, dressed in a rich extra virgin oil and torn leaves of basil. A bottle of red wine was placed on the table and they sat in silence, listening to the sounds of the night all round them and a guitarist playing early Hadsadaki, music from before the '67 Junta took over Greece.

Anoushka leaned her chair back against the white-washed garden wall. Page thought she looked lovely and relaxed in the candlelight, the trumpet vine draped all round her, its elongated cream blossoms partially closed for the night but still looking as if they were waiting for Gabriel to come blow them. They had not spoken since they had given their order to the proprietor and seemed quite content just to be there. Sally poured the wine.

Apropos of nothing Anoushka said, 'My mother was forty years old when I was born. That was in St Petersburg. Not the city you see in black and white movies, still magnificent and in its glory as it was at the turn of the century, but a skeleton of that beautiful and glamorous place. She was a doctor, extremely beautiful and refined-looking, glamorous for a Russian. She was resented by her colleagues for all those reasons and for her aristocratic background, though she was a staunch communist. My father was a painter, not a very good or successful painter but a man who believed unequivocally in communism. He was well in with the regime and the power brokers of the party who bought his paintings. I never knew him. He died when I was eighteen months old. Cirrhosis of the liver.

'We were poor, middle-class and poor. Imagine a doctor being poor. Only in the Russia my parents loved could that be possible. But that's the way it can be when you are not politically correct in the Soviet Union, or what was then the Soviet Union. The regime of my father's time had gone, a new one was in place.

'Four years after he died my mother met a man, a rising star in the party. He worked in the diplomatic service: Serge Kuznitzikoff. He was completely besotted by my mother. She was charismatic, and now when I think of her I realise what a sensual and flirtatious creature she was. She could have been an actress in the old style, a blonde Garbo, a Dietrich. He moved us from the dreary back two-room we lived in, in a once famous palace that we shared with seven hundred other people, to a dacha just outside the city. a new life began for us. He doted on my mother and me.

'As he advanced in the party, so did our standard of living. My mother had more success in her work but finally gave it up for Serge and me, to be with us. I called him "uncle" but I always thought of him as my father.

'At the beginning, when he started travelling abroad, we didn't go with him, and our life at those times was very empty. You see, he was our world. we yearned for his love and protection. I could hardly wait for him to come home, to feel the touch of his hand, to have him pick me up and kiss me, to be caressed by him. I felt so bright and alive when he took me by the hand and showered all his attention on me. My whole world revolved round Serge. He spoiled me, and so did my mother.

'By the time I was eight years old we were travelling with him wherever he went. And lived with him in the cities where he was posted: London, Paris, New York, Tokyo.'

'Hence your ease with languages,' said Page.

'Yes,' said Anoushka, and refilled their wine glasses.

The balmy night and the scent from the trumpet vine, the odour of roasting meat and rosemary, the music, all seemed to add to the nostalgia of Anoushka's story.

'Serge was a diplomatic trouble shooter, a very important man who knew where a great many skeletons were buried, and in whose closet. That meant that we lived on the fringes of the official diplomatic service and were able to keep a degree of privacy. People did not want to ruffle Serge's feathers. He had power, a quiet, discreet power, but power nonetheless. And that was a good thing because he never married my mother.

'He was a handsome man, tall, broad-shouldered, heroic-looking, what every child wants her father to be. He was, too, very ambitious for me to be educated and cultivated, a fitting companion for him in his old age. There were private tutors, no bad schools for me. Abroad there were private schools, but never for long. We seemed only to get settled when he was re-posted. He instilled in me a love of reading, something that kept me apart from other children, I learned to like my own company and that of those I loved, no others'. We were free spirits, Serge and my mother and I, behind the prim and proper image: the coarse plebians the party liked to portray themselves as.

'From early childhood, I have nothing but fond memories of men, having grown up in Serge's arms. Being petted and caressed and loved and coddled by him, first as a child and then as an adolescent, instilled in me a love for him and for all men. The scent, the feel of a man's skin, his touch, a kiss . . . it's excited me as far back as I can remember. It was natural, naive of us maybe, the three of us, my mother, Serge, and I, to think it was not out of the ordinary to want each other carnally as much as we did. We bathed together, sometimes slept in each other's arms. We were a part of each other's sensuality and probably didn't realise it until it was too late to turn back.

'When I was twelve my mother became ill and Serge became even more my world. As my mother slowly receded from life I began to take her place, was more his companion than she was, became the woman at his side. We were in Paris. "La Traviata" was at the Paris Opera House and Mother was too ill to go. She insisted that I take her place. It was horrible – I was happy that she was ill. I can remember it even now, a child in love with her mother's lover. That night was the first time I realised it, the night of "La Traviata". She lent me her favourite Balmain gown and her best jewellery, and sent me to her hairdresser to have my hair put up for the first time. She made up my face and pinned camellias Serge had sent me in my hair, and then she presented me to him.

'My mother and Serge were sensuous libertines who had handled their love of all things erotic with discretion, and until that night I had had no idea about their active sex life and how it had affected mine. They had been priming my libido for years. I was, by the night of the opera, an erotic soul in search of sensations to satisfy my sexual drives. They had known that I was ready, what I craved, even before I did. All those years they had been teaching me the excitement of the sensual, wanting me to know every nuance of the beauties of the sexual experience. I had been yearning for it for years and they had until that point been able to satisfy my yearnings, but I had come of age, things had to change.

'That night after the opera and supper at Maxim's we returned to the flat where we were living and Serge took me into his bed and we had sex for the first time. It was the most exciting night of my life. He was wonderful. I could not get enough of him. He was an exquisite teacher and I the most compliant and willing of pupils.

'My mother and Serge had been decadent, depraved in their lust for each other, but they loved each other as well. My mother gave me to Serge because she loved me and knew that he would never harm me and that we would make each other happy in bed. That he would be a wonderful first lover for me. Five weeks after that night my mother was dead. I was fifteen years old.

'Serge and I were a well-kept secret, party politics and all that. We were passionately in love, a teenage girl and a man still handsome and virile but old enough to be her father. The party could have had him shot for a scandal like that.

'Regimes change and Serge must have sensed his power would soon be fading. We had had four blissful years together. A return to Russia? Our relationship could not survive there, we both knew it. And he saw changes and great problems ahead. I had spent most of my life living abroad with Serge. He was worried about my future and could not see it back in Russia. We had always spoken about a time when a new love would come into my life and had promised each other that if that happened we would never let what we were stand in my way. But neither of us ever believed we would let it happen.

'And then, one last time, fate stepped in. Serge was given a posting in Egypt, to Alexandria. I was as usual with him as his step-daughter and a part-time personal assistant, but of course was really there as his lover, the light of his life. Our sex life took a new turn in Alexandria. Serge became friendly with several of the towns more erotic games players. Whereas we had been able to fool everyone else, we were not able to fool these men. Serge could not bear for any scandal to taint me and my future. A sheikh from one of the Gulf States became besotted with me and courted me. He was not the first, but Serge took him seriously as a prospect for my future. He wanted a new and better life for me.

'Sex was easy for me, it was natural, something I yearned for and had been brought up to believe was an essential part of my being. I agreed to meet the sheikh. But it was clear that no love was involved here. I was a sexual possession to be played with, an object of desire to be purchased.

'He was to have been only the second man I ever had. But something extraordinary happened that very first night we were to consummate this erotic courtship of his. He liked me even more than he wanted me. Found me vulnerable and in need of something better than he was prepared to give. Strangely, that made him angry.

'He didn't want to have me as a friend, nor to feel anything for me that didn't fit his fantasy. He knew he could not do right by me or Serge. That night, supposedly *the* night, he had some friends and some willing ladies to dinner.

'I was introduced to one of the men, my host's doctor, Robert Rivers. Even as a young man Robert had a successful career and a certain degree of fame. He was handsome with an incredibly attractive personality, and I fell instantly in love. As did Robert. Now, when I look back at that meeting, I can see why. Young, virile, and handsome, under the influence of his host and exotic Alexandria, a straight-laced serious New England doctor, having been handed over a young woman as a gift, a depraved gesture he could not refuse. A young woman with the looks and manners of a proper lady yet sexually free, a girl experienced in all things erotic. We made love only hours after we met, and had a sexual encounter never to be forgotten. Robert never had a chance, he was instantly seduced.

'Hours later we still could not keep our hands off each other. A mere slip of a girl had set this experienced man sexually free as he had never been before. When had a man like Robert Rivers even been handed a sexual slave? In books, in films, in men's fantasies, maybe, but this was real life.

'The sheikh lent his beach house in Marsa Matruh to Robert, and there we stayed. Sex for three days and three nights. We ate into each other's sensual souls. From there Robert was to go to the South of France for a month's holiday. He took me with him. The holiday over, he was still besotted with me and the strange life I had led. I was devoted to him. We couldn't bear to be parted, and when he learned that if we were, I would go back to Serge for whom I still had a deep attachment, he went mad with rage. Robert deplored even the idea that I would give myself to any man other than him.

'He took me home, to Lakeside. But Lakeside wasn't Alexandria or a holiday in France, and certainly not sex in Marsa

Matruh. The holiday was over but we were not. For him I was the luscious depraved side of his life that he loved too much; he wanted to legitimatise his feelings but he couldn't. I didn't know it then but I do now – he was in love with someone else. I was an object of desire he still craved, and he was in too deep to get out. I became pregnant. He did the honourable thing. And I have been trying to live down who and what I am ever since he slipped that wedding band on my finger. Anything I was or did before I became Mrs Robert Rivers became null and void. That's how he got control of my life.

'Now that I have found myself again I know I made one great mistake with Robert, I told him about my past. He used it against me, manipulated me, almost to death, and that's why I hate him. For that reason and because he deceived me, didn't love me, or respect the love I had for him or all that I had given up to make him happy.'

Anoushka's story seemed to have tumbled out, almost as if she were relating someone else's dark secret. When she finished she raised her glass and brought it to her lips. She drank the wine slowly and replaced the glass on the table. No one said anything. The women remained silent and listened to the night. The waiter arrived with a platter of grilled lamb chops, salad and a stack of white plates. The clatter and clang and bad service by the waiter broke the spell of Anoushka's story and the night.

Anoushka pronged a chop with her fork and, carrying it to her plate, addressed Page and Sally. 'Robert is right about one thing, I never have had any friends. I had always been worried that I might give myself away, the real me, the one I tried to kill for his sake, for love. I wanted you both to know where I'm really coming from, not the pretend me you'll see in Lakeside.'

Again silence took hold until Sally said, 'My goodness, Anoushka, when you play the truth game you *really* play the truth game.' The three women burst into smiles. Someone laughed. It was Anoushka.

Page wanted to ask what happened to Serge but thought better of it. Instead she reached across the table. Taking Anoushka's hand in hers, she squeezed it and said, 'Welcome home, Anoushka. It's really nice to know you.'

Chapter 14

Crisis Of Faith and the Roman Catholic Church Of Jesus Christ: there had been other books and countless essays by Oscar Kroner but none would be more damaging to the church he loved and the God he believed in, for whom he gave up Judaism and the woman he loved. To lock himself away in years of retreat to test his own faith, to steep himself in theology and its relation to man, had been his objective. Now he was going home. At last he was free.

Oscar lifted the manuscript from his small leather suitcase and one more time fanned the pages with his thumb. A work that was the culmination of a lifetime of love and despair at the theological dilemmas that haunt the church and those scholars who follow it as devoutly as he had. Loss was the central theme; not only loss of love for Jesus but the loss of the Church's humanity in the twentieth century.

He was forty-five years old and the church, theology, philosophy, had been the lodestars of his life. As a man, he understood the seriousness of loss: for one who had chosen God over the woman he loved, for a priest in danger of losing his faith not in God but in the church.

A man of the cloth, he found the church seriously lacking in its central themes of God and humanity. The church did not condone his criticism but he had a powerful rhetoric, and as a priest he opened up questions that made the church look like progressive thinkers.

Oscar had tried, studied and, during the years of his work since he left Page, tested himself and his own faith and that of his church. Now it was over. When he finished the manuscript in his case, he had finished with the church once and for all. He could make no more excuses for himself or for his church. They both had to change, return to their essential selves. He had. And that had meant giving up the priesthood and returning to a life and love that was more valid for him.

The church was uneasy with his success but continued to put

him on his artistic mettle. And there he had lived in mild unhappiness until he knew he could live there no longer. He missed love, intimacy, carnal life. He was a poorer man for giving up those things.

The demands of the Catholic church: a life of abject subordination in which Oscar had no power was unacceptable to him. He felt he had a moral responsibility to himself. He knew that there were people in this world who believed they didn't exist unless the church told them otherwise. Oscar was not one of those people. Did that make him less a son of God?

Once when he had been young and foolish, he had been helpless to extricate himself from the thrall of love for the church. Now a mature, wiser man, it was no longer a problem. His dilemma had been solved by the realisation that it had not been the church but God that had enthralled him. Faith in a supreme being, whether it be for Jesus Christ or the lord Buddha.

He had always known in his heart and had always made known to the clergy that he believed all heroic men must set out on a quest. His was to overcome the obstacles that clouded the mind and the heart, his own failings, and finally to be able to return home, whether it be to the church or elsewhere. In his case he knew now it meant Page.

To give up his collar was no easy task. He was a leading figure in the theology of Roman Catholicism. Though his archbishop had always known that Oscar might defect from the church, he had tolerated that possibility because of Oscar's writings.

Had they ever thought that it would be over? Did he? When Oscar posed those questions to himself, he had had no answer. Thinking about them now, he realised Page had always known it would end. She had been more wise than he or the church, she knew him better than he did himself. She had a greater faith than he did. But then he had always known that about her. A quiet faith, solid as a rock.

In the end he had been no more than a writer who got lost in his subject. It had been months now since he had decided to leave the church and had asked to be relieved of his vows. Now at last the final papers had been signed, the formalities were over, and he had said good bye to his greatest mentor in the church.

Cardinal O'Malley bid Oscar farewell saying, 'Oscar, you've been good and you've been bad. Mostly you've been good, and always brilliant. Your greatest attraction for us was your forthright honesty. You were always more a literary man who was a believer than you were a priest. Your love of women and life was

204

always greater than your love for God. We all prayed that you would see the error of your ways.

'We've heard your confession and know who you are and yet we held on to you in the hope that you would honour your commitments to the church. But, for you, God always came after literature. Literature is your vanity, you love words more than the church.

'For you, Oscar, to live properly is to live for literature and philosophical thought. That's how you lost your way as a priest and why you cannot obey or accept the church as it is. You want the church to justify itself in contemporary cultural terms. It doesn't have to, it doesn't want to. The church regrets losing you. But you've made your choice, and may God forgive you and bless you.'

Oscar went to the mirror and adjusted his tie. He was not used to it. He ran his fingers through his blond hair and noticed that it was peppered with silver. He had never been a man to deceive himself. He knew the man in the mirror very well, what he would be once he walked from that room, both a star and an embarrassment to the Holy Roman Catholic Church. He had not been the first in the long history of the Catholic church and would not be the last, and he took heart from that. He had wrestled hard and long with himself and his love for the church, and now his fight was over, his work complete.

He took one last long look around this room that had been his home for so many years. The magnificent huge chamber, the most perfect of rooms, a double cube with a thirty-foot ceiling, carved and painted and gilded. Seven arched windows whose glass doors opened on to a terrace that overlooked the formal gardens and fountains and the Tuscan Hills, and nothing more for as far as the eye could see. The peace and tranquillity had a special feel, as crystal clear as the clean fresh air.

To have lived and slept in this room, this library, famed for one of the finest collections of theological books and manuscripts that scholars for centuries had come to study, that had been the real gift he had received from God and the church and for that he would be ever grateful. His eyes rested for some minutes on the faded terracotta silk damask draperies tied back with elaborate seventeenth-century silk ropes and tassels in what had once been luscious jewel-like colours. The sun and time had done their work on them but still they hung in faded grandeur, the odd streak of their original brightness showing through. The walls from floor to ceiling were lined with leatherbound books, there was dark rich honey-coloured cherrywood for shelves and pannelling, and on easels stood Renaissance religious paintings rich with love and passion, trying to evoke the crucifixion of Jesus Christ.

The opulent and beautiful seventeenth- and eighteenth-century furniture: Chinese vases from the Hahn and Ming and Tang dynasties; carpets over the dark wood-planked floor, impressive for the quality of colour and design; sofas and chairs and library tables where for the last hundred years the brightest of minds, men of many denominations, teachers, writers, and great spiritual leaders, had come in retreat to sit and learn from this library.

Others came to meet and speak with Father Kroner, to discuss his work and exchange theological thought. It was here that he met for the second time the Dali Lama, who had accepted Oscar's reciprocated invitation. Here too that he met His Holiness the Pope when he had come to stay in the palazzo. And it was here where often he would sit with the ghost of his friend Primo Levi and speak not of theology but man's inhumanity to man, and of forgiveness and redemption.

This room was not for the church but for men and women and life. A life that included love, passion and laughter. It was this room with all its knowledge and all its secrets, all its questions both answered and unanswered, that he would walk away from with a lighter heart than he had ever known. He had not left it physically, yet mentally, emotionally, he found himself already distanced from it. It was as if he were no more involved with this library than just another transient visitor.

He looked at his robes lying across the seventeenth-century fourposter bed heavily draped in its original hangings of silk-embroidered white flowers on a dark plum-coloured silk velvet, placed to one end of the room. The crisp white bed linen trimmed in heavy cream-coloured lace was covered by a blanket of Russian wolf skins and large embroidered cushions of hunting scenes, a wood of many shades of green and dusky blues, unicorns hiding in the leaves and ladies and noblemen of the seventeenth century riding voluptuous white stallions.

Once he was out of that door they would remove the bed from the library, wipe all trace of him from this room that had been his home and his world for so many years. His vanity was piqued. Every man likes to leave his mark. How unpriestly of you, Oscar, he chided himself.

He walked to the bed and, taking up a robe, folded it neatly and placed it down again. From the pocket of his Armani jacket he took his silver cross and laid it on top of the robe. Oscar walked round his bed for the last time, picking up each of his items of priestly clothing and doing the same thing. His rosary of amber beads felt warm in his hands. He raised them to his lips to kiss them and then laid them too on another folded robe. Brushing his biretta with the palm of his hand, he placed it back on the bed along with his shoes. He would take nothing with him.

He walked from the room with nothing but his worn and battered leather case, the manuscript, several Armani shirts, boxer shorts and pairs of socks, all bought in Milan several weeks before for his return into the main stream of life. He left the church and all its trappings behind as he closed the library door.

He heard the click of his heels on the marble floors echo as he walked swiftly through the corridors and down the grand staircase to the ground floor. He felt light-headed, as if a great burden had been lifted from his shoulders. His work was done, his faith was stronger than ever, unfettered by dogma, any formal doctrine or tenets of the church. Love soared from his soul for every little bird, leaf on a tree, for every man, woman and child, for the sound of the sea, for Page. It had all been there always, he had never let it go, this love for the world and his fellow man, his love for Page and the life they'd had together. At night, alone in his bed, he would speak to her. He would tell her, 'Page, I see you all the days, all the nights. I see your every breath, every glance of your eyes, every movement of your lips. You are a part of my soul.' That love for her, so sensual and deep, had become a part of his heart, his soul, his very being. But he had somehow let it recede into the mist of other forces pulling at his soul, but only recede. He had never lost complete sight of it, never let it go.

He had already been committed to Jesus Christ, was already a man of the cloth who had taken his vows, when she had come into his life. He had not toyed with his love for her, the carnal attraction that drew them together. They had known their love was shadowed by his mortal sin, that his loyalties were divided by church and Page. That had never been good enough for this love triangle. They gave each other a long lead, and time to get on with their lives, to test themselves and their commitment, and now each knew where their loyalties lay. The triangle was broken.

Oscar had many successes to his credit; he had won his many battles with the demons of the soul, with his work, and loved the church again even more now, but in a different way. He understood it in relation to Jesus Christ and man, life and death.

The sixteenth-century palazzo of a hundred rooms was one of

extraordinary beauty, filled with treasures owned by the Vatican. Palazzo Goldolfo Navarone was a favoured summer retreat, a luxurious prize for the church's hierarchy. A jewel in the Vatican's crown. There were always dignitaries there on a visit or in residence, wined and dined by an archbishop and his numerous staff of priests and nuns who were in charge of all that went on in the palazzo. They, plus the house staff who worked there, had seen to it in the years Oscar had been there that he had privacy, total freedom, and control of his domain, the library. They had cared for him and his every need.

Today, from the moment he awoke, he had seen no one. Now, walking through the rooms for the last time, the palazzo's other inhabitants might have been invisible. And another thing: there were usually fresh flowers, huge arrangements of them in marble vases. Now the peonies, delphiniums and roses were all gone. Not a sound but that of his own footsteps could be heard in the house. Were they mourning his death?

The sun cast wide swathes of light through the windows on either side of the massive carved and metal-studded wooden doors. He pushed them open and the creaking sound splitting the silence was like thunder. Oscar stood on the threshold for several minutes, not hesitating but so as to breathe in deeply the fresh mountain air, then he took his first step towards Page. She was right there with him in his thoughts and in spirit, taking that first step with him.

The big black Mercedes, the several Fiats, the black BMWs, not even a pick up truck or an estate car belonging to the palazzo was parked outside at the foot of the stairs. Gone, all gone, like his brother priests and sister nuns, the maids and cooks and cleaners. Just the sound of many birds, the warmth of the sun, the scent of things growing: tall and elegant the cypress trees, needles of pine, and blossoms more pungent still for having the early-morning dew still on their petals. Only they were there to bid him farewell. A smile crossed Oscar's lip.

In a crunch of gravel a taxi swept round the fountain and screeched to a halt at the bottom of the stairs. The driver leapt out. He had been summoned from Perugia. Was Oscar his customer? Oscar walked down the stone steps and shook hands with the driver. He got into the front passenger seat, his precious case balanced on his lap. The taxi swept round the fountain. Oscar caught a glance of the formal gardens rolling away from the house. The fountains were playing and the stone sculptures in the morning light looked as fresh and impressive, as powerful and mysterious, as they always did at that hour. They had a habit of taking on different aspects as the light changed throughout the day. At night the human figures were brooding hulks locked in stone, the animals dead beasts turned to marble. On the nearly mile-long drive now, an avenue of Cypress trees, tall as five-storey buildings, Oscar caught other glimpses of the estate. A rough wood where he had often ridden on one of the mounts from the stables, the artificial lake where he had done his swimming and boating and even some fishing, and finally just a brief glimpse of the maze, designed, planted, and kept in perfect order for more than a hundred years. There he had wandered and thought of and sometimes spoken to God.

These last years of privilege in such luxurious surroundings were a reward from the church for the years spent in remote parishes in Africa and South and Central America before the world and its theological scholars, a clever publisher and readers the world over, gave him the success he so richly deserved.

It was a strange sensation to see all that at one glance and have it recede from his mind in very nearly the same instant, consigned to the past. Oscar felt himself stepping out of his skin and observing himself. He liked what he saw, loved himself for who and what he was. He was centred on life and in this moment of truth was content and at peace with himself and the world.

The car sped away from the palazzo. At the end of the drive massive ornamental iron gates hung from stone pilasters topped by charging lions carved from shiny black marble. Each lion held a cross in one paw, standing guard as if keeping the world out and the church in. Unusually, not one of the thirty gardeners who tended the grounds was to be seen. Unbelievably, the gates had been left open and unattended by the gatekeeper.

They went through the gates and turned on to the paved road. Several hundred yards and another turn and they began to descend the mountain. They wound their way for nearly two miles before they went through the hamlet of Monte Goldolfo Navarone, owned by the church and where most of the staff who worked at the palazzo lived. The street that ran through the hamlet, the only street, was deserted, every door and shutter closed, not a face to be seen. Even the chairs and a table that always stood in front of the bakery had been removed. Not a sign of life to bid him farewell.

The road twisted and turned precariously through olive groves. Now they were winding their way up another mountain, then through a decent-sized village that was just coming to life. Oscar had the driver stop at the café and invited him to breakfast. At a small table on the street they ate fried eggs and thick slabs of bacon and drank hot black coffee. Oscar made an arrangement to be driven on to Rome. He was taking no chance of missing his flight to Athens.

The plane had been in descent for some time and at last broke through the cloud. There it was below, sparkling blue in the late-afternoon sun: the Aegean Sea. No matter how many times Oscar saw that first glimpse of the Aegean, or that special light that is Greece, an artist's agony and ecstasy, he always thrilled to it. Home. He was coming home.

The first time he had flown over the sea he had been nine years old, a child on holiday with his parents. He'd thought it was magic because his mother had told him, 'This is a sea made by a god for all the gods. One day this great god thought the people occupying the land that is now Greece needed a jewel to make them proud and wealthy for all time. So he lay on his tummy on a great white cloud and he huffed and he puffed and blew a wind. It swirled round and round and turned the most beautiful blue and formed a great ball. The god grabbed it with his hand and he threw it down from the sky to the earth. When it landed it made a huge hole and changed from wind to water and flooded the land and became the Aegean Sea.'

Oscar smiled. He had thought the story his mother told him then to be true and that the Aegean Sea was the home of gods. Now the tale came back to him and he wanted to believe it. Looking down, he still thought it was magic: the sun on the sea and a craggy coastline with a white city rolling back from its edges.

The plane swooped in low over Athens, a concrete jungle crawling with motor cars of all shapes and sizes, that could still sparkle white in its bath of sunshine. Greece with its history, its mythology, still crawled into Oscar's heart no less than it had done when he had been a boy. With every return to the country since that first holiday with his parents he had left something behind, some useless piece of excess baggage that made his life lighter and which he never looked back on.

The plane was in a holding pattern over Athens airport and kept circling the city. There, out of the mayhem of traffic and surrounded by buildings, could be seen enclaves of beauty, reasons to visit Athens: the cemetery of Pangrati, the Acropolis with the Odeion of Herodes Atticus. He strained his neck and just caught a glimpse of the Agora with the Byzantine church and Hephaisteion, just a flash of the small exquisite temple, as the plane flew above it and out over the sea again. It circled the city once more, then made its final approach for a landing.

It was hot, the air chokingly polluted. Oscar wanted to cover his mouth and nose with his hand, but braved the air for the scent of the city was still there to be savoured: heat and dust, a hint of pine and wild rosemary blown down from the hills of the surrounding countryside, the smell of the sea.

The usual chaos of the airport was easier for Oscar than the other passengers. He had nothing but hand luggage to open at customs control. And then there was a taxi. He sat in the front seat with the driver who shot, as if he were a Formula One driver, into the afternoon stream of traffic inching its way back into the city after the afternoon siesta.

Oscar felt a surge of excitement: the traffic, the people, the hustle and bustle, he even felt some affection for the ugly concrete apartment buildings they passed, if only from imagining of the teeming life going on inside them. The talk, the idle chatter of the taxi driver. Oscar hung on his every word, laughed at his every joke.

In front of the Hotel Grande Brittagna the two men spoke for several minutes. Oscar greeted the doorman with a handshake and a smile. They were old friends from years of comings and goings. A pat on the back from Oscar for the driver and a deal had been made. He would wait.

Oscar took the stairs two at a time and in the lobby was greeted by a porter, with more hand shaking, and Oscar's literary agent, Michael Benson. The two men also shook hands. Oscar waved the small leather case at him, a tease.

'Finished?' asked Michael.

'Finished,' he answered.

'That's great. Can't wait to read it.' A moment of silence passed between agent and writer, two old friends who had been together for a very long time. And then Mike spoke. 'I almost don't know what to say.'

'That's impossible,' said a smiling Oscar.

'Oscar, we're not going to be coy about this.'

'Of course not. Don't look so embarrassed. I'm not the first priest to take this step.'

'No, but you're one who's going to get a lot of media coverage from it. Are you all right about it?'

'I'm just great about it.'

Together they walked over to the desk. Hotel staff converged

211

on Oscar to greet him, old faces who had grown older together. It was just like coming home. At the desk yet another hand to shake before he signed the register. There was no embarrassment from the hotel staff, who were used to seeing Oscar in and out of his priestly robes. He signed the register Oscar Kroner rather than Father Oscar Kroner.

'Your key, Father.'

For a moment he thought to correct the man then changed his mind. What could he say? 'I'm a defrocked priest now. Call me Mr.' No, he thought not.

He did not correct the concierge. Soon enough the man would get the message and act accordingly. It was then that Oscar realised it was going to be just as hard for strangers and acquaintances, even close friends like Mike, to come to terms with the change he had made in his life. More civilised, gentler on them, to let them find out in their own way. That would cause the least embarrassment for them. They were, after all, used maybe not to defrocked priests but certainly to Greek Orthodox priests who did marry and have children. The Greeks, a most tolerant, humane and generous people, would understand and be charmingly accepting of such a life change.

'Let's go,' he said to Michael, as he turned from the concierge, rejecting the key and handing over his case for safe keeping. 'I've kept the taxi.'

'Where are we going?'

'To the Acropolis. I have this tremendous longing to stand among its stones. Then down to the Agora to walk past the giants at the Odeion of Agrippa.'

'How about a drink first?' invited Mike.

'Later, if you don't mind. Right now I yearn for the white marble stones of ancient Greece. To stand before the Parthenon, the Temple of Athena Nike; to return to the Erechtheion and blow a kiss to the Caryatids.'

He smiled at Mike who smiled back at him. 'I'll buy that. I've never seen you like this. It's great to see this new, happier Oscar Kroner.'

Amazingly there were few people on the Acropolis so late in the afternoon, the bus tours had long since gone and the crowds of tourists: too much to see, too late to do it all before closing time. Perfect for Oscar and Mike. The two men were swept up by the power and beauty, the timelessness of the place. They scrambled over the stones that seemed always to speak to Oscar. Mike followed him, swept up in his storm of enthusiasm.

212

Oscar had about him something mesmerising. It was in his writing, teaching and lecturing. In his own quiet way he was able to transform his audiences' thinking, raise them to a higher level.

He was physically more than just attractive: tall and slender, broad-shouldered, he was handsome but not at all in a movie star fashion. Instead his face was sensually and ruggedly handsome: his nose was crooked; clever, hooded dark blue eyes smiled seductively, with lines at the sides that signalled that here was a face that lived with passion. The slight furrows in his brow added character. A not very good skin, pitted in places, but a mouth and lips that would have been beautiful on a woman. The reddish-blond hair fell boyishly to one side over his forehead and he had a habit of flicking it away with a slight movement of his head.

That was it, he had a boyish look about him for a man his age, and a boyish charm that was both endearing and mesmerising. As was his voice, one of his many assets: husky, slightly raspy from cigars and whisky, ardent and earthy, a voice that could make the smallest statement seem important, urgent, unforgettable. With its almost cut-glass vowels and New England twang, he used it adroitly, playing on certain words and every pause. As a man, a romantic, a poet, he could melt the hardest of hearts with that voice, his looks and seductive soul, as he had done to so many women who had loved and lost him, to Page Cooper who had loved him and loved him still, and never lost him.

The two men were standing together looking up at the Erechteion, Caryatid Porch. There was a relaxed, almost sentimental beauty about it and the four Caryatids, ladies with marvellously dressed hair of stone and faces worn away by the centuries, still statuesque and voluptuous in their gowns of draped stone, capitals balanced on their heads, holding up the roof. They were bathed in a rich golden light from a sun now turning pink against a bright blue cloudless sky. They were overwhelmingly beautiful and seemed to speak to anyone with the will to hear their words.

Oscar looked at Mike and smiled then looked back at his ladies once more before they walked away from them across the marble stones of the Acropolis for yet another view of this wonder of the world. Oscar stopped. Looking from the Acropolis out across the city to the sea, a ribbon of blue in the distance, he recited:

213

'Deprived, not I, blessed,
The God Eros, then Page, lust and love,
I kiss your eyes, lick your lips and remember.'
It took some time for his emotions to settle and when they did he said to Mike, 'I have a woman to meet, a destiny to fulfil. Let's go.'

Chapter 15

'Nothing flash, nothing conservative. Right down the middle. Young and glamorous, but not too obvious.'

Sally, Page, Anoushka and Jahangir were sitting in the back seat of a large Mercedes on their way into Paris from Charles De Gaulle airport, the women having travelled by ferry boat from Hydra to Athens, and from Athens by plane to Paris. Anoushka appeared to the other two women as calm and collected in herself about this traumatic return to her sons and the States for the first time since her unhappy departure. On their arrival at Charles De Gaulle Jahangir had been waiting for them. He had greeted each of them by pinning a white camellia to her jacket and giving her a kiss on the cheek.

'What are you talking about?' asked Sally.

He raised her hand to his lips, kissed it and said, 'You have no idea how traumatic it is for the boys when the parents come to visit for a day, never mind a weekend at school. The mothers are always a problem. I know, I and one of my brothers went to Eton. My father felt that two of us should be educated in England, hence Eton and Cambridge for Rangi and myself. His younger sons were educated in the States, by coincidence Groton for prep school, then Harvard.

'We boys were far better equipped than our parents or the school to know what the right form should be in dress and behaviour so as to make ourselves acceptable to our school chums, because that is after all what we cared about. Unfortunately parents don't listen to their children, but act on the premise that they know best. Their knowing best has made many a boy miserable, I can attest to that. Now here I must be brutal . . .'

The women looked at each other. Anoushka remarked, 'You, brutal, Jahangir? You're a pussy cat.'

Everyone began to laugh. 'Isn't he wonderful?' asked Sally, looking terribly starry-eyed.

'I am serious about this, ladies. You women can laugh but for a boy at school, his classmates and the kudos he has with them depends a great deal on how his parents look and behave, and especially the mother. Boys can be cruel. A flowered hat with too big a brim could break him.'

The women did not laugh this time but were not, however, able to keep a smile from their lips, thinking him ridiculous.

'Boys don't want a mother their friends can hold up to ridicule. Twinsets and pearls are out. Hats are always an embarrassment. If a mother fawns and dotes, dares to kiss her son or hug him in public – all black marks. That sort of thing has to be done strictly in private. No, Jahangir knows best. No cashmere jumpers or tweed suits, no pearls, very discreet with the jewellery, and most definitely no hats. So we're going shopping.'

Shopping. A magic word for Sally. 'Isn't he wonderful?' she asked again. And again Jahangir kissed her hand.

He turned from her to face Anoushka who was sitting opposite him in one of the small jump seats. 'I can be brutal, ruthless even. Anoushka, you don't want to embarrass your boys, do you?'

'Well, of course not.'

'You want to return in triumph and win them over to you again, don't you? That is the object of this exercise in this visit we're all making, isn't it?'

'A little subtlety wouldn't go amiss here,' warned Page.

'Well, we don't have much time, so we must face things the way they are. Well, Anoushka?'

'That's true.'

'Good, then I've got it right. Some ground rules then. The dress code for us all has to be right. Then transportation. Boys at school are seriously interested in what parents drive or fly. The right car can make or break a boy in school society.'

Sally tugged at his arm. 'You're doing a takeover, Jaha, we *are* capable. We could have made this trip without you. Instead we're making it *together*.'

'Yes, well, I do have that tendency. But on the other hand did you go to Eton or Groton? Are you an adolescent, young man? Have you ever been adolescent? Well, I have.'

'He's got a point,' said Page who knew from past experience how sensitive and intelligent and clever Jahangir was.

'Yes, I suppose you have, darling,' conceded Sally. 'I just don't want you to think we're not capable of doing this trip together, just two friends helping another out.'

'Believe me, Sally, I know your strengths. Remember who's

216

been doing the chasing these last months. I just want to make it easier for Anoushka and her boys. We're family, aren't we? Or will be after the wedding.'

There could be no answer to that. Each of the women in her own way was quite overwhelmed that he was taking them all on, and each knew that he meant it. Anoushka recovered herself enough to reach out and take his hand in hers and give it a squeeze of gratitude. He smiled at her and patted her hand. All was going to go well.

'None of you is able to judge the right thing to wear so I'm going to choose for you.'

'But none of that's necessary,' said Anoushka. 'We have a change of clothes in our bags. We're trying to keep it easy, so we can travel fast and light and not get caught up waiting at airports for luggage.'

'Not to worry your head about that. I have it all well in hand.'

'Isn't he wonderful?' repeated Sally.

He kissed her hand again. With all that kissing it was obvious to the other two that not only was he besotted with Sally but was deeply in love with her, unable to keep his hands off her, much as he was trying. 'Yes, he's wonderful,' said Page.

'I'm being repetitive, aren't I?' asked Sally, and all the other three people in the back of the Mercedes said in unison: 'Yes.' She removed her hand from Jahangir's and looked quite embarrassed. 'Look like Barbie is OK, act like a Barbie not on,' she said aloud. And then everyone broke into peals of laughter.

'I'm serious about this. We simply can't walk in looking in anyway embarrassing for Mishka and Alexis. I can't stress enough what this means to boys at school.

'So let me tell you what I've done. I've called my brother, a Groton old boy, and he's called the head master and we now have official invitations from the school for Sally, Page, and me. You, Anoushka, have one automatically. I then called the head master and we had a long talk but I'll tell you about that later. Now, back to our shopping. As we don't have much time, remember the criteria: whatever you buy must look pretty, sexy in the eyes of young teenage boys who are horny, fantasising and frustrated, without being vulgar. What your boys want to hear from their school mates is, "Wow, your mom and her friends are terrific. I wish my mom looked like that. I don't remember your mom being so terrific, you're a lucky one Rivers." That is, Anoushka, how you'll win your boys back.'

'You're assuming that I've lost them.'

217

'You have. To a husband who is there, and to his new wife, who's trying to take your place.'

Sally, who felt very protective towards Anoushka, broke the silence that followed. 'You really can be harsh, Jaha, I don't think Anoushka needs you to spell it out.'

'Yes, dear, she does. But I'm not just thinking of Anoushka, I'm identifying with Mishka and Alexis, and remembering what it was like to be at school when I was a boy.

'At Eton, no matter how clever I was, how good at sports, how popular, I was still a wog and my friends wanted desperately to forget that. It was not a problem for me, I had no insecurities about who or what I was, but the torture over how my parents behaved towards me when they visited was no different than the other boys'. When my parents came it was always an embarrassment for my brother and me.

'The first time my mother visited she was wearing a very elegant sari and over it a full-length sable coat. That was very bad form. The next time she came dressed in Balmain, that wasn't much better, too grand, too elegant, too sophisticated for the tweeds and the twin sets of cashmere and the obligatory pearls, that were just as much an embarrassment to the other boys. The next time she came, she wore the tweeds and that was worse. Then, finally, she just stopped coming and it was a relief. We all wanted our mothers to look like Bridget Bardot or Jane Fonda and dress like Marilyn Monroe.

'Dad had it worked out. He always came in the right car with a huge hamper from Harrods and another from Fortnums, for my brother and me; we were told that they were from our mother for us and our friends. You see, any form of food was acceptable.'

'What was the car?' asked Page.

'A Rolls driven by his chauffeur when my mother was with him, a vintage Mercedes Benz with a soft top when he drove alone.'

'I get your message, Jahangir.'

'Good,' he said with a smile.

The grounds were teeming with people: schoolboys and parents, sisters and brothers, teachers and caterers. It had that strange atmosphere of being a festive occasion, a family reunion, a country fête, with all the anxiety and fun that comes with any and all of those occasions.

Anoushka and Page were walking together, followed by Jahangir and Sally. They were on the path heading for the headmaster's office. Anoushka looked round and smiled at them, then turned to Page. 'He's so clever, I'm so happy for Sally.'

'I suppose what you're referring to are those admiring looks we're getting from the boys?'

It was true. There were groups of them standing together, some with parents, some without. Anoushka had even heard a loud whisper from one boy to another, 'Who do you think they belong to? Wow!'

Page, of course, was the most dazzling with her green eyes and auburn hair worn long and nearly straight for the occasion. She was dressed in a leather suit of dove grey, the skirt tight to her body and hanging to just below her knee. The short jacket finished snugly at the waist and was the same shade of grey in suede, trimmed in the polished leather of her skirt. It looked like the most refined biker's jacket with its large revers and two rows of silver studs round the waist band. Her long shapely legs were in cream-coloured stockings and her flat-heeled shoes were grey snakeskin trimmed in black crocodile. Jahangir had declared mothers tottering on the grass in high heels, even worse if they were stuck into the grass lawns and had to be yanked out, a most serious embarrassment for a boy. Immediate laughter on sight. She carried under her arm an envelope bag of black crocodile. Glamorous but not flash, young but not ridiculously so. Perfect had been Jahangir's opinion, thinking of himself as a young teenager starved for a woman.

Anoushka was looking ravishingly attractive. Her silvery-blonde hair shimmered in the sunlight. In Paris they had cut it short and it was wavy and worn off her face to show off better her high cheekbones and classical aristocratic Russian good looks. The silk and linen jacket of tiny checks in black and white hugged her body. It had great charm with its slightly puffed sleeves at the shoulder that fitted snugly to her arms and its short peplum that fish tailed provocatively just above her bottom. The form-fitting skirt only accentuated the cut and dash of the suit that was more like a two-piece dress since she wore no blouse beneath. Her cream-coloured calfskin shoes and handbag matched. Page's comment on seeing Anoushka had been, 'Oh, you must have it. It's Lauren Bacall's suit when she met Bogart in their first movie. Well, almost.'

Of course heads turned for Anoushka and Page, but eyes lingered longest on Sally. She was every boy's dream, petite, provocatively pretty, a doll of a girl. She, like Page, had chosen leather. Her suit was a polished coral colour, a hip-length jacket

219

over a skirt finishing a few inches above her knees.

Jahangir too drew the attention of the boys as being very smart. He had chosen cream-coloured flannel trousers with turn ups, a rich blue Turnbull & Asser shirt, a red and white polka dot tie, and a navy blue linen jacket, worn with its sleeves pushed up and open to show a tobacco-coloured herringbone waistcoat of linen.

Was it Anoushka's imagination that everyone looked frightfully dull? No, not so much dull, there were a great many well-dressed and pretty women, handsome and well-turned out men, just an air of people taking themselves, and the event, and their children, too seriously.

About a hundred yards from the entrance of the building was the headmaster's office. She had made arrangements to meet Robert and her boys there. Anoushka felt suddenly strange. Not at all the Anoushka Rivers she had been, her children had known, her husband expected. She had lost some of her insecurities about being anything other than the Mrs Rivers Robert had wanted. She was being reunited with her sons and that was what they expected, who they loved and wanted to see, but she was no longer that woman, only a fraction of her was left. Yes, she felt decidedly strange.

Mishka and Alexis saw her before she saw them. They were cutting across the lawn heading for the headmaster's office, and not knowing why they had been summoned. At Anoushka's request, her arrival had been kept as a birthday surprise. It was Alexis who recognised Page first from photographs Anoushka had been sending them of herself and her friends.

'Mishk, I think that's Mom's friend, Page Cooper. What a knock out! It does look like her. Fancy Mom having a friend like that . . .' He stopped in mid-sentence.'

'Alexis, that's Mom with her.'

'I thought it was, but she looks so different. Boy, she sure looks good.'

They broke into a run across the lawn and rushed up to Anoushka and Page. 'Mom, what are you doing here?'

'I'm a surprise for your birthday. And I brought my friends.' It was difficult for her to hold back tears of joy but she managed it. 'Don't suppose you could manage a hug for your mom?'

'Not here, not in public!'

That wise Jahangir, she thought, before saying, 'Well, I can at least shake your hand. That is permissible?' Finally Alexis gave her a hug, but it was quick and afterwards he looked round in the hope of not being discovered.

'Mom, this is a great surprise.'

The boys looked so happy to see her, it gave Anoushka all the courage she needed to get through the weekend. 'This is Page.' They shook hands with her and were quick to thank her for the birthday gift she had sent. 'And this is Jahangir.' The boys immediately launched endless questions at him about the polo equipment he had sent them, and when Jahangir interrupted them to introduce Sally they suddenly became dumbstruck and fell in love. Every school boy's dream to have a Sally to prance round with at an open day at school. She charmed them with more than her looks, and asked all the right questions about the events of the day. They made up a jolly and attractive party and every few minutes one of Anoushka's sons would remark how different she seemed to them or how different she looked. Of course they were right, she was different, she'd been through hell and back again and you don't make that trip without changing.

After fifteen minutes it was Alexis who said, 'Oh, Mom, we were supposed to be at the headmaster's office twenty minutes ago.'

'I know, so were we. That's where we'd planned to spring this surprise, and meet your dad.'

All the fun and life seemed to drain from the boys' faces and they went very quiet. Finally it was Mishka who asked, 'Mom, you're not going to have a fight with him and say terrible things to him or make a scene like last time we were all together? That was terrible. You were kind of crazy, very scary. It's not going to be like last time, Mom? You wouldn't do that, would you?'

Then Alexis spoke. 'If you're going to make a scene, please not in front of the headmaster. That would be so embarrassing. Or any of our friends. We'd never live that down.'

'I'm not going to make a scene. You have my word on that. And not in front of *my* friends either.'

Smiles reappeared on the boys' faces. 'Well, that's all right then,' said Alexis happily. Mishka looked relieved. The atmosphere was relaxed again.

En route to the headmaster's office they were stopped several times by boys who would approach Mishka or Alexis seeking to be introduced to their mother and her friends.

She could never remember seeing such pride in her boys' faces or hearing it in their voices when they said, 'This is my mom. She's flown in from an island in Greece just for Parents' Weekend. These are her friends, the ladies she's going to sail the Atlantic with.' And then they would very deliberately introduce everyone to each other. It was therefore a very happy party that finally burst into the headmaster's office.

'Boys, you're late. This won't do. Your father has been waiting. Oh, I see you have your surprise.'

Anoushka greeted the headmaster, introduced her friends to him and then apologised. 'It was by accident that we bumped into each other on the way here, and I delayed us.'

That seemed to smooth things over with the headmaster who did not seem very cross but actually more interested in Jahangir than anyone else. Anoushka found it difficult to take her eyes off Robert and Rosamond who were standing at the window.

Sally and Page were watching her with some concern. Both of them felt a new admiration for her for what she was doing. How brave to be fighting back, they had declared to each other. Mishka and Alexis were obviously happy to see Robert and Rosamond and did nothing to hide their affection for them, kissing Rosamond on the cheek and shaking hands with their father who ruffled their hair. Anoushka thought her heart would break. They had had to think twice about giving her a hug, and the kiss had never happened.

Jahangir, standing next to her, whispered, 'Remember, boys don't kiss mothers in front of other boys.' That helped. Anoushka closed her eyes for a second and took a deep breath. She was all right, in control of herself again. How had he guessed what she had been thinking? Had it been showing? She simply could not have that. She could and would carry off this weekend, and on her terms.

Introductions had to be made. That eased things, distracted the emotions. It gave her time to organise her thoughts. Finally she was able to say something to her ex-husband. 'Robert, you're looking very well.'

'So are you, Anoushka. In fact you look marvellous.'

Rosamond had not left Robert's side. Anoushka faced her but was unable to bring herself to speak to her. The others were at the far side of the room looking at framed photographs of former pupils and searching for Jahangir's brother in them. So Anoushka did have a modicum of privacy for this awkward meeting. It was Rosamond who spoke first. 'I hope we can be friends?'

Not wanting to make a scene, Anoushka dropped her voice so that it was just above a whisper. 'Oh, I don't think so. But I'm calling a truce for my sons' birthday.' And then she walked away to join the others.

It was an exhausting day, with a continuous programme of field

222

sports, some theatre, a concert, rowing, and sailing events, lunch and tea. The socialising with other parents was the most exhausting of all. In the evening there was a dinner dance at the school, black tie and evening gowns, and Mishka and Alexis and half a dozen of their close friends joined the Riverses and party. All in all it was a great success and no one was in doubt that Anoushka Rivers and her friends had made a great contribution to the festivities.

By evening Anoushka, Sally and Page had become the centre of attention for parents as well as boys and staff. They all wanted to know about the plan to sail the Atlantic. Why were they doing it? How? When? From where to where? Some wanted to know about their trekking in the Himalayas, others what it was like to live on a Greek island. They were adventurous, and boys and parents found them fascinating. Mishka and Alexis kept asking their father, 'Isn't Mom different? And terrific.'

'A great surprise,' Robert would reply, relieved that all was going so well.

Throughout the evening and all the attention heaped upon Anoushka and her party, Rosamond behaved impeccably. She joined in and was charming to everyone, including Anoushka, whenever the occasion arose. At one point while everyone was dancing Anoushka found herself alone at the table with Robert.

'You're making the boys very happy. You're making a hit.'

'And you?'

'You surprise me pleasantly. But I would be grateful to you if you would be nicer to Rosamond. She misses you as a friend. She bears no malice towards you.'

'Robert, please don't be stupid, it doesn't suit you.'

He bristled. 'There's no need for you to talk to me that way.'

'And there's no need for you to defend Rosamond. There is no defence for her behaviour. She stole you from me, and my home, my children, my life. What malice could she possibly bear towards me? She got everything she wanted. Why should I be nice to her? I said there was a truce and I'll stand by that. But you expect too much.'

'The lost years? The children we might have had? But let's talk no further about this. There's no point. We're here for the boys.'

'Maybe you are, Robert, but I'm here for the boys and me. If that means being civil to Rosamond, I will be. She's a part of their life and has been for almost all of their lives, now more so than ever, but if she wants to stay that way she had better be damned nice to me. I suggest you tell her that instead of lecturing me on how to behave with her. Now excuse me.' Anoushka rose from the chair and walked to the far side of the room to join her friends.

The following day at the school was more or less the same as the day before but Anoushka was with her boys and she had won them back. That for her was everything. There were odd moments when they expected her to behave as the mother they had always known: permissive of everything they wanted or did, vague, indifferent to their criticism of her, accepting of the little jokes about her bad housekeeping and lack of organisation. They sometimes sounded as if they were mimicking their father. The new Anoushka saw and heard things that she could no longer equate with herself.

Her greatest problem though was not her boys, or even Rosamond. It was Robert. She still found him handsome, sexually charismatic, charming. She still could not divorce herself from the years of happiness she had had with him. The security of home, a family, status in the community. She still wanted him sexually. She would have gone with him to any corner in that school, behind a hedge, anywhere, if only he had asked her. He could still trigger in her erotic feelings so intense she wanted to weep for his rejection of her, his deceit, the years of lies and disloyalty, but more than all of those things put together, for not wanting to have sex with her any more.

Anoushka struggled with that but kept it well hidden. She could see in the way he looked at Rosamond, his every touch, every word was filled with love for her. Sexual desire for her shone in his eyes when he looked at her across the crowded room. There was no hope for Anoushka. No reconciliation was even remotely possible. Had that been what she had hoped for?

Now for the first time she understood what those looks she had seen exchanged between Robert and Rosamond for so many years during her marriage had meant. They had always loved each other and she had refused to see it. She had been in the dark, whether by choice or ignorance. Should they not have taken her by the hand and led her into the light? How they must have hated her when all the time she thought she was bathing in their love for her.

Anoushka was aware that this was the new, the very changed Anoushka seeing the truth of her past life with Robert. The new woman could not feel the pain of that realisation as the old one would have. Anoushka had learned during her exile from marriage how to harden her heart, to love herself. She had stopped

224

beating herself up for someone else's faults.

It was no longer a matter of getting the weekend over with. She was enjoying being in the States, being a parent again, seeing her boys and their friends, their admiration for her, and the new life she was carving for herself. She was aware that it was in part thanks to her friends.

Jahangir had, of course, triumphed in his organisation of the journey from Groton to Lakeside. She was certain the boys at the school would never forget the vintage cars that swept the party away to a private airfield where they boarded a small plane. Anoushka told him, 'Your organisation of things is making this such a joy for me, however did you manage it all?'

He replied, 'It's easy when you have a string of polo friends to help you out.'

She had fantasised so many times what it would be like to return to Lakeside, to see it again. The reality was nothing like her fantasies. It was difficult, she had expected that, but in a different way than she had imagined. She found Lakeside even more beautiful than she already knew it to be. And the house, when they drove up to it, all but took her breath away. It was home. The only real home of her own she had ever had, the only home she had ever wanted. Though she no longer wanted it, it still remained a palatial, beautiful place with all the grace and charm of New England at its best. To have allowed herself to be thrown out of this house and this town that she'd loved, she knew now she must have been momentarily out of her mind. It was at that moment, standing with Page and Sally and Jahangir, that she knew why she had insisted they stay in the house. She was laying ghosts that might haunt her all the rest of her life had she not faced them.

A few people were already there for the party when they arrived. Mishka and Alexis ran out to greet them, and Rosamond showed them to the guest rooms. That was almost unbearable for Anoushka, and certainly awkward for Rosamond and Robert. Just as she had predicted, however, they all managed to hide their feelings from the boys.

For Mishka and Alexis, having them all together again, mother, father, and Rosamond, and having a good time as they used to, gave them a sense of security about their future. They kept talking about it to the three adults. Anoushka had accomplished what she had set out to do.

If her friends and even Robert and Rosamond made it as easy as possible for her, Robert and Rosamond's friends, people she

225

had known for most of her married life, did not. Neighbours and their children, Robert's colleagues, the children's best friends and their parents, all found Anoushka an embarrassment, an intruder. They thought her appearance with her friends there to be in the worst of taste and that she should impinge on Robert and his new wife, vindictive. They were neither subtle nor kind about it. Only sensitivity to the boys' feelings allowed them to be just civil to her.

It was so obvious that it prompted Page to say to Sally, 'What could she have done to make these people dislike her so? How did she get it so wrong? How did she alienate herself from them so completely?' Page and Sally were her friends and they would never think of discussing it with Anoushka but they could between themselves. As usual it was the down-to-earth Lancashire lass who got it right.

'Look at Robert, he's sensationally attractive. Knowing her story as we do, and I'm sure no one else but Robert does, put two and two together. She loved him, had possession of him, had everything she wanted, and was in the nicest possible way cocking a snook at them. "Get stuffed, I've got it all and you haven't," was what she was saying, and they thought she did. She flaunted, they were jealous. She was always the intruder. Poor sod!'

Page and Sally loved Anoushka more for her having had such bad luck.

Robert and Rosamond put on a great party for the boys and the house seemed full of fun. Anoushka kept up for as long as she could but suddenly knew she had done it all. She kissed her boys and went to her room, promising to be down for breakfast with them before she left. The chorus of thanks from them and their friends had made it all worthwhile. In the room, alone at last, all Anoushka could think about was sleep.

A knock at her door and Rosamond entered the room. She asked, 'Have you everything you need?'

'Yes, I have, thank you.'

'I'd like to talk to you, Anoushka. I think what you did coming here was very brave and right, and I was wrong not to want you here in the house.'

'Is that what you've come to tell me? You haven't come to apologise? Not that you can. How does one apologise for ruining someone else's life? Stealing their husband and their children, their home, not to mention their dignity. Next you'll be telling me you haven't been disloyal to me, a liar, a cheat?'

'No, I can't tell you that. But what I can tell you is that I tried many times to go away. To leave Robert for you and the boys' sake.'

'Not hard enough. Just go, please, Rosamond, leave me in peace.'

Rosamond left the room without another word. She walked down the stairs and her heart lifted. This was her house now and it was teeming with people who were happy and laughing and having a good time. People were dancing to the steel band and singing, they were spilling out on to the lawn. Waiters were still serving all the boys' favourite food, washed down with beer and wine for the adults, root beer or milk shakes thick with ice cream for the girls and boys, all forty of them.

There was a crack and a rumble, then a bang as a million fireflies burst on to the night sky. Not fireflies but fireworks. A whistling sound from the lawn and a rocket burst in a shower of pink stars that rained down over the lawn. Another burst of noise, and another, and another. Several explosions at the same time and the night sky lit up like high noon. People rushed from the house on to the lawn, wanting the best view of the display, the culmination of the boys' birthday party.

Both Sally and Page saw Rosamond walking down the stairs and into the drawing room. 'Is Anoushka all right?' Page asked.

'Well, I don't know about that.'

'Do you think I should go up?' asked Sally.

'No, I don't think that's necessary. Sorry, I think I might have given you the wrong impression. What I wanted to say was, I think she's all right but I'm sure she can't help but be somewhat upset. She's still very angry with me.'

'Well, Rosamond, you really can't blame her, can you?'

'Yes, Sally, actually I can. No one ever wants to listen to the other woman, her side of the story, least of all the ex-wife.'

Rosamond began to walk away but Sally, with a gentle hand on her arm, stopped her. 'I'm sorry if that sounded rude, Rosamond, you have been as gracious to us all as anyone could be, and so hospitable. But can you blame us? She is our friend.'

'Look, if she's your friend, really your friend . . . Oh, never mind.' And once more Rosamond tried to walk away from the girls.

'No, please, what were you going to say?' asked Sally.

'You don't know how lucky she is to have made friends with women like you. Anoushka is wonderful but there are two sides to this story, and as I said, no one ever listens to the bitch who steals another woman's man. If you were really her friends you

227

would listen to my side of the story, and then maybe you could help her to leave her bitterness behind her and really get on with a new and better life for herself. For as long as I am her enemy, and she will not see our side of it, she will carry the wound that Robert and I have inflicted upon her. You can't imagine that either of us wants that for her, even though we no longer want her in our lives.'

'Are you speaking here as the other woman or as a psychiatrist?' asked Page.

'Probably a little bit of both.'

'She still loves Robert, doesn't she?' asked Sally.

'I don't know. I think she probably hates him more now than loves him, which in a way is a good sign but not great. Great would be if she just let us go, neither loved nor hated any more.'

'Now that *is* the psychiatrist speaking,' said Page.

'Yes, I suppose it is. But she *should* hate him. He was foul to her. He is a remarkable and wonderful man, charismatic and vital in many ways. Women fall in love with him all the time. Nurses are devoted to him, they see him as god-like and a man they would like to know and care for; his colleagues look to him for direction. Robert has many facets to him, but he can be a bastard when crossed. She was constantly crossing him, and he was a bastard to her.'

'And he isn't to you?'

'No, he has never been that to me. You see, we've been in love for a very long time. The Anoushka you know has come a long way since Robert left her. She is quite a different person. Some women are not at their best when they're in love, especially if that love is obsessive and possessive.'

'Do you know her background?' asked Page.

'No. As well as I knew Anoushka, she was always very secretive, playing her cards close to her chest. I may have been interested once, I am no longer. She's out of my life, on any intimate level anyway. Our paths will always cross because of the boys but that's just about it. It's counterproductive for me to know anything about where she came from at this stage in our relationship. However, I don't think it would have been counterproductive for her to have heard my side of Robert's and my love story. I just tried. She doesn't want to know. I might be wrong, she might be right. What does it matter? We've all started afresh, only she needs more help than we do. She's been wronged, but isn't blameless either in this story.'

All during their conversation the din made by the fireworks

228

never stopped. It seemed to grow louder and louder, Rosamond could just about hear Sally when she said, 'I'd like to listen to your side of the story, not so you can try and justify your behaviour but for Anoushka's sake. You know she has found someone? He's in love with her and she's putting him off, asking him to wait while she gets herself wholly together. I have a vested interest in that relationship. Yes, I think I would like to hear what you have to say.'

'Anoushka says she has no room in her life for a second bad marriage,' added Page.

'You see, she knew it was a bad marriage but she was happy in it and so it didn't matter to her. I'm glad to hear she doesn't want another one. Come into the study away from this noise. We can see the fireworks from there and I really would like to tell you a few things. I'll be brief and I promise that to listen to what I have to say will not be a disloyal act on your part if that's what's worrying you.'

'It does,' said Sally.

'How clever of you to understand this conversation does bother us,' added Page.

'Don't let it. Anoushka will never know. And I would never have said anything except that the bond you three women have forged is so obvious it gave me the courage to speak up.'

In the study Rosamond closed the doors. She had the privacy she needed. 'It's all quite sad in a way. Sad for everyone concerned. I was married to a man called Dr Harley Rogers. I was twenty years old when I met him, a scholarship student at Harvard Medical School. I was dirt poor, and I do mean dirt poor. I was one of those born into genteel poverty, all the trappings of a good family and no money. I was in one of the wealthiest schools in the country, and always starving and in hand-me-downs donated by my sorority sisters. But I had a burning desire to become a doctor, and I was of course young. The way we met was quite simple and terribly romantic.

'The renowned Harley Rogers was at Harvard giving some lectures. I hadn't enough money to eat regular meals and fainted in the street. He took me home and fed me. Recently widowed, he was much sought after by women – terrifically handsome, a young sixty year old, and very fit. We fell in love. He bedded me, and I knew for the first time what it was to be in a state of sexual bliss. We married on condition that I carried on with my education and internship, then started a practice. He was the founder and bright star of the Harley Rogers Clinic here in

229

Lakeside. It was heavily endowed with old money, his as well.

'I never knew or cared about his money. I fell in love with the man. He was remarkably attractive and kind, a medical genius who was not a bore but an exciting and vital human being. There was a scandal at first: the age difference, me being off at school most of the time, not being what was expected of a wife of such a famous man. But no one challenged Harley. People soon saw we were a real love story and they accepted me and learned to respect me for making him happy and having a successful career of my own.

'Then Robert came into my life when he became my husband's protégé. We fell in love. It was platonic love. We never touched each other, that would have been unthinkable. We loved Harley too much. The sexual attraction we had for each other was simply set aside. We never dreamed of being anything to each other but platonic lovers with a deep, and abiding affection for each other. Our love was set apart from my love for my husband. It was years before we declared ourselves to each other.

'Robert and I always agreed that though I was first in his life, he could be nothing but second in mine. We remained deeply in love on those terms for all the years Harley was alive and then he died. It was more of a loss to me than I imagined it would be because Harley and I had always discussed what would happen to me in the event of his death. Our age difference made it a near certainty that he would die before I would. For years he prepared me for that and to take over some of his work at the clinic. All that talk and preparation vanished in the wake of real loss. I wasn't prepared for it, no matter how much I thought I would be.

'Suddenly I was an extremely wealthy woman, one with responsibilities, keeping his work at the clinic on the right track. And I had lost the man I loved and revered. I needed time to grieve. Robert respected that and gave me the space I needed to heal, so that I would be ready to take on a second love, as full and rich as the first.

'During that time it was not unusual for him to go abroad to operate or to spend time at heart clinics teaching other surgeons his technique. So I thought nothing of it when he went to Egypt and then arranged to take a month's holiday in France which he had agreed to break into to give several lectures in Paris. We agreed that was to be our last separation and on his return we would set the date. It never happened.

'He met Anoushka in Egypt. It was quite simple – he became sexually besotted with her. A kind of sexual madness took him over. A decadent, exotic, erotic life he had never known or experienced before opened up for him and swallowed him whole. Our love went momentarily out the window. When he returned to Lakeside with Anoushka, he woke up from the dream of lust as a way of life, and knew immediately that his relationship with her was over.

'He came to me and told me what had happened. That he had been caught in a trap that was not easily escaped. He told me that Anoushka had a pathetic story, one too depraved to talk about, and that she must be let down easily. Nothing more than that about her. He had made the dreadful mistake that men sometimes, to their own detriment, make. He mixed up erotic sexual overdrive with love. It didn't matter, this hiccup in our love story. A mistake is not necessarily the death knell for a love such as ours. He was going to send her away. In the end he was unable to, she became the pregnant. The rest is history.

'So far I still see Anoushka as an innocent victim, Rosamond.'

'She wasn't to us, Page. We were two people who understood what had happened to us. But that didn't make it easier for us. I didn't see Robert for a long time. I couldn't bear to. To see him married to another woman and trapped in a marriage that he despised and didn't want, the marriage we had wanted so desperately for ourselves, was too painful. I took a year off, and came to terms with his marriage to someone else. The children were born. And the moment I saw them I loved them as if they were my very own. They were the children we would never have. He returned to me, and I could not stay away from him. We resumed our platonic love again. At least, that was the way it was at the beginning, and I embraced Anoushka and her family as my friends.

'I never had any malice towards her but from the beginning you could see that she could not handle marriage with Robert, raising the children, running a home the way he wanted to live in it. She was too obsessed with Robert and her relationship with him. That was her life, her world. She would do anything to keep him happy and her marriage intact.

'Early on, it was Anoushka who kept dragging me into her life. She was wily, saw how happy Robert was when I was with them. It's true, I was happy to be with him, to add something to his home life which seemed to be a series of concessions and more concessions to make the marriage work. I was in love, he was in love, we did what we could for each other and to ease the pain of not being together.

'Anoushka used me to keep her husband. She will never admit that to herself, it will always be me who has to be to blame. Me who will have to carry the tag: deceiver, cheat, thief. And I was all of those things and not at all proud of it. But she helped to make me what I became.

'Yes, Robert was wrong. He should never have married her, but he wanted his children. Yes, he should have gone to her and told her the truth about us. I begged him to, believing it cruel of him not to. Those first years, I believe he did try to make it work, and when it didn't he tried to ignore to the best of his ability his unhappiness. We were used to loving each other, we were bound together in love, and so I became his mistress. It was the best we could do, because the children were too young to break up the family life they had. He could not imagine Anoushka bringing them up alone.

'If anyone ever tells you it's easy to be a mistress, don't believe them. She flaunted her love for Robert in front of me and everyone else, and Robert and I had to live with that. Over the years he gave her any number of reasons to open her eyes and see how unhappy he was with her. She saw nothing. In the end, he saw his life ebbing away and himself an unfulfilled man with too many regrets and bitterness beginning to seep into his soul. He couldn't bear it, not one more day. End of story.'

'I think you *are* trying to justify your behaviour, you know,' said Sally.

'You see, I told you, no one wants to hear the other woman's story.'

Chapter 16

The sky was a dead grey colour and rain was teeming down. Drops were hitting the tarmac with the force of lead shot charged from a gun. They sent up sprays of water round the quartet's ankles. Huddled together, holding large black silk umbrellas over their heads, they seemed oblivious to the bad weather. Having arrived in Paris from New York aboard Concorde, they were still riding high on their successful weekend.

'I don't know how to thank you all,' said Anoushka.

'You can't thank people who have shared a good time with you,' said Jahangir.

'Isn't he wonderful?' Anoushka and Page mimicked Sally in unison and then burst into laugher.

'You got me,' she said, smiling.

'I hate goodbyes,' said Page.

'We're all getting soaked standing out here,' said Anoushka.

They all seemed reluctant to break up the party. Jahangir was on his way from France to Pakistan where he was going to play in a polo match between Pakistan and India, a match of tradition and great fame that was played every year on the most remote field in the world in a spectacular setting, the mountainous region of Pakistan. Men had been playing polo there since Jahangir's great-great-grandfather's time. It was an event that brought people from the far corners of Pakistan and India.

Sally and Anoushka were bound for Cap d'Antibes and the *Black Orchid*. Page was en route back to Hydra. Each was changing direction, shifting gear, leaving the others behind, none of them quite wanting to do so. But they did want to get on with their lives. Somehow, standing there in the rain, not one of them could quite say: The party's over. So they just kept making inane conversation to delay the women from mounting the stairs into the small Lear jet that would take them from Paris to the South of France.

'All a man's life he waits for the bell to toll,' Jahangir suddenly

233

declared. 'To hear that ring of real happiness that makes him come that little bit more alive to himself and the world. It's a sound like no other, neither loud nor soft. It doesn't even have to be particularly sweet, only clear. When a man hears that there is no looking back, there's no looking forward, merely an acute awareness, bliss, an extraordinary sense of contentment. I hope you too have heard it, Sally.'

He raised her arm, the one that was holding the umbrella until it was high up over her head and then moving out from under his, he dropped his umbrella and took shelter under hers. They watched the umbrella roll several feet away from them. From his pocket, he removed a ring and took her hand in his. 'It was my great-grandmother's. I did promise you a ring.' Then he slipped it on her finger.

It was a large square-cut diamond set in a single row of emeralds and then a row of dark blue sapphires. Sally dropped the umbrella. Jahangir swung her up off the tarmac and into his arms. They kissed amidst a confusion of tumbling umbrellas, rain drenching them, Anoushka and Page trying to cover them with their own umbrellas. Jahangir slid Sally slowly down his body and away from him and placed her, as if she was a delicate piece of porcelain, on the rain-swept tarmac.

'You see, the party's never over. If you're clever you just move the venue. I have to go.'

'You have the instructions, how to reach me on board?'

'Have no fear, I have the instructions, I'll call you every day.'

Jahangir led a by now drenched Sally to the several steps leading up and into the six-seater Lear jet. Anoushka and Page followed. As soon as the three women were aboard and the door securely closed, he picked up one umbrella, shook the rain from it and held it over his head. The other he closed and tucked under his arm, then he walked away from the plane across the tarmac towards a waiting car.

The plane spluttered to life and after a short warming up period took off almost immediately. By the time the pilot told his passengers it was safe to remove their seat belts the sun was shining in a blue sky. Rainy Paris was left behind. After some fussing to dry Sally's hair and clothes with a hair dryer supplied from the luxurious bathroom, the three settled into their deep comfortable chairs and swivelled them round to face each other.

'This is some life for a middle-aged, middle-class house-wife . . .'

But before Anoushka could finish her sentence Page interrupted. '*Has been* middle-aged, middle-class housewife. You can hardly call yourself that now.'

'You're right, Page. I don't much feel like that has been middle-aged, middle-class housewife anymore. That's what I was when I met you, what I have been for thirteen years. The memory bank has to catch up with the emotions and deposit the changes so I don't slip back into the past. I stand corrected. What I was going to say was, I've learned so much about myself and life through this friendship with you two, and now Jahangir. How could I not think like you, Sally, like Jahangir? Why didn't I realise that life can be a party and you just keep it going. You take the bumps, the tragedies, all with the good, ride them out as life just doing its business. I have never felt that way, ever. Suddenly after this weekend that could have been so hideous for me, I realise what I have been missing. That bell that has tolled for Jahangir, Sally, did you really hear it?'

'Yes, I did. That very first night we met at the Taj Mahal when he chose me and neither of you. It was more a click in the head for me. All the pieces of my life seemed to come together. The moment he took me by the hand and looked into my eyes, I was in step with him, and myself, and the world. He heard a bell, I heard a click. I was suddenly aware of life and all things beyond. It was kind of like an instant Nirvana. Buddhist monks say you can enter that moment of truth and awareness at any time, in any place. For some it happens when you give yourself up to love. A click in my head, the bell tolled for Jahangir. A slap in the face, the sight of an incredible sunrise, a great painting, a single poppy in a field of high yellow grass . . . it can be anything. I suppose all you have to be is be open and ready to hear it, receptive enough to accept it. Did you hear it with Robert?'

'No. I know now that I never heard that click, nor Robert that bell. There was never that moment of awareness of being one with each other and the world you talk about. I understand what you're saying, but I can hardly conceive it. It was passion, enormous lust, admiration, aspiration, that was what governed my love for Robert from the very first time I saw him and until he left me. Survival through love, the erotic. I was constantly manufacturing happiness and living in a state of bliss and in a secure world in order not to die or just fade away, exactly as most people do. And I did find happiness, and haven't as yet known any better than that which I had with Robert even though I am out here, alone, and working on it.'

235

Sally wanted to ask, 'And what about Piers?' But she couldn't bring herself to, and was somewhat relieved when Page spoke up and she missed her opportunity.

'It rang for me.'

Neither Anoushka nor Sally spoke. Page smiled at them. 'What, no questions, no curiosity?'

'Oh, yes. I've always been curious about you, Page,' Sally admitted. Always thought there might have been someone. But you're such a private person, you never gave us the merest hint *the* man in your life might exist or had existed.'

'I suspected,' said Anoushka. 'I've met two men who know you, Hervé and François, but it was Hervé who told me there had to be a secret love, a great love or a great disaster that made you cast off any man who became too deeply involved with you. He claims you are a legendary femme fatale for the many suitors who couldn't capture your heart. He says that you use men as most men use women. I never believed it to be quite true.'

'But it was, it is. There have been many men. I've had a wonderful, full and rich sexual life with them, and romance, and yes, even love, but they could never be *the* man. You see, I'm one of the lucky women of this world for whom the bell did toll, like it has for Sally now. I see it in you and Jahangir, that same commitment that I have to one man, one love. I've found my life-mate. Until I met Oscar and it happened for us, I never believed that kind of love existed. Never dreamed that I could look at one person and fall deeply in love, that a life could come together just as Sally has described, and there could be for eternity peace and contentment.'

'But where is he?' asked Anoushka.

'He left me, abandoned me for what may be a greater love.'

'So that's what we three have in common? We're women who have been discarded by men. Until now, I thought Sally and I were the only ones,' said Anoushka.

'But you're the only one of the three of us waiting for him to return,' said Sally.

'Well, not exactly waiting. If you mean that all life is suspended, that my heart is broken, that I'm pining and in despair, that time might heal a broken heart, no, it's nothing at all like that. My heart never broke. I wait for him alone in the house in Hydra for three weeks every year. During those three weeks he is in the forefront of my mind, my dreams, every minute of the day and night. The rest of the year I just carry him in my heart and get on with life without him, which includes other romances, other men, great sex, my work, friends, and now best friends. Till you two came along, I never did have any women best friends.'

'Will he come back?' asked Anoushka.

'I don't know, not for certain I don't.'

'But in your heart you think he will?'

'No, not in my heart, in my total being. I have utter and complete faith in what I have with Oscar. You see, I think, for special reasons, that our love has been blessed by God, all the gods. As ridiculous as this may sound to you both, it's almost irrelevant whether he does or does not come back to me. You see, we're apart, out of communication, but we never *really* left each other. It's more that circumstances . . . well, it's difficult to explain. It's an impossible love, let me put it that way. Impossible unless Oscar comes to terms with it. The sacrifice he has to make to return to me is tremendous. He's a man torn between two great loves, for a woman and for the Holy Roman Church. He needed time to resolve his conflict.'

'Oh my god, he's a priest, a man of the cloth!' said Anoushka, looking very shocked at this news.

'Yes.'

An awkward silence settled over them, then Anoushka said: 'Needed? You said needed, past tense. Does that mean that he has come to a decision?' asked Sally.

'How strange that I should have said that. Almost as strange as my speaking so openly about him to you girls. Something has happened, I feel sure of that now. The idea is so thrilling it's making me feel quite queasy.' Page took a few deep breaths.

'Are you all right?' asked Anoushka.

She was smiling again. 'Yes, it's passed. It was rather as if someone was walking over my grave. I'm fine now, feel wonderful.'

'I don't quite understand, Page. He's considering giving up the church?'

'We agreed to part but never to stop loving each other or wanting to be together. He's a famous theologian who has always had a great many conflicts about the church and where it's going, celibacy, the human factor between doctrine and believers. He's always been a renegade priest who challenged the church, but a believer who loves Christianity. By the time I came along he was a powerful voice for reforms in the church and a redefining of Catholic philosophy. You have all at some time or other read him, heard him, or at least his name: Oscar Kroner.'

The look on Sally and Anoushka's faces told Page all she

237

needed to know, they had indeed heard of him.

'And you've carried this tragic love around for how long?' asked Anoushka.

'No, Anoushka. Not tragic, and it's carried me – us. We made a calculated decision to give each other our freedom to have other loves, other passions and interests, to put ourselves and our faith to the test. I really should explain, but where to begin? The house in Hydra, I'll start there because you both love it and understand the magic of the place. It's not mine. It's ours. He bought it for himself and then gave it to me.'

There was no cabin attendant on the plane but before they had taken off the co-pilot had shown them the coffeemaker and microwave. Page rose from her chair and went to the small kitchen. There she placed a jug of coffee and warmed croissants for them on a tray and returned to her still stunned friends.

The women drank their coffee and looked at each other reassuringly. Finally, it was Sally who spoke. 'You're not going to leave us dangling. Surely there's more that you can share with us. We're your friends, we would like to know.'

'I would, in fact, like to tell you about Oscar and me.'

'You're still in love with him?'

'Oh, yes, and I have no doubt that he's still in love with me. I think I would like to start at the end. It was always a bit unfair not to tell you the truth about the house in Hydra. It might end up being a house just for me, but like the captain who haunts it, Oscar is always there and always will be in spirit if not in the flesh.'

'Did you live there together?'

'Yes, soon after he had bought it. When it was mostly a wreck.'

'Then you rebuilt it together?'

'No. We designed it together, spent months and months working out how to restore it, and then he went away, left me, and I have been for the last five years carrying out our plans. I said I'd start at the end to tell you about Oscar and me, but maybe I had better start at the beginning.

'It seems so strange to be talking to you about him, to anyone for that matter. I never have, you see. I never had best friends to confide in before. I've held him and our story close to me because ours is an impossible love, a secret love, sinful. And we are talking sin on a big scale. But not in our eyes. What we are together has never been that to us. Now that I want to talk about it, I don't actually know where to begin. First I was going to start at the end, then at the beginning, and

238

now I think I should start even further back before that and tell you a little about me, before Oscar and I ever happened. Maybe you'll understand me better and our love story even more.'

Anoushka stood up and refilled their coffee cups. Sally said, 'Hold it, don't begin yet!' and rushed off to return with more croissants.'

'As delicious as these are, my mother would have disapproved,' said Page. 'She used to make the most mouthwatering croissants ever. My mother was a cook, and my father head gardener on a Long Island estate. The north shore. I was the only child born below stairs in that household, and so was spoiled rotten by the servants and the owners as well. The Van Meers were real Long Island high society. Old, old money, one of the first Dutch burgher families to settle in New York. Conservative.

'Mrs Van Meer was a wonderful woman, extremely nice to me. She was a keen gardener with a passion for flowers, and it's really thanks to her and my father that I have the same love. When I was no more than five years old she had me helping her with her flower arrangements which were always spectacular. Of course then it was holding a flower at a time while she talked out how she was going to use them. I adored her. She was an absolute beauty and so sweet, she drew everyone to her, had a power over people. I wanted to enchant, as she did, and followed her about everywhere, and at any time I could.

'She had five children of her own. They were my playmates. I grew up with them. I had the run of this marvellous estate and not quite the run of the house. It was an idyllic childhood. She saw a kind of beauty in me that she was always wanting me to make the most of. My mother and father, the other staff in the house and on the estate, tended not to know quite what to do to add to my life, they just let her bring me up.

'Though I was an only child, I was never lonely, I had the Van Meer children to play with. They learned tennis, I learned tennis. They learned to sail, I learned to sail, swim, and so on and so on. One of the boys was called Bradley and was four years older than I was. He had known me ever since I was born. He was my god, my best friend, and we fell in love. I was five years old, he was nine.

'We were inseparable, growing up together running wild and free until he was sent away to school. That made little difference to me, I had the other four for friends. Though I missed him, so did they. We kept him with us by talking about him all the time, and reading his letters over and over again. He would write to us about the world outside the Van Meers' estate, every letter for us was an adventure story. The moment he came home, he was in the kitchens looking for me and off we would go together as if he had never been away.

'We took a great deal of teasing from everyone, but never minded, we were one big happy family. I learned what it was to be adored, to be loved, to have a man passionate over me from Brad Van Meer. It was he who made me understand how my body could excite a man. He liked to make love to it. It was so innocent and natural, this craving for each other's flesh, discovering our sensual natures. We used to take all our clothes off and I used to lie back in the long grass in the south field and he used to caress me, kiss me, lick my little budding titties, suck on my nipples. We thought it very adventurous when he discovered my cunt and licked and kissed it. The excitement I felt made me squirm with pleasure, his made him erect. We woke each other up to the sensual and sexy. I was nine years old. It got better at ten, and at eleven years old I knew how to use my body to excite him and keep him enthralled.

'I suppose something of the sensual, like a strong perfume, told people not what we were doing but that we were passionate children just waiting to grow up. Everyone teased us for our togetherness, above stairs and below, and were charmed by our children's love story. We didn't care, it was true and we were all children together having fun.

'But his mother, Beatrice Van Meer, and her flowers and fondness for me, were more important to me than puppy love and sex. I used to work with her in the garden whenever she had the time, and fetched and carried for her all over the house while she worked on her arrangements. She taught me everything about flowers and arranging them, about how to dress, manners and how important they were, what was beautiful and what was vulgar. She loved me.

'When other girls came into Brad's life it never worried us. We knew we were drifting apart and accepted that one day other men would take his place in my life, other women mine in his. Though we still had erotic passion for each other and had sex together at every opportunity, which by the time I was seventeen had taken on adventurous and experimental overtones, it was love and respect for me that held him to me. It took a long time, that drifting away from each other, until only sexual togetherness remained. He was sexually possessive about me, wanting always for me to have nothing to do with any sexual encounter that was anything less than what I had known. It was he who produced my first dates, my first lover, other than himself.

' "You don't take the cook's daughter out unless she's something special, ravishingly beautiful, interesting and sexually exciting," he kept telling me, and so I went out into the world of men and sex with great self-assurance, knowing very well how to enthrall men. I liked beautiful young men, and when they professed love, life became even sweeter than it had always been. Suitors were plentiful, romances came and went. After university where I read English Literature, I opened my first designer flower shop and started to travel. Life was unconfined and exciting.

'I had an education and a talent with flowers, a relatively good head for business but no real money behind me. I was interested in success and money but soon realised that one is easier to achieve than the other when you are out there all alone. I was not averse to taking advice. Early on I realised the sort of men who could further a girl like me, and those who were attracted to me, were one and the same type: educated, successful, well on the way to their Swiss bank accounts. Money makes money. I listened and learned and acted on tips adoring swains were happy to give me. The wealthy always like their friends to have their own wealth, it makes them secure. And frankly, I found these men romantic and just as easy to date as poor ones.

'By that time I understood my looks and sexual charisma, and that those two things could probably get me anything I wanted, and so using them became part of my psyche, as I suppose it always had been ever since I was that little tot who could charm the Van Meers. I always felt quite whole and secure in myself and so, not so strangely, I never needed to look for *the* great love, never really quite believing that it did exist. Nor did I have that urge most women have to find a fabulous catch for a husband. Love, and romance just happened for me, I never had to make an effort.'

'How lucky you are, Page. It seems to me I've been chasing after the right man all my life. After a while it gets demeaning. Would that I could have been more like you,' said Sally.

'For me it was different. That chasing after a man for love happened only when I saw Robert and wanted him. I never stopped running after him even after he had married me. Sally's right, it is demeaning, only I was so stupid in love I never realised it. Sorry for the interruption, Page, do go on.'

'One early-September, I suppose, just about the time you were having babies, Anoushka, and you, Sally, were probably just an innocent Lancashire adolescent, I felt a real need to get away from it all. The glamorous New York, London, Paris life that I would flit in and out of to work on floral commissions, the fun of those cities, my sex life, had somehow slipped into high gear and I needed to distance myself from it all, get back to some basics. I was desperate to be alone, go off by myself and lie down somewhere in the sun. To look at the sea, steep myself in it, swim naked for long distances, do nothing more than empty my mind.

'It was rather a matter of: is this all there is, what my life is always going to be like? As good as it was, as great as it was, I somehow felt that I was missing something, that there had to be more. My world seemed too narrow, small. I knew a Dutch broker for the best pure white tulips you can imagine, and I remember he told me that once he ran away to Greece and the place healed him. He had not known he was sick until he had been healed by the simple life he lived there. It was the best holiday of his life. I called him and he arranged for me to rent a house, one he had seen just a few days before he was leaving the area. He said, it had magic.

'I rented it. It was a primitive little white house with bright blue shutters and a porch with a reed roof for shade. Two rooms, a bed, two chairs, a table. No electricity, oil lamps, the bare bones of a kitchen, set all by itself in the centre of a cove on a white sand beach about twenty feet from the water. A sea that glossy posters promise, clear and clean, and the colour sometimes of emeralds, others of sapphires twinkling under a hot, hot sun.

'You could reach it only by boat or by scrambling down some steep hills thick with scrubby bushes and covered with olive trees, a few peach trees, several lemon and orange trees all heavy with fruit at the back of the house. The scent of the place was glorious. It smelled of the sea and the sun, wet sand, ripe fruit: lemons and peaches, oranges and figs, olives. A little Eden, and yes there was a kind of magic to the place. It was remote, a very special and secret place. It was on the mainland, the Peleponnisos. If you were to sail a direct line across the water you would arrive at the island of Hydra. It was, however, too far to see with the naked eye.

'It was not an easy climb from the back of the house to the top of the hill and then you had to walk for some distance through more olive groves to the tarmac road that took you to the nearest village large enough to have shops where you could buy supplies. It was still the Greece of old, for the romantics of this world not the cheap package tourist. The owner of my hideaway lived in a larger house about a mile up the beach. He kept a small sailboat anchored two coves from the house, which I had access to.

'I never wore any clothes except at night, when the sun was down and cooler air moved in, and then nothing but a thin cotton batiste sarong. I used to spend hours in the sea, floating with my face up into the sun, swimming out as far as I could and back, diving to the bottom and swimming underwater then up again to float and rest until my energy returned. On to the sand to bake in the sun and then back again to cool off in the water. It was that kind of holiday, simple, without artifice.

'I had been there for about six days. It was unusually hot for that time of year, well into the nineties. I was walking naked out of the sea when I saw him. He was on some rocks several feet above the sand on the promontory that formed one side of the cove. He too was in the nude. I should have been surprised but somehow I wasn't. His hair was very blond, streaked white in places from the sun. At first sight I thought he was a young boy in his early-teens. He had such a young and vulnerable face, incredible brown, soulful eyes. He was lying on his side watching me. Then I saw his was not the body of a young boy. It was the mature body of a virile, exciting man. He had broad, broad shoulders and was very slim. Not at all a muscular body except for his thighs which looked strong. He had wonderful arms, so strong, and large hands with slender fingers. He looked sensitive, and though not beautiful or particularly handsome he had a male charisma that was almost mesmerising. I thought him a romantic poet, a writer of some sort, a painter. It was the face, so young and bright and yet boyish, innocent even. Or if he wasn't he wanted to be.

'There was no towel on the beach for me, no robe or shirt to cover myself with. I felt no embarrassment and neither did he. You could see that from the way in which he was looking at me. Instead of walking away from him to the house, I walked towards him and the rocks. It was instinctive. He raised himself first to a sitting position and then stood up. Without haste, he scrambled down. I remember thinking he had fortitude. Those rocks were burning hot under his bare feet and on the sand it was hardly better. He walked towards me. Oh, his smile – slightly crooked, it warmed my heart and was somehow exciting and full of promise.

'I loved his body, found it incredibly sexy. And the way he moved: a walk with a slight rolling gait. I found it difficult to direct my eyes away from his penis. It was flaccid and even in that

243

state large by any standards. He was circumcised and I was transfixed by its beauty. It was incredibly erotic the way it swayed slightly from side to side as he walked, revealing at times a beautiful scrotum. He was like a young god cast down upon the earth, come to play with me. He was thrilling in the same way you would find an early Grecian statue of a young man carved from the finest piece of white marble exciting. So perfect, so god-like, yet innocent.

'I wanted him before he even said hello. And I knew that he wanted me. His eyes were devouring me. I had never seen a man hunger for me in the way this man did. I could imagine him sucking on my nipples, caressing my breasts. He licked his lips and smiled broadly. He was close enough to take my hand in his. He did, and raised it to his lips and kissed it. Still holding it in his, he turned me round to face the water and together we walked into the sea.'

There was a catch in Page's voice as she told of her first sight of Oscar, and she had to wipe the corner of one eye. The tears were there but they were not sad tears, merely a mask of immense emotion which was not wasted on her girlfriends. Anoushka reached over and handed her a glass of water. Page took no more than a sip. She could not have stopped telling her story even if she wanted to. Years of silence now ended, it spilled forth like a glorious waterfall.

'The sun burned us from above, the sea cooled us from below, the water caressed us. I remember thinking fancifully that I was being baptised, blessed by something beyond reason or mere faith. He never let go of my hand, not even when the water was over our head. We began to swim, each of us only using one arm. Then finally he released me and we continued to swim together far out from the shore. When we stopped swimming we floated on our backs until we were rested and then he pulled me into his arms. The water was up to our chins. He placed his lips to mine and his kiss was the most gentle I have ever known. His hands caressed my breasts, my hips, my bottom, and he drew me close to him and impaled me on him.

'I was drowning but not in the water – in sexual bliss as he moved me on and off him. He floated on his back with me on top straddling him, he was fucking me by raising and lowering me on and off his rock hard penis. He was throbbing inside me, holding me very still with one hand while the Aegean waves rolled over us and caressed my breasts, my back, and bottom. Then he spoke to me for the first time.

' "You're a gift from God. I've been waiting all my life for you."

'And you know, I knew it was true. And although I didn't know it before, I knew at that moment that I had all my life been waiting for him to find me. We came together and I had never known sexual intercourse like that ever. That was when the bell tolled for us. Alone in the sea, swimming in our own come, in that remote place we found ourselves. We had left everything behind. Our personae, our lives as we had been living them, even our clothes. All thought of yesterday or tomorrow.

'We stayed together there in that little house, that secret place, for five days and five nights. I had brought some books with me: the Greek Myths, Robert Graves, Shakespeare's Sonnets, Marcel Proust. We read to each other and swam in the sea and ate from the orchard and all of the little food I had in the house. We fished from his caique, that he had sailed from Hydra in and had anchored in the next bay.'

'That same caique that you still have in Hydra?' asked Sally.

'Yes, the very same one. We sailed along the coast in it and fished for our dinner. We almost never wore clothes wanting always to take each other whenever sex took our fancy. The more we fucked, the better it got for us. An erotic world opened up for us. We were wholly besotted with one another. The erotic extreme became the norm for us. It was unbelievably physical.'

At this point Page interrupted herself and asked, 'This doesn't embarrass you, my talking so frankly about the sexual impact we had upon each other? If it does I can stop, but there's no other way I can explain our story.'

Sex had never been a taboo subject between the women. They had many times talked about it between them, but up to now never as explicitly and always in guarded terms. Now that they had come so far together, they told Page to speak frankly, assuring her they had all at one time or another wanted to be more explicit when confiding in each other.

So Page did continue. 'As I said, the physical aspect of our coming together was overwhelming. He had only to look at me and he was lost. You could actually see it in not only his face but every fibre of his body, sense it in his soul. I was all that he could ever want, I excited him beyond all reason. If you think it was any different for me, you're mistaken.

'Just to look at him at any given moment was to make my heart beat fast. I would look away from him to try and break the spell. Impossible. I would have to look back at him. There was something more than the sensual about him, there was a passionate nature that

245

drew me to him. It was something beatific, a youthful innocence. I fell in love, at once and forever. I'm telling you about our beginnings and what we meant to each other now because I feel exactly the same way about him all these years later.

'Finally we ran out of all supplies in the little house. We put on some clothes. He had a pair of old worn chinos and a white batiste shirt, a pair of leather sandals. We sailed up the coast to the village, dropped anchor and walked from the beach the short distance into the old town. Even with clothes on he had a special kind of charisma that was inexplicable. Men would talk to him, follow us, offer us gifts of food, any help they could. We picked up a trail of children and the women, normally reticent with strangers, would speak to me and ask about him. His Greek was perfect, a joy to hear spoken, a scholar's Greek, not your average man in the street's Greek such as I spoke.

'Several days after we had returned from our trip to the village, he told me, "I've never loved a woman as I love you. I will never love any other woman as I will love you." I knew that he was telling me the truth. "Tell me all about you. I want to know everything: what you were like when you were a little girl, how and where you grew up. Your first love, your first sexual experience, the men you loved, the men who loved you. I know there have been many, and I want to know why you never loved them as you love me. I wish that I had been with you from the moment that you were born. I would have liked to have been a part of your skin then as I have become now."

'I told him my story, he told me his. Incredibly I was neither shocked nor disturbed to find that he was a Roman Catholic priest. It's difficult to explain how that could be. It was probably because it didn't affect how we were living together, the way we felt about each other. Whether there was going to be a future for us together or there wasn't didn't come into it. We just knew that something had happened to us called love and that we were together and that it would work out. Whatever way it worked out, we were richer and better, more alive for having been together. He told me he had no anxiety about breaking his vow, about loving a woman more than Jesus Christ.

'But having no anxiety about breaking his vow of celibacy does not mean that he did not have many conflicts with himself and his role in the church. By then I knew who he was. His name and what he represented was familiar to me. He did have, at the time we met, some celebrity as a result of his writing but not nearly the fame he does now. Who and what he was didn't seem to divide us

246

in any way. We continued our life exactly as it had been before we revealed ourselves to each other.

'Another week passed and he took me home to Hydra. We sailed away from our cove and the Peleponnisos. Were we leaving behind this romantic idyll, the erotic world we'd created for ourselves, this earthly but not quite earthly place? Were we sad to leave it? Not a bit, we knew we were taking it with us. We were excited about the future, about landing in Hydra and living together on the island in the romantic ruin he had bought. It never occurred to me to be concerned that I was living with a priest.

'It was as wonderful living with him in Hydra as it had been in that little hidden cove and the white house with blue shutters. We never lost the magic. We wore clothes more often, that was the greatest difference. We saw people and spoke to them, not hiding the love that we had for each other from them. Some knew he was a man of the church, others didn't. It didn't stop us taking the caique out, shedding our clothes and diving into the sea on the far side of the island where we had our privacy. Nor did it stop our nights and days of unbridled sex in his ruin of a house overlooking the port. His house had become our house. We planned its future rather than our own.

'The ghost visited us one night when we were way out over the top sexually. Actually it was at that moment just after we had come together in a powerful and long orgasm that stole every vestige of control from us, leaving us to scream into the night for help so that we might not linger too long in that moment of little death and be unable to revive ourselves. He wrapped himself round us and wept with joy and we imagined we heard the words: "You've come home." I never saw the captain's ghost again after that night.

'Eventually you always have to leave the island of your dreams. And we did, together. I for my Park Avenue shop in New York, he for a monastery in central America. That year we were together whenever it was possible, and the following year, and our love grew stronger. Our sexual hunger for each other never diminished. Every meeting, every sexual encounter, was a confirmation of the strength we had to be true to ourselves. For our second anniversary he gave me the deeds to the house in Hydra.

'The following year we had two months together. Fame was taking him over. Christ and his work had been his life until I had come along, and we both knew that I too was part of his life now. I could live with his devotion to the church but the church could

247

not live with his devotion to me. Oscar and I gave each other our freedom to live our lives outside the one we lived together because we loved each other and could never make light of each other's needs. That only drew us closer together. Each of us knew we had to work out our life for ourself and that ultimately that was what would determine our future.

'Finally we came to a decision to part. Not see each other at all nor communicate for a given length of time was the plan. He wanted to return to the church alone, without being influenced by his love for me, to make his decision to remain in the priesthood or to leave it once and forever because he could not in truth and heart be the man of the cloth that Roman Catholicism demanded he be. We gave ourselves seven years to get on with life without each other. If at any time during those seven years he came to terms with leaving the church, he would return to the house in Hydra and to me.

'We both knew that he had an enormously important work to complete, a church to obey, and unless he accomplished those things to the best of his ability, all would be lost for us. We made a pact. I would be in the house in Hydra for three weeks, those same three weeks every year. During that time, if he had resolved his conflicts, he would return to claim me and his house. I could wait. But he wouldn't allow me to promise that. The only promise he would allow me to make was that I should be in the Hydra house during those three weeks. If during his absence I were to find someone to love more than him, I was to send word through his publisher that I would not be in Hydra. If that were to happen he wanted the house to be mine. This is my fifth return to Hydra for my vigil.'

'Do you think he'll be there?' asked Sally.

'I have never asked myself that question. I just go there and enjoy myself and think about him, sometimes pretending that he's there with me. Crazy? Well, love is crazy, I can attest to that.'

'Hence your rush to get back to Hydra,' said Anoushka.

Page began to laugh. 'As if one day would make a difference! Who's to know, maybe it will.'

Chapter 17

The speed boat inched itself away from the dock. With a thrust of the motors it rose up in the water to cut a wide arc and aim towards the *Black Orchid* anchored about a quarter of a mile offshore. Anoushka, Page and Sally were standing aft, gripping tight the cross bar, all eyes on their greatest adventure yet, the boat they would sail across the Atlantic. They exchanged looks with each other, smiling broadly. The speed of the boat, the spray of the sea shooting past them, the black schooner with terracotta-coloured sails tied to three masts. It was all very exciting. Here was the beginning of their challenge of a lifetime.

Anoushka shouted above the din of the motors, the wind and the spray coming off the sea, 'Yes! Yes! Yes!'

The three women began to laugh, forgot safety and let go of the cross bar to hug each other, almost immediately losing their balance and falling all over each other. Hands went instantly back on to the cross bar. Page shouted above the noise, 'We'll make it! We'll do it! Oh, she's such a beauty lying there in the sun just waiting for us. Sally, we owe thanks to you for this. I wouldn't miss sailing her across the Atlantic for anything. Watch out world, the adventure is on!'

Sally shouted back, 'Piers's guilt, that's what we can thank!' And all three laughed again. Anoushka for once not taking the remark, as she took any remark about Piers, as personal, since his declaration of love for her.

On board they were greeted by the captain and his crew. The skipper of the schooner was straight with them. 'You do realise, ladies, you will have to be very good – better than good – top notch sailors before I will turn this boat over to you for the crossing? You will have to know every inch of her, every instrument and how it works, the feel of every rope, how to handle every sail. This boat will have to be part of you, your very heart and soul. And what about the ocean and the winds? You have to have a feel for them. To master the boat is one thing, but master the ocean? The Atlantic is its own master, it would be good to remember that. In fact, you might take that as your first lesson.'

'You don't think we can do it,' said Page.

'I didn't say that, ma'am.'

'But you're thinking it. I can assure you, we will. We three women *will* sail *Black Orchid* across the Atlantic and into the Caribbean Sea.'

The look she received from the captain and his crew made her smile. She told them, 'We may look like cream puffs to you at the moment, and not at all the part, but we will. And not only that, we'll *be* the part.'

It was true they hardly looked like young salts in training to challenge the Atlantic in the same chic clothes they had left Lakeside in, and bare feet. Each of them holding a pair of Maude Frizon shoes in their hands, Hermès handbags slung over their shoulders, Sally with a massive gem on her finger. The captain smiled. Page could do that to a man, make him melt, look beyond reason. She charmed him into an admission.

'I can assure you, Miss Cooper—'

'Page,' she insisted with a smile.

'—Page, with character and a will of steel, hard work as a priority, a quick mind and better than good reflexes, all of which I am guessing you have in abundance, you will be drinking champagne in the Caribbean.'

Smiles appeared on everyone's faces. Arms shot out and hands were now shaking others in a real welcome on board. The air had been cleared, everyone understood each other.

Clothes that were appropriate for crewing were already below in the ladies' cabins having been sent ahead before they left for the States. Sally and Anoushka went below to change. Page remained with the captain and crew above, walking the deck, admiring the beauty and condition of *Black Orchid*.

'It will be difficult for you and your crew, going as ballast instead of sailing her across the Atlantic, Captain. We don't need resentment with all we have to learn,' she said.

'I hope that I'm right in thinking that's more a plea for help rather than an insinuation that we'll not do our best for you all, Page?'

'Yes, I think you could say that. Now let's presume you find us as seaworthy as your boat. Up to taking over *Black Orchid* and sailing her, three women, across the Atlantic. The real challenge for us would be if you let us make this voyage on our own, and you and the crew flew over to the Caribbean and met us there.'

The men standing round her looked appalled. 'No way, Page, no way. Don't even think it. It would be foolhardy. To sail the Atlantic a crew needs years of experience. She's a lot of boat to handle, and she's not yours. Remember your arrangement with Piers. You sail her, we watch. No interference, ballast you may call us, but we're there. And if at any time I think lives or the boat are in danger you can't handle, I take over. I hope that settles it?'

'Those are your only criteria?'

'You have my word.'

Page stuck out her hand and shook the captain's. 'You can't blame a girl for trying. Under the same circumstances you would have done the same, now wouldn't you? All of you?'

The captain was once more charmed by her. A hint of a smile crossed his lips. Fortunately Anoushka and Sally were back on deck and joining them in time for him to escape having to answer Page.

It was another celebration and all Anoushka kept thinking of was how right Jahangir had been. The party does go on. Lunch, as ordered by Piers over the telephone from wherever he was, was smoked salmon sandwiches and champagne, served on deck with his compliments. There had been no other word for Anoushka. Piers was holding to his resolve. For that she was relieved, having still not sorted out her guilt about Sally's feelings via-à-vis Anoushka and Piers being together.

'I understand that you have to go, Page, But I wish you could stay. That we were all starting off together.'

'There's so much to learn, Anoushka, I know that. But I'll catch up with you once I'm on board. We'll still have nearly four months to sail together, to get it right. I won't let you down.'

'I wasn't thinking that you would. You have to go, I understand that, but I wish you could stay or I wish we could go with you. Now that we know the facts, I can't help but think, as Sally does, that it's a lonely vigil you'll be keeping.'

The plane buzzed the schooner and all faces turned up towards the sky, hands shading eyes. It circled once more and then landed on the water and taxied towards *Black Orchid*. All joy and excitement went of Sally and Anoushka's faces as the pilot cut his motors and the crew caught the plane's tow line and held it fast. Everyone was at the rail watching the plane bobbing up and down in the water, the waves slapping hard against the pontoons. The women hadn't spoken for some time, having been distracted by the business of holding the sea plane in tow for Page to board.

She turned to face her girlfriends. 'What, sad faces? Now, now, what's this?'

'I can't bear it if he's not there,' said Anoushka.

'I never think that way. I'm not a woman who tortures herself over a man, no matter how much I love him and want him. I never have been, never will.'

'Then why are you going back alone?'

'Probably because I never had friends like you before to come with me. Because I made a vow to myself and to a man I love that I would be there during these next three weeks. And mostly because I want to. I have faith, complete and utter faith in myself, in Oscar, in what is right and what is wrong for us. Ever since I met him, he has done nothing but add to my life. So, please, no sad faces for me. You two work hard and learn well, and I'll join you when you sail into Hydra and begin my tuition then. We have an ocean to cross, a great adventure, and we all three of us are going to be ready for it.'

She made haste to kiss Anoushka and Sally. Then she turned to speak to the captain, who had with his crew heard most of what had been said between the women. Rather than looking embarrassed, he looked admiringly at her.

'Thank you, Captain, for your hospitality. Take care of my friends for me. Not the best of jobs, training three ambitious ladies with a quest to fulfil. I'm sure that's what you're thinking. But we won't let you down. Why, you might even get to like the job! I look forward to coming on board for my training when you arrive in Hydra.'

One of the crew went ahead, descending the ladder followed by Page and then another crewman. The first sailor jumped on to the pontoon, opened the plane's door, and then held out a hand for Page who stepped gingerly from the boat ladder to join him. The water was choppy. The sailor held her steady with an arm round her waist, the co-pilot appeared at the open door and extended a hand. Page grabbed it and found the foot hole on the side, stepped into it, and was helped up into the plane that was to fly her directly to Hydra.

Seconds later the plane was drifting away from *Black Orchid* even before its door was closed. The tow lines having been pulled on board by the co-pilot, the plane's motors sputtered to life. It taxied bumpily through the waves to clear the boat before it picked up speed. Sally and Anoushka stood at the rail watching the plane shimmy and shake as it cut through the sea and then slowly achieve lift off and a climb at a gentle angle into the sky.

'Impossible love, impossible choices for both of them. How could they have concocted such a heart-breaking plan? How could our sensible, lovely Page have become involved with that? From where does she gather her strength for such an unachievable love?' asked Anoushka of Sally.

'Not strength, faith. She's solid with faith is our Page. It's her belief in something more than life itself that gives her the strength to love like that. When I lived with Piers I never had it. I wouldn't have understood it even if I had had it, but now that I'm with Jahangir, I do.'

She looked at her ring sparkling in the sunlight. Anoushka could not help but smile. She patted Sally on the shoulder and took her hand and held it up to have a better look at the ring.

'He's done you proud there, Sally.'

'He always does us proud, doesn't he?'

The two women looked again across the water and then scanned the sky for any sign of the plane and Page. Nothing.

'We'll call her tonight,' suggested Anoushka.

'No. If she wants us she knows how to reach us,' said Sally.

'Do you think he'll show up?'

'Does it matter? She's living her life the way she wants to, and he's there in it, the only way he can be. That's good enough for Page, and so it has to be good enough for us. I wouldn't venture a guess. If Page is happy with what she has of him, then what does it matter if he shows up or not? Now we'd better start learning how to sail this tub,' said Sally, punching Anoushka playfully on her arm.

Long after she flew away from the schooner, Page kept thinking about Anoushka, Sally and herself. They had come a long way together. Had she understood when the three had first met how serious their emotional troubles had been? Only now in retrospect could she really understand the despair that had taken over each of their lives. All because of men who were through with them.

It was not returning to Hydra and the house, the waiting for Oscar, that made her think about women cast off like worn-out clothes, by their great loves, who could, for whatever the reason, no longer sustain a life with them. It was Dr Robert Rivers that made Page think of them. Dr Robert Rivers and his cruelty to Anoushka because he loved another woman and had been unable to make a life with her. Page had gone along to support her and was not in the least sorry for having done so. She could see the positive effect confronting a return had had on Anoushka, but there had also been something haunting, a kind of ugly aura that had hovered over that unhappy triangle of Robert, Rosamond and Anoushka that Page found disturbing. The only really negative factor in Anoushka's return.

Page sighed. Relief? Yes, that she had escaped anything as soul-destroying as the past Anoushka was still and probably would always be living with. Page had no doubts that Anoushka would carry the scars of Robert's cruelty, the sexual manipulation-cum-love she had been indoctrinated in by Serge forever.

To see Sally and Jahangir was a joy, but would the scars inflicted by a man who threw her out vanish for good? When Page had first met Sally, she too had been cast off by someone she loved and had built an entire existence around. She had done nothing to deserve having her lifestyle torn away from her. To have been a convenience rather than a man's love – how humiliating. Needing to have a man who is through with you pick up the pieces of your life and find a way for your survival because you are too beaten up to construct anything for yourself. Serious abuse, utter defeat.

Page covered her face with her hands in despair for what her friends had been through, and for the millions of other women much less fortunate even than Anoushka and Sally who had suffered the same humiliations, defeats, destruction of self-esteem, in the name of love or worse, just to keep a man tied to them.

And what of herself? She had placed that ad in the *International Herald Tribune*, not because she was so wounded by a man but because she was so loved by one. Impossible love does not necessarily mean pain. No, she had not suffered pain as her friends had, merely a deep loneliness that none of the men she had been with since Oscar had been able to assauge, no matter how much they had tried, what good times she had had with them. A lady alone who needed adventure and the companionship of other women of like mind was what she had become so she could leave behind those that filled her life but were not love, just men.

Anoushka, Page and Sally pulled each other up by the boot straps from where they had been, strangers who had become best friends and somehow through each other learned about love, the good kind and the bad. Love slipped into proper perspective with the rest of their lives now. They had a new viewpoint on themselves and men and loving them. They owed each other a great deal, their new lives. That was Page's last thought as the drone of the planes motors hummed her into a deep, dreamless sleep. The sleep of a baby. Contentment.

It was dusk when she saw the coastline of Greece, the port of Piraeus, and Athens crawling across the landscape like a white amoeba. They skirted the bay, clogged up with ships in transit, huge oil tankers side by side, rusting in the afternoon sun. A graveyard of ships.

Flying low, the sea plane followed the coastline: the island of Aegina came into view. It was a mysterious and bewitching time of day to fly low over the water between the mainland and the islands of the Aegean. Dusk was coming down fast, they were racing against nightfall. They were flying in daytime, night descending from above, the sea below them like a voluptuous woman, beautiful and powerful, unfathomable, their haven, spread out ready to receive them. Ahead of them they had a clear view of both night and day as they flew towards Hydra. It was an eerie, seductive sight, and strangely erotic, something like being swallowed up by the elements.

The island of Poros, its small white church on the edge of the port, came into view, another island of white-washed houses. This one was famous for its pistachio trees and the vendors down on the docks selling them freshly roasted to the ferry boat passengers. It was short flying time now to her island, the race against nightfall still on. Suddenly there it was, Hydra, barren rock, some scrubby wind-swept green, rising high and magnificent out of the sea. Her heart began to race.

She told the pilot, 'Make your landing just this side of that promontory,' and pointed the area out for him.

'No problem,' he told her.

'If we could cruise round the point and into port that would be great. I'd like to make the least dramatic entrance possible, otherwise we'll have the whole island down in the port to see who's arrived. The water's somewhat rough this side of that rock face but it becomes calm the moment you make that turn into the harbour. We can taxi in then without too much of a fuss.'

The pilot signalled thumbs up. He knew very well what excitement a sea plane causes. The landing was a good one but as Page had predicted on a rough and choppy sea before they made the turn into the harbour and the town came into view.

It was as calm as a lake, the caiques were already in for the night and bobbing lazily up and down in the water. The crescent-shaped port and town rose dramatically like the most perfectly shaped amphitheatre to the top of the island. White house upon house, upward and upward, shimmering in the heat, with a hint of pink from a sun en route to setting.

The motors were cut to slow cruise, and they made their entrance into the harbour just as lights began to appear in the windows of the houses: the glowing light of candles or of stars. The port was quiet at this hour, a few drinkers trading the day life of the port for the night life or making ready for it; the cooking smells wafting from the restaurants, tables being laid, waiters sweeping.

Page had eyes only for her house. Whenever she came home and had that first glimpse, she thought, 'There's the captain's house, he's on watch for me.' Strange for a woman who could hardly be considered fanciful.

It looked glorious in the evening light. The way the building broke for a courtyard here, a terrace there, for a flight of steps to yet another level. The old fig tree, the ancient date palm. The perfect marriage of architecture and natural terrain. The house was closed up but still had tremendous presence as it always had whether inhabited or not. It was much admired and sometimes envied by all who were lucky enough to sail into the harbour.

It felt good to be back, *and* on the day she had set for her return. It hadn't been all that easy to manage it. *Black Orchid*, being stateside, Groton, the school shenanigans, Lakeside and all that went with that trip had been fun, thanks to the effort everyone made, but somewhat exhausting. It had only been five days since the three women had left Hydra.

Children were shouting at the sea plane as they ran along the quay, curious Hydriots having their early ouzos abandoned them to have a closer look at the white and silver sea plane. Who was arriving on the island in such style? was the question on everyone's lips. All along the port where the caiques were secured, people were lining up to have a guess and a gossip. The tables of expatriates living on the island stopped drinking, some stood up for a better look.

The plane was secured at the very end of the quay with the help of the two port authority people. The co-pilot was the first out of the plane, Page followed and then the pilot. The onlookers were both impressed and disappointed. They wanted to see Sophia Loren, Tom Cruise and his wife, Sylvester Stallone. The ultimate for them would have been Clint Eastwood, a big movie star. Any movie star would do. But a sometime resident? Impressive to come home in a sea plane, yes, but a let down too. Some of the locals did shake her hand and remark about her mode of transportation: where had she come from, how long had it taken, when would the plane take off again, was a ride possible?

Page gave her passport to one of the port authority men and once it was established that the plane was taking off in a matter of minutes, after a drink and something light to eat for the pilots, the officials agreed to forget the formalities and watch the plane, which otherwise would have been crawling with the curious. The pilot, his co-pilot and Page then walked along the port to a café where she bought ouzos and a plate of char-grilled squid.

Page chose that same table any time she could get it because from there she could look past the moored boats, out across the small well-protected harbour and up at her house with the rest of the town rising up against the skyline.

The pilots didn't linger. They had stretched their legs and had a drink to revive them from the long flight from the south of France and were anxious to leave, wanting to make Athens and an overnight stop at Vuliagmeni before dark. They would not allow Page to walk them back to the plane, so it was handshakes all round and she watched them walk back to the plane, wanting to get off as fast as possible.

They taxied the plane across the water at a greater speed than they had entered the harbour. Loudly roaring engines cut the quiet of the lazy port and drew everyone's attention as they churned up water and spray, leaving a trail of choppy waves. Noise and speed. Just what the Greeks liked. Macho living. The sight drew crowds along the quay, children running on the stone path along the edge of the rocky island that rose so sharply high out of the sea. Finally the plane had lift off. A roar of approval from the onlookers and in seconds it was high in the sky and out of sight, swallowed up by twilight.

Page ordered another ouzo. It felt good to be home, so right just to be having the time to think about Oscar. To indulge herself for the next three weeks with him in the forefront of her mind was her greatest luxury. These were the weeks when she worked on the house with the builders, or read, or swam, or fished, alone with her destiny. She always felt buoyant during these three weeks when she was there for her and Oscar.

It didn't take long for the world, Anoushka, Sally, and the past five days to slip from her mind. She kept looking up at her house and each time she glanced at it she was aware of its beauty, how good it always felt to be there. She came other times during the year, whenever her schedule allowed. Would this be the last June pilgrimage she would make? The last vigil she would hold? Only on the last day when he had not arrived or sent word of any kind would that question arise. She never had an answer in advance.

She leaned back in her chair and ran her fingers through her hair, gazing yet again up at the house. It was love she saw there, and home, belonging. She smiled. And then right before her eyes she saw, without warning, a room spring to life with lamplight, the ground floor hall off the terrace. Next the open arched loggia lights were switched on. Page sat up in her chair. Her bedroom. The shutters were being opened, several windows overlooking the harbour shone in the soft yellow of incandescent light bulbs. Another room, and another. The guest rooms in the wings of the house. Room by room the house became ablaze with light.

Page was mesmerised to see the house looking so very lived in. Never had she seen it like that. Neither had anyone else. For years parts of it had been continually under construction or redecoration. Only now did she realise what a massive work she had undertaken. How clever she and Oscar had been in designing it. She realised something at that very moment that she had not understood before: the house was complete, it was a home. People sitting at the next table were talking about it. Someone passed her and patted her on the shoulder, saying, 'Marika has gone mad with your electricity, Page.'

No, not Marika. Even as a welcome home for Page she would not have opened the house so extensively. One person, not even three as when she, Anoushka and Sally had been living there, had opened all the house. She began to understand: there was to be no vigil this year or any other year. Oscar had made the most important decision of his life. He had come home. He had chosen life with her above the church.

The realisation of what he had done overwhelmed her. Tears slipped slowly from the corners of her eyes. She had to lower her head and cover her face with her hands. Not wanting to draw attention to herself, she willed herself to composure. Page wanted to dash from the table, to run across the cobblestoned port, through the narrow stone streets and up the steep white-washed steps that twisted and turned up to her house. But, limp with emotion, she had no strength to make such a dash, her legs had turned to jelly. Her heart raced and her mouth was dry. She needed to gather her strength and calm herself further before she would be able to walk past the people who had by now wandered down into the port. Another passed her table and commented,

'Page, it looks as if your ghost has returned to claim his house and wants us all to know it.'

That brought a smile to her lips. A warmth to her heart. It stopped racing. She answered the butcher, 'Yes, my ghost has come home. But then he really never left.'

She regained her legs, left some money on the table and walked slowly, eyes always on the house round the crescent-shaped port, unable to keep a smile from her lips, her heart from singing. She passed the post office and Marika's house below and was just turning up the narrow street to begin her climb when Marika came rushing out and threw her arms round Page. 'He's come home, madam, he's come home for good! I never thought he would come home for good!' Tears were streaming down the woman's face.

'Shush, Marika. Shush, I know. The house is ablaze with him. Isn't it wonderful?'

Page gave the loyal Marika, who had been with Oscar even before Page had met him, a kiss on the cheek and turned her round and sent her home. One last look at the house, now a place of warmth, the sunshine of their lives, before she took that first step of the climb and it vanished from sight behind other white-washed houses.

A deep breath for the climb and then she took her first step and then the next and then another. Too slow. She began to race up the steps. Halfway to the house, having to catch her breath, she had to stop and lean against a wall. A neighbour, a very old Hydriot, always dressed in widow's weeds, stepped out on to her small wooden balcony that leaned practically on top of the wall surrounding her house. In Greek she said, 'Page, God bless you both. Be happy. I'll light a candle for you and for your man.' And with that the woman cut a single white rose, full blown, and tossed it down to Page. The rose had been carefully nurtured by the widow, it was her pride, her joy. A generous act. Page had so many lost loves to live her own for. The flower's scent was so sweet.

That was all she needed to spur her on. She took the steps now two at a time. She couldn't get to him fast enough. Every second he was out of her sight was a torture for her now. She called out, 'Oscar, Oscar!' as she approached the walls of her house.

She heard his footsteps before she saw any sight of him. She imagined him racing across the terrace and through the gates. His footsteps echoed down the narrow walled-in path as he raced down towards her. It was dark now, a crescent moon had appeared just above and in front of Page. Its bright white light shone down the path, illuminating the steps and the high white walls. The sky was midnight blue, millions of stars peppering it. A bend in the path. He raced round it, and she saw him. He was exactly as she remembered him: youthful and blond-haired, a sensitive, vulnerable, yet virile and exciting face, the incredibly sensuous body. They crashed into each other's arms.

Neither could speak for the tears, emotions striking them dumb. They kept wiping each other's tears from their faces. Finally, arms wrapped round each other, tears speaking where words would not come, they walked together up the remaining steps and through the old wooden doors set in the wall. Together they turned to close them.

What price love?

Chapter 18

Immediately he saw her, Hadon Calder knew that it was Anoushka. The sight of her as she was now brought a smile to his lips. She came out of the *boulangerie* with a dozen French sticks under one arm and a handsome young man on the other. She was laughing and the Adonis with a body builder's physique, dressed in white tee shirt and navy blue sailor's trousers, fly buttons of white bone, reached over to smooth a lock of hair from her forehead. This sailor, instantly recognisable as a member of crew of *Black Orchid* by the uniform he was wearing, was clearly besotted, and Hadon was clearly amused.

It was difficult to equate this happy smiling woman with the one he had rescued on board the *QE2*. There was nothing dowdy about this Anoushka and she certainly didn't look as if she needed to be rescued. Trimmed down, hair smartly cut, she was dressed in jeans that could have been custom made for the way they clung to her body to show the sensual, sexy Anoushka he had had and had enjoyed so enormously. She too wore a white tee shirt, her breasts and nipples, their ample size and stunningly good shape discernible under the tight top. A reminder of what a surprise she had been sexually. His eyes rested on her leather belt with a large and attractive antique silver buckle, a handsome chunk of turquoise its centre of attraction. Navaho, he guessed, Ralph Lauren, about ten years old.

He watched her walk down the *boulangerie*'s two steps to the pavement. Even her walk had changed, the way she moved. For several moments he watched her standing on the pavement talking to the young man. A slip of paper was produced from his pocket. A shopping list, guessed Hadon. Early-morning shopping? They wouldn't have much luck with that. Only one or two places were open at that hour. Hadon was intrigued by Anoushka's being there. Even more so when Akito too walked from the *boulangerie* with three baguettes under his arm and she stopped him for information.

Hadon was taking a genuine pleasure in the change in Anoushka, some pride too for having, on first meeting her, spotted that she was far more than what she had become. She had surprised him beyond imagining when she had proved that first with her talent for languages and then sexually.

He never thought to get out of his vintage Mercedes to make contact with her. It didn't even occur to him to call out her name, though he could have easily since the soft top was down.

He watched her walk away, and wanted her. She had suddenly become an object of desire, his sexual desire, as she had unexpectedly on board the *QE2*. Having never given her a second thought from the time she had left his cabin, it was now that he remembered keenly how great she had been sexually. What had happened to her since he'd rescued her? Whatever it was, he liked it. She piqued his interest, something she had not done when he had had his first encounter with her. Akito slipped into the front seat next to Hadon and closed the car door.

'What did she want, Akito?'

'To ask if I knew what time the *charcutier* opened for business. I told her about Mercier's the last time we met in the bakery shop.'

'Did she tell you where she lives?'

'Oh, you are being naughty, I can hear it in your voice, Mr Calder.'

'You're not my keeper, Akito.'

'Oh, no?'

'Well, of my house and a good part of my life, maybe, but not of my soul.'

'Oh, now the soul comes into it!' Akito's laugh was mocking. He knew his employer very well.

'Is she local? Renting a house here on the Côte d'Azur, close by?' asked Hadon.

Akito found the questions unusual. Hadon Calder rarely showed interest in anyone other than himself unless it was to do with his work. Akito was enjoying this. He rarely had the chance to take a dig at his employer who usually had the drop on Akito and could, in the nicest way, tease him unmercifully.

'Oh, you haven't heard? You really don't know? Everyone is talking about them. Everyone wants to meet them.'

Hadon rose to the bait. 'Them, Akito?'

'She and two other women.'

'A *ménage à trois?*'

'No, no. She and two other women are going to sail the *Black*

Orchid across the Atlantic from Nice to an island in the Caribbean.'

'Just three women?'

'That's what they say.'

'I can't believe it's true.'

'It is. That young man, he's one of the crew on *Black Orchid*. Didn't you recognise him?'

'No. If it were true Rab Nesnet would have told me.'

'You haven't seen Rab for months. You haven't seen anyone for months. remember, you told me no visitors until the manuscript is completed.'

'Has it been that long?'

'Yes, Mr Calder.'

'I've met that woman before, Akito. I have no doubt that if she were well trained she would be capable of sailing the Atlantic, but I cannot believe she has the desire or the courage to do it. You really do surprise me with this news. Where is she living?'

'On board *Black Orchid*. She won't be here for much longer though. They're taking *Black Orchid* for a sail round the Greek islands very soon now.'

'You seem to know a great deal about all this.'

'In the mornings when I see her at the *boulangerie*, she talks to me. She speaks Japanese.'

'What do you think of her?'

'Very pretty. She speaks like an American but she's not, and her accent in my language is not the way an American who has learned Japanese would sound. A nice woman.'

Hadon kept a straight face but smiled to himself. Exciting in bed would be a better description, he thought, delighted with himself for having had her and surprised too that he was wanting her in just that way again.

The village streets were empty of people at that hour, only the odd shop was open for taking deliveries and serving. Hadon sped through the streets and down on to the coast road where he headed the car for home.

This was a rocky peninsula of land jutting into the Mediterranean close to the Eden Roc Hotel. A poor boy all his early life, Hadon had understood the importance of owning land, and the security that went with it. When money and success did start rolling his way, he put it into land and houses. For years he had been buying land, parcel by parcel, hectare by hectare, period cottages and farmhouses on the spit of land he could now call his own.

They were approaching the gates, unimpressive, solid rusted sheet metal. He pulled off the busy road right up to the gates and Akito hopped out of the car and opened them. After closing and securing them with a chain and padlock, he returned to the car and Hadon drove slowly up the quarter-mile drive through a tangled wood of knotted trees indigenous to the Côte d'Azur, heavy undergrowth and many ferns. The wood thinned out and suddenly they emerged from the cool of a shady forest into bright sunlight and a first sight of the spectacular view of the bay, an endless view of open water beyond. Marvellous hanging gardens tripped down from terrace to terrace carved from the cliffs and to a small sand beach sheltered by rocks jutting out from the cliffs.

Hadon drew up to the handsome Côte d'Azur house built in the twenties with all the charm that went with houses of that period in the South of France. He cut the motor and turned to Akito.

'When do they make this crossing of the Atlantic?'

Akito shook his head. 'Mr Calder, she works very hard learning to sail that boat. She has not time.'

'You leave that to me. When do they go?'

'Not for a long time.'

Hadon walked directly through the house to the patio over-looking the sea. From there he had a clear view of *Black Orchid* riding at anchor almost opposite the house and about a quarter of a mile into the bay, Rab Nesnet liked to anchor in that spot or close to it when *Black Orchid* was in Cap d'Antibes. How game of Piers to let three ladies have their adventure on his schooner. And how Rab would be hating having to give his boat over to them. The very thought caused a smile to appear on Hadon's face.

He and Rab Nesnet had become all-boys-together kind of friends since Rab took on the job of captain of *Black Orchid*. Hadon really coveted the schooner; he had his own fantasies about sailing it across the Atlantic, or to Australia. He looked at it now, so long and sleek with its three masts and rust-coloured sails. *Orchid* was a honey when she came in under full sail.

Coveting, wanting, that was one thing, but committing yourself to a boat such as *Black Orchid* was another. An extravagance and a responsibility, a commitment Hadon was not prepared to take on. His houses and gardens were all the commitment he could handle. For all his success and wealth, he was a man who liked to keep his life pared down, simple, uncomplicated, but extremely comfortable. Writing was all the commitment he wanted.

He was a creature of habit. Up at five in the morning, then an hour's work. Into the sea for his morning swim, weather permitting. At six o'clock another hour's work, usually at the beach house. Once a fisherman's cottage, it was built into the cliffside above the old wooden dock where he kept a speed boat and his sixty-footer, a good sailing vessel but not approaching the class of *Black Orchid*.

Rickety wooden stairs with equally rickety handrails crisscrossed the cliffside from the water's edge to terraces filled with potted trees and flowering shrubs, weatherworn, wooden chaiselongues for sunning, umbrellas for shade. The dining terrace was midway between the top of the cliff and the house. And it was there every morning, weather permitting, that he breakfasted. Always the same breakfast: mango, a pot of hot black coffee, half a dozen croissants still warm from the *boulangerie*, and peach preserve thick with fruit, a hint of brandy and slivers of almond. Strips of either Parma ham or streaky bacon, three times a week with poached eggs, completed the fare.

It seemed strange that Anoushka Rivers should have been under his nose all this time. He watched *Black Orchid*'s speed boat returning from shore to the boat. Writer's curiosity: how had she come this far and in so short a time? Then his breakfast arrived and he realised he was ravenous and forgot her for food. After his breakfast, he went not to the house but to another cottage a five-minute walk from the main house. This was his primary work place; no telephone or fax, no interruptions, except for a clear view of the sea. He worked there until two o'clock when he broke for lunch, had a siesta and then another swim. If the energy was still there he would work for three more hours, have a light supper and go to bed. No matter how much he would have liked to have a sex scene with Anoushka, his schedule and work came before that. Firmly he put her out of his thoughts for another day.

Rab Nesnet, captain of *Black Orchid*, was never surprised by anything that Piers Hazlit asked him to do. He always rose to the occasion. Even more than that, he responded with enthusiasm. Piers was an adventurer, Rab had always been a soldier of fortune, together they had been a good team now for nearly ten years. But this! Training three inexperienced women to sail the Atlantic with only four months in which to learn . . . not only had he thought Piers mad, he considered him out of line in asking Rab to take on such a boring and impossible task. Rab, of whom the

265

term male chauvinist would have been a flattering description, liked his women off boats and in bed, the kitchen or a whore house.

Now, after ten days with Sally and Anoushka, he was not so sure Piers had gone mad. Of the two, it was Anoushka who was the greater surprise. Rab had thrown every menial task that had to be done on *Black Orchid* to the women. It was rise and shine at five in the morning and work until they fell into a dead sleep at nine in the evening. Not once did they flinch or complain or deliver less than the best of themselves. This was no lark; they intended with every fibre of their being to make that crossing.

Rab Nesnet had the sea in his blood; his father had been a captain, his grandfather and *his* father before him, all Massachusetts men of the oceans, whalers and fishermen, later shippers and owning shipping companies. He had sailed solo at the age of six, and travelled the oceans and the seas of the world from the time he was a teenager. From all the men he had come across at sea, he had learned one thing: there were those who had a feel for the sea and the sail, who knew the winds, how to pit themselves and their craft against those two great untamable forces. Anoushka had the sensibilities of a keen sailor. Every question she asked, the way she took to the charts and navigation, used the instruments, indicated that. After ten days Rab understood what Piers had seen in these women to have loaned them *Black Orchid*. They had adventure in their souls, and courage to break out and fulfil a dream. Having been handed a chance to make their wish come true, they had grabbed it in both hands. And for that alone they had to be admired.

In two days' time they would sail for Hydra to pick up Page. From there he had planned a voyage, one he liked to make, through the Greek islands along the coast of Turkey. It was tricky. Hot, dry winds blew in from Africa, and they were difficult seas. A terrific training ground. He would give them the benefit of doubt and make his judgement in four months' time. For the moment he'd decided he liked his protégées, and was believing more daily in their ability to achieve the crossing. He was keen to see what they could do, and dared to think that they just might make it.

'I'm giving us all twenty-four hours' leave,' he announced to his crew which now included Anoushka and Sally. 'We'll kick off with lunch ashore.'

The morning after Hadon had seen Anoushka, Akito was pouring his breakfast coffee and Hadon was scanning the bay and

266

Black Orchid through a pair of powerful binoculars, something he did every morning.

'And was she there this morning?' he asked.

'No, the other lady was there.'

'Oh.' Hadon lowered the binoculars and placed them on the table. 'And what's she like?'

'Very pretty.'

'And you speak to her too?'

'No. She says "good morning", that's all.'

The following morning at breakfast Hadon made the same inquiries, Akito's answers were the same. On the third morning after Hadon had seen Anoushka, the questions and answers were the same. By the fourth morning he had lost interest as to whether or not Anoushka had appeared at the bakery. He posed no questions to Akito. He knew where Anoushka was and he could find her whenever he wanted to, if indeed he ever did want to. But Akito surprised him.

'Your lady.'

'What lady?'

'The lady in the *boulangerie*.'

'Oh, that lady.'

'I saw her this morning.'

'Oh?'

'They're going to lunch at Stephano's, captain's treat. The entire crew has twenty-four hours' leave. It's a reward for their hard work, and because they're sailing: a practice cruise, the Greek islands.' He smiled knowingly at Hadon and then walked away.

Hadon's immediate reaction to this news was that he would miss the sight of *Black Orchid* in the bay. The luxury of watching anything as beautiful as that schooner leaving in full sail for a day's cruising, or returning with a setting sun for a backdrop, was something he would miss. It was as if his best neighbour was going off on holiday.

Another ten days, two weeks at the most, and he would be free of his book. He might take *Easy Rider*, his own boat, on a cruise. The sixty-footer was no *Black Orchid* but Hadon knew how to get the best out of her. Sailing her had always given him enormous pleasure. He looked at her now, moored one side of his wooden dock, the speed boat on the other side. The idea spurred him to get on with his day.

Three hours later, during his coffee break, he surprised even himself when he jogged up to the house to tell Akito, 'I'm

267

lunching out. Call Stephano and tell him to save me a place. My usual table, I'm dining alone. I'd like a cold supper later. Leave it set up in the kitchen. Flowers on the table, Chablis, and place settings for two. Take the evening out if you like. And do me the courtesy of wiping that smile off your face!'

'Shall I take a car out?' asked Akito, trying to hide his surprise and amusement at this break in the working schedule, almost unheard of for Hadon.

'No. I'll take the power boat.'

After coffee, Hadon returned directly to the work house. He knew Rab's form. He would take his party by water to Stephano's, Hadon's guess was at twelve o'clock. Right on schedule he watched *Black Orchid*'s speed boat circle round the schooner and head in towards shore. He could see everyone on board quite clearly when Rab swerved away from shore to ride parallel to Hadon's property. The boat vanished from Hadon's view when it rounded the point. From there Rab would follow the coast to the next cove and two others before he would tie up at Stephano's jetty.

Stephano's was one of the French Riviera's best-kept secrets, the perfect restaurant that one dreams of discovering on the Côte d'Azur. It was what every diner dreamed of, what cookery writers wrote about but never found. Not at all prepossessing – something between a string of fishermen's cottages and a French farm house, built among huge rock formations and caves – it could be reached by boat up rocky steps from its jetty where guests tied their boats fast. Above the house the land flattened out into fields farmed for sunflowers. In the 1990s it was one of the last unspoilt treasures the Côte d'Azur had to offer. Stephano and his family held on to their sunflower fields and their restaurant; no matter what the offer, no real estate developer was getting it in its owner's lifetime.

Stephano, an Italian, had married a local French girl after the Second World War. The land had been in her family for generations. Before the war he had worked as a chef, and afterwards decided to go back to his old trade. The vegetables came from their fields, the wine was throaty and local, and his Calvados was a dream come true.

The restaurant was unimpressive: dark, low ceiling, white-washed walls, blue-and-white-checked table cloths, white napkins big as a baby's nappy, two tables seating ten people, and two that sat four, one small table for two. Where you ate depended on the weather, what you ate depended on Stephano.

You could reach the restaurant by boat. Large sailing yachts and motor cruisers dropped anchor off shore and took dingies or power boats in. Or you could drive off the main road, down the dirt track through the sunflower fields, and walk the rest of the way down the hill on stone steps to the front of the house to enter the restaurant. That is if you knew how to get there. There were no signposts, and Stephano never advertised.

One table outside and two tables inside were already taken, some of the diners knew Hadon by sight. They stood up to greet him and shake hands. Rab and his party were seated at a table for ten, inside. All eyes were on Hadon as soon as he entered the room. It was cool and inviting inside out of the hot midday sun. A light breeze was blowing through the small casement windows, rippling the blue and white gingham curtains hanging limply on either side of the glass.

Hadon received a rapturous greeting from Stephano and his wife Charmaine. An enormous hug and a kiss on first one cheek and then the other from Stephano which Hadon returned with nearly as much enthusiasm. His wife stopped serving a table to do the same and their teenage son, who waited table, shook Hadon's hand. Before he could get to the small table by the window where he always sat by himself, or with an elegant and expensive lady of the night, he was handed a drink: a rough white wine chilled to perfection and poured from a jug. They were still standing by the entrance, the sea clearly visible crashing against the rocks behind them.

Rab excused himself from his table and went to greet Hadon. They patted each other on the shoulder and shook hands.

'Join us?' suggested Rab.

'Too many people. You know me, if I'm not in the mood.'

'It's an age since I've seen you. I hear you're locked away, all visitors forbidden. Is the book finished?'

'No. I've just escaped from it for a while. Giving myself a twenty-four hour break.'

'What a coincidence, so are we. Come on, join us.'

'No, I think I'll keep it simple this lunchtime.'

'But I have two terrific ladies for you to meet.'

'We'll skip it today.'

'As you like, old boy. Nice to see you, Hadon, let's get it together soon.'

He sat down at his table and only then did he look past the smiling happy faces and directly into Anoushka's eyes. He could see that his entrance had had an effect on her. She was startled.

Rab said, 'That's Hadon Calder.'

'Oh!' said Sally, knowing very well that it was his book that Anoushka was translating.

Before she could say another word Anoushka shot her a look that demanded silence. Sally picked that up immediately and changed the subject. 'Anoushka, try this.' And she cut a slice off one of the half dozen salamis stuck in a wicker basket on the table, and handed it to her.

'That's a *salame toscano*, mild, sweetly peppery, and the infusion of garlic is done with a light touch. My favourite. Maybe we can get Stephano to sell us one for your crossing,' said Rab, and handed her a piece of rough home made bread to go with it.

Anoushka and Sally were thrilled. That was the first indication they had from their captain that they might be making a crossing. They played it cool, knowing that it was early days, anything could happen yet.

The table was already groaning with platters of *antipasti*, including *bruschetta* with a garlicky, dark and delectable purée of aubergine. A pottery dish contained a warm tangle of fennel with a caramelised shiny glow to it. Loaves of several different kinds of bread, including olive bread dense with thinly sliced olives, were lying on the table. The anchovy butter was a gourmet's delight.

The same fare was put on Hadon's table. He never thought he was hungry until he had that first whiff of the Stephano cuisine, and now he was ravenous. Today's choice of pasta, always the first course at the restaurant after the *antipasti*, was no problem for Hadon. Wide straw-coloured ribbons dressed with *porcini*, or ropes of it served with a clam sauce. Or else *gnocchi*: mashed potatoes bound with herbs and flour and whatever other magic ingredients the master chef Stephano used were rolled out and pinched into fat little ears, dropped into boiling water, drained and served with a pesto sauce and freshly grated *Regiano parmigiano*. *Gnocchi* always won his favour, hands down.

Today he chose to follow with rabbit studded with juniper berries, fennel seeds, and needles of rosemary, both braised and roasted – one of the great gourmet rabbit recipes of the world.

Hadon glanced over at Anoushka several times until at last their eyes made contact. Just as a woman knows when a man wants her, a man has that same sensibility. They were in like mind about each other. She was digging into her food and enjoying every morsel of it. Anoushka was hungry, but not nearly as hungry for food as she was for him and sex. She had not forgotten their last encounter; he could feel her heat even across the room.

It gave him enormous pleasure to watch her. A plate of soft white goat's cheese topped with a local silky, smooth, honey was placed down in front of him. Hadon spooned it into his mouth. Sheer ambrosia. The taste triggered his sexual memory. He could think only of the taste and the texture of her cunt. It had been as sweet and exotic as the dish placed before him.

He went to the kitchen door and asked for a bottle of Stephano's home-made golden *grappa*, flavoured with oranges. Once he had it in hand, he walked from the kitchen door directly to Anoushka and without a word to her or anyone else at the table, took her hand and kissed it. She rose from the chair, they smiled at each other, and she said, 'I thought you'd never ask.'

Before they reached the door everyone in the restaurant was clapping, raising glasses of wine to toast them, the crew wolf whistling.

Rab called out after them, 'We sail tomorrow, all hands on deck at fourteen hours. That's two o'clock, Anoushka.'

She turned and looking over her shoulder, blew him a kiss and told him, 'I'll be there. wouldn't miss it for the world.'

271

Chapter 19

They walked in silence from the restaurant down the first flight of the weatherworn wooden stairs and on to a landing. There he pulled Anoushka up short and, placing an arm tight round her waist, asked, 'Why didn't you come to my table, acknowledge me? Can you only want me when you're in distress?'

'I'm acknowledging you now,' she said, slipping her hand under the belt of his trousers and caressing him, feeling the swell of him in her hand. 'Ah, I see you remember me.'

He laughed and removed her hand and kissed it, then taking it once more firmly in his, he pulled her down the next flight of steps. 'You look fantastic, and that's no exaggeration. I could hardly believe it was you when I saw you in front of the *boulangerie* several days ago. Akito is my housekeeper.'

'Why didn't *you* say something, acknowledge me?'

'I'm a man of habit. It had been great sex, it was over. I never rekindle things. We'd agreed a one night stand and that was that. No future, remember?'

Anoushka gazed intently into Hadon's eyes. Finding men's demands and ultimatums no longer of interest o her, she said, 'Good, I hate lukewarm anything. Then we'll have to begin again.'

She broke away from him and ran down the remainder of the stairs and on to the jetty. Very sure of herself and him, she waited for Hadon to reach her.

'Here, take this,' he said, and handed her the bottle of *grappa*. He jumped down into his boat and reached up, arms at the ready. She jumped into them. He pulled her to him. She felt good. Her audacity excited him.

In one quick movement he put her away from him and slid her tee shirt up over her head. He stood back to have a better look at her naked breasts and without hesitation clasped one with both his hands, caressing it, and fed the nipple into his mouth to suck on it voraciously.

She tensed immediately. It was sexual tension, the sort that comes from wanting not to hold back, but to hold on to every nuance of sensation she was experiencing. He unbuckled the Navaho belt and unzipped the blue jeans. He felt the flesh of her mound in his hands and squeezed hard on it before finding her willing slit. With deft fingers, he parted the cleft and his fingers toyed with the soft, warm, silky inner lips of her cunt. His hands were large, his fingers long and slender, very sexy.

He knew what she could do, how much she could give, what excited her. Unceremoniously he thrust his fingers deep inside her and was amazed as he kissed her wildly, sucked her tongue into his mouth, bit hard into her lips, how much he wanted her. Unable to stop himself, his lips went from her mouth to her breasts. His sucking was urgent and powerful, unrelenting. Hadon felt her giving in to him and his rage of passion for her became more violent. His lips moved to between her breasts and there he licked her flesh, sucked it into his mouth. She tasted sweet. He calmed himself somewhat when he felt that tiny shudder and her first orgasm flow over his fingers. Reluctantly and with some finesse, he relinquished her cunt and placed his fingers in his mouth, sucking them, wanting to share in her bliss.

Anoushka was so moved she had to place her hands over her face, if for no other reason than to break his lustful gaze. Their erotic desires had somehow taken them over, commonsense had been abandoned. They were in too public a place for how they felt about each other and where they wanted to go with that. He caressed her shoulders with a degree of tenderness that made her want to melt. He closed her jeans and buckled the belt, took her hand in his and held it while keeping her close to him. Turning the key, Hadon started the motor, Anoushka pulled in the line, and he swung the boat away from the jetty. At full throttle, he sent the boat speeding across the water. It was a rough ride at such speed and in such a small craft but they hardly noticed.

She was quick in hoisting herself up on to his dock and tying the power boat fast to it. She leaned over the boat and her still naked breasts, so large and fully rounded, swung provocatively above Hadon's face as she extended a hand to help him on to the dock. Did she know how much she was teasing and taunting him with her sexuality? He was quite mad to have her.

She broke into his thoughts when she reminded him, 'My shirt?' He had handed her the bottle of *grappa* but had indeed forgotten her shirt, preferring her naked and vulnerable to him. He was quick to retrieve it, and then with it still in his hand, was there on the dock beside her.

There was about them both a pent-up sexual energy asking to be released, begging to be made the most of. There was too sexual chemistry, erotic freedom, between them. They knew that, not only from their mutual erotic hunger for each other now but from a one night sexual past. Together they had tasted real sexual honey, sexual ecstasy, bliss, oblivion, those same things that they wanted from each other now.

Anoushka walked up the cliffside on the stairs that criss-crossed it, past the beach house, the work house. She was enchanted. She had somehow not imagined Hadon would live in such natural splendour – but then, she had not imagined him or anything about him at all.

From the water's edge to the patio doors of the drawing room in the main house all she could exclaim was: 'Wonderful!'

Hadon was no sooner into his drawing room than he was peeling off the blue and white checked shirt he was wearing and dropping it on the floor. Anoushka had forgotten how much she had liked his naked flesh. She caressed his shoulders and a shock of pleasure, warmth, went through her.

Once again he unbuckled the Navaho belt. This time he pulled it sharply from the loops of her jeans and tossed it on a chair. He was out of his own jeans, naked and with a massively erect penis when he turned her round. He wanted to see the back of her, that delicious bottom in tight jeans that had provoked his hunger for her when he had seen her in front of the *boulangerie*.

He placed his hands on her hips and caressed them while he indulged himself with a long and hungry look at her buttocks. He embraced her thighs, her bottom, liking the way she filled her jeans. She felt incredibly taut and sexy in his hands. He fondled her flesh through the seam between the cheeks of her bottom and followed it down to between her legs, scratching and teasing the denim that covered her cunt so solidly. The flesh so tightly bound in denim – buttocks, cunt, thighs, pussy, hips, the flesh mound, sexy tummy – provocative as hell, as was the way she moved to his caresses, begging for more without saying a word.

Hadon was losing himself to his pleasure: making love to this body in his hands. He spun her round to gaze into her eyes, and pulled her tight against him. With barely room between them for his hand to open her jeans, he did and pulled them down to below her hips and just above her knees. Now he was able to caress her naked buttocks, the back of her thighs, to grab a fleshy orb firmly in his hand. Hadon bit hard the soft skin but firm flesh of a breast.

Breathlessly, in a voice husky with lust, she told him quite unashamedly, 'Hadon, it feels so good, your wanting me, to feel my cunt throbbing for cock.' She whispered in his ear, 'Come and come again and again, until I'm drowning in your come.' She spurred him on, telling him, 'Whatever it takes, to get there, to get to that sexual high, do it for *us*!'

'And what if it's everything? Beyond even reason or morality, and we sink into sexual depravity?'

'If we trust each other, we'll come to no harm.'

His kisses now were more urgent, more passionate. 'Then there's no turning back for us,' he told her as he swept her off her feet and carried her to the sofa. He removed her espadrilles, dropped them to the floor and roughly yanked her jeans off her legs.

Anoushka was a lady who enjoyed her orgasms and had them in abundance once she let her ego drop away. It was then that she became all female sexuality and nothing else. He liked that in women, but there were few who understood that over the top sexuality was the norm for them. Anoushka did and that is very seductive to a man. It was to Hadon. It set her apart from most women.

He knew what she wanted, and what he wanted to give her: deep penetrations, to fill her fully with penis, so that neither of them knew where penis began and cunt left off. A sexual intercourse where they were together as one, cock and cunt in total accord.

He barely looked at this body he was so eager to possess; urgency didn't allow for such a luxury. He pulled her off the sofa and bent her over the back of it. Spreading the cheeks of her bottom and her cunt lips open he was able to view her in all her most intimate glory before he entered her in one fell swoop. His thrust was swift and deep, and before she finished calling out in a scream of uncontainable passion he had found his pace and was fucking her sublimely.

Hadon gave Anoushka not a moment to catch her breath between such powerful thrusts and withdrawals. She was limp, passive, the perfect receptacle for him. Having no defences against such an onslaught of lust, she took it all, and wanted more. But the libido knows how to eke out every last vestige of will to go that much further, experience always that little bit more, when searching for that elusive sexual moment of bliss. He

276

sensed her holding her breath, her body being made rigid, how she was holding on and holding on, for as long as she could. Release. She went lax, let go her breath, gave in body and soul to coming and orgasm, her passion for sex and all things sexual, to her love of men and cock, of being penetrated. She yearned for Hadon to come, to fill her with sperm.

Anoushka went with her emotions, she spurred him on with lustful rantings that excited him to fuck her without mercy. She braced herself against the sofa so he could pummel her with his cock.

It was so thrilling, this fuck with Anoushka, so delightful to take her from the rear like this, to hear her lewd and flattering talk about his virility. She was giving him everything he liked. He was on the edge, ready to fire hot warm seed into this ravishingly exciting woman, but Hadon was a master of sexual control. He withdrew, held himself back for a few minutes.

He kept whispering in her ear while using his fingers to pleasure her; how he wanted to give her more, to inflict upon her his sexual dominance. She brought out all his male fantasies and they became even more exciting for his knowing she would allow them to become reality. She moved her bottom to the rhythm of his penetrating fingers. He loved her bottom, so provocative, so very sensual, so untamable. The Navaho buckle caught his eye. Without thought he reached for her belt and wielded it against the smooth soft skin. She cried out, more from surprise than pain. A pink welt rose against her skin, and again he whacked her. She tried to reach behind her to grab the belt. She needn't have bothered, his sadistic act steered his lust to love her, not beat her. He threw it across the room and plunged his still hard and throbbing penis into her with all the passion that erotic love demands.

He wanted to take not only her cunt to make his own but all her orifices. All that held him back was that he was too big, she was unprepared, and they needed a scented cool cream to ease the way. The very thought of sodomising her was too much, he could no longer hold back. He came in a long and strong orgasm. He grasped her to him, held her tight, his hands caressing her breasts. He was not normally a man to come with such abandon as to scream. Now he did, and cursed, and pulled on her hair and bit into her back. For a few seconds they both sailed together into a sweet sea of come and ecstasy.

Hadon held Anoushka there in that awkward position until he could gain control of himself. Had he not, they might have collapsed to the floor, so weak were they from their coupling. Minutes went by, he resting his head on her back, listening to their hearts pumping. Finally, with a great sigh, Hadon withdrew and swept her into his arms. He carried her through the house and up the stairs to his bedroom. There he laid her on the bed and lay down next to her. They turned on their sides to face each other. Tears stained his cheeks. Sheer release, pent-up emotion set free, surprise, fear. Like it or not, he had fallen in love.

Anoushka kissed his eyes dry and then his lips were the recipient of her kisses, sweet kisses, loving kisses. She nibbled at his lips and licked them with the point of her tongue. She climbed on top of him, straddled him, and her hands caressed him. She worked his nipples with hungry lips and sucking mouth, a tongue that kept them moist and shiny. She watched his penis come alive again. She liked the excitement in his eyes. The taste of his noble penis. Their orgasms, his and hers, were for Anoushka an aphrodisiac. She slid herself down his body, gathered his penis in her hands and held it to her lips. She licked it and the inside of his thighs, caressed his scrotum with her tongue. She tried to gather all of him into her mouth, wanting to make love to him, wanting to nurture him and excite his lust, his sexual hunger, his new found love for her.

He watched her, seeing her in a different light. That of a man in love with a woman who understand male sexual needs, the sexual fantasies that occupy so much of a man's life. He was moved by the way she made love to him, slowly, taking command of his body, taking control of their sexuality.

She slipped off his body and lay on her side next to him, leaning on an elbow. He had forgotten what a voluptuous creature she was, this Anoushka who had stolen his heart. He gazed now at every inch of her body, and realised why he had found her mound so seductive. She no longer had the blonde silky triangle of hair. She had shaved her mound clean, it was smooth as a child's yet not like a child's for she had left an inch-wide band of pubic hair clipped short down the centre of it. It was unbelievably erotic. He had had an expensive Chinese lady of the night who had groomed her pussy that way. He had found it quite delectable to go down on her and subsequently had asked of several of his amours that they groom themselves like his Chinese lady. This surprise delighted him. He found it beautiful; so feline, erotic, irresistible.

He couldn't bring himself to speak of it to Anoushka, so moved that even in this she pleased him. Instead he kissed the narrow band of clipped pubic hair, licked it to leave it moist with his

278

saliva. Then he lay back against the pillows, his arm round her shoulders. She leaned into him, rested her head on his chest, and they watched him fondling the cleft in her decorative mound, he stroking her clitoris while they lay content with each other and the erotic world they were creating for themselves.

He could tell when she was coming. She had that way of holding her breath when she came near her moment. Her body tensed for several minutes, then a shudder and orgasmic release, a moan of pleasure. Once, twice. The third time he reached into the drawer of the table next to the bed and found a pot of cream, an amber dildo in the shape of a penis, carved with skill, a work of pornographic art.

How sensuous, how exciting, the feel of the cool, scented, white cream caressing her genitals. His massaging fingers, slipping and sliding in the thick cream, searching to excite yet more sexual thrills for Anoushka. So many erotic sensations with Hadon but this was somehow frighteningly thrilling. He was deliberate and controlling, yet obviously wanting to seduce her by his expertise in creating sexual situations she would find irresistible. Another erotic sensation to trigger her lust. Anoushka whimpered with anticipation.

She was silky-slippery, moist and luscious: mound, her cunt, between the cheeks of her bottom, her intimate orifices. There too he had anointed her with the cream. Every muscle of her body was relaxed. She lay open and ready for him, wanting only to be taken possession of.

They were still lying on their sides facing each other, he whispering in a voice rough with lust for her how wonderful and exciting she felt in his hands, what he wanted to do with her, what he was about to do to her.

'Yes, please. Oh, yes, now, Hadon! I want it all now,' she told him between kisses and while using her own caressing hands on his pulsating penis. She made it doubly exciting for him because she too was using the cream.

Slowly this time, savouring the feel of her cunt thick with cream, he took possession of Anoushka. Before he commenced his fucking, he allowed himself to rest deep inside her, to feel himself throbbing, her cunt gripping tight his penis. He kissed her eyes, her nose, and then her lips, all the while whispering of his passion for fucking her. They were tender caring kisses, as tender and caring as his fucking was this time.

It was different, this satiny sensuous fucking. He found his rhythm, created a beat to fuck by, and her cunt joined him in tight grippings. Their hearts were pumping fast to the beat of sex. Gently, he used the amber dildo; or as gently as sodomy can be. She held her breath to contain her excitement for the pain that wasn't pain but a new sexual sensation. She bit the flesh on the back of her hand for fear he would stop.

Hadon was a master at deflowering women in that way. Women who liked it and wanted it. And now Anoushka was being had by him and his amber artefact, his deep and passionate kisses. Between them he told her, 'The moment I saw you again, I knew I had to have you. I resisted, but it was useless. I don't fall in love easily, I'm warning you that. I'm not even sure I like it, but I love you.'

As if his declaration had changed things, his fucking became more exciting for them both. He used himself and the amber penis at the same time and with skill. It drove Anoushka mad with excitement, and almost immediately into orgasm, intense, long and exquisite. She felt herself dissolving, vanishing into sexual oblivion. All reason gone.

She received Hadon sexually in the way most every man dreams of being received: in total trust, accepting of all things erotic he could deliver. This time she was peaking and he sensed it and let himself go. They came together, tearing at each other's flesh, pulling at each other's hair, driven by the power of lust.

In their moment of ecstasy they found oblivion, over the edge of erotic lust, and were the richer for it.

They dozed off in each other's arms, and when they awakened praised themselves for having been able to give themselves up to each other so completely. This was sex without artifice, no games playing, pure animal feeling that comes from the libido, from the soul, the very core of being.

Lying in each other's arms they talked and drifted off into sleep, only to awaken and feel the joy of being together. Secure in themselves and their togetherness, they would doze off again. This went on all through the night between bouts of lovemaking.

The sun was up when they awakened and Anoushka asked, 'Am I alive? Pinch me. I have to know I'm alive and what's happened to me is not a dream, that you aren't a dream. That I haven't died in a moment of ecstasy.'

It was as if she had stolen his thoughts. He pinched hard and she reacted with a shout of pain. Then he knew too that he had not expired in lust. Every man's dream: to die and be resurrected in lust, for eternity.

They bathed together and dried each other with large white

bath sheets of soft towelling. He picked her up in his arms and laid her on the bed. 'Don't move, I want to look at you, remember every inch, every curve of your body.'

He took his time, and when he had registered her in his mind forever, asked her to open her legs wide. He went on his knees between them and lowered his head to her shaved mound, kissing it and the narrow band of pubic hair. He raised her bottom on pillows for a better view of her and opened her cunt lips and looked at her. He fondled the inner lips and then kissed them. He moved away from her to lie on the bed next to her and take her in his arms.

'Now when you're away I can think of you, your blonde hair, the wonderful face, how wonderful your cunt is, and how much I like the taste of it.'

What man had ever spoken to her like that and meant it? What man had ever revelled in her lust and approved of it enough to tell her? What man had ever loved her for the real Anoushka? Maybe Serge. Not since him, and she had been a young girl then, had a man made her feel so wanted. There had been Robert and great sex for many years, but he had never done that, wanted to etch her cunt, her whole being, into his psyche; never once had he declared his love voluntarily once they had married. There had been Hervé and Piers, but they had been nothing like this, what was happening between Hadon and her.

There was something about Hadon. As hard a man as she sensed he was when she had first met him on the *QE2*, she had been able to appreciate his forthrightness. His attraction then had been his honesty, that he spoke straight from the heart. She knew from the first where she was with a man. No man, not even and maybe especially Serge, had ever been as straight with her. She looked at Hadon and felt whole and in control of herself, her emotions and her life. Right from the beginning that had been what he had wanted for her.

It was her turn. She raised herself and gazed deeply into his eyes, etching his rugged good looks and how he was with her at that moment forever in her mind. They would change places. Her turn to be the sexual aggressor, his to be open and vulnerable to her. She took his body over, tamed it and made it her own. She intended for him to feel every sensation of sexual pleasure she had. To that end she used every resource of her own and what she found in the drawer of the bedside table. And he, as she had done, gave himself over to her in lust.

281

Chapter 20

It was hot in the sun so they breakfasted under a large white umbrella on the terrace. Akito's serving was impeccable. He was obviously making an effort and had placed a bowl of white tulips on the table.

Hadon and Anoushka had been talkative until they arrived on the terrace and sat down, then the spectacular view and the sight of *Black Orchid* lying at anchor on a blue sparkling sea, under a near cloudless sky, commanded all their attention. Being together in this place brought a powerful sense of contentment.

Hadon liked her silence, the way she looked at him and his haven: with the eyes of a woman in love. He liked the immediacy of their relationship, everything about the way they were together. He cleared his throat.

'This is twice that I've given myself to you as I have never done to any other woman.'

'Never?'

'No, Anoushka, never.'

'And so?'

'And so you're dangerous.'

'How dangerous?'

'You have the ability to enslave me sexually.'

'And you mind that?'

'Not as much as I thought I might, or should. No, in fact I quite like it.'

'Well, that's a relief.'

'That does not mean, however, that you're not dangerous to me and my lifestyle. I'm not going to marry you, Anoushka.'

'I don't remember asking you to.'

'In time you might.'

'I won't, you know.'

"How can you be so sure?'

'Because, like you, I don't want to be married.'

'Then shall we settle for being in love with each other and live with that?'

She began to laugh. 'Is this the same man who told me on the *QE2* we would never see each other again?'

'Can you honestly say this is the same woman?'

'Yes, the same woman. But with a difference.'

'A big difference, Anoushka. Liberated ladies, ones with courage and adventure in their hearts, have always excited my interest, in and out of bed. Especially ones who keep surprising me as you do.

'I see in you now something I never saw that first time we met. You want to eat up the world as if it were a cup cake. You're a lady ready, able, and willing to live. Someone who has taken control of her life. You have no idea how appealing that is to me. I'm a selfish bastard, I don't want the responsibility of your life on my hands. Can you live with that?'

'I don't want to live without it,' she replied.

'Come here.' He scraped his chair back from the table and patted his knee. Anoushka sat on his lap, taking her coffee cup with her. He placed an arm round her neck and watched her sip hot coffee from the cup. He broke off a piece of croissant and buttered it, draped a piece of near transparent Parma ham on it and fed it to her. Then he gave her an affectionate peck on the cheek.

'I can be hard and ruthless.'

'I've seen that side of you.'

'Good, then you know what I can be like.'

'But I have seen the other side of you too, the tender lover, the passionate sexual being. You don't coddle me, you're straight with me. I could love you for that alone.'

Anoushka placed her cup and saucer on the table and this time it was she who fed him with croissant and peach preserve, trying to hide the overwhelming feelings she had for Hadon Calder. She was struggling to keep a tight hold on herself and remain calm when she told him, 'I do love you, Hadon Calder.'

'Good. That's settled. We have to go. I promised to get you back on board for two o'clock and I have to get back to work. You're the only woman I have ever broken my schedule for. For the sex, yes, but for more than that. That inexplicable, elusive something that can happen between two people.'

He kissed her, this time because they understood each other, and eased her off his lap. 'We have to go,' he told her.

Only minutes later they were in the power boat and he was

taking her back to *Black Orchid*. 'Hang on to me,' he told her.

She clung to him with one arm round his waist, a hand holding tight to a chrome grip attached just above the dash board. He threw a throttle full forward and the bow of the boat rose from the water. They sped towards *Black Orchid*, lying majestically in the bay.

Anoushka turned to look over her shoulder at Hadon's cliffside estate, in time to see Akito waving farewell. He knew that she would be back, that she was already a part of their lives. She had a sense of home and, realising how much she had missed that, felt suddenly choked with emotion. How grateful she was to feel so alive again, to have survived the ordeal of utter rejection, the death of life as she had known it.

She took a deep breath, sighed, and looked at Hadon. Instinct made her throw both her arms round him and give him an enormous hug. He looked away from the sea to her and smiled. Understanding was in his eyes. The wind was blowing her hair back off her face. Anoushka felt giddy. She threw her head back and laughed, feeling as if she had beat the devil. 'I love your home,' she shouted above the roar of the turbo jet motors.

'Good,' he shouted back at her. It seemed only seconds before they pulled alongside *Black Orchid*. Their arrival brought Rab and the crew to the rail.

'Permission to board, Captain?' called out Hadon, unable to keep a smile from his face, so amused was he by the reception he and Anoushka were receiving.

'Permission granted,' replied Rab, and sent down one of the crew to sit in the power boat, another to keep a line on it.

Anoushka and Hadon boarded and Sally went to her and placed an arm round her shoulder. They had big grins on their faces. Rab and Hadon shook hands and Anoushka introduced Hadon to Sally.

'Hadon, I'd like you to meet one of my two best friends.'

It was she who brought up to the subject of the work Anoushka was doing translating his novel, something that had been completely forgotten in their preoccupation with the carnal side of their natures, trying to cope with the shock of falling in love.

'She's so clever and works so hard on every word, and she's always saying she couldn't bear it if she were to lose one iota of the passion and beauty of your writing.'

'I'll send you your copy of the translation when I've completed the work, in about five weeks' time,' Anoushka told him.

'No. Don't. I'll come and get it. I finish my book in two weeks' time. You get on with your schedule and I'll get on with mine. Afterwards I'll take you to Japan for a holiday, in celebration of the completion of your first translation.'

'When?'

The light in her eyes made him feel good. 'Well, we'll have to work out dates. I'll be in touch.'

Hadon left Anoushka with Sally. No great goodbye or kiss, a mere squeeze of her hand and he walked to the rail to descend the ladder. Rab was waiting there for him.

'You old devil! Can still pull the best birds, I see. But what about that little blonde? Isn't she a doll? And if you think these two are special, wait till you meet the third one of the trio. We're picking her up in Hydra. A honey to look at – very seductive stuff.'

'Will they make the crossing?'

'Let me put it this way – I wouldn't bet that they won't but don't tell them that. These two have got guts and determination, and Anoushka has a real feel for the sea. Page, the one yet to come on board, I have no doubts about. Beauty and guts, adventure in their hearts, and me training them . . . have *you* any?'

'Not a one, except love might step in and bust up the trio.'

'You don't know these women if you think that. They're not making this crossing to forget a broken heart. They're making it because they want an ocean adventure. These ladies are buddies who have put together a dream, and no man's going to bust that up for them. I hope you're not thinking of trying?'

'Me? Not me, old buddy. I like their spirit, real-life heroines. I'm rooting for them.'

'Me too, but don't tell them that either.'

The two men laughed. 'I'll be calling you, Rab, might be joining you for a few days when your schedule permits.'

Hadon was over the side and down the ladder. Soon as he had cleared the schooner it was all hands on deck, sails unfurled, and *Black Orchid* the training ship was on her way to Greece.

Piers Hazlit was on a river expedition in Guyana. They were charting rivers, estuaries, waterfalls, following a course down the Essiquibo from the North Atlantic Ocean across the length of the country into Brazil and Jauaperi River. The Jauaperi flowed into the Alalau and that flowed into the Amazon, the end of their journey, across relatively undiscovered land and water ways. They were also recording flora and fauna. The expedition had been in the planning for three years, and was his kind of adventure. Interesting, undisturbed places and people, uncharted territory, with competent, experienced colleagues including a doctor who had taken leave from Guy's Hospital, and serious documentary film makers in tow. They were a party of nine.

At night, exhausted from the heat and the humidity and a day's hard travel by motor boats, one of which carried a dismantled micro light plane, sitting round a camp fire with a gin in his hand. Piers's mind would sometimes stray from the jungle and wander back over other adventures, other expeditions. His findings safely recorded at the Royal Geographical Society were always an anti-climax for him. Adventure, discovery, that was the real reason for making his expeditions; that and to write his always anxiously awaited travel books. This journey was no different than any other, with the exception of one thing.

During his previous travels he had always known that there was someone at home waiting for his return: Sally. He had not realised until this expedition how much he'd enjoyed having the security of someone keeping the home fires burning, or at least the illusion of Sally doing that. How important it had been to know that Sally was sleeping in the bed at Chalfont or in the house in Hays Mews. That life had been going on in his absence: civilised, normal, boring even.

For all her silly parties and girlie lunches, the gossipy, frivolous and endless phone conversations, Sally had at least always been there for him when he wanted her. He thought of her now and how she would jump at his bidding, meet him wherever he wanted her to be.

He thought of Anoushka, her homely qualities and new adventurous spirit, her children whom he would take to his heart as he had taken her. He knew that he could give her the home she yearned for, an even better lifestyle than she had lost.

He met her, fell in love with her, felt compassion for what she had been through, and bedded her. The sex had been better than good, they had had sex on a grand scale, but that had come after he had fallen in love with her and had decided what a good life they could have together.

He had wooed her as best he could in the short time they had been together and it was a great affair, but that was not what he wanted from Anoushka Rivers. He wanted marriage or nothing. In her, he sensed the things he had missed all those years with Sally: love for him, not love for what he could give her. A wife, the mother of his children, his hostess, his best friend to travel with. Those same things Sally had wanted from him, he now wanted from Anoushka. He had to be strong with her. He would have marriage or he would have nothing.

Piers, a man whose life was always full, rich and rewarding, was not a man who pined for anyone or anything. That was how he assured himself of never getting hurt. He only really wanted what he could get on his terms. It had been easy enough for him to leave Anoushka behind emotionally. He had no problem with waiting for an answer as some men in love might. He would be there on the dock waiting for Anoushka's answer as to whether or not she wanted him when *Black Orchid* completed her crossing at Mustique. But in the meantime he would contact her and say that if she wanted to be with him, she must agree to marry him. It was as simple, as cut and dried as that. On many levels he wanted Anoushka, she satisfied his needs, his passion, but he wanted a wife more. He could appreciate that she had a great deal of past to be finished with before she could give him an answer, and she was right to hesitate. He travelled light emotionally, she had to be the same. At least Sally had been right about that.

Whereas Anoushka and Hadon had little to say to each other about their pasts, and Jahangir and Sally were only living in the immediate present every day for fun and each other, Page and Oscar spent their first three weeks together after years of separation making love, having long and exciting sexual trysts, and talking.

In Page's arms one night, after a particularly erotic night of lovemaking, Oscar told her, 'The priesthood was an unnatural place for me. The mind wanted to be there, the heart believed that it belonged there. Uncertainty had always been my nature: love for women and freedom, a voracious libido, pride and belief in myself as an individual . . . I met you, and in your arms I found my true nature could be denied no longer. There's nothing unnatural about my life now.'

They spent time talking about their lives during their years of separation. It was a way for each of them to bring the other into those years, a way of dissolving the time lost between them. They hardly left the house, wandering from room to room, touching every window, every wall, opening every door, every cupboard. Making their mark on their house together.

'It's beyond my wildest dreams, beyond anything I imagined it would be. And you did it all by yourself without me, for us.'

She could see how moved he was, and he was right to be

moved. Now that he was here with her, she could view the house from a new perspective, through his eyes, and afresh for herself. She too was moved, could understand even more why Anoushka and Sally had been so drawn to the place, how it had wrapped itself round them and enchanted them. It had, besides simplicity and majesty, beauty and an incredible peace, an other worldly feel. It had always been a house built on a foundation of romance and love. First the sea captain, who still walked as a ghost through the rooms, then Oscar and Page.

'I'll make it up to you. For the rest of my life I'll make it up to us. It's marvellous, it's wonderful. You're marvellous, we're wonderful. It's just as we planned it, but the reality is far better.'

Like almost everyone else when Page had said she was sailing the Atlantic with two girlfriends, Oscar told her, 'You're an outstanding woman.'

'I know!'

'And Anoushka and Sally sound terrific.'

'Oscar, you'll be surprised by this friendship. We're all so completely different from each other but somehow we came together and have become best friends, closer than sisters. When we sail into Mustique, it will be very nearly a year since the first time we met. Almost to the day, come to think of it. A year, Oscar, and we will have been through a lifetime of changes in ourselves and our lifestyles. We will have been through things together that none of us could have faced alone.'

She told him all about Sally and Anoushka, the most intimate things she knew about them. He listened and understood the bond that tied them together. Was not such friendships, such togetherness, what the human condition should be? He had had friendships, still did, and was close to his male friends, but there were no bonds nearly as strong as he was hearing about from Page.

She said, 'It's not disloyal of me to tell you these intimate details of Anoushka and Sally's lives, because I want you to know them and what we have been through together. Soon, in a matter of months now, our voyage across the Atlantic will be over. But not our friendship.

'It's already happening, our separation. Each of us is going our own way, entering a new phase of our life with a new companion of the heart. Sally will marry Jahangir and return to the world she loved, waiting for her man, having fun and parties and playing with life, having the grand life style. Anoushka has Piers if she wants him, and can be a wife and mother again. And I have you.

'I've no doubt that Anoushka and Sally feel as I do, that no matter how much I love you, or they love their men, no matter if we will be living very different lives and probably separated not by miles but continents, we will always be there for each other as friends. We would not want to let that go.'

'I wouldn't want you to. They're an essential part of your life, and as such will now be part of mine. They'll always be welcome with us, wherever we are, and surely you must understand that I would appreciate your going to them whenever you like, for fun, or need, or even for no reason at all. I understand what you have going with your best friends. Because we're making a life together, doesn't mean you have to give up a life of your own.'

'I knew you'd feel that way but it makes me even more happy to hear you say it. Any day now they will be sailing into harbour and then I'll be joining them for training here in the Aegean.'

'Do they know about us?'

'That you've returned? No.'

'Don't you think we should tell them? A call, make contact in some way.'

'No. We'll surprise them.'

'Surprise? Am I right in thinking that they knew you were waiting for my return but had doubts that it would happen?'

'Something like that. I'm afraid neither one of them is very strong on faith. They saw our love as impossible.'

'Page, say it. They didn't think I would give up the church for you. In time they'll understand. I gave it up for you, and for me, and for love. Because I believe I can serve us and humanity and God out of the cloth better than I can in it. I wouldn't want you, or them, to think you have to carry the burden of such a monumental decision. That, my dear heart, is all mine, and in fact no burden at all, only a merciful release.'

'We won't have to tell them that, Oscar. They'll only have to meet you, see how we are together, and know you for a few hours to realise all that.'

'OK, we'll surprise them,' he told her. 'And Anoushka?' he asked.

'What about Anoushka?'

'Will she marry Piers? Or is she still not over her husband?'

'I don't know. Piers is a very interesting man, and Anoushka is beautiful, complex, much more than she seems. She has a great deal going for her but I'm not sure what she wants. Piers wants marriage, but can he pin her down?'

'Can I pin you down?'

'Is that a proposal?'

'It is if you say, "yes, Oscar, I'm pinned".'

Page gave a sexy toss of her head, her shoulder came forward just enough to tease. His already melting heart dissolved. She gave him a throaty, breezy, laugh and throwing her arms round his neck, she told him, 'Yes, yes, yes, Oscar, I'm pinned, I'm pinned, I'm pinned.'

She ceased covering him with kisses only long enough to lead him to the bedroom. They sated themselves with sex in the delicious knowledge that what they had together was going to be forever.

Afterwards Oscar said, 'When you sail off on your training cruise, I'll go into Athens, and get the details worked out so we can be married here in Greece. Would you like that, or would you prefer to be married in the States, China, Timbuctoo, anywhere? It's our first and last wedding.'

'I'll marry you wherever you choose. I don't care. You work it out, and tell me where and when. Surprise me. I did the house, you do the wedding.'

'Are you sure?'

'Very sure. Only one thing – I'll do the flowers!'

'I'll talk to the captain of *Black Orchid* and find out his schedule, where you'll be moored and for what length of time.'

'You do understand, Oscar, about my not wanting to give up this chance to sail the Atlantic? Aside from wanting the thrill and experience of the crossing, and not wanting to let the girls down, I want to feel the vastness and power of the ocean, that sense of aloneness with nothing but myself to pit against the elements.'

'Of course I do. I want you to make this voyage. I could never deprive you of such a great experience.'

'I think I knew that.'

'I'm sure you did.'

'During this training period, sometimes we'll only be day sailors.'

'Then at those times you can be a night wife. We'll work it out so I'm where you are when you're free. You're not to worry – sailing first, and I'll fit in. That's from now until November when you hope to make the crossing. I'll be at the other end. We'll have Christmas in the Caribbean.'

'You're wonderful,' she told him.

'One has to be if one has an adventuress for a wife.'

'What about you and your work?'

'I'm not thinking about me or my work for a long time. I'm

291

thinking about you and me, and just enjoying life.'

'Can we afford that?'

'Yes, I think so. And your greenhouse. We'll make that my wedding present to you. I'm actually quite comfortably off. My books make quite a lot, and if truth be told, for most of my life I never needed money so there's my savings to live off.'

'I have some too, quite a bit, to throw into the pot.'

'When the sailor comes home from the sea, we might throw a party in celebration of our marriage.'

'A small party. You really wouldn't mind that?'

'Why small? Why would I mind? We no longer have to be discreet, and I have no intention of being reclusive. A large party with all your friends and mine. I want the whole world to meet my wife.'

They were on the terrace off their bedroom. Page raised her face to the sky and threw her arms wide. 'I'm reaching for the sun, I've already got the moon and the stars. Oh, Oscar, there's nothing like having it all!'

She danced around him and he laughed and laughed and thought himself the luckiest man in the world.

Chapter 21

Anoushka was the first to arrive at Nice airport. She had flown Concorde from New York to Paris, had stayed there for two days to meet a Japanese writer friend of Hadon's and to pick up a contract to translate a book of his poems, then took a plane to Nice. She was late but so were the others.

Page was flying in from Athens and Sally from London. Start off as we mean to go, they had decided. No seeing-off parties, no grand gestures or fare thee wells from loved ones. That was the way they wanted it and that was the way they were going to have it. With that decided it made sense to wait for each other in the airport. They would take the first step towards their long-awaited journey across the Atlantic together, arms linked, best foot forward.

Twelve noon, give or take an hour, Nice airport, 11 November. The women had worked out their schedules, they'd be there. At midnight, all hands on board *Black Orchid*, anchored off Cap d'Antibes. At dawn on 12 November they would set sail: Marseille, Gibraltar, Tangiers, Casablanca, Las Palmas in the Canary Islands last stop before the crossing.

Anoushka watched people rushing into the terminal, shrugging off rain, shaking dripping umbrellas.

A better day would have been preferable. It was bucketing down, almost dark enough outside for street lamps to be lit; cars pulling up to the entrance of the terminal were already using headlamps. Not the best of weather for travelling or to sail away in. Never mind, for Anoushka it might have been sunshine. Nothing could mar this day for her. Butterflies in the stomach, a constant tingle of excitement, eyes twinkling with delight and anticipation. A rain storm? What chance had that of dampening her spirits?

She was watching every face in search of Page and Sally. After a period of time she felt hypnotised. Her eyes became heavy. She decided to close them, rest for a while. A cat nap would have been nice but she found it impossible to drift off. Instead she ran through a mental review of the last few incredible months, the most amazing time of her life.

Neither she, Sally nor Page had stopped for a minute. Their lives were running in high gear and top speed, and it had been one exciting event after the other. Learning to sail under the guidance of Captain Rab had been thrilling. She had had no idea she would take sailing to her heart as she had. Sally had been a surprise too, far more accomplished than anyone imagined she would be. Page was simply brilliant. They had been dedicated pupils, learning fast, working incredibly hard, sailing so well. And *Black Orchid*: what a boat! It was almost as if she had waited to be sailed by women, playing with the wind and the sea, she the mistress and they her acolytes.

The cruise to Greece and Hydra had been hard work for the yet inexperienced Anoushka and Sally, but it had been thrilling too. It was really then that Anoushka found her stride as a sailor, then that it became a part of her life forever. Cruising through the Greek islands and down the Mediterranean coastline of Turkey had been memorable. Then she thought about those first few days when Page had joined them. It had been as if she had been sailing with them right from the first. Rab and the crew? When Anoushka thought of them, it amused her as to how much their attitude had changed towards her, Page and Sally. They were now firm friends and proud to be their ship mates.

So many highlights in such a short period of time. *Black Orchid*, Hadon . . . meeting Oscar had certainly been one of them. She had really had no idea what to expect when they sailed into Hydra's port, but it certainly hadn't been that he would be there standing next to Page, welcoming them with open arms and a happy smile. She and Sally had received a description of him from Page but Anoushka had found it difficult to summon up an image of the man. She had considered Page's love affair with him as such an impossible situation that she tried if anything not to conjure one up.

They had been so busy bringing *Black orchid* in under full sail, Oscar had been the last thing on her mind. She remembered it so well. They had brought the schooner about, shortened sail and proceeded to tack across the harbour, Sally and Anoushka handling the boat with the crew as back up. The two women's best effort ever.

She saw him for the first time when they were safely in the harbour and ready to tie up. After her initial surprise and the hellos and welcomes and words of praise, she was able to see a man with a special kind of handsomeness. His face had in it something of the ethereal, a boyish innocence, incredible charm. Yet there was a maleness about him, rugged and strong but somehow not obvious. He was an exciting vital man, and unimaginable as a priest. There was something uncanny about his looks, so youthful yet so quiet and wise. They had about them an undercurrent that Anoushka had found incredibly erotic, so much so it made her blush. It was there too in his voice, the way the man moved.

Not hours but minutes after their first meeting, she could understand Page's love for this man. He was dynamic in the most subtle way. No wonder the church couldn't keep him. He was larger than life, more seductive than a warm summer's breeze, very sexy. He and Page were so much alike. Hervé, François, men whom Anoushka had thought of as terrific in every way, seemed like cardboard figures, mere puppets, in comparison. What chance had they against a man like Oscar when it came to winning Page's love!

Just thinking about Oscar and what he meant to her friend was to remind her of Hadon. Not a word had she had from him once they had set sail for Greece. Weeks had passed, and then one day when they sailed into the port on the island of Simi, close to the coast of Turkey, there he was, sitting at the café having a drink. After meeting Page, and receiving a warm welcome from everyone on board, he offered the crew of *Black Orchid* lunch ashore at a taverna on the water's edge, kissed Anoushka's hand and walked off with her without a word, just as he had done the last time they had met at Stephano's. He fucked her all through the night and morning in a small deserted house on the beach far from the town, returning her to *Black Orchid* after they had breakfasted.

Long after they had sailed, leaving Hadon on Simi, Anoushka had found two first-class air tickets to Tokyo in her jacket pocket. It seemed that everyone on board had known what was going to happen and had kept the secret from her.

She sighed and opened her eyes. She took a walk round the terminal. For a quarter of an hour she stood at Arrivals scanning faces but could not see the ones she was looking for. She returned to a seat but this time took a different chair where she could get another perspective of the terminal. Once more she closed her eyes.

The weddings. First there had been Page's marriage to Oscar in the church of the monastery in Patmos. The ceremony had been performed by a Greek Orthodox priest, a friend of Oscar's who arrived from Mount Athos for the wedding with two fellow monks to assist him. Jahangir had brought their dresses from Paris. On pain of death he had followed their telephone and fax instructions as to what they wanted: cream-coloured, St Laurent, anything suitable for the occasion, no veil. Hadon flew in the flowers Page had ordered from the South of France by sea plane.

The ceremony had been more than moving, something everyone there knew they would never see again. A dozen Greek Orthodox monks gathered out of respect for Oscar to chant prayers that were as rich and as pure in sound as Bach fugues. The tiny church was thick with white smoke and the heavy scent of incense emitting from silver and gold censers hung on long chains and swung back and forth in the hands of the black-clad, high black-hatted monks. The atmosphere was Byzantine. It transported them from one world to another.

Their vows had been memorable, for their significance, the price each had paid to be able to utter them, the commitment they signalled. The monastery, the church, the drama of the Greek Orthodox ceremony, the monks, scholars and friends in the church, the sun beating down, the sea surrounding them . . . for a few hours they were raised to a place of extraordinary faith and love. Even now the memory of that wedding sent a feeling of having been touched by the divine through Anoushka.

By contrast Sally's wedding was dramatic, on a much larger scale, exciting, amusing, full of colour and pageantry. It had thousands of people attending, as against a few best friends and a boat crew. A three-day event in a thousand-room palace in India with a procession of brocade-draped elephants and vintage cars. A reception for best friends in a white marble palace in the middle of a lake. That was how it was done for an Indian prince and a lass from Lancashire. They had all been there: Oscar and Page, Hadon and Anoushka, and her two boys, all of Sally's London girlfriends, dazzled but not surprised.

The children had been on summer holiday. It hadn't been a very successful one for mother or sons. It had started off badly with the boys arriving two weeks late. That had been Anoushka's fault, she should not have given in to Robert. But he had the boys and had been on the telephone pleading to allow them to change plans. A place had been found for them at a summer workshop for young musicians up in Lenox near Tanglewood, the Boston Symphony Orchestra's summer home. A friend of Rosamond's had found them places, having by accident heard them play at The Plaza at their mother's farewell party.

Anoushka reluctantly gave in. She knew what their music meant to them, and how very talented the twins were. What choice had she? Mistake. Once more she let her heart rule her head, once more she placed her children above her own need to be with them, see them, be a part of their life.

By the time they arrived in Greece it had been high summer and no matter how Page or Sally or she had entertained or amused them, they had barely raised themselves to the occasion. They seemed lost in Hydra, preoccupied. They had been rude, asking constantly how long they had to be there, and when could they join Robert and Rosamond who were in Portofino?

The only thing that seemed to work for them had been being with Oscar. They followed him round everywhere, full of wonder that he had once been a priest, and with endless questions about God, hanging on his every word.

If they had suffered culture shock in Greece, which they shouldn't have, having travelled with their parents there before, then their arrival in India for the wedding, which before their arrival they had been enthusiastic about, left them stunned. They had been thrilled by everything they saw and did, but devastated by the heat and dust and poverty of India.

Impressive, dramatic, romantic, luxurious . . . the wedding. That part of it they did appreciate, though for thirteen-year-old boys who loved New England it was not their idea of a fun time, more like hard work. Only Hadon and Oscar saved the day. It was they to whom the twins clung, they whom they had a good time with, not Anoushka or Page or Sally. There was little of their holiday left when Hadon extended an invitation, offering them one of the guest houses on his Cap d'Antibes compound. All three grabbed at the chance.

'The South of France is more our style, we can cope with that,' Mishka announced.

And it was true. They were both bilingual and liked French food. But still, at that moment, Anoushka thought she really disliked her boys. They were much more like their father than she had ever realised. When they had seen the compound they were really happy. At least it hadn't ended as badly as it had begun, and for that she had Hadon to thank.

One day she was walking through the wood from the guest house to the main house when she came upon her sons and Hadon, cording wood.

'You look very busy,' she said.

'We are, Mom, you shouldn't interrupt us. This is boys' stuff.'

'You know women cord wood too, Alexis.'

'Mom, you don't cord wood. You can't even bake a decent cake.'

'See you later, Mom,' said Mishka, dismissing her having not even given her a sideward glance.

'See you later,' she replied and walked away, not thinking much about the incident.

She stumbled and caught herself and sat down under a tree to rub a bruised ankle. She hadn't meant to eavesdrop but she did overhear Hadon. His voice was not so much angry as decidedly firm.

'Put those tools down.'

Mishka kept sawing. 'Mishka, I said put that saw down, and Alexis, place that axe carefully on the ground.' The boys obeyed immediately.

'Why are you such shits to your mother?'

They remained silent.

'Answer me. By God, I will have an answer!'

'We're not shits to her.'

'Well, you could have fooled me. That was a shitty thing to say to her. And a shitty way to behave. And it's not the first time I've seen you two behaving that way to your mother. I want to know why. Come on, out with it. She doesn't deserve treatment like the sort you dish out. She breaks her ass to keep you guys amused. What's going on here?

Anoushka's first reaction was to go to Hadon and tell him to forget it. But then she saw what an awkward position she was in. He had not meant her to hear his conversation with the boys. She remained silent and where she was.

'Haven't you any respect for your mother?'

'We do. It's great, all these far out things that she's doing.'

'You don't act it, buddy. And it's not enough to respect what she's doing. How about what she is, who she is? Why do you treat her the way you do?'

'It's the way we've always treated her.'

'It's just not good enough, guys. It's just not good enough.'

'Dad never said anything.'

'Well, maybe Dad should have. Why don't you talk to her? Don't you talk to your parents?'

'We talk to Dad,' said Mishka.

'We talk to Rosamond,' said Alexis.

'Not the same way you talk to your mother, I'll bet.'

'We speak to Mom,' said Mishka.

'Yeah, when you need something, you're hurt, you want something.'

'Are you angry with us, Hadon?'

'No. Just disappointed with your attitude. It stinks. I would just like to know what's going on here? Is it some kind of tug of love story because your parents are divorced? Is it attention from your dad you're seeking by being less than nice to your mother? Or are you being nasty to her so that she will go on continuously trying to win your approval? Are you playing two unhappy people against each for your love? Cheap shots, kids, real cheap shots. Now, Alexis, pick up the saw. Mishka, help me heave this log on to the block.'

Alexis spoke up, a tremor of nervousness in his voice while he did what he was told. 'My mother never loved us, not the way she loved my father. My father loved us, really loved us, and still does. He's always been terrific, and I don't mean just because he buys us things or takes us places. He teaches us all the time about life and all sorts of things. He loves us.'

'Spare me that one. I don't want to hear that clap trap, even if it's true. You're old enough to know that people love in different ways. If you didn't know it already, you know it now, boys.'

'Does my mother love you?'

'I hope so. But if she does it's not the same way she loves you, or the way she loved your dad.'

'You're not angry with us?'

'No, I told you that. I just don't like your attitude to your mother. She doesn't deserve it, and it makes you look like snotty little brats when I know you're a heck of a lot better than that. But an attitude problem is not serious. You can always change an attitude.'

And they did. They made an effort from that very day on. And Anoushka stopped trying so hard. The conversation with Hadon had had a terrific effect on the boys and Anoushka. It prompted her to turn her back on her marriage and Robert, once and forever. It was also what prompted her to take some final steps for herself and her future.

Yes, that incident had to be classed one of the highlights of those last few months. Anoushka opened her eyes just in time to see Sally struggling into the terminal, loaded down with luggage and looking prettier than ever. Upmarket Barbie doll Maharani. It did make Anoushka laugh. She leapt up from her chair and all but ran to greet her friend. She called out: 'Sally!' raising her wrist and pointing to her watch. They hugged each other, Sally dropping the luggage to the floor.

'Sally, I can't believe it! For the first time since I've known you, you are absolutely on time.'

'On time?'

'Yes, you're only forty minutes late.'

'Not my fault.'

'It's never your fault.'

Sally shrugged her shoulders and the two women kissed each other French style, once on each cheek. Anoushka found a porter and the luggage was disposed of. The two women sat down.

'Page isn't here yet. Miracle of miracles, she's not on time. How are you, Nooshky?'

'Happy, excited. And you.'

'The same. What happened in Lakeside?'

'Oh, I'll tell you all my news when Page gets here. How was London, Jahangir, marriage?'

'London's great, Jahangir in top form, marriage . . . I'm blissfully happy in it. But I've missed you, worried about you. You know, I would have gone to Lakeside with you.'

'You're a good friend, Sally. But don't worry about me. You can't fix it for your friends, you have to do it for yourself. That does not, however, mean that it isn't a great deal easier when you have a support system going for you like I have in you and Page. Everything went well, I'll tell all when Page gets here. Right now my head is filled with only one thing – we three sailing the Atlantic ocean on *Black Orchid*.'

'Me too. I think about it all the time, I even dream about it. Sometimes during one of my girlie lunches at San Lorenzo's I'll drift off into thinking about us bucking the North Atlantic, the trade winds, forty-foot swells. I'm worried that I'm obsessed, and Jahangir's thrilled that I am.'

They had hardly settled into a gossip when Page arrived. Her first words were, 'I'm so thrilled we've made it! God, it's good to see you two.' She hugged and kissed them both and a porter was summoned. He pushed his trolley through the terminal loaded with what seemed like an inordinate amount of luggage for three women sailing the Atlantic in a three-masted schooner. They followed, full of chatter and an effervescent charm that drew people's attention.

'Rab is going to go crazy when he sees the amount of stuff we're toting,' said Page.

'Well, it's not exactly an overnight hop, is it? Fourteen days to Las Palmas, and sixteen to eighteen for the crossing to Mustique,' said Sally.

'Any excuse to go shopping,' teased Page.

'You'll be happy for my luggage, all of you. It's not all for me. Two of those cases are a result of a raid – well, several raids – on Fortnum's and Harrod's food hall. It's a long voyage and I didn't think goodies would go amiss. I sent the champagne by courier right to the boat.'

'And I sent the claret and some tidbits from Paris. I was worrying about getting bored with shipboard cuisine, captain Rab-style.'

'I have a whole Mortadello and a wheel of Regiano in my case, dragged them all the way from Tuscany back to Hydra and now here.'

'That brings me to something I wanted to talk to you about,' said Sally. 'I think we should dress for dinner every evening.'

Page and Anoushka burst into laughter. But in only a few minutes they had decided that Sally was right and if they banded together and discussed it with Rab they could swing it their way. A smile of complete satisfaction crossed Sally's lips. Both women looked at her. They knew that smile.

'Confess, Sally.'

'I bought black silk ties for the men, and white dress shirts. Jahangir thought I was right so he's sent a gift to Rab and the crew: dinner jackets with gorgeous black satin lapels from his Savile Row tailor, 1940s style. we might as well make a party of it.'

The three women once more burst into laughter. 'You'd better twinkle at Rab with an extra bit of sparkle to pull this one off, Sally.' Rab had a soft spot for her, and there was little he could refuse her when she made her mind up to it.

They stood at the glass doors and watched the rain pelting down. Gusts of wind sent drops into spins and twirls creating waterfalls of rain.

'It's a bloody storm,' said Sally.

'Maybe it'll blow out to sea,' said Page.

'Oh, thanks, Page,' said Anoushka.

'I'm famished, where shall we go to eat?'

'Good question.'

'Hold everything. Look, Anoushka, isn't that Akito? Oh, you are clever, getting him to come and pick us up.'

'I didn't.'

'Then how . . . Hadon. God bless Hadon!' said Sally.

In the car spirits were high, especially with the women not having to think of where to lunch or how to get their luggage to the boat. Hadon had arranged everything for them. They sat in the back seat together, Anoushka in the middle, talking in Japanese to Akito.

'Well, where are we having lunch?' asked Sally.

'I have no idea. Akito says he knows a place that will serve us at this hour, so just let's leave it to him. I thought we'd lunch then go to Hadon's for tea, if that's all right with you girls? Just long enough for me to say goodbye.'

All was agreed and then they fell silent, looking at the rain, hoping it would go away.

Finally it was Anoushka who spoke up. 'I think I'm overexcited.'

'At seeing Hadon?' teased Page.

'I am always overexcited at seeing him, but you know very well what I mean.'

'I do indeed, dear. I'm that way all the time about this voyage. But now that Maharani Sally has decreed dressing for dinner I don't think I'm quite as ready for this crossing as I thought I was.' Page made the statement as a joke and was made to laugh once more, as was Anoushka, when Sally replied, seriously, 'Oh, I thought as much, so I went shopping. Short, smart, dead chic but simple. Evening cruise ware.'

'Incorrigible!' was the word that Anoushka and Page used.

By the time they had arrived at the small dirt road to Stephano's the storm had blown out but the rain was still pelting down. Only when they were making their way down the slope did they realise where they were, none of them ever having been there by road. The restaurant looked warm and inviting, lit by candles and lamps, a fire crackling in the stone fireplace.

Nothing could have been more delightful than to see their fellow diners. There they all were: Hadon, captain Rab, and *Black Orchid*'s crew. 'Don't be angry with me, this is no party, just a good meal on shore, and if truth be told I couldn't resist seeing you three in your moment of glory together, a dream realised. But I promise, no toasts, no scenes, no dramatic goodbyes, no words of wisdom.'

With that Hadon removed a very wet hat from Anoushka's head and shook it out. She smiled at him, put her arms round his neck and kissed him. A kiss of thank you and of passion.

Hadon and Anoushka said their goodbyes in the rain, standing on the dock waiting for their luggage to be loaded. The Riva was too small for all the luggage and the crew so some of the men remained in the restaurant and waited for the second run to *Black Orchid*. Anoushka remained on shore waiting for the second run too, only she and Hadon did not go inside. They found instead a darkened doorway and huddled there in the shadows, talking and kissing, until finally lust took them over and he pressed her against the locked door and raised her skirt. He caressed her near naked bottom, the exposed flesh of her thighs between the top of her cream-coloured stockings, held in place by long garters that hung from the lace belt she was wearing. He tore the tiny slip of silk from between her legs and shoved it in his pocket. Then he fondled her cunt.

Anoushka was lost to Eros and Hadon. She wrapped her legs round him and he plunged deep inside her and they fucked to the sound of the rain and the wind and came together, unable to hold back the urgency of their passion for each other. All this between relentless kissing, and hearts and minds racing together to their moment of sexual oblivion. Breathless, exhausted, they leaned their weight against the door and rested before he withdrew and they adjusted their clothes. This then was their goodbye.

Chapter 22

At ten o'clock when everyone was asleep the rain was still falling in a heavy downpour. By dawn's early light it had stopped, the winds were moderate and Captain Rab called for all his crew to assemble on deck. He had an announcement to make.

'There can be only one captain on a boat and I have made my decision. I'm retiring as captain of the *Black Orchid* for this crossing. Anoushka, you're in charge, you make the run across the Atlantic as captain of this schooner. I'm making this crossing as an observer, and will be at your shoulder any time you need me. That goes for the rest of the crew, just think of us as ballast. Only one thing can change these orders. We hit bad trouble where boat or life is in danger, I take over.'

Anoushka's first order from the wheel was: 'Weigh anchor, Sally,' and the three women experienced their proudest moment.

Oscar surprised them in Casablanca, much the same way as Hadon had surprised Anoushka in Simi.

The weather had been all any sailor could have asked for: sunshine, the right amount of wind, clear blue sky, starry and moonlight nights. The women sailed *Black Orchid* without a hitch, confidence riding high.

Only when Jahangir arrived in Las Palmas and they were all dining with him on shore for the last time until Mustique did the women realise it had been Rab who had been choreographing the support system for his lady sailors.

Eleven days out of Las Palmas and they hadn't had it all their way. After weathering a three-day mid-Atlantic Force Eight storm they were now riding very uncomfortably in the trough of a long swell. By now they were used to such swells: walls of water cresting at times fifteen or twenty feet high. But they had ridden out the storm with no damage to the boat and relatively few bruises, none fortunately to their ego. They had handled themselves and their craft admirably.

The sun was high in the sky, lunch was being cooked below,

most of the crew was sun bathing or reading in the bow – no easy
task for the pitch and roll of the boat, but hungry for fresh air and
sunshine they managed as best they could. Sally was at the wheel,
Anoushka sitting close by. They had the trade winds behind them
and were making serious speed considering the rough ride Mr
Ocean was giving them, though it seemed to all on board a lake
compared to what they had been through. Page was scanning the
horizon and *Black Orchid* was cutting through the ocean like a
hot knife through butter.

'This is more, much more, than I ever dreamed it would be!'
shouted Sally to Page and Anoushka.

'I think this is the closest to God I will ever be,' said Anoushka.

It was true, there was something religious about being afloat
under sail in the middle of the ocean. It was magical and mystical,
deeply spiritual. Page understood exactly what Anoushka meant.
She motioned to her, suggesting they go below for a hot cup of
coffee, and then to Sally. Ten minutes. They'd return to relieve
her in ten minutes. Sally gave them a thumbs up. Below the two
women had the galley to themselves. They shrugged out of their
coats and sipped from their mugs.

'That tired old expression "leave the world behind",' said
Page.

'You certainly do that out here. What is the world? Eleven
days out of Las Palmas and I've forgotten about it. This ocean,
sailing, it's disorientated me, and yet it has somehow put my life
in perspective.'

'Do you think any of us will ever be the same after this
voyage?'

'No, never. Enhanced by it.'

The two women remained silent. Listening to the sounds: the
creak of the boat, the wind in the sails, the sound of the ocean.
They didn't speak for several minutes.

Finally Anoushka commented, 'This is real freedom. It seems
I've been getting ready my whole life for this crossing. Oscar,
Hadon and Jahangir knew so well what we wanted to experience.
How was it that at first we really didn't.'

'I certainly didn't but maybe I had an instinct, a desire for the
experience of real freedom.'

'It was their support, their understanding and appreciation of
what we are doing, without laying expectations on us, that's
heightened this experience for me. I don't want any man ever to
lay any expectations on me ever again. I've been there, had that,
thank you.'

'They must love us very much to understand the friendship between the three of us. Piers did too, that's why he offered us *Black Orchid*, it wasn't just guilt over Sally. He wanted her and us to experience real freedom, the way men do,' said Page.

'I've been looking for an opportunity to talk to you and Sally but one hasn't arisen. One of us has always been on watch or someone has always been hovering. There are things to be said, things I want you both to know. I've taken some serious steps.'

'Is this good or bad news, Anoushka?'

'Good. Great.'

'Oh, thank heaven for that,' said Page, looking very relieved.

'Let's take some coffee up to Sally. Maybe the wind has dropped, the sea does feel a little calmer. If the swells are subsiding then I'll be able to tell you what's been going on.'

But the swells did not subside, not until the following morning when Anoushka was at the wheel. Then the weather was some of the best they had seen on the entire crossing: a bright sun, an easy ocean to ride and perfect trade winds. They were at full sail, a ride on the Atlantic that every mariner dreams of. Everyone was on deck taking advantage of the morning but a good distance from the three women round the wheel. Sally and Page were sitting facing Anoushka, their faces to the sun.

She just plunged in. 'I haven't mentioned it before because I haven't really had the chance. The last few days of the boys' holiday back in August, I overheard a conversation between them and Hadon. It gave me quite a shock. Made me see the light, so to speak. I won't go into what was said, merely the upshot of it all.

'I can't cope any longer with this tug of love between Robert and me for the love of my boys. Something the boys said to Hadon made me realise that Robert stole their affection from me long ago, when they were small children. It's him they love. Not that they don't love me, they do, they just love him more. It's not good for me, trying as hard as I do to win them over, and it's no longer good for them: my constant trying, their constant rejecting, my constant accepting of the situation.

'They know I love them, that I'm always here for them, but last summer's holiday and their behaviour towards me was a nightmare, I'll not put myself through that again. The years of being treated as the crippled member of the Rivers family are over.'

'Do Robert and the children know how you feel about them now?' asked Sally.

'Yes, and they know that if they want me they will always be

307

able to find me, come to talk, talk to me. I'm not rejecting the boys. I'm just putting our relationship on an even keel. Hadon told them I deserve to be treated better than they treat me, and he's right. As it stands now things are moderately better. All three of us seem to have changed our attitude and that's working for us.'

'Are you all right with this?' asked Sally.

'Very all right. Very, very all right. You're my best friends and I wanted you to know, but don't think I'm unhappy about the changes, I'm no longer even unhappy about their feelings about me.'

'Something did have to be done, and it's great you got up the courage to do it,' said Sally.

'Courage was riding high so I made a clean sweep of some other things.'

'Like what?' asked Page.

'I've cut all ties to Robert, except of course those that relate to our boys. I've sold the remainder of my antique coin collection too. I did *not* sell to Robert. I put the money in a Swiss account. I went back to Lakeside to tell Robert how I feel about the boys and that I'd sold his precious coins.'

'Oh, how he must have loved that!' said Page.

'Let's just say he played a bad game of wait and see, and lost. He did not take the news at all well.'

'Oh, dear, will he make trouble?' asked Sally.

'He would like to but he can't. They were legally mine.'

'All I can say, old girl, is well done. I was always afraid you would soften and return the coins to him.'

'I might have, once.'

No one spoke for several minutes. The ocean and the sun and the sky, the thrill of their isolation, seemed to wrap itself round them, hug them. They stood up to embrace.

'Well, it seems we three have arrived somewhere in our lives,' said Page.

'We sure have,' agreed Anoushka.

'I'll say so,' added Sally, and placed an arm round Anoushka's shoulders. Page's arm went round her waist. Three beautiful and serene women standing entwined like that at *Black Orchid*'s wheel was reminiscent of a glorious classical statue: the Three Graces, which, in a museum in Side in Turkey, they had viewed with admiration not many months before.

More days passed: days of silence and an incredible otherness.

They did dress every night for dinner and the crew and captain

308

alike rose to the occasion. There was something very gallant about their evenings at table, and they spoke to each other, all of them, of things they would never have mentioned had they not been sailing across the ocean.

There was always one of the three on watch throughout the night. After dinner the other two would go up for a night cap. One particularly beautiful night with a clear sky and a perfect half moon, as white and shimmering as ever they had seen, a sky hardly visible for the stars, the women had their nightcap of whisky and spoke about love and the erotic life.

They were less than two days' sail from Barbados and heading for Mustique. The excitement and thrill of arriving in the Caribbean, of having sailed the Atlantic virtually on their own, filled them with tremendous self-awareness, a more complete knowledge of who and what they were than they had ever known.

They all three knew that Anoushka had love choices she must make. Little had been said about that during the voyage. It was Sally at the wheel this time, and she took it upon herself to talk about it to Anoushka and Page.

'I think it should be said, Anoushka, that nothing will change between us if you choose to marry Piers. I won't love you less, and it will make no difference to our friendship. I would never allow that.'

'Piers should have married you, Sally. He was a fool to let you go.'

'Throw me out. Let's get it right.'

'What are you going to do, Anoushka,' asked Page. 'You won't get marriage offered from Hadon.'

'Oh, I know that. I don't want to be married ever again. I wouldn't give up my freedom now for any man, especially a man like Piers who demanded it. I've done that all my life. No more. I have my sons, I have my independence, financial security, a budding and rewarding career, a man who loves me and leaves me free to do my thing. Hadon Calder adores me, looks after me, protects me, the real me that Robert has never seen or respected. Why would I give all that up for marriage?'

'Then you've chosen?' said Sally.

'Yes, I guess I have, just now.'

'Does Hadon know?'

'I haven't told him but he might have guessed.'

'Piers?'

'No.'

'Poor Piers.'

'Don't feel sorry for him, Sally. I can assure you he would have done to me what he has done to you, only I would have had a ring on my finger. He would have been another Robert, in a different style. And I would have become once again the old Anoushka, chasing after his love. No, don't feel sorry for Piers.'

'She's right, you know,' said Page.

'I know, but it still hurts to admit it,' said Sally.

'He's going to be in Mustique waiting for my answer as to whether I will or will not marry him.'

'Let's hope seeing us sail *Black Orchid* in safe and sound will take the edge off his disappointment. Do you think there's some poetic justice going on here? I'd like to think there is. It would actually make me feel a little better about having been tossed away by him. Vindictive? Well, maybe. Nobody likes having to carry a scar round for the rest of their life, not even if it's barely visible.'

'Well, that's going to be quite a reception committee waiting for our arrival: Piers, Hadon, Jahangir, Oscar, waiting for the sailors home from the sea.'

'Not for me it won't,' said a smiling Anoushka.

'You've got something up your sleeve?'

'I told Hadon about Piers a long time ago, not long after we met. That last night we were together in Cap d'Antibes, he told me he was not a man for scenes. I had a decision to make, and though it involved him, I would have to make it alone. He had no intention of standing on a dock next to Piers waiting to be picked. I think his expression was "Like a ripe fucking plum off a tree". Much as he wants to see us all sail in after an Atlantic crossing, he won't be in Mustique.'

'Oh, no!' wailed Sally.

'He can't miss our arrival. I'll really be disappointed if he won't be there for our moment of triumph, he's been so supportive of the three of us,' said Page.

'He doesn't have to. He's researching a new book in Barbados, he's been there very nearly since we left France. What he said was, "If you're looking for me you'll find me in Barbados in a large house facing the sea, a place where one can have a great view of the boats coming in from an Atlantic crossing." I'll be jumping ship in Barbados, ladies.'

There were tears and hugs and kisses, a great deal of happiness for Anoushka. She too had found her man, the right man.

As captain of *Black Orchid*, she called the crew and Rab Nesnet on deck for a meeting. She felt, as did Page and Sally, that she had to explain her situation and ask for their support. They had come too far, been through too much together, for her to leave them out of her decision. They considered how she could abandon ship, since Rab's orders from Piers had always been to complete the crossing at Mustique. Rab took over and choreographed the event. Anoushka called Hadon.

They had a brisk wind and at seven o'clock the following morning Sally was on early watch when she sighted land for the first time in eighteen days.

'Land! Land! I see land!' she shouted, ringing the ship's bell, and screaming and laughing. Everyone having breakfast below rushed on deck. They had done it, it was over, they were right on target, the island was Barbados. The three women broke down and cried, uncontrollable tears of joy and pride. They had between them brought *Black Orchid* across the North Atlantic Ocean. Someone ran down for champagne. Everyone seemed to be shaking everyone else's hand, everyone kissing everyone. They took great draughts from the bottles of vintage wine, some of the crew whooping and hollering.

Two hours later they were all still on deck and sailing parallel and close in to the white sand and coconut palm-fringed beaches of Barbados. They had dropped sail and were scanning the deserted shore for any sign of Hadon when quite suddenly he appeared out of the tropical bush and on to the sand at a run, arms waving, and shouting. Behind him were Mishka and Alexis. Anoushka could hardly believe it. All aboard were thrilled. The boys were jumping and running and calling out, 'Mom, Mom, you made it!'

Anoushka peeled off the shirt and sarong she was wearing. She stood barefoot in her swimsuit with her friends and shipmates all round her. They kissed and said farewells.

'I don't know if this is the best or the worst part of the voyage, I've never jumped ship before. Rab Nesnet, you're once again the captain of this vessel. I resign. Reluctantly, I might add.'

Everyone laughed, but there was just a hint of a tear in every eye. Page passed the log book over to Rab.

'You'll be all right, Anoushka, there was really no other way. My first loyalty has to be to Piers. His orders were to bring *Black Orchid* to anchor in Mustique after the crossing. We can't stop like some packet ship to drop you off. Be brave a little bit longer. If you mastered the Atlantic ocean, you can swim a few hundred yards in the warm Caribbean Sea.'

They were already at the rail of the boat, He shouted to

Hadon, 'You want her, come and get her. She's all yours.'

They watched Hadon and the boys charge into the water and start to swim. Rab hoisted Anoushka on to the ships' rail, 'Balance yourself well before you dive,' he ordered.

She was steady as a rock when only seconds later she turned to throw kisses to Sally and Page then took her dive.

She cleared the boat and vanished under the water for what seemed like an age. She surfaced halfway between the boat and Hadon and her sons. A shout of relief rose from all aboard. Anoushka turned to wave one last time and then swam hard and fast towards her future.